Richard

To Richard
with love

EClm 2018

Owl
Woman

Elen Sentier

Pea Green Boat
Britain

Also by Elen Sentier
Owl Woman
Toad in the Shadow Lands

and shamanic how-to books
Dreamweaver
Numerology: the Spiral Path

Owl Woman ©2002 Elen Sentier

Jacket art © 2002 Anny
Jacket design by 2002 Anny
Interior design and layout by Anny

Edited by Fiona Dove
magpiewolf@googlemail.com & 07798 571441

ISBN 978-1-4452-8941-0

Pea Green Boat Books

For Goldy
and all the Gang at the Shapeshifter's Arms

With particular thanks to everyone at Pea Green Boat; Fiona Dove, my faithful and long-suffering editor; Martin Ludgate for the oracular Welsh poem; and Paul for putting up with and encouraging me.

All pictures by Anny ...
Front cover – Karen, a dancer friend; Nectan's Kieve; Arianrhod's Bay, Snowdonia; owl and foxgloves by Wendy Davies.
Back cover – a picture of Tarr Steps and the Barle river on Exmoor.

Elen Sentier

I live in the Golden Valley, in the Black Mountains of the Welsh Marches. Archenland, my home, is a mile from any road, full of peace, quiet and wildlife. I share it with my husband and our two cats who watch with interest as I grow vegetables and fruit, write and teach Celtic Shamanism.

My mother's mother was a witch from the Isle of Mann, my father a somewhat reluctant shaman and engineer. One of my uncles was a gardener who talked to his plants and did lots of biodynamic-like things, another was a farmer who could call a wild hawk to his wrist. Many nights I sat under a tree, by his side, while all the night creatures of the wild woods came right up to us.

Over the years, I've worked with Caitlin & John Matthews, C Maxwell Cade, Colin Bloy, Hamish Miller, Tom Graves, Michael Poynder and Paul Devereux on the Dragon Project.

I've done lots of things this lifetime ... contemporary dance (Laban and Graham); finance officer for fighter-trainer aircraft then project manager of software design for Defence Sales in the Ministry of Defence; transpersonal therapist; garden designer; biodynamics.

http://www.elensentier.co.uk/ – for links to the Celtic Shamanism and Biodynamic Gardening sites, my Blogs as well as Facebook, YouTube & MySpace.

The Hollyman and the Lady

The lady stood at her own front door
As straight as a willow wand,
And along there come a holly man
With a great branch in his hand, and he said

CHORUS
Bide, lady, bide,
There's nowhere you can hide,
For the holly man will be your love
And that'll lay down your pride.

"Well may dress you, you lady fair
All in your robe so red,
But e'er a year and a day go by
I'll have you in me bed," and he said
"Away, away, you green holly man,
Would you do me this wrong?
To think to have me maidenhead
That I have kept so long!
"I'd rather I was dead and cold
And my body laid in the grave,
Than a husky, dusky holly man
Me maidenhead should have!"

Then the lady she held up her hand,
And she swore upon her soul,
She never would be the holly man's love
For all the cup of gold.
But the holly man held up his hand
And he swore upon the Tree,
"I'll have you for me love, my gal,
And the gold cup is the fee."
CHORUS

So she became a little grey mouse
And ran into the barns,
But he became a black tom cat
And fetched her in his arms, crying
CHORUS

She turned herself into a hare
And run upon the plain,
But he became a greyhound dog
And he fetched her back again, barking
CHORUS

She turned herself to silver salmon
And swam upon the sea,
But he became an otter bold
And after her went he, saying
CHORUS

The lady changed to a white barn owl
And flew up in the air,
But he became a falcon bright
And they flew pair and pair, and he called
CHORUS

And the lady ran to her own bedroom
And she changed into a bed,
And he became a green coverlet
And he gained her maidenhead.
And watch ye how he held her soul,
And still he bad her bide,
And the holly man became her love
And she laid down her pride.

Celtic lore has many variations of this initiatory song, a *fith fath* song (pronounced *fee faw*). It tells of the shapeshifters' chase between the goddess and the god, the Lord and Lady, the Queen who is the Land itself and the King who is guardian of the Land. The goddess holds her maidenhead, as prize, to test the god, to see if he is capable of being her guardian. He must win her, and she will run from him, shapeshift, to see if he can not only keep up with her but catch her. She wants to be caught … but only if the god can manage it. Vicki and Merle take on these roles in the story. Being human they are not fully aware, until the end, that this is what they're doing.

Death

Vicki

Vicki wrestled silently with her invisible captor. She knew it was a dream, one of those terrible ones where you're out of control, no way out, but there was nothing she could do. Fear, cold and palpable, gripped her and she couldn't move. Then, suddenly she was free, flying over the tree-tops, darkness rushing beneath her, moonlight blinding her. Then it all came into focus and she found herself hovering above the tower, as a barn owl.

A man stood below her, on the edge of the waterfall, something golden in his hands. He held it up to the light and now she could see it was the cup. No! He mustn't do that! She tried to call out to him, tell him, but only the screech of the owl came out.

He ducked, startled, let go the cup and fell. She watched him plummet down the fifty foot waterfall and hit the pool, like solid concrete. His body plunged through and carried on down to the bottom where he smashed his head open on the rocks. Slowly, he floated up to the surface again, pinwheeling like one of Van Gogh's crazy stars.

She hovered over him, unable to cry, unable to speak.

Something bright glimmered in the water near him. He turned towards it, his finger pointing. It was the cup. How the hell was it floating? She strained to speak to him, but it was no good.

He caught her eyes. He could see her. Somehow he wasn't dead yet. He tried to turn, to reach for the cup but, just as his fingers touched it, it slipped away from him and sank down into the water. He looked at Vicki desperately, his lips moving.

'Remember!' he said soundlessly. 'Remember!'

Everything went hazy. Now, when she wanted to stay in the dream, stay with him, she was coming awake. She felt herself falling backwards down the long, dark tunnel towards the point of light at its end. She concentrated on it as the feeling left her body and consciousness slipped away into the mist.

Lightning jolted through her. She sat bolt upright in the bed just as the phone began to ring.

'Vicki? Vicki?' she heard Vera's voice dimly through the fog in her head. 'Vicki, Jacob is dead. Your father is dead.'

She sat still, clutching the receiver, hearing Vera's voice calling to her but not knowing it.

'Mummy? Mummy? Is that you …?' she began.

'Vicki, luv, tis Vera here. Luvvy come back, speak to me.'

The fog began to thin.

'V-vera …?'

'Yes, deary, it's me, Vera. Can you hear me all right? Vicki? Vicki? You sound so far away, luvvy. Speak to me.'

'Dad's dead?'

'Yes dear, your father is dead.'

Vicki sat staring, silence inside her and out.

'Vicki …?'

The fog was nearly gone now. 'Dead? … He's dead?'

'Yes … dead.' Vera waited.

'Oh Shit! Damn!' Vera could hear her banging her hand against something. The noise stopped. Silence, then,

'Daddy … I never said goodbye to you!' Vicki whispered.

Vera choked off a sob herself, waited, then,

'W-what happened?' It was the child's voice. The same child who asked where her mother was twenty-three years ago.

12

'It was me as found 'im. He was in the Tower Pool, drowned. Us don't know no more. Joe's called the police. Will … will you come home now, me dear one? … we do surely need y'.' Vera's voiced trailed off into silence.

'I'm coming,' Vicki said at last. 'I'm coming home. I'll be there as soon as I can. Oh! Vera … Vera?' but the line was dead.

She sat staring blankly at the receiver in her hand.

'Daddy …? Where are you …?' she cried out softly, but only her own voice echoed an answer.

Groggily, she switched on the light, pulled a blanket round her and stumbled down to the kitchen.

She could still feel the feathers on her face and see trees beneath her. She felt in limbo, hanging between worlds. She knew in her head she was in the kitchen of her own flat in London, that it was her tribal rug beneath her feet, not a forest. But her heart told her she was in the Wilderness.

She made tea, with sugar, choking on the sweet, syrupy liquid. I'm OK, she told herself, just in shock, nothing special about that, and she began to giggle, shaking the tea all over the floor. The giggling turned into shivering, crying. Oh god, I'm going mad, she whispered and hugged the blanket closer. Something in her auto-pilot made her pick up the phone and call Faye.

'Hullo …?' the groggy voice queried after several rings.

'Faye … it's m-me, Vicki.'

'What?' the voice snapped into focus. 'What is it darling, what's happened.'

Vicki tried to speak but nothing came out, she choked and sobbed into the phone.

'Vicki? Vicki … it's OK darling, I'm here, I'm here …' Faye began to mumble on into the phone, giving Vicki time.

'D-dad … d-dead …' Vicki managed at last.

'Hold on there, I'm on my way. OK? Vicki? You hear me? I'm coming to you, hang on … OK?'

'O please be quick …' Vicki sat clutching the receiver, the coldness ran through her. She wanted to run away to the place between the worlds where nothing happened, nothing hurt.

'What am I going to do?' she whispered into the silence.

13

Faye found her clutching the dead phone. Gently she wrapped her in another blanket and tipped Rescue Remedy down her throat. Vicki could feel Faye's arms around her, the world began to come back into focus.

'What are you going to do?' Faye asked once she was fit enough to sit by herself on the sofa.

'Go home.'

'Are you OK? Can you drive? Shall I drive you?'

'No!'

Then she turned back to Faye.

'No, please. I'm better, look,' and she held out her hand, 'it's steady now, no more shaking. See?'

'I don't know …'

'But I do.' Vicki walked a straight line to the kitchen and back. 'Look, no wobbles.' She came and sat on the arm of Faye's chair. 'Let me go. I have to go by myself. I need to. It's no good with you, I'll give up and let you look after me.'

'Vicki … are you really sure?'

Vicki nodded. 'I must go alone.'

'OK … OK,' Faye held Vicki, kissed her. 'Can I help you pack? Get you something to eat?'

'Food would be good. I don't want to eat but I should, I suppose.'

'Yes, you should,' Faye watched Vicki's back as she went up the stairs. 'Fly well, dear one,' she whispered.

As though she heard, Vicki turned and smiled down at Faye.

Later, Vicki took the car up the ramp from the underground car park and out into Vestry Street. The roads were quiet, silent, strange for London, even at half past four in the morning. She slid round the roundabout and up Old Street heading for the M3 and home. Merle would be there.

14

Merle watched the owl's face grow in the computer screen until it blotted out all the costings he'd been working on. It changed, swirling, shapeshifting, becoming almost human, the eyes dark wormholes, holding his, dragging him down.

Just before his head hit the keyboard he came to. He'd passed out for a moment. Now he sat up, breathing hard, blinking, trying to regain focus, but still mesmerised by the owl face on the screen. He watched it fade, watched the costings return. The thing had blinked and he could smell it. He wanted to hope it was just the burgundy and camembert he and Jacob had put away earlier. But he knew it wasn't. The owl face had dissolved into hers. God damn! he thought, that was over ten years ago.

The loud, trailing 'khree-i' of a barn owl shattered the silence. Goldy sat up, bottling her tail, jumped off the desk and headed for the door where she turned to look at him.

'What is it, girl?'

The cat stared at him out of huge, unblinking silver eyes. He groaned, the wind was rising, it was late, but he followed to find her stood by the kitchen door. She trilled sharply.

'OK! OK! I'm coming!'

He dragged on boots, a thick coat, found a scarf. He was about to open the door when the cat trilled at him again.

'Eh? Oh yes!' He went to the pantry.

Goldy led him across the yard into the lane, past the stone pig-herm who guarded his gate and down to the river. The moon made a path across the water to the island by the clapper bridge. He scooped the cat up and carried her across into the shaw of hollies. She jumped onto a tree stump and sat curled, waiting.

Merle collected some kindling and built a small, hot fire in the shelter of the hollies. Its white smoke rose in a thin column until it came above the tops of the trees, then the wind took it. He took a small bowl out of his pocket and got some water from the river. He muttered over it, took a sip and set it down by the fire, then he sat on the other tree stump to wait.

The clapper bridge was a white dragon-skeleton in the moonlight, the birch trees glimmered ghostly along either bank. How long would it be?

He looked at the pile of wood, it would last a while yet but he built up the fire. The trees soughed wilder than before, the winds were rising again.

Would it come? A movement caught his eye from the far bank and he saw the owl launch from a tree at the other end of the bridge. It flew silently across the river, wing-beats strobing in the moonlight, to land on a branch at the entrance to the holly-cave.

'Come, friend,' Merle whispered. He fished the meat out of his pocket, offered it.

The owl stooped down, snatched the meat from Merle's hand and took it back to the holly branch where it sat tearing at it thoughtfully, watching him.

Goldy gave a low mutter in her throat, arched, then set her tail around her paws and sat still as stone.

Merle stared into the flames. The image came. He was up by the waterfall with Jacob. A scream shattered the silence, they both ducked but Jacob slipped and fell. Merle stood bodiless, helpless, at the top of the cliff, watching as Jacob fell into the pool. The vision changed, now he could see the cup, it came closer and closer. He reached out to take it but the image exploded into pain. He came to and found he had put his hand into the fire.

He crouched beside the stump, hugging his hand under his armpit, groaning and swearing. The owl flew down and rubbed its beak on his burned hand. He stared into the golden eyes.

'Help me!' he heard inside his head.

Vera & Joe

Vera came away from the window. The night air still flowed in like a dark, chilly stream, wrapping her round and making her shiver. Downstairs, she pulled on a coat and went out, leaving the door open so the brightness from the kitchen flowed out to light her path. Not that she needed it. These lanes were in her bones, her blood, had given birth to her. She turned up past the crown of ruins on the hill, oak leaves crunching brownly under her feet and her ears still full of the cries of owls. Vera trudged on in the bright moonlight, her breath coming out as frosty smoke.

16

The way seemed to take forever and, despite her fifty years' familiarity, she nearly missed the way into the Wilderness. The gate creaked. Beech trees surrounded her, reaching up their grey arms, and a huge holly twisted whitely skywards. She followed the ride to the middle of the wood and stopped still. He wasn't there. How not? She had seen the owls, followed where they led, but the glade was empty of all but the circle of stones, sitting up out of the grass like tall hares. The central stone stood stark and white in a splash of moonlight.

Her feet took her back towards the lane. The gate onto Tower Moor was open and she stared at it, not wanting to go up to the ruins. She'd never liked the place, even as a child she wouldn't join the other children to play there. Cold, dark, treacherous, she muttered, what's 'e want to go opening all that up for? But he had. Reluctantly she went towards it.

Fumbling in her pocket, she found the torch and screwed her eyes shut as the sudden light blinded her. She clambered round blocks of masonry and piles of earth. At the top, the hole gaped before her, breathing out an ancient dank smell of leaf-mould and wet soil, like an old garden. Vera leaned over to look. The torch showed nothing, an empty pit.

She made her way round to the west side. Here, where the cliff fell fifty feet, a waterfall shot out of the ground and down through a circle of rock into a deep pool. There was a seat by the head of the fall, Vera found her way to it, sat down, and looked.

Jacob floated face up in the water, his body pinwheeling left and then right in the eddy from the falls. Vera's breath stopped. Sometime later she realised she was crying. Later still, she found her way down the precipitous stone steps into the glade surrounding the pool. Ferns dripped wetly and caught at her bare legs. Her slippers were sodden. She stood on the pebble beach watching him turn. What am I to do, how can I get him out?

A movement in the rhododendrons on the other side caught her eye. A splash of white? She watched, but it took her a little while to accept what she was seeing. She felt a tickling inside her head, then words came, *Find Joe! Owlpen woods!* came the voice in her head. Vera blinked and rubbed her eyes, but the owl-like figure was gone. If it had ever been, she thought.

Wearily, she found her way back. Going across the garden she noticed the study lights were on and the French windows open. She didn't stop. The gate at the end of the garden let her into Owlpen Copse, not far down the path she tripped over Joe where he lay in the grass. On her knees beside him, she felt for a pulse but immediately he groaned.

'Argh!' he said. 'What happened?'

'How should I know, silly man! I only jus' got here m'self!' Vera told him with the crossness of relief from one who thought she had two dead bodies to deal with.

'Ugh! Oh! What happened?' Joe tried again.

'Jacob's dead' Vera sat back on her heels.

'Ugh!' Joe lay still, holding his head.

Men! Vera thought crossly, you has to tell 'em everything fifteen times afore it sticks. And then they don't remember. She stayed quiet to give Joe time to get the significance of what she'd said. He sat up slowly. She passed him a handkerchief. He wiped his face, not looking at her, thinking.

'Where?' he asked after a few moments.

'In Tower Pool. Drowned.'

'Accident?'

Vera shrugged. 'There weren't no-one else there that I saw 'cept …' she caught her breath, stopped, then said again 'There weren't no-one else there.'

Joe shot a look at her then pulled himself up, reached down a hand to help her.

'We'd better go see' he took her arm, as much to help himself as her.

They went back to Tower Moor, and the pool. Joe stood watching the body pinwheel.

'How's we goin' ter get 'im out?' Vera asked after a bit.

'We're not,' Joe said. 'Better get the police.'

'Is there summat …?' Vera's voice trailed off.

'Don't know. But we have to call the police. Come on, love. We both need a cup of tea and I'd better tell Olive where I am and what's happened.'

In the kitchen, Joe dialled 999, Vera made tea.

'Where's Hecaté?' she asked him when he got off the phone.

'Oh lord! I'd forgotten her. I'll go look, you stay here.'

Vera sat at the table with her mug of tea, staring at nothing. She started awake when the door opened. Joe had a small black bundle in his arms.

'She's not …?' Vera jumped up.

'No, she's OK. I found her in the bushes by the pool, crouching, watching. I was afraid she'd scratch when I went to pick her up but she didn't, just butted my hand and began purring.' He put the cat on the kitchen table. They both examined her, there seemed to be nothing at all wrong.

'She saw it though!' Vera said.

'Whatever it was,' Joe added.

Dick

Dick got back from lunch to find the phone ringing. It was Jacob's solicitor.

'Hello, Dick. I'm sorry to ring you at the Museum but I needed to catch you as soon as possible. Are you alone? I'm afraid I've very bad news. Jacob died last night.'

Dick spluttered slightly and then remembered to breathe. He could see nothing, his eyes were full of water.

'Dick? Dick? Are you there? Did you hear me?'

'Y-yes, I'm here,' Dick managed.

'It all happened very suddenly last night, or rather early this morning …' Delagardie rambled on gently, giving Dick time to take it all in. 'Will you be going down to the funeral?'

'Err … umm … I … err … well …' Dick mumbled.

'No matter, dear boy, no matter. You're mentioned in the will you see, you have to know. I'll go down myself for the funeral, and to read the will. Now, is there anything I can help you with in regard to the Museum? Can you let them know? Set off procedures and such? Probably better done in house than by me.'

'Yes, James. I can do that,' Dick's stutter left him. 'I'll be in touch. I think I need to sit down and take this in. Oh god!'

'Dick, call me any time. Don't forget.' Delagardie rang off.

Dick sat down at the desk, staring at Jacob's papers, all laid out before him. He could focus on nothing. There was the beginning of an empty pit growing in the middle of his stomach. He called the personnel office quickly and began setting wheels in motion, before he lost it completely. The afternoon was spent with people popping their heads round the door, offering condolences and asking him to sign or agree things. At four o'clock David Ranley-Hall, the big boss, called him in.

'Dick, this is dreadful!' he hardly let Dick sit down. 'Can you carry the show for the time being? Is there anything happening I should know about, anything I've forgotten? You'll want to go to the funeral. So will I. D'you know when it is?'

Dick felt he was in the firing line of a gattling gun.

'Yes, no, no, yes, yes, no.' Dick answered in sequence.

Ranley-Hall blinked and his spectacles slid down his nose.

'Thank you, Dick. Knew we could rely on you. Dreadful thing though, dreadful. How will Vicki manage?'

I don't need this, not right now, thought Dick.

'David, I haven't a clue,' he said. Agaiin he was surprised at how well his stutter was keeping in the background. 'If you don't need me I'll finish up here, then I'd like to get home.'

'Of course. Go off as soon as you like. We can all manage. You'll be all right to come in tomorrow?'

'Yes David,' Dick smiled wryly at his boss. 'I'll cope.'

Sylvie

Sylvie watched. It was like watching a TV screen, only silent, no sound. The picture showed her Vicki, struggling to escape the dream, her hands convulsing, clutching at the duvet.

'I've enchanted you now, girl, trapped you inside the owl,' Sylvie whispered, her voice sweet and sticky, like honey. 'You are my owl woman. You cannot escape me, you will do my will!' her mouth curled in triumph.

With her mind's eye, Sylvie steered Vicki towards the tower. She watched the owl's white wings hungrily cupping the air as she swooped over the eight-spoked wheel of the Wilderness. Then she saw Jacob standing on the rock shelf above the pool, by the tower. He was holding the gold cup.

'I have you now!' and Sylvie filled Vicki's mind with fear, forcing her to fly down towards her father.

'She knows! She knows!' Vicki cried out.

Jacob heard only the ghostly screech of the barn owl and felt the rush of wind as the bird flew low over his head. He ducked away from it.

Sylvie watched, revelling. Jacob's feet slipped out from under him on the wet mossy stone and he fell towards the shimmering water. His body plummeted to the bottom, his head hit the rocks and he sucked in the deadly water as he floated to the surface. His broken body turned first this way then that in the water currents. The grieving owl-woman watched from a branch by the edge of the pool. Sylvie was satisfied.

'Well, Jacob, you are gone and I will have the cup now,' she laughed aloud. Then she realised that somehow Jacob was still conscious. He could see the owl-woman, and he knew who she was. Sylvie ground her teeth. She watched Jacob smile to his daughter before his eyes dimmed.

Sylvie spat, snuffing out the candles, and turned on the desk lamp. The stuffed owl was quiet again in its glass case, the spirit which had animated it was gone.

Return

Vicki drove down the A303 on auto-pilot, her head full of memories. Merle and she had grown up together. Both only children and natural solitaries, they had gravitated to each other. Her mother wrote magical children's stories, his was an artist and musician. Their fathers were old friends, his the local doctor, hers the lord of the manor.

'Going on for bloody centuries!' she snorted, putting her foot down to pass a lorry.

They loved woods, the river, gardens. Joe, who ran his own herbery as well as being gardener at the manor, taught them about gnomes, as he called the elementals of the soil.

'The TV gardening programmes call biodynamics witchcraft. Hocus-pocus!' he waved his hands in the air and pulled a face. 'Cow dung instead of snake oil! But you can see what it does for the land, how the plants grow.'

Jacob loved it. It was what his grandmother had done. But he'd always been too busy rootling about with bones and history, so the old walled garden had fallen into disrepair. Dad had been glad when Joe came.

'I learned all this from my dad,' Joe told them. 'And he actually met Rudolph Steiner. And his dad, my granddad, was one of the ones who gave Steiner the old lore which he built his agricultural lectures on.'

They had been impressed. Especially after they'd discovered who Rudolph Steiner was and Jacob had told them about Vicki's grandmother, how she had gardened that way. And that she, too, had met Steiner.

'It's a small old world,' Jacob had said.

They'd told Joe things they'd learned from the fey folk. Joe listened, and taught them to dowse. Merle taught him how to listen to the water, to hear underground streams. She taught him how to hear animals. They both kept horses, rode together, were childhood sweethearts. Everyone assumed they would marry. Perhaps that was the beginning of the trouble.

Merle went to Oxford to read maths and philosophy. She followed him to read English. He got a first and went on to a PhD. They left together. He asked her to marry him.

'I was so happy … at first,' she told the windscreen. 'I made all those plans, how we could convert the clock house until I inherited Bridewell. Then, after the gods know how long, I got out of my own head and actually looked at his face!'

Vicki banged the steering wheel with her hand.

'Ye gods!' she accelerated past another lorry, 'How could I have been so bloody crass?'

But her memory wouldn't stop its replay.

'I love Bridge Cottage,' he said one day.

'Oh so do I,' she had enthused.

'I don't want to leave it,' Merle didn't look at her. 'Would you … could you … ?'

His voice trailed off. She didn't answer. He turned away and walked back home down the path through Penny Woods.

'So blind. So stupid,' she cried out loud in the car. 'I didn't follow him … Oh why, gods, why? No! I ran away to London, took the software job. Bought the warehouse flat, hid there with my lovers and my roof-garden and my work. Life was fun and full and satisfying, or so I kept telling myself,' she said savagely. 'Faye kept me sane … And there was Dad …'

She pulled in for petrol and stood staring up at the dark sky, sucking in the cold, damp air. It had the smell of home.

She saw the accident again, the blood, Mummy dead. And the woman peering into the car, a pale golden halo of hair and eyes like pits into which Vicki had fallen. Now, twenty-three years on, she wasn't even sure it had actually happened.

She got back in the car and headed for the M5, her mind still playing old films. She turned the radio up very loud, trying to drown out her thoughts. But a little part of her remembered the foxes. Merle had rescued her then.

Advent

There is no beginning. There is no end.
There is only change
Bob Toben
Space-Time and Beyond

Owl Noises

'I saw it, Vera. Just like the pictures in the old books. Just like the mask Vicki wore on the feast day.' Joe stopped. 'I knew I was dreaming but I knew who it was.'

Vera could tell from his eyes he was still seeing it. 'Go on,' she said. 'What happened?'

'It was all golden. And I could hear water, like the waterfall.' He stopped again, staring into space.

'Get on, man! What did she say?'

'She said the cup must come home,' Joe frowned. 'I didn't know it was gone.'

'N'more did I,' Vera stopped, thinking. 'P'raps Jacob did find it after all.' She got up and pottered about the kitchen. Joe let her. He could wait. She just had to get her mind round it, whatever it was she wanted to tell him.

'I was sleepin',' she began. 'I saw this owl hanging over me. She spoke to me, said he had taken her soul from its bed and so she was able to be caught. Then she made that weird noise owls do make and I saw the stone circle in the Wilderness. Next thing I knowed I was awake, sat straight up in me bed with this terrible owl-cry going through me. I got up and went to the window but I couldn't see nothing, so I pulled on a coat and went down to the Wilderness but he weren't there. Then I knowed he'd gone to the tower. I went up and saw him floating there in the pool, turning round and round. I went down to the poolside then, to

24

see, and I saw the owl again, for real this time. It said to go find you.'

'Do you know if he found the cup?' Joe asked.

Vera was quiet for a minute, then,

'I see'd him. In the study 'twas, just afore midwinter. He was all hunched up over by the fire and muttering, I could see his lips moving. And 'e 'ad something in 'is hands.'

'Where were you, for goodness sake?'

'By the French windows. There's a nice bit a holly grows up the wall there an' I was cutting it for the decorations. He looked so strange crouching there beside the fire 'e caught me eye. Didn't last more'n a few minutes. Then he was over t'other side. And there weren't nothing in his hands then.'

'He must have found it,' Joe breathed.

'Mebee Sylvie found him with it and killed him.'

'That'd make sense of the owl asking us to get it back. She said the land'd be wasteland until the cup came home.'

'And so it have been since Sylvie an' that toy-boy of hers capped the well,' Vera grunted, 'and started the bloody bottling factory. Nuthin's gone right since. An' he threw her out right after she went and took up with young Julian.'

'Damn!' Joe smacked his fist on the table. 'Jacob should have known better. It's all in his damn history. And I'll bet you Dick doesn't know anything about him finding it. Bloody old fool.'

The Police

BRIDEWELL

The police came. Went. Came back. They spent the rest of the night cordoning off the pool, setting up forensic, taking finger-prints, asking questions and complaining about the number of footprints around the poolside. Joe and Vera had to have plaster casts made of their shoes so the police could identify which prints were theirs. It seemed like a farce.

25

'Accident,' said the DI. 'You don't know of any reason why the deceased would take his own life?' he asked them both.

They shook their heads.

'Bloody slippery up there,' the DI went on. 'Nearly fell in m'self.' He took another sip of the now cold coffee Vera had made for him two hours past. She'd offered him fresh.

'Give me indigestion!' he said. 'Too many years have gone by since I last drank hot coffee! And what did he go for a walk for, at midnight, in January, anyway?' he went on.

Again Joe and Vera shook their heads.

'He liked going out alone at night,' Vera offered. 'And there was the ruins and the dig. He were all fired up over that. He might go out there just for the fun of it.'

'Fun …? The DI's eyebrows scaled his hairline. 'D'you know what he did earlier this, no last, evening?' he continued.

Vera hesitated, then, 'He had dinner with Mr Hollyman.'

'That's Merle Hollyman who runs the software company, Pontifax ain't it or something like that?'

'Yes,' Joe kept his face straight. 'Means bridge builder. Merle does a lot of work on databases, bridging between networks and people's businesses.'

The DI looked down his nose. Was the man vamping him?

'Where's he live?' he asked.

'Bridge Cottage,' Joe couldn't help grinning now. 'Down the bottom of Firebeacon Hill, by the Bride Steps. Know the place?'

'I can find it,' he glowered. 'I'll be off down there then.'

'Go out the drive and turn left. You'll come to a ford at the bottom of the hill. It's not deep at the moment but go through slow and steady. You don't want to stall.'

'Thank you, Mr Millar.' The DI said acidly as he got into his car. Then he stuck his head back out of the window, 'You carry on here,' he called to his sergeant. 'Call me if you find anything.'

'Right, Guv,' the man grinned over his shoulder to his chief.

Bridewell Manor was still full of policemen and forensic and photographers and Uncle-Tom-Cobley-and-all. Joe sighed.

'Merle Hollyman?'

The DI made a play of looking studiously down at his notebook, but he was surreptitiously watching under his eyelids to see how Merle would react to being visited by the police at four o'clock in the morning.

'Yes?' Merle stood blocking the doorway.

'Detective Inspector Hardacre,' the DI said.

Merle didn't move.

Hardacre fished in his pocket and pulled out his warrant card. Merle took it and held it under the porch light, studied it, then checked the picture back against the actual in front of him. He handed the card back.

'What can I do for you?' he said.

'I'm afraid I've got some rather distressing news,' Hardacre replied, watching Merle to see if he was being distressed. 'May I come in?'

'What is it?' Merle asked.

'I believe you know Professor Jacob Bryde?'

'Yes.'

'He's just been found dead, sir.'

Merle sagged visibly against the doorpost. It was true then, what he'd seen with the owl.

'You'd better come in.' He moved back from the door and let the policeman into the kitchen.

'I've just come from Bridewell Manor,' Hardacre continued. 'I understand Professor Bryde had dinner with you this evening.'

'That's right. It's a regular thing. We usually have a meal together every week.' Merle busied himself at the sink, filling the kettle, putting it on the Rayburn, anything to keep from thinking. 'Will you have a cup of tea, inspector, or are you all tea'd out?'

'Thank you, sir. I could do with a hot cup,' Hardacre said graciously, belying his previous statement to Vera and not mentioning that he hated tea. When they were both sat at the kitchen table he went on, 'Can you tell me what happened this evening, sir? What time did Professor Bryde arrive?'

'About seven I think. He was a bit later than usual, we both tend to eat early.'

'Did that surprise you?'

'Well …' Merle raised his eyebrows. 'I didn't think about it. We don't have to be avidly punctual. We're friends.'

'Did Professor Bryde give any reason for being late?'

'No.'

What the hell was going on? This was beginning to sound like a murder investigation. Merle was thinking on his feet, keeping his face bland but mobile. Jacob had arrived as excited as a schoolboy and obviously full of secrets, Merle wasn't about to say anything until he knew more.

'We sat down to eat pretty well straight away,' Merle added; which was true, he thought thankfully.

'What did you talk about?'

'Well, you probably know, he's got … had … this dig going at the Folly on Tower Moor. Discovering what his ancestors got up to. That's been a main topic for some weeks now. I can't get up there very often, too much work myself.' Merle smiled at the policeman, who took it stonily, on the chin. 'So Jacob would bring me up to date on the latest stuff.'

'Was that all you talked about?'

'I told him about my latest project with an old wine company near Toulouse in France. Jacob is … was … quite a connoisseur of wine and I hoped he and Albert de Seligny might meet one day. Perhaps I'd be able to take Jacob to France with me. We talked about that, but he said he couldn't spare the time what with the dig.' Merle paused, looking out into space, then brought himself back. 'He never will now,' he finished grimly, then, 'What happened? Can you tell me how he died?'

'I gather that you've not yet been to bed, sir.' Hardacre was looking at Merle's jeans. 'Can you tell me what time Professor Bryde left? What have you been doing since then?'

So there is something more, Merle thought.

'Jacob left a bit before midnight. I didn't look at the time particularly. I went back to my study to do some more work on the database for the Jolys Company. About half one I needed a break so I went out for a walk. Sat by the bridge for a while, listening to the river, even built myself a little fire. Then I came back. I was still restless. It wasn't long before you turned up.'

'Was there anyone with you, out by the bridge?'

'Only my cat,' Merle gave the policeman a wry grin. 'She's not much of an alibi.'

Hardacre looked down his nose.

'I suppose you could get forensic to test the ashes of my fire, see if that confirms my times at all,' Merle added acidly.

'We will if we need to, sir, be sure of that,' Hardacre gave as good as he got.

'Can you not tell me what happened?' Merle backed down.

'Professor Bryde was found by his housekeeper, floating in the pool below the tower. It appears he drowned.'

'He fell? It was an accident?'

'We don't know that yet sir. However, it is very slippery up there. Miss Gardner says he would often go for a walk at night, up to the ruins or down into that wood they call the Wilderness. We'll know more after the autopsy and when forensic come back with their results. We're looking into all possibilities at present.'

'Yes, he did like his night-walks,' Merle was thinking of the ones they'd done together. 'And he might well have gone to the tower. He was very full of the discoveries he hoped to make over the next few days.'

'What were those sir? If you can tell me?'

'Well, the tower site is quite like some of the underground structures in the Orkneys and Jacob thought … hoped to show … that it too was an oracle shrine. The Iron Age Celtic religion involved the worship of nature spirits and springs or wells, which goes along with the Bridewell legends. Jacob was hoping to dig up things which would confirm all this. What he'd got so far made it a definite possibility.'

Privately Hardacre thought this was a load of moonshine, as bad as the name this bloke Hollyman had for his computer company. But academic types were only too likely to hare off after some legendary stuff which had no relation to everyday life. Heads in the clouds, he thought to himself, like this man here. But he looked at Merle again, from under his eyelids. There's something, he thought, something he's not telling me. He would wait and see. He got up to leave. At the door he turned back.

'Professor Bryde didn't leave you anything, I suppose, sir?'

Somehow, Merle managed to look up quietly and normally.

'Eh?' He headed to the sink, teacups in each hand. 'Should he have?'

29

'I don't know, sir. It was just a thought that came into my head. You would let me know if you found anything, wouldn't you, sir?' Hardacre stood in the doorway. Butter wouldn't melt in his mouth.

'Naturally, Inspector.' Merle smiled back at him.

'Well … goodnight, then, sir.'

Finally, Hardacre shut the door. Merle forced himself to walk naturally over to the sink and get on with the washing up. He watched the inspector walk slowly up to his car, unlock it, stand a moment looking round and peering up into the sky. Then he got into the car and, a few moments later, chugged out the gate. He forgot to close it.

Merle went out and shut the gate. The stone pig-herm was grinning up at him.

He was exhausted after the interrogation but still unable to sleep. Goldy crept down the stairs, from where she'd been keeping watch through the banisters on the strange human who had come to her house. She jumped on the table, purring and rubbing herself against him, she even touched her nose to his.

'I'm OK, girl,' he told her, rubbing behind her ears. He picked her up and took her to sit with him in the rocker beside the Rayburn. Joe found them there, asleep, a few hours later.

HARDACRE

Hardacre drove home slowly, thinking all the way. There was something funny here and yet he couldn't put his finger on it. That question about the professor leaving something had been a pure shot in the dark but he'd seen the infinitesimal hesitation, the slight tension around Merle's eyes. It seemed he'd hit a nail on the head, if only he could find out what nail. And how had the man burned his hand? He would bring that up later.

Professor Bryde had been eccentric. That was one of his plus-points in the area, making him something of a cross between a sacred cow and a tourist attraction. He was obsessed by his research, his work. Well, Hardacre could understand that. His own obsession with his job had cost him his marriage. It seemed the bible was right, a man could only have one wife. Hardacre just wished it had been more specific earlier in his life, or that he had understood what the preachers were saying from their high pulpits. The Methodist mafia of West Milton were another form of masonry to him, and he disliked it just as much. He would never rise above DI because he didn't have the right handshake, or a wife who took a leading part in all the chapel coffee mornings and such things. The police mafia were as thick as the thieves.

Hardacre parked the car, locked it carefully, and made his way up the path to his own front door. He unlocked that carefully too. Inside, he took ice from the fridge and a bottle from the cupboard and sat down at the kitchen table with his notes. He put neat ticks beside each of the people on his list whom he had spoken to once. He would see them again.

Most of all, he wanted to see Vicki. That would have to wait another hour or three. He had asked Vera to phone him as soon as Vicki arrived home but he knew she wouldn't. No matter. He would turn up at Bridewell around midday. She should have arrived by then but it would be too soon for her to have gone out again. With luck he would find the two women in the kitchen – just where he wanted them.

Bridge Cottage

Joe tucked the blankets around Vera as she sat in the rocking chair by the kitchen stove. 'I'll be back later but I must go down and see Merle.'

'I know' she told him. 'Olive's yere now and we'll manage together. This lot'll be yere forever,' she added, waving at the hordes of police marching about outside.

Joe set off again down the path across Owlpen Copse. Vera'll be all right with Olive, he told himself, and Olive with her too. In some ways this death would hit his wife more than Jacob's housekeeper. Vera was born and bred in the village. For her, death wasn't something horrible to be avoided at all costs, life and death could be sad but they were part of everything. She would cry but she would go on. For Olive, it was as though she'd lost her father a second time. She had very much taken to Jacob, looked to him whenever she was unsure of things for herself.

'It's different if you lived in an extended family, like I did,' Joe muttered. 'Watched your grandparents, and older aunts and uncles, grow old and die. Or even grow ill and die, like Mother.' Joe paused in his walking, seeing her again.

'But Olive's an only child,' he carried on talking to himself. 'Lost her dad when she was just a little kiddie, barely six. And her damn mother never allowed her to forget that it was an eternal tragedy. Life stopped, for Olive, at that point …'

Joe found himself back in his own kitchen with no idea of how the way had been getting there. On auto, he grimaced. Ah well! He grabbed the car keys and went out again. Thundering up Owlpen Hill, he slipped the clutch and accelerated round the left turn at Honeybeetle Cross. He shot past Bridewell and down Firebeacon Hill at a steady fifty to arrive at the ford grinning like a schoolboy. He braked and went through the water at a demure five miles per hour, putting up a speedboat-style wash all round him. Satisfied with his little rule-breaking trip, he parked sedately in Merle's yard and shut the gate.

Knocking produced no response whatever so Joe opened the door, country-fashion, and stuck his head round.

'Peace and love, man!' he waved two fingers the right way round at the figure in the rocking chair. Again, no response.

'Waste of time!' he muttered as he crossed the kitchen and realised that Merle was dead to the world. Goldy, curled in his lap, roused and chirruped. He stroked her head. She dug her claws into Merle's leg.

'Ugh! Ow! Huh?' Merle opened both eyes and stared at Joe as if he was a Martian. 'Wossamatter?'

'Tea?' Joe asked rhetorically, taking the kettle to the sink.

Later, when they were both sat at the table, Joe asked him,

'What did the policeman say to you? Or rather, what did you say to the policeman?'

Merle grinned. Joe had known him for most of his life, been one of the towers of strength that had helped him grow up.

'He said as little as he possibly could. So did I. I don't think either of us fooled the other,' he finished.

'So … what can you tell me?'

'Not a lot more really. Jacob came to supper last night, a bit later than usual. He talked a lot about the dig but I'm not really sure he said very much, and what little I think he did say I'd rather keep to myself for now.

He was very full of himself. Stolen a march on Sylvie was what he said. Then he wanted to know about the de Seligny contract, and we spent quite a while trying to work out when he could come to France with me for a bit of holiday. And,' Merle smiled wistfully, 'who would do the driving. That got to be quite an argument which, come to think of it now, was probably stage managed to keep me off the scent of whatever it was he was up to. He eventually left a bit before midnight.'

'What happened then?'

Merle looked up at Joe. There was something in his voice as he'd asked the question. 'What d'you mean?'

'You could start with how did you burn your hand.'

'You're as bad as that bloody inspector,' Merle growled. 'Well, OK. I wasn't sleepy so I went back to do some more work on Albert's database. Then I felt like a walk and went and sat by the bridge for a while, built a little fire, sat dreaming.'

'You just felt like a walk?'

'What are you getting at? What d'you want me to say?'

'OK.' Joe sat back in his chair and looked at the younger man. There was more to it, but he knew Merle far too well to think he could get him to say anything if he didn't want to.

'I was out too,' he began. 'It must have been near one o'clock when I woke. It was the owls, calling and calling. I had to get up, had to go out. Like something was pressing down on me, almost stopping me breathing. And I knew where I had to go too, to the tower, so I set off across the copse. I'd been out about five minutes when there was a rush of wind, sounded like hundreds of birds flying over me, and everything went dark. I caught my foot in a root, fell and knocked myself out. I dreamed I saw Jacob standing at the top of the fall, then he fell into the pool below. When the ripples subsided he floated back up to the surface and his body slowly pin-wheeled in the current. Next thing I knew, there was Vera kneeling over me and telling me Jacob was dead, just like in my dream.'

Joe stopped, looked at Merle. They were silent together for a few minutes.

'I was working at the computer,' Merle began, 'doing the costings. Suddenly, I found myself staring at an owl's face in the computer screen. It blotted out all the page of costings. Then the owl blinked at me, its eyes moved, like it was real.' Merle paused. He wasn't going to say about it turning into Vicki's face.

Joe nodded.

'Then the costings returned and I heard the 'khree-i' of a barn owl, real close, over the cottage. Goldy heard it too, dragged me out to the island by the bridge. I found some firewood and built up a blaze, partly to stop myself being scared out of my wits. I got some water from the river, set it in my silver bowl so the moon caught it, then we sat and waited. Goldy sat beside me, purring, and I found myself humming along with her. Then the owl came swooping across the bridge, to the shaw. I offered her some meat and she sat with us. I stared into the flames.

'It was as though I was with Jacob. He had the cup in his hands. I saw the owl fly over his head, heard it call out to him, warn him it seemed. But Jacob was startled. He slipped, dropped the cup and fell into the pool. Then he came up again. He looked like one of Van Gogh's white stars, spinning slowly first one way and then the other in the black water. I must have reached out or something because I came to with a bang, found I'd stuck my hand in the fire, burned it.' He held the hand out for Joe to see.

'The owl was gone. Goldy said the show was over, time to go home. I knew something was up but I just couldn't bring myself to phone Jacob. I kept telling myself it was too much burgundy and camembert. Then this policeman knocks on the door and I knew it wasn't. I really had to think on my feet, I couldn't tell him I was seeing visions in a computer screen. Fortunately he never asked about my hand.'

Joe looked at Merle. 'Know how you feel! Wasn't about to tell him I was seeing visions either. I told Vera though, she saw much the same thing. Seems we all did.'

Both men were silent again.

'I'd best get back,' Joe got up. 'Olive's with Vera, she'll be even more upset if I stay away too long. Vera called Vicki,' he added as he got to the door. 'She'll be here today.'

Merle said nothing. Joe let himself out.

Vicki rolled down the long drive and stopped by the clock house. She pulled the bags out of the car and stood a moment in the dark, feeling home. Tears began. Before she was half way across the grass the door opened and Vera came out to her.

'Here! Gimme they,' Vera took the bags and led the way into the kitchen where she dumped them down and set to with the kettle. 'Set yersel' down, girl. You need summat to drink.'

But Vicki went over to the washing basket by the door.

'Oh Hecaté,' she knelt down and buried her face in the black fur. The cat began to purr. After a moment she sat back. The cat yawned, showing a magnificent set of fangs. Vicki picked her up and hugged her, brought her to the table.

Vera brought the teapot. 'There's some o' me own Victoria sponge if you want it or a few shortbreads left from Christmas. Bit weird at this hour, but there ...' she poured the tea.

Vicki held the cup in one hand and stroked the cat with the other. The two women were quiet for a little while.

'The polic've not long gone,' Vera offered.

Vicki looked up.

'They 'aven't a clue,' Vera continued.

'Can you tell me about it?' Vicki put down the cup and reached her hand to Vera's. 'I'd like to know before I see anyone else. They've taken his body ...?'

'Oh yes. All done up in a black plastic bag, like a condom.' Vera had never been mealy mouthed. 'In the coroner's meat wagon. I suppose they'll let you see him, mebbe later today but not until after they done an autopsy. Gotta make sure he wasn't drunk or summat,' she answered the question in Vicki's eyes. 'There was a huge crack on his head. I could see that, even when he were floating in the water. But I don't think there was any other mark on him. Nor do Joe.'

'You both found him?'

'I got there first. I saw him, but I just didn't know what to do. There was a voice in me head said to go find Joe. So I went off to the Owl House and near fell over him lying in the middle o' the path on me way.'

'What?'

'Oh, he were all right. Just tripped on a tree root and knocked hisself out, but he was already coming to when I found 'im.'

'How'd you come to be looking for Dad?'

'Heard the owls, didn't I,' Vera said softly. 'All the owls in the world it sounded like and they made a great, dark cloud in the sky. Covered the moon right up, they did. And a rushing noise as they came over, like the wind. I 'ad to go out, follow 'em. Thought they was going to the Wilderness and so I think they did. But I had to go on, up to the tower.' Vera shivered, even the memory made her go all cold inside.

'You went up to the tower ...' Vicki prompted.

'Aye. An' set down on the rock seat there by the falls. Then I looked down. He looked like a great big Catherine wheel, turning and spinning there in the pool, under the water-shoot. I don't think I really took in what it was I was looking at, not at first. Then I did. Then I had to go down and see for meself.'

Vera stopped. Vicki knew there was something more.

'I saw her,' Vera was whispering. 'I saw the owl.'

Vicki sucked in her breath slowly.

'You saw the owl woman?'

'No, not her. She wouldn't show herself to me. The owl.' Vera looked directly at Vicki.

They were still again for a little time.

'I'd best be getting y' to bed.'

Vera got up slowly and picked up Vicki's bags. Vicki followed her into the hall and up the stairs. Her feet took her without thinking, straight to her old room, she turned on the light. Nothing had changed.

'I've put out clean towels for you and the water's all hot. You'd best have a soak and then a sleep.'

'What are you going to do?' Vicki asked her. 'You're not going home are you?'

'Nay. I'll be here. I was just going to lie down on the sofa in the housekeeper's room, get a couple of hours' nap. Not a doubt but thicky darn perlicemen will be back soon enough. Shall I call y' in a couple of hours? With some proper breakfast?'

36

'Only if you wake up,' Vicki kissed her. 'Otherwise I'll get the breakfast for both of us.'

Vera closed the door on her quietly and went back down the stairs. She stood a long while at the kitchen door, only going in when the blackbird began to sing. Unusual that, she thought. Sign of a bad winter if they be singing in January. She shut the door and went to lie down on the sofa.

Vicki turned on the bath. Vera was right, a soak and then, hopefully, sleep. She couldn't take it all in, it felt as though it wasn't really happening, that she was an actor in a play. But, in another way, it felt as though it had all been happening forever. After the first tears it seemed she was all dried up, only an empty feeling inside which ached, but wouldn't rouse into an all-out pain where she could scream. She felt in limbo. Between worlds. Neither here nor there. She would have to wait. The pain would find her eventually, she knew.

The bubbles were up to her ears, the house quiet now, what wind there had been had cleared the sky, Vicki could see through the window. There was a frost. But, for now, the hot water was leaching away the tiredness of driving and the pain of loss.

In the dim light, through half-closed eyes, Vicki imagined she saw her father sitting in the Victorian nursing chair under the standard lamp on the other side of the bathroom. She smiled sleepily. The image smiled back.

'Hello darling,' it said.

Vicki opened her eyes wide. The image was still there, looking remarkably solid.

'Dad …?' she breathed.

'Yes, it's me. I don't know how long I can stay, it's getting late and I shouldn't be here at all.'

Vicki sat up. The bubbles covered her.

'What is it?' she asked him.

'The owl woman. I know she sent the owl, although I didn't know it at the time. You must stop her. It's the cup.'

'Eh? Who? The owl woman?'

'No, no!' Jacob was testy, as always, when she didn't get his shorthand speech. 'She has the right to it. Sylvie!'

'Sylvie is the owl woman?'

'Of course she isn't! Well, yes, maybe she is in a way. She hijacked the owl that frightened me into the pool.'

'I know.'

'Eh?'

'I was there.' And Vicki told him her dream.

'Ah! So you know, about all her spells and witchery and stuff?' Jacob stopped, pursed his lips, looked shamefaced and tucked his chin into his neck. 'I … err … well … err … I'm sorry.'

It all came out rather uncomfortable and self-conscious. He tried again. 'I really am, my dear. You were right and I was wrong. I should have listened to you.'

'Oh Dad!' Vicki was exasperated. Her bath was seriously interrupted. It was just like old times, as though he hadn't died. He so often irritated her this way, it was a wonderful, warm, comforting feeling. He was so real.

She climbed out, wrapped herself in a robe, then added more gently, 'Thank you. It's good to hear it. But what are you talking about? Sylvie has the cup? How? When? Where?'

'No,' Jacob's form flickered, faded a little, then came back.

'Dad! Don't go!' Vicki cried out. Reality was running away from her again.

'Can't help it,' he said quickly. 'Sylvie knows I have it, had it. She got rid of me because she thinks she can find it herself.'

'And can she?'

Jacob was fading badly now, most of him gone, just the eyes and the mouth left. Like the Cheshire cat. 'Merle …' he whispered. Then he disappeared.

'Dad …?' Vicki went slowly over to the chair. There was no sign, but then she caught the faintest trace of rosemary and lavender. She began to cry.

Dawn was coming up as Vicki woke to see the owl standing on the window-ledge, staring at her. She got up, went over and stroked the silky feathers.

'Khree-iii!' it whispered softly, ruffling its feathers and pecking at fleas under its armpit.

'What is it?' she asked.

'Khree-i!' it said again, more stridently. Then it climbed onto her wrist. Vicki winced as the sharp talons gripped her bare arm but, surprisingly, it didn't hurt.

'What is it?' she asked again.

The owl nibbled at the hair behind her ear, then flew out the window. Vicki leaned out to see where it had gone. Yes, it was sitting on the Pan statue just below, looking up at her.

'You want me to go with you?'

The owl blinked at her.

Vicki pulled on jeans, sweat shirt, grabbed a coat, scarf and gloves. The night was cold. Downstairs, she slipped out of the French windows. The owl was waiting for her, called softly, then floated away on silent wings. Vicki followed it to the Wilderness.

'May I come in?' Vicki stopped beside the gate.

The owl blinked once. Vicki closed the gate behind her and followed the bird up one of the rides to the Troytown. There it sat on a stone beside the entrance to the maze. Vicki made to enter but the bird flew at her. She ducked. The owl chittered and settled itself on another stone, glaring and clicking its beak.

'What do I do?' Vicki asked warily, in case it decided to fly at her again.

It stared into the centre of the maze. Vicki followed its gaze. She could see something moving there, like marsh-mist and fire-flies. It took the shape of a cup. The owl chittered again and Vicki stood back as the misty shape came towards her. As it passed, all her hair stood on end. She reached out to touch it and got a jolt down her arm like a mild electric shock.

The owl took off after the cup and Vicki followed down the Greenway, into the village.

They turned into the churchyard. The owl sat in the porch, waiting for Vicki to open the door. It groaned reassuringly and she followed the bird up the nave to the apse on the north side, where it stood by the stone covering the saint's grave. Vicki pulled a kneeler out of the nearest pew and sat down to watch.

39

Nothing happened for a while and her eyelids began to droop. Then the owl moved slightly and Vicki saw a sliver of light falling onto the stone. The marsh-mist effect began again and, as the cup took shape, it seemed there were hands holding it. She watched as the woman sat up out of the stone, holding the cup out to her.

Warily, remembering what had happened last time, she reached out her hands. Cold! So cold and silky it felt. She looked into the woman's eyes.

'Find my cup!' she heard inside her head.

Next thing she knew she was waking in her own bed, sunlight streaming through the window.

'Did I dream it?' she thought, but there were marks on her arm. They looked like owl's talons.

Sylvie

Sylvie watched the pictures go past her mind's eye. How many years was it now? Twenty-three since Jacob found the bronze tablet in the saint's grave in Bridewell church. It had made his name. She had wanted it to make hers.

She had seen the news of the dig in an archaeological journal while she was still a professor at Pennsylvania. Straight away she had applied to join and, thank the gods, been accepted. She flew to England.

David Ranley-Hall was an easy target, her lip curled. Jacob had been far more difficult. Neither Dick, Jacob's assistant, nor his wife, Caroline, had liked her. Both had tried to persuade Jacob not to take her, but Ranley-Hall had prevailed.

She had been there, seen the name "Iwerydd", the picture of the cup and the village story on the bronze tablet. All the legends had been vindicated. Somewhere, everyone now knew, was the Bridewell grail. And the picture on the tablet showed it to be very similar to the Rillaton cup they found in Cornwall, back in the nineteenth century. And the Rillaton cup was four thousand years old. It was likely the Bridewell cup would be the same age. Jacob was like a dog with two tails.

Then someone had said the team must be dismantled. It wasn't

Ranley-Hall, she knew that for certain. She'd been sleeping with him at the time. She always suspected Dick of those machinations. The team had been down-sized, again her lip curled. 'Just small enough so I had to go,' she spat.

Then Caroline had the accident. But that hadn't done any good either, and that she put at Vicki's door.

She had bided her time. No more had happened for years until she heard Jacob was planning to dig the old folly tower. It coincided with the Oxford conference and she got herself invited to speak. David Ranley-Hall was there, she remade the old acquaintance. After that it had been relatively easy to entrap Jacob. He had a hazy memory of her. She set herself to charm. And Dick had not been there.

But it hadn't lasted. She blamed Vicki for setting Jacob against her, for he changed, became suspicious. Her lip curled, well he'd been right to be. Then there'd been the final row. And Julian.

As she thought of him the door opened and Julian walked into her study as if he, not she, owned it. It always irritated her.

'Well, Sylvie? What now?' he drawled, leaning over the back of her chair, putting his hands on her.

She didn't answer.

'How'd you do it, Sylvie?' Julian whispered into her hair.

Sylvie turned on him.

'What d'you mean?'

'Kill the bastard, of course.'

'Don't you ever, ever, say anything like that again, you hear?'

'What is it, my precious?' Julian raised his eyebrows, laughing, then he leaned forward and bit her cheek. He drew back, looking at her quizzically.

Sylvie hit him.

'You heard me?' she hissed into his face.

He caught her wrists and held her, breathing hard. She was suddenly terrified, looking into those ice-blue eyes, there was no expression in them at all.

'Don't you ever hit me again, darling,' he said softly, 'or I'll make you regret you were ever born.'

41

They stayed a moment at bay, then Julian let go her hands and smiled. He leaned forward, kissed her, then left the room.

Sylvie sat back, shaking. She pulled the bottle out of the desk drawer, along with the glass, and poured herself a large scotch. She sat sightless for a few moments, sipping the liquor, allowing it to work its calming magic, until she was able to put the glass down without her hand shaking. She needed Julian, and mostly she could control him but not always, that was the attraction. Sylvie pushed aside the vision of his face, those eyes, the feel of his hands. No! Not now, she thought.

She turned back to the scene of Jacob's death, following it through in her mind. Was the cup in his hands when he fell? She watched again. No, she couldn't see. She would have to look for herself, and that would need Julian's help. And soon, before the damn police went sniffing about. The last thing she needed was them finding it.

She found Julian in the kitchen. Coming up behind him she put her arms around his waist and snuggled into his back.

'I'm sorry,' she said. 'I'm just so on edge. And I need you, will you help me?'

Julian turned and took her in his arms, kissed her long and hard, then walked her back across to the kitchen table. He turned her and laid her across it. She wriggled delightedly. She was warm and soft as he entered her.

Later, in bed, she asked him again.

'We should go before she has time to think about anything.'

Julian grunted assent.

'Don't you want us to find it?' she asked him.

'Only if it means I can get something out of it,' he said, staring up at the ceiling.

'You can. You will. We both will. Finding that cup will make my name. And it will kill Vicki. That's what you want isn't it?'

Julian turned to her again, nuzzling the blonde silk hair.

'What a pair we are, eh? Glued together with lust and hate.'

Breaking Fast

The two women were sitting in the kitchen. Vera had fixed breakfast, putting food in front of Vicki and encouraging her to eat as though she was a child. So she is still, in a way, Vera thought as she held the teapot poised over Vicki's cup. It would be good for her to be able to sit still a bit and catch up with things here in the village. But that wasn't likely to happen.

''Twas a terrible row they had. All about her stealing his papers and trying to get 'em printed in them archaeological magazines, or so he said later.' Vera looked as though she didn't altogether believe this explanation. Vicki waited to see what might come.

'We kept our ears pricked, out in the inner hall, and it went on and on until we heard the crash. Then Joe an' I ran in on 'em. She was standing with the poker in 'er hand and 'im lying out on the floor with his leg all scorched and bleeding, and the rug smouldering and nearly on fire. I just went for 'er and grabbed the poker off 'er. Joe got him to the hospital.'

'And what did she do?' Vicki asked.

'Oh, she let go on it ready enough, standing there, all white about the gills and panting. I put the poker back in the grate and took a look at the leg. She'd stabbed 'im in the ankle with it, all hot from the fire. An' that's odd come to think on it.' Vera stopped, looked at Vicki. 'For what would they 'ave been doin' with the poker in the fire so long it got hot?'

'You think she meant to do it?'

'Wouldn't put nuthin past that cow,' Vera spat.

They sat silent again, then Vera said, 'I seen the white owl, once, when he was settin' in the study.'

'I saw her last night.' Vicki stared into her teacup.

'Seems as several folks 'ave seen her,' Vera said. 'Even them as 'as no imagination, like Mrs Partridge over the post office.' She stopped and watched Vicki from under her eyelids for a moment, then she went on.

'Mr Jacob's been huntin' around like nobody's business all the midwinter. He seemed like he'd got a lead and was following it like a fox after a rabbit. He was very jubilate deo and then, after Christmas, it all went hush. He was in the study morning, noon and night. I'd knock and he'd come to the door to get a plate o' sandwiches or some tea. Lived on bloody sandwiches for over a week, so he did! I never got no dustin' done in there for days.' Vera smiled wryly at Vicki. She would remember how her father was once he had the bit between his teeth. 'Then all on a sudden he upped and went to London, just for the day, right a'rter New Year. Then 'twas back to work all the hours god gave until yester ar'ternoon, when he stuck his 'ead round my kitchen door and told me to bring a great pot of Lapsang and lots of cake. I found him in the library for once, with a little leather bound book in his hand. "Don't you go saying a word," he told me, grinning from y'ear to y'ear. "Now would I do such a thing, Mr Jacob," I told him. "I bin keeping the secrets in this family for nigh on thirty-two years and I bain't gonna change me ways now!" "I'm going down to dinner with Merle tonight," he told me, "don't wait up. You get along home. I'll be fine. I'll see you in the morning." And that's the last time I see'd him.'

Vera's voice had gone husky, eyes cloudy with tears. Vicki put a hand on hers and they both looked away.

'How did Dad get on with Merle?' she asked.

'Oh they two was thick as thieves. He'd go down to Bridge Cottage for dinner one week 'n then Merle'd come up here the next. Sometimes more. It was good to be cooking proper dinners again and 'aving a bit o' company in the house. You know his parents died?'

'They said it was an accident, didn't they?' Vicki said.

'Aye, so they said. Dr and Mrs Hollyman went over to Hurlestone Point so she could do some more of her watercolours and he could watch for puffins or terns or summat. They found them both at the bottom of the cliff. You know how slippery the grass can be up there. The police didn't want to make no trouble, I think, for Merle. And she had the cancer you know, only months to live. But they'd never told Merle so he didn't know nothing about it.' Vera paused. 'He needed you to come home then … but I s'pose you couldn't.'

Vicki said nothing.

'He'd just come back, after his marriage broke up. Never did think that'd last,' Vera muttered. 'Anyroad, he hadn't bin back more'n a couple o' months when it happened. Mr Jacob was down there quite a bit after that. Seein' to things and keepin' an eye out. Merle was very upset, I think he really appreciated the way just about everyone helped. He got his computer company going and it just seems to 'ave gone from strength to strength. An' he plays the organ again. An' he's got a good little jazz band goin' an' they get to play all round the moor. They even roped him in for the bell ringing and the village won the competition last year.' Vera finished triumphantly.

Hardacre Perspectives

BRIDEWELL MANOR – VICKI

The quiet morning of catching up for Vicki and Vera was interrupted by a car grunting its way up the drive.

''Tis that perliceman again,' Vera peered out the window. 'I might 'a guessed he'd be along bright and sharp. He know'd you was coming down overnight an' he's going ter try an' catch you out afore y've had time to turn around. We'll ''ave 'im in 'ere an' I ain't going nowheres.'

There was a knock on the door. Vera went up the hall to answer it. The DI followed her back to the kitchen.

'Good morning Miss Bryde, Miss Gardner. I hope I'm not too early?' Hardacre stood in the doorway, holding his hat, watching them from under his eyelids.

'Come in.' Vicki stood up wearily, thinking he's in already.

The policeman took the chair she offered.

''Tis coffee you like, Mr Hardacre. Black, no sugar. I'll make y' a cup.' Vera's chin was well tucked in.

Hardacre settled himself at the kitchen table, thought about taking out his pipe and changed his mind. No need to antagonise them further. Shortly Vera came with the coffee. Neither of the women had volunteered any conversation, something his slow, waiting tactics usually produced in nervous people. These two were very contained, masters of themselves. Mistresses, he began to correct himself and thought again, no, mastery was the word.

'I'm very sorry about your father, Miss Bryde,' he began the conversation himself.

'Thank you,' Vicki replied. 'What can I do for you?'

'It's just really to confirm what you know of your father's doings, his work and that.' Hardacre paused.

Vicki raised her eyebrows and smiled faintly.

'You know your father had dinner with Mr Hollyman the night he died?'

'I do now.'

'You didn't?'

'Not until Vera told me, when I arrived home this morning.'

'Was this a common practice of his, do you know?'

'Mr Hardacre, you don't understand. I knew a lot about some parts of my father's work and doings, what happened in London and what he'd tell me. And nothing at all about other bits. I haven't seen Mr Hollyman, or spoken to him, for years. We, er, fell out. Dad wouldn't be so gross as to talk about him to me.'

'So you'd know nothing of what they may have talked about, why he would have gone there.'

'Nothing at all. I assume he went for pleasure. Vera tells me they were in the habit of dining with each other every week. I didn't know that until she told me. Consequently I've no idea what they would have talked about. I can guess, of course. Dad would likely have been on about his latest project. I dare say the same would go for Mr Hollyman. Vera tells me he's doing very well in his computer business and various village activities. I knew nothing of this until a few hours ago.' She paused and poured herself a cup of tea. 'Can you tell me why all the interrogation? I understood my father slipped and fell into the pool, and drowned. Is that not the case? Is there something else?'

'I can't say as yet, Miss Bryde. We're looking into everything.' Hardacre felt he sounded like something out of Agatha Christie. Probably a good idea, he grinned internally, he didn't want her to know him yet. He changed the subject.

'When did you last see your father?'

'Before Christmas. We had dinner together in Soho.'

'You didn't spend Christmas with him?'

'No.'

'Was this normal?' Hardacre felt getting blood from a stone would be easier.

'Yes.'

'You didn't get on with your father?'

That hit something in her. He watched closely, hiding behind drooping eyelids.

'We were very close,' Vicki managed, her voice breaking. 'I didn't get on with his mistress, so I've not been home for years. Dad and I would meet up in town, visit each other. As long as she wasn't there.'

'It seems there's a couple of people you are not on the best of terms with down here, Miss Bryde?'

'It does, doesn't it?' Vicki stood up. 'Mr Hardacre, if you've really nothing else to the point to ask me, I'm very tired. I've been up all night driving and just had a couple of hours sleep. My father is dead. I would like the space to mourn him in peace.'

'I think that'll be all for now.' Hardacre stood up too. 'I'm sorry again for your loss, Miss Bryde. And for troubling you at such a time, but I have to look into your father's death. It's probably all quite straightforward but you wouldn't thank me if, later, it turned out there was some foul play and I hadn't been rigorous in my investigations now. Thank you again for your time. I'll let myself out.'

And he was gone.

The Owl House - Olive Millar

Detective Inspector Hardacre drove up to the top of the drive and stopped. He sat speculating which way to turn but there was really no question, he knew where he was going. There's no getting away with it, he told himself, you need to see all the women, and as soon as possible, before they get to chittering amongst themselves like so many sparrows. He made a wry face, shifted to first gear and let in the clutch.

At Honeybeetle Cross he turned right again and slipped along until he came to the corner, and the lane to the Owl House. He knew she would be alone, he'd seen Joe trundling the old Victorian water cart through the gate of the walled garden and down to the pump in the stable yard. Joe'd be at his work. Olive would be at home, if the gods were smiling on him, and he thought they were. He could feel it in his bones.

He rolled up the lane between the high banks, the tyres scrunching on the new gravel. She would have advance warning if she was outside.

Rounding the last corner, he saw she was hanging out the washing.

'Morning, Mrs Millar,' he called as he got out of the car. 'Nothing like a bit of frost on the sheets to get them smelling good, is there? I do that myself.'

He was smiling cheerily as he walked over the hard standing and onto the path up to the front door. He stopped by the chestnut arch which divided the garden from the yard and waited, watching, while the Sealyham yapped excitedly and wagged his back half madly. Tail's too short to wag just that, thought Hardacre as he reached down to stroke the dog's ears.

Olive left the rest of the washing in the basket and came over to him. He held out his hand. She took it.

'I'm Detective Inspector Hardacre,' he announced, looking apologetic. 'We met after a fashion last night, under very sad circumstances. I wonder if I might ask you a few questions?'

Olive's lips pursed. 'I don't know that I can tell you anything,' she began.

'Oh, it's just to get an idea of Professor Bryde from those who knew him. I gather you knew him fairly well?'

Olive pulled herself together. 'Please come in,' she said leading the way into the cottage. 'Can I get you anything?'

'Well, only if you were going to have something yourself,' he replied, reminding himself that an iron constitution and an infinitely expanding bladder were essential for good police work.

'I wasn't really,' Olive looked at him quizzically. 'As you saw, I was in the middle of the washing.'

Hardacre's eyes crinkled. 'I'll try not to keep you too long. I meant it about the frost,' he added.

'I agree!' Olive sat down at the table, indicated he sit too.

'You knew Professor Bryde quite well?'

Olive took in a breath. 'Yes,' she said. 'Yes I did.'

'Can you tell me a bit about him?'

'What sort of thing? How would it be important? I understood it was an accident, he slipped and fell.'

'It looks that way at the moment but we'll have to wait for the post mortem to tell us the cause of death. He could well have slipped. But I would like to know more about him, get more of a picture of him. It's important not to let Miss Bryde down at this time. It will help her to know all the circumstances surrounding her father's death.'

Olive looked at him, considering.

'How long have you known the professor?' he asked.

'Nearly ten years now. Since Joe first brought me down here before we were married.'

'You knew him before you married Mr Millar?'

'Oh no. Well yes. I mean Joe brought me down as soon as we were engaged. He wanted us to meet. He works … worked … very closely with Jacob and he wanted us to make friends.'

'And did you?'

'Oh yes! Everyone loved Jacob,' Olive's voice caught, she swallowed hard.

'His death must be a great shock to all who knew him,' Hardacre said sympathetically, while he watched Olive carefully.

'Yes,' she paused. 'He was like a father to me. I lost my father when I was hardly more than a baby and Jacob seemed to take his place. I shall miss him. So will Joe.'

'Did you know about his work?'

'Only what everyone knew. What he was doing at the tower, with the dig, and looking into what his ancestor did. It was very exciting, especially when they had the man down from London with his radar equipment, felt like being on Time Team! And there were a whole lot of students down for a few weeks helping with the digging, after the men had done the heavy work dismantling part of the tower so they could see the foundations. Jacob was ever so excited. He came round to supper a few times and told us how it was going. I went up to watch a bit, at first, but it's very slow work, worse than cricket!' Olive smiled tentatively. 'They seem to have to sift tons of soil for every tiny bit they find but there were some lovely pieces of Roman work and then the Tintagel ware and then some very old stuff. Thousands of years BC I think Jacob said.'

Hardacre smiled back. Funny way of saying it, he thought, only what everyone knew. Why would she think he was asking about secrets? Perhaps because there were secrets. She's not used to walking around the truth, he thought. And she'd really like it if Joe came in right now to rescue her, but I hope he doesn't.

'So he was excited by his work, happy, no worries?'

'Oh yes, certainly. He was really hoping for a breakthrough. He's been on the tale of his ancestor, Richard Bryde, all his life. He had no worries on that score.'

'So on what score did he have worries, Mrs Millar?'

Olive swallowed again. She realises she's told me more than she meant to, he thought.

'I suppose you know about the water?' Olive asked him.

'I understand Mr Courtney and Mrs Villiers have capped the village spring, and are bottling the water and selling it.'

'Exactly! It's unheard of! The water's always belonged to the village, and no-one ever thought anyone would do such a thing. It's wrecking everything, the water table's gone down, the cottages are subsiding, the apples are failing. It's terrible.'

'I believe you do the books for Julia Courtney at the Cider Press, is that right?'

'I do. Did. Still do, as long as Julia can keep going. She's in a terrible state since her husband's death.'

'Ah yes. Very sad. Suicide, wasn't it?'

'Yes.' Olive shut her lips firmly.

'What happened there, do you know?' Hardacre had seen her mouth but he thought it was worth a try.

'You'll have to ask Mrs Courtney,' she said.

'Yes, of course. And so I will,' he watched her under his eyelids. 'And do you know Miss Bryde at all?' he changed tack.

'No. I've not met her yet.'

'Really?'

'Oh no. She never comes home now. She's not really been here for several years and, the few times she has, she's just been at the manor and not gone about. And then only for the odd weekend. I think even Joe hardly saw her.'

'How's that? Didn't she get on with her father?'

'Oh they were very close.'

50

Hardacre raised his eyebrows.

'I don't really know the story but I believe it was to do with an old friend. Really you'll have to ask her.'

'Yes, I will,' Hardacre said again. Damn, he thought, what I need is gossip, and she's realising that now and clamming up.

'I suppose the capping of the spring is very unpopular in the village, people upset, angry at young Julian Courtney.'

'And Mrs Villiers!' Olive couldn't resist the bait. 'Most people think it was largely her fault. She put him up to it. And they think it's spite against Jacob.'

'How's that?'

'Jacob had an affair with her. Then there was a row and they split up and she took up with Julian. It's bad. Julia can hardly look anyone in the face now her son's become village gossip, yet again. Sylvie Villiers must be twenty years older than him.'

'Toy boy, eh?' Hardacre grinned.

'It's horrid!' Olive was upset.

It's only horrid because it involves Jacob, Hardacre thought. This woman didn't look as though she was usually straight laced. He had the feeling she was more than half in love with Jacob herself. But she doesn't know that, he thought, she won't admit it to herself. I wonder if Joe realises? Bet he does, no flies on that one at all.

'So the village is angry over the water?'

'Indeed they are, most of them. Some of the younger ones, who work at the bottling plant, like it of course. Julian pays well and the water's making him huge profits. But that doesn't help the village as a whole.'

'How did the professor feel about all that?'

Olive's jaw tightened again.

'I think he was very angry about the whole thing. He wanted to get the water back but there was no way legally. The well itself belongs to Well Cottage, so whoever owns that owns the well. It's just that nobody ever thought of stopping the water before and so nobody thought anybody ever would,' she repeated.

'Umm! Yes. That sort of thing does happen.' Hardacre said as Olive seemed to seize up again.

'But we didn't need it to happen here!' the words burst out.

This was something very close to the bone for her, Hardacre thought, but what bone? Her love for Jacob, almost certainly.

'So really, you'd agree, the professor's main worry at this time would have been the water rather than his work?'

'Ye-es. The water problem bothered Jacob a lot. He and Joe were trying to find ways round it, since the lawyers said there was no way to contest the bottling plant capping the well. But his work on the tower seemed to be going really well and he was always very chirpy about that.'

'So you don't feel there might have been any reason why he might have wanted to take his own life?'

Olive stared at him.

'Good god, no!' she said. 'Jacob would never do such a thing! He loved life. And his work. And he wouldn't want to give up on the village about the water either. He would have tried everything he could think of to make things right. There's no way Jacob would ever have committed suicide!'

'Well, that's very good to hear, Mrs Millar. And thank you very much for giving me your time. It really has helped me understand a lot more about Professor Bryde. I feel I can go on more confidently now.'

'Do you really think it'll all be sorted out soon?'

'I really do hope so, Mrs Millar, I really do.' Hardacre realised he was being sincere in that statement.

He turned the car carefully, avoiding driving onto the grass. I wonder, he said to the steering wheel, I wonder if her own father committed suicide? She really seemed to be far more upset than I would have expected at that question, she didn't even get in such a state over the toy boy bit. No, that one hit home somewhere.

Well, he thought, they've given me some leads to follow up. And I'm just in the mood for a spot of lunch.

He came down Owlpen Hill, turned the car into the square and parked. He stood tapping out his pipe thoughtfully, looking around at the pretty white and cream cottages, the thatched roofs, the bright gardens. It was a pretty place, Bridewell. It looked prosperous and all the history said it was. But now? He rather thought things had changed drastically in the recent past, and he felt that Professor Bryde would have taken it quite personally. He would go and see what was being said in the Green Lion.

52

Perhaps that landlady, Pat Elworthy wasn't it, would not have too many customers so he could talk to her. She looked a jolly sort and well up to snuff. And, if he couldn't enjoy the cider, it looked as though they still served a good pint of beer.

THE GREEN LION - PAT ELWORTHY

Hardacre walked down the flagged corridor and opened the oak door into the bar. Immediately he smelled the fire, apple wood he thought. Hmmm! I hope they're not already cutting down the apple trees, he thought, a pity if they do. Things could always get better as well as worse in his opinion.

The bar took up most of the back of the old stone building. There were deep window-seats and a door into the conservatory which looked out south, over the apple orchards, and caught the winter sun, reflecting it back into the bar. The floor was flagged, softened by rugs and tapestry cushions in the window-seats. The fire crackled merrily in a huge chimney on the east wall. Ingle, he grinned to himself and then, influenced by the place and its people, he said *aingeal*, the old Gaelic word for hearth.

'Good afternoon,' said a cheery voice from behind the bar. 'It's cold but it's bright. A good winter's day.'

Hardacre went over and stood looking at the array of pumps. He smiled up at the woman, 'You've a goodly selection,' he said. 'I'm spoilt for choice.'

'D'you like a dark ale or a light?' she asked him.

'I'll have a dark today. I'm very partial to Old Peculiar.'

'It's a good ale,' she agreed. 'But I wonder, if you like that sort of thing, if you've tried Riggwetler? It's another Yorkshire brew, Black Sheep Brewery up near Hebden. Their black ale is beautiful, and we have it on draft here. It's quite strong.' She finished.

'Riggwetler?' Hardacre managed the word.

The woman laughed.

'It's Yorkshire dialect for a sheep that won't get up.'

'If it's as strong as you say perhaps that's why!'

'Aye! One of the Theakston family set up the Black Sheep brewery. He used the money he got when the family sold out to wet up his own small traditional brewery. They sell some seriously good ale!'

'Well, the Theakston pedigree is a good recommendation. I'll try a pint.'

'Jug or straight?' she asked him.

'Jug, please.'

She looked at him again, then turned to where some elegant china pint pots hung at the back of the bar. She took one down and drew the beer. Hardacre took a sip, careful not to lose any of the head. It was good. He put the jug down and looked at the painting. It was a green lion, but the head was also a green man, half human, with leaves coming out of its mouth.

'A theme for the pub, is it?' he asked.

'And for the village itself. The green man is the man-of-the-woods, the Hollyman, who rescued the unborn child from the owl woman's body when the harvesters cut her down. We have the owl too.' She took a china pot from the other side of the bar. This one was like a Toby jug but in the shape of a barn owl.'

'It's quite a legend you have here,' Hardacre mused.

'Indeed we do! You know it then?'

'Bits and pieces, yes I do.'

'A local man?'

'I am. But I spent twenty years working in London before I came home again.'

'Ah! It's good to go away and see the world, but it's good to come home too. I got my training in the Grosvenor by Victoria Station. Good fun it was, but very hard work, and stands me in good stead as the landlady here. I got to be a housekeeper before I left,' she said with a wry smile. 'I've seen you about I think?'

'I'm investigating the death of Professor Bryde.'

'Policeman is it? Should I call you superintendent?'

'Only detective inspector,' he said modestly. He had seen the smile in her eyes, but he could also sense her shrewdness. She would tell him what she thought he ought to hear, but that would be useful too, he would know what to ask of his next victim.

'Ask away, detective inspector,' she grinned. 'After all that's what you're here for, as well as my beer. Can I get you something to eat? Questioning's a hungry business. We've got some local pork sausages today which the girl's made into a very nice toad-in-the-hole. and some of Joe Millar's cabbage and potatoes too?'

'That sounds very good, Mrs Elworthy.'

'Saw my name over the door, did you?' she laughed. 'Well, my license is all in order but you're not interested in that today.'

'I was wondering what you could tell me about the professor and his family. It seems Miss Bryde hasn't been home for many years and it's like there's a bit of a mystery about it.'

'Oh, no mystery. I daresay people think it's family business and are not willing to gossip to strangers, such as yourself, about the affairs of the Big House.' Her eyes twinkled and her voice spoke the capital letters, amused but indulgent.

'Are you willing to put me in the picture?' he asked.

'Why not? You'll know sooner or later, and sooner is better for it'll put your mind at rest on that score. You've met Merle Hollyman? Well he and Vicki Bryde grew up together, everyone thought they'd make a match of it, including Jacob, but when they were both at university things got a bit strained and they parted company. She went off to London, after she'd got her degree, and got a bang up job with a major software company, done very well, by what I hear. He ran off to France. His mother was half French and he had friends there, I think. Anyway, that didn't seem to last and back he came. Then he took off for London too. He's another computer freak, went into partnership with a bloke he'd known at university and got married, but again that didn't last. I think the story goes she got off with his friend, anyway they divorced, he split out of the company and came back home. His mother was very ill with cancer, but they'd not told him. She died in a tragic accident, fell off the cliff at Hurlestone Point, along with her husband, so Merle didn't have a happy homecoming at all. That was five years ago now. He inherited Bridge Cottage and set up his computer consultancy, settled down. Doing very nicely now too.'

'Ah! So the childhood sweethearts fell out, is that it?'

'Yes. But it wouldn't surprise me one bit if Jacob's death doesn't bring them back together.'

'Did the professor get on well with Mr Hollyman?'

'Oh yes. They were always in and out of each other's pockets. Until he took up with Mrs Villiers.'

'Mr Hollyman?'

'Certainly not! And don't you go playing the innocent with me, detective inspector,' she grinned. 'I expect you've already heard that Jacob had an affair with Sylvie Villiers. She was a colleague in the archaeology business, I believe. They met up again at some conference and into bed they fell. Natural enough. She's a very attractive woman, and he's been a widower for over twenty years. I don't think it went down very well with Vicki, though. She was mistress of the house since her mother died and wouldn't take kindly to another woman in her place. I seem to remember too that there was no love lost between Caroline, Vicki's mother, and Sylvie when she first came here. That was at the time of the coffin discovery which made Jacob's name. I daresay the daughter feels much as the mother did.'

'Would you say there was enmity there?'

'On a sort of smouldering level, perhaps. Neither Vicki nor Sylvie like each other, but they've both got lives, and plenty to do besides having a go at each other, if that's what you're thinking.'

Hardacre had been working his way through the toad-in-the-hole while he listened to the landlady. Her staff were taking care of the few other customers and it seemed she was quite happy to give him her time. Now he pushed the empty plate away with a sigh of contentment.

'Good job the pattern's firmly stuck to the plate,' she took it. 'Or you'd have licked it off, I think! Good?'

'Very good!'

'Can I tempt you with some more beer?'

'I think I'd better have some coffee to wash it down,' he said. 'But the beer is excellent too. How about Julian Courtney?'

'Mary! A pot of coffee please!' Pat Elworthy turned back to Hardacre. 'Young Julian? A nasty piece of work there. A pity too, he could have been a very clever man, and done well for himself, if he hadn't always had himself at the forefront of his mind. His selfishness has made him stupid quite often.'

'Can you tell me about him too?'

'Well you know he's the son of the Cider Press?'

Hardacre nodded.

'Very well off they are, the Courtneys, or were. They had a daughter too, but she's married to some American and spends most of her time abroad now. She flew home for her father's funeral, but was off again the next day, couldn't stay to care for her mother. But then, she hadn't been home for four years before that either.'

'Sounds as if there's a selfish gene in the family?'

'Aye, well …! Julian was brought up in the country, but he's not a country boy. He was always hankering after the bright lights and the excitement. As soon as he could, he went up to London and got himself a job in one of the big advertising agencies, did very well too, for a while, until his itch got to him again. He's always got to be number one, have an edge, be ahead. Nobody knows what really happened. There were stories of embezzlement, sex, taking bribes, all of which I'd say are well within Julian's remit. Anyway, whatever happened, he turned up here again a bit over eighteen months ago. Things were cooling between Jacob and Sylvie. She was here one evening, sitting in that window over there, all on her own with a bottle of wine, when in comes Julian and claps eyes on her. It took him about three minutes to get his own drink and find his way over there. They left together fairly soon after, and everyone watched them go. I expect that was it, really. He's a very good looking young man, very personable. And I dare say she's as fly as he, so there won't be any misunderstandings there. If it wasn't for the water I'd say good luck to them.'

'But it is about the water, isn't it?' Hardacre looked at her.

'Yes, it is.'

'You know, it doesn't make the least bit of sense, really, to the honest but struggling police mind,' he grinned at Mrs Elworthy. 'But I think the water is the crux of the matter. This whole thing, Jacob's death, is all about the water.'

Pat Elworthy nodded slowly. 'It wasn't an accident then?'

'Oh, everything points to that. It's very likely he slipped and fell. It's just my gut feelings,' he smiled wryly, 'and policemen aren't supposed to have instincts nowadays, but we all do.'

'And what now? Is there anything more I can help you with?' she asked him.

'Not just at the moment, Mrs Elworthy,' Hardacre took out his wallet, offered her the ten pound note and took the change. 'But I might call back.'

'Do,' she said. 'And try to come when you're not on business.'

'That'll be a day when there's a blue moon!' he laughed.

He walked back to the car and stood slowly filling his pipe. No, he thought, I'll walk. He turned about and set off back down the square, past the Green Lion, to the path through the orchards.

THE CIDER PRESS - JULIA COURTNEY

The lane between the Sunday School and the pub was hardly more than a footpath, just wide enough for the residents to bring their cars down. The houses were new, compared to the rest of the village. Just after World War Two, Hardacre thought, by the look of them. Ah yes, there was a row of lock-up garages at the end, partially screened by honeysuckle climbing a wooden fence.

There was a good, new, wooden five-bar gate at the end of the lane with a small kissing-gate beside it for pedestrians. The path through the field was metalled, it seemed people used this way quite often, a public footpath probably. He went through.

The path ran beside the remains of the stream-bed. He bent to touch the dried primrose leaves, it brought back his boyhood. There'd be wood anemones too, and daffodils in the spring, if there was any water to feed them. He understood the village anger at anyone who tampered with the stream.

He looked at the apple trees, they seemed dry. Difficult to tell at this time of year, trees always look asleep in January but he went over to one and wriggled a finger down into the hard earth. It went too easily, the earth was dry, it should have been hard with frozen water on a day like this. He wiped his finger against his coat and puffed up his pipe, at least the pipe-bole was warm and kept his fingers from going numb.

The path led through the orchard. He imagined it in blossom, buzzing with bees, and the scent. Avalon. He chuckled as the picture came … himself riding his mother's broom-handle round the yard, with a saucepan on his head and waving the wooden sword he'd made. He'd been so proud of that sword. Borrowed his father's tools and made it himself. Even Dad thought it was good. Little knight on a white charger, wasn't I? And here I am still at it! Wonder where that sword is now? He felt tempted to hunt in the attic when he got home. But I was a kid, he thought, the people here seem to live this stuff for real.

The path was longer than he'd thought, but eventually he found himself at another wooden gate. The stream bed beside him was a couple of feet deep now, but still dry. The water should be fairly rushing along at this time of year, but only the east wind sang through the stones at the bottom. A weird note, it made the hairs on his neck stand up. He went through the gate.

Now, he could see the water wheel which powered the apple-pressing machinery. It stood still, waiting hungrily for water. Damn! He thought, I'm right, I know I am. Water is at the bottom of this whole bloody mess, it's even the way that poor bugger died. But I'm not going to get that past the Super. Superintendent Haddick was a careful man, he went by the rules, followed the book every inch of the way. He was also a modern man. He had a mobile phone, knew how to do text messaging, send pictures of the crime scene. He had a laptop, kept abreast of the statistics and managed his life with one of those new-fangled computer diary thingummies. And he was always trying to insist that Hardacre should do the same.

'This is the twentieth century, Hardacre!' Haddick would burst into his office, his eyes searching around for some space to sit. 'Damn nearly the twenty-first century!'

Haddick would protest loudly, glaring, resigning himself to standing. Every available piece of furniture was covered with precarious piles of paper. In his heart, which he practically never consulted, Haddick knew Hardacre maintained his office just so in order that no-one would ever be able to sit down and interrupt him. Haddick was envious of Hardacre's self-sufficiency and, just occasionally, he allowed himself to wonder how he managed it. But, of course, there was no way he would ever ask.

'Here you are, Hardacre,' he would glower down, 'still bumbling along like Sherlock Holmes. It's embarrassing you know. Sets a terrible example for the younger men.'

'Yes sir,' Hardacre would reply, and keep his head down.

His years in the Met helped ease the pressure. That and his MBE. My Bloody Effort! he scowled to himself, listening to the singing stones. Damn near got killed! Maybe it would have been better if I had … No! Stop that right now! He pulled himself back together. The wind singing in the stones echoed his thoughts back to him. Damn this place! I'm getting in a mood. He stood still, spent a few moments cleaning his pipe and putting it away. The careful ritual helped to calm his nerves.

The old stone house was three stories high, with gable windows in the dark slate roof. He felt as if it was crouching over him. Ye gods, he swore at himself, this isn't Stephen King! Get a grip! He marched up to the door and knocked.

Nothing happened. Where was she? All his instincts told him she was here. He knocked again. Then he heard feet. A small, blonde woman carrying a trug emerged from between the laurel bushes and the house wall.

'Hello,' she began. 'Can I help you?

'I hope so. Mrs Courtney?

'Yes …?'

'I'm Detective Inspector Hardacre. I'm looking into the death of Professor Bryde. I wonder if I might ask you a few questions, just so I can get a picture?'

Hardacre watched the smile fall off her thin face at hearing the professor's name. Were all the women after him?

'Oh … well … you'd better come in.'

He followed her up the steps and through the glass-panelled double door. She dumped the trug unceremoniously onto the big table. Hardacre surreptitiously stoked the dust off it while she crossed to a door at the back of the hall. The grain was beautiful, it looked like elm.

'Louisa!' she called. A girl came out of the back of the house. 'Can you get us some tea please? You'll take a cup, won't you?' she turned to Hardacre.

'Thank you very much.' He thought of his iron constitution and asked it to handle the tea so it didn't upset his superb lunch.

The woman led him into a large sitting room. The windows gave onto a deep, muddy pit. The mill-pool, Hardacre guessed. Dry skeletons of bamboo rustled along its edge. Was that the remains of a gunnera? Not much chance for it, without the water.

She indicated they sit down in over-stuffed armchairs, either side of a low table.

'What can I do for you?' she asked.

'I'm very sorry to trouble you, Mrs Courtney. I really just need some background information on Professor Bryde and the family. Just so I can get a clearer picture. You knew the professor quite well I suppose?'

'Yes. Our families have always been friends. My husband ...' she stopped, gagged, started herself up again. 'My husband and Jacob were boys together. I married Brian not long before Jacob married Caroline. We were all much of an age.'

'I see. His unexpected death is quite a shock to you?'

Julia Courtney choked slightly and sat biting the side of her finger for a moment.

'You know about my husband's death?'

'Yes. I was very sorry to hear about it. A colleague of mine had the case. It was something to do with the water here?'

'Yes.' She stopped again, looked out of the window for several minutes and then turned back to him, seemingly having made up her mind. Hardacre waited patiently.

'It's my son,' she said. 'We've never really understood Julian. He was always a difficult boy. Brilliant but erratic at school, and the other boys, in general, seemed afraid of him. In fact, we nearly had to take him out of school on a couple of occasions, when they told us he was bullying the younger boys. It was very hard to accept, but there'd been things at home, here.' Julia Courtney stopped, sat chewing her hand, then resumed her testimony. 'He had a spate of shooting at everyone's pets, and the animals and birds in the woods. Jacob found out, and told Brian. We locked up all the guns after that. I think the other boys in the village had a go at Julian about it too.'

'I don't expect that endeared them to him?'

'No.' She bit her hand again, then realised what she was doing and fussed, moving magazines off the table so the tea tray would fit when the girl eventually brought it.

'Julian became even more withdrawn and sullen after that.' She stopped fussing and sat back in her chair. 'He asked to spend the holidays with a school friend he'd actually made, rather than come home. It was as though he walked away from us, we didn't know what to do.' Julia stopped again. 'I don't know if you've heard about what happened at the well-guardian ceremony?'

Hardacre shook his head.

'Well, the daughter of the Bryde family is, by tradition, the guardian of our spring here in the village. It all goes back before Roman times. I don't really know the history, but I do know it's very important to everyone here. I'm an incomer you see, I was born on the other side of the county. I met Brian and we fell in love. Now I've become part of the village. Anyway,' she took a breath, 'Vicki became the well-guardian on her thirteenth birthday. It's odd that, her birthday really is on the same day as the feast day, rather a fluke, I suppose. There's the ceremony, which is really very good and moving, and then there's a big party at the manor. All the village takes part.

'At the ceremony, Vicki has to run the maze in the middle of the Wilderness wood. When she gets to the middle she has to call the boys to come and get her. Then they run a race through the maze and the first one there gets her and becomes the representative of the Holly Man in the legend. And that's odd too. You know Merle's name really is Hollyman? His father came to be our doctor here a bit before I married Brian. There was Jacob, Jack Hollyman and Brian. They were really close friends. I got on very well with Caroline Bryde and Jill Hollyman too. We were all friends together … except for Julian. I used to walk him in the pram, with the others, but even then he didn't seem to want to play with them. They'd be playing away and he'd sit on the side, just watching. It was really strange to see a baby watching so intensely. Later, when Lizzie, his sister, was born, she'd play with Vicki and Merle, and the other children, but still Julian would go off on his own or just sit staring, watching.' Julia gave an unconscious shudder as she spoke, as though her own son was an alien to her.

'I'm drifting from the point,' she said, just as the girl brought in the tea. There was a plate of little triangular sandwiches with the crusts cut off, home-baked cakes in paper cups and bread and butter triangles, along with dishes of different coloured jams. Hardacre's stomach threatened to rebel.

Julia waited until the girl had closed the door behind her.

'On the feast day, everyone expected that it would be just Merle who would run the race. He and Vicki had been childhood sweethearts. And there was the funny coincidence of his name. Like her birthday. But, just as the blacksmith called for the runners to come up, Julian stepped forward. I didn't know whether to laugh or cry. In a way, it was good to see my son actually take part in something in the village, but I was also afraid of what he might do. I'd lived with him for seventeen years, he'd never missed a chance to score over anyone in that whole time. He'd had ways of making me do what he wanted, even as a baby.

'The race began and straight away Julian was fouling, barging Merle, knocking him down. Merle knew what he was about though, and got past him without assaulting him in return. He won. Julian lost. And sprained his ankle to boot. Later, at the party, he hobbled about with bottle after bottle of beer in his hand then, about ten o'clock, he disappeared. I heard what happened later from Jill Hollyman. Apparently Julian followed Vicki and Merle down to Bridge Cottage. When Merle went home, Vicki came to walk back up through the woods, by the Owlwater. She'd done it all her life, all the kids walk through there. Julian followed her, found her and tried to rape her. Merle came in time. He said he'd been called by the foxes Vicki was playing with when Julian found her. He knocked Julian about a bit, which was a good thing really or I think Brian would have killed him else. The story crept its way round the village and nobody would even look at Julian for weeks. I found it terrible to go into the shops and the post office. In fact, I started to go into West Milton to do my shopping rather than face everyone here. Not long after that, Julian got the advertising job and went to London. Brian gave him money to get set up there. We were really relieved he'd gone. It was possible to go into the village again, and everyone was very sympathetic.'

'That was a very difficult story, Mrs Courtney. Thank you very much for telling me. It gives me a good picture of how things must be between your son and the Bryde camp. I would doubt there's any love lost there at all.'

Julia Courtney gasped.

'I'm sorry, Mrs Courtney. That was rather blunt. I beg your pardon.' Hardacre watched the widow from under his eyelids.

'No,' she took a deep breath. 'I think you're very right. However the truth is not always good to hear, especially when you've been hiding from it as long as I have.'

'What happened with your husband, please?'

'Well, you know Julian has set up with Sylvie Villiers after she broke up with Jacob? She bought Well Cottage when she first began seeing Jacob, so she could be here, and see him, without living in the house. There was no way Jacob could've done that. Vicki would never have spoken to him again. And I suspect Sylvie also wanted to make sure she had a bolt hole in case anything happened. She's a very careful, far-thinking woman.'

Hardacre grinned at Mrs Courtney. 'That's a very charitable way of putting it!' he said.

She had the grace to smile back. 'Yes! It was, wasn't it! No, you're right, I don't like her, but it's not just because of Julian. She was on that first dig, when Jacob found the owl woman's grave, the bronze tablet which had the story of the cup and all that. He was chasing that cup all his life. Anyway, Caroline didn't like her, felt she always wanted the kudos for herself. Sylvie was certainly very peeved when Jacob's papers were published and his career made for life. We all thought she wished it had been her.

'Anyway, there was Julian with Sylvie. And not too long after that they set up the bottling plant. Somehow all the permissions came through like clockwork, before anyone had time to register an objection. Jacob was away, lecturing in America I think. And Vicki was never here. So there was no-one we could turn to. One day the water stopped. We didn't believe it but it was all too true. It's never come on again. The stream from the well was the major feed for our orchards so the trees started to suffer. Many of them are dead already, and the rest are dying. A couple of years ago Brian got a very large loan from the bank to modernise all the machinery in the press, and in our bottling plant too. Ironic that, Julian sets up his plant just like his father's. He'd never had any time for the business before but he must have been watching, he certainly knows how to do it.

'Once the water was gone the business began to fail. There were no profits to pay off the loan, we were on our last legs. Brian went to ask … no, to beg Julian to give the water back.' Julia stopped and bit her hand again. 'Julian … Julian laughed.'

She broke down and sat shaking with silent sobs. Hardacre watched, waited. She would be better to come out of it herself, probably jump out of her skin if he touched her. Gradually the sobs subsided and she came back to herself. She was quiet for a moment, then,

'Brian killed himself that night' she said baldly.

They sat together in silence for several minutes.

'I'm so very sorry, Mrs Courtney.'

Julia looked at him, a terrible hopeless expression in her eyes. He found it difficult to look back. He waited again. After several more minutes she sat up straighter.

'I hope that's all been helpful to you, inspector.'

'Indeed it has. Thank you again, Mrs Courtney. It's most useful. I have a much clearer picture of everything involved.'

'You do believe it was an accident, don't you?' Julia's eyes pleaded. 'I'm sure it must have been. He was often going up there and it can be very slippery ...' Her voice trailed off.

She realises that too many words will set off all my suspicions, he thought grimly. And so they are. Why does everyone want me to believe it was an accident, I wonder? Why do they care so much? This is going to take further pondering.

He did some of the pondering as he walked slowly back to the village through the acres of apple trees. Suddenly he stopped. His head was turning, hunting, listening, then he set off into the heart of the orchard. He stopped beside an ancient, gnarled tree. It had the remains of a rope hanging down from it. He looked up. Yes, he could see how you could climb the tree, fix the rope around the branch, put the loop around your neck. Then all you had to do was jump.

WELL COTTAGE – SYLVIE & JULIAN

Hardacre arrived at the mouth of Orchard Row and paused. There was a light on in Well Cottage, just as he'd hoped there would be. He knocked out his pipe, walked slowly across the road and up into the huge square. The church tower loomed down at him from every inch of its one hundred and fifty feet. Then the bells began to ring.

He knocked and waited. He could hear nothing over the ringing so he knocked again. The door opened immediately.

'Yes?' The tall, fair young man looked down at Hardacre over his aquiline nose.

'I'm Detective Inspector Hardacre,' he held out his warrant card. 'Is Mrs Villiers in? I'd like a few words with her.'

'Sylvie!' the young man called over his shoulder. 'It's the Bill. Are you in?'

There was a silvery laugh from down the corridor and a slight woman came out of a room at the back. Hardacre watched her. He knew she must be in her early fifties at least, but she looked about thirty-five.

'Darling!' she exclaimed gracefully to the young man. 'Of course I must be in to the police. Bring him in. Put the kettle on, he's bound to want some tea. Isn't that so, Inspector?'

The slight American accent was very attractive. Hardacre could feel the spell of her looks, her voice, tugging at him. He smiled back at her, thinking attack was probably the best form of defence. The young man also smiled and opened the door wide. As Hardacre stepped past him he felt the hairs rise on the back of his neck. He followed Sylvie through to the large sitting room. She pointed him to a comfortable looking chair.

'Put some Lapsang on for me would you, darling, and …?' she turned to Hardacre.

'Do you have any Darjeeling?' he asked rashly, never having drunk the stuff in his life, but he recalled it was said to be like good champagne for tea connoisseurs. Sylvie's eyebrows went up and she looked at him again. I said the right thing, he thought grimly. Then, yes Vicki, he said to himself, you have quite some opponents here.

'We certainly do. Make it Darjeeling for two, or three if you want to join us, love. Is that OK, Inspector?

'That would do nicely, Mrs Villiers.' Hardacre's mouth slid around a smile. It seemed they understood each other.

'You probably realise I'm looking into the unfortunate death of Professor Bryde,' he began.

Sylvie inclined her head.

'I understand you had a relationship with the professor for some time but it was ended at the time of his death. Did you see him at all?' Then Hardacre coughed. He realised he'd lost himself under the spell of those silver-blue eyes. He retrieved himself, asking the right question at last.

'When did you last see Professor Bryde?'

Sylvie's smile told him she had enjoyed his mistake.

'I saw Jacob in the post office on the morning of his death, but we didn't speak. In the terms you mean, I hadn't seen him for several weeks.'

'So you had no idea what he was working on?'

'Oh yes! I knew what he was working on. What he was always working

66

on whenever he was down here, and probably a lot of the time he was in Town too. That blasted grail legend. Jacob was totally obsessed, you know.'

'And you had been helping him with that?'

'Yes again, while we were lovers. And before that too. You probably know, I first met him when he was digging the grave here in the church, where he found the bronze tablet confirming the legend. We were just professional colleagues then. We didn't have our affair until very much later, when we happened to meet at an Oxford conference a few years back.'

You're giving me a nice lot of information, Hardacre thought. What is it you're trying to hide in this smoke screen?

'I understand there was some row and you split up?'

'That's right. The usual sort of thing between professional archaeologists, who owns what paper and who can publish it. It's funny when you can stand back.' She laughed gently. 'We're a pack of children really. My ball! No! My ball! Swat! Biff! But it's only verbal biffs, you know, we're all much too committed to resort to the physical, except in that Agatha Christie novel. We spend a quarter of our lives going through the professional journals looking for mistakes to point out to our colleagues. Point scoring is a very sweet cup.'

Now why is she disclaiming any physical violence quite so readily, Hardacre wondered.

'But, I believe there *was* some physical stuff in your row, wasn't there?' Hardacre called up memories of the internal police file on the 'domestic incident' which had been reported after Jacob had landed in the local hospital.

Sylvie's eyes narrowed.

'I see you've been doing your homework, inspector,' her voice was very soft. 'Yes, Jacob and I came to blows. He went for me and I defended myself with a poker.'

'I see. And weren't you present too, Mr Courtney?'

Julian's eyes narrowed, a nasty smile crossed his face.

'Yes, I was there. I was worried about Sylvie. We'd recently begun our affair and I know, to my cost, the Bryde family is notoriously jealous. I felt I should be around when she was trying to get her papers back from the professor.'

'Ah, yes,' Hardacre watched Julian and Sylvie. 'Of course you've known the Bryde family all your life, haven't you?'

'I was born here in the village. It's very difficult *not* to know the Bryde family. They take such a great interest in everyone, and everything, here, one cannot avoid knowing them.'

'You seem to be telling me you tried?'

'But not very successfully as you can see, inspector. Here I am, still involved in their blasted affairs.'

'Where were you on the night the professor died?' Hardacre sprang the usual police question. The trap worked. Julian flushed up, even Sylvie's carefully controlled breathing missed a slight beat to his trained eyes.

'I was here. With Sylvie. Do you want precise details of what we were doing?'

Hardacre allowed his eyes to crinkle at the corners, showing Julian he acknowledged the hit.

'I don't think that will be necessary,' he said softly. 'Provided Mrs Villiers can confirm you were with her.'

'Oh yes, inspector. I can indeed do that. Before we went to bed I was in my study, working.' Sylvie anticipated his next question.

'May I see your study?'

That caught her off guard.

'Why, yes,' she said, after an instant.

Hardacre followed her across the room and through a door he hadn't noticed. He was immediately aware of the smell.

'I'm a herbalist in my spare time,' Sylvie watched his nose wrinkle. 'That's wormwood you can smell. I use it as a cleansing herb. It can be very useful after someone you know has died.'

Hardacre looked round the room. She kept the lighting low, his eyes took a moment to adjust, then he saw the stuffed barn owl in the glass case on the mantelpiece. Its eyes caught his. For a moment, he could have sworn they moved.

'Thank you, Mrs Villiers,' he turned to leave the room.

'Has all that intimate gossip helped you at all?' she asked him, her voice smiling but her eyes hard.

'Yes, actually, it has,' He smiled back at her in a very genuine way.

Suddenly he wasn't frightened of her any more and realised that he had been when he first entered Well Cottage.

Julian showed him to the door.

Hardacre sat for a couple of hours, sipping his whisky beside the fire in the sitting room that night. Yes, there was professional jealousy there. And she'd told him, rather in the manner of a spin-doctor, that Jacob was obsessed with the cup. That told him that she was equally, if not more, obsessed … and obsessed people did strange things. He felt in his bones that she would do anything to get that cup. She wanted kudos ... and more. The smell in her room reminded him of something but he couldn't remember what it was. Then his mind took him back twenty-odd years.

He was standing in the dim living-room of the cottage down at Kitnor, a young constable on his first solo case. He'd been called in because there was a missing person. Some American woman had gone walking along the beach below Porlock Weir, despite being been warned of the tides. She and her daughter had been staying with the old woman who owned the cottage. There had been a similar smell there then.

The old woman was famous in the district as a herbalist. The local people, even his religious mother, all went to her. She'd sent some stuff when his father had the shingles and it had worked too, much to the West Milton doctor's surprise. Then he had gone on holiday and Dr Hollyman had come for the last visit. He'd been pleased to see old Lilly Clocks' herbs. 'That'll do the trick,' he'd said. His mother had been glad Hollyman approved, it gave her confidence, and Dad got better far more quickly than anyone had expected.

Hardacre tootled across the moor early the next morning and took the car down the track into the Kitnor valley. At the bottom, he leaned on the bridge, listening to the water and looking at the tiny spire, perched like a witch's hat on top of the church.

'Morning!' said the witch, coming up beside him. 'You want to come down to the cottage then?'

She was carrying a bundle of sticks and a leather bag bulging with moss and herbs. The valley was wonderfully alive and warm. It didn't feel like January here.

69

'Thank you,' he said, smiling down at her. She gave him a toothy grin in return.

Inside, the cottage was just as he remembered. Every available surface contained an animal, either sleeping or washing itself, or else jars and bottles full of brightly coloured concoctions. There was wool on the spindle of the spinning wheel, it looked like she'd been working it recently. She took the big kettle and filled it from the pump by the sink, then hung it back over the fire.

'You could do with some mint tea,' she said. 'Bin knocking your insides about by the looks o' you.'

'True enough, mother. That's how it is with police work!'

'Aye, I remembers you. Just a young lad with your shiny new uniform the last time I see'd you. Bin doing a lot o' things since then, have you not?'

'I have.'

'And now you'm here about Jacob Bryde.' It was a statement, not a question.

'And can you tell me anything?'

Lilly Clocks pottered about, getting mugs and herbs, then the kettle began to sing and she made their drinks. Hardacre sipped his tentatively, then took a longer drink. He felt better.

'Still works, don't it?'

'Yes, mother, it does.'

'What d'ye want to know?'

'I don't know,' he said. 'I know there's something I need to know, but I don't know what it is.'

Lilly sat down at the spinning wheel. It clacked and hummed rhythmically, he felt his eyes closing.

He was back in Sylvie's study. He watched her take the glass case with the owl and put it on the table. She took three candles and lit them, setting them around the owl and then put some incense on the charcoal in the bronze dish in front of the case. The smells were strange, pungent, even in his dream they made him want to sneeze. Sylvie began to speak, it sounded like Welsh, whole mouthfuls of consonants, and a mist began to grow inside the case. Her hands wove patterns around the glass.

Suddenly the owl moved. He stared at it. It seemed to have a human face, Vicki's face, he realised with a start. The bird seemed to be struggling, trying to get away. He looked at Sylvie and saw her eyes narrowed, a triumphant look on her face.

'I have you now,' she whispered.

The owl flew off and Hardacre followed in the dream. It went over the Wilderness and on to the tower where Jacob stood at the top of the waterfall. He, too, looked triumphant. He was holding a gold cup.

The owl shrieked. Jacob fell. Hardacre found himself back in Sylvie's study. He felt frightened now, he wanted to wake up, this dream was getting nasty.

The owl was back inside the glass case. Sylvie was putting away all her paraphernalia when Julian came in.

'It's done,' she said to him. Her voice was tired but the note of triumph was still there.

'You have the cup?'

'Not yet, but I will soon.'

'And Jacob?'

'Dead.'

Julian sighed with pleasure. He stood behind her smelling her hair, then he put his arms around her, reached up and opened her shirt. Her small breasts were like turned wine-cups, firm like a virgin's, her skin like silk.

Hardacre struggled, he wasn't a voyeur. He began to hear the clacking and humming of the spinning wheel again and shook his head. Lilly stopped her spinning and got him more mint tea.

'I see,' he said, 'I think.'

'I be thinking so too,' Lilly agreed. 'She's wanted that cup since she first read about it way back in her university days in Americky. It's been her whole life, and everything she's done has been with that in mind. Still is. Oh yes, she takes her pleasure with that young man, but he's her tool too. His anger, need for vengeance on Vicky Bryde and Merle Hollyman, she uses them for her own ends. She wanted to get the cup by easy means, by Jacob finding it for her. She imagined herself like the goddess, as if he would bring her the cup, like it says the old priest did in the legend. And she sees Vicky as Iwerydd, the one who thwarted the stepmother's ambitions in the story. She'll do her best to make sure she's not thwarted again.'

'That sounds like she's a reincarnation of the old story?'

'So she is. And so is young Vicky. And Merle. The poor buggers have got to play out the story. And don't you go helping 'em in the wrong way, mind, and cocking it all up!'

Hardacre laughed. 'And how do I stop from going wrong then, Mother?'

'Keep your nose clean and follow it! And don't you go meddling if you ain't asked. Or at least,' she stopped and looked at him, knowing perfectly well he wouldn't be able to follow that advice, 'you ask 'em afore you goes messing about.'

'Will you be there to help me, mother?' he asked as she showed him out the door.

'Nay. You all got to do this by yourselves. But I think there's one o' my kin might be around to give y' a hand. Not that she can do anything much, we none of us can. This is for the owl woman to sort out. And she'll only use her own people, not mine.' She pushed him out the door.

'Come and tell me about it when it's over,' she called as he went down the path and opened the creaking gate.

'I will,' he called back. 'If I'm still alive!'

He heard her cackle as she shut the door.

Robin

Vicki sat thinking. The interview was over and Hardacre gone. Being here, her life in London felt like a fairytale, Bridewell the reality. In London it felt the reverse. She was torn by the shock of her father's death and the excitement of seeing Merle again. And the terror that they might become close.

She watched Vera potter about the kitchen. It was obvious she assumed the two of them would tie the knot. Merle's marriage to Kate had just been a hiccough in Vera's books, and everyone was allowed one mistake. No doubt others in the village felt the same. It was a burden. It was why she hadn't come home again once she'd left. London was cool, distant and delightfully cosmopolitan. She had friends, but no-one tried to arrange her life for her, fix her lovers, tell her who she would marry.

But the electricity was there, in the air, the chemistry at the thought of him. It would be just too easy. Her body spoke for her now, as it always had. The ties went deep into the bone.

She got up and went to the cloakroom, pulled on a coat, went out towards the woods. As she crossed the lawn she felt a wind come behind her. She ducked as the white owl swooped over her head. Damn! It was like living in a bloody legend here!

The air was still freezing. Everything sparkled in the bright sun. Her feet crunched in the icy grass and the gate into the Wilderness creaked gently. She felt something soft brush her hand as she shut the gate, but could see nothing.

She walked up the ride. A robin chirped from a tree branch.

'Hello,' she said softly.

It chirruped again and flew to the next branch. Vicki followed. It gave a trill and flew down an animal track leading off the ride.

She saw the woodsman's hut through the tree trunks. It was old, unused now and the forest was reclaiming it. Mosses covered the shingle roof and dripped down over the eaves like a green fringe. Ivy covered the walls along with frost-rimed old man's beard. Sunlight lit down through the canopy of bare branches so the greens shone. It was a fairy house.

The door still worked. The woodsmen used to have their tea here in the old days. She stroked the table, under the dust and mould the wood was silky from years of use and hand-grease. She sat down in one of the two chairs by the black woodstove, facing the open door. Her eyelids drooped.

'I used to come and play here, as a boy,' he said. 'You did too, when you were little. We lost you one evening, but I found you here curled asleep in the chair, like you are now.'

'Hello, Dad,' Vicki mumbled. She was warm and cosy with her feet up in the carver chair, unwilling to move. She could see Jacob clearly this time, he wasn't wavering.

'It's because we're here, in her wood. She helps me stay solid.' Jacob answered the question in Vicki's mind.

'What's going on, Dad?'

But Jacob didn't answer. There was a movement now at the door and a feathery light came into the little hut.

The figure was tall. The feathers on its head brushed the roof and went on through. It was translucent.

'Soooo,' it whispered with the wind, 'yooo come home.'

The words were slurred and long.

'Yes,' said Vicki softly.

'The king is dead. Long live the king.' The wind in the feathers sounded mournful. Then, 'The cup is gone from its resting place, you must return it.'

'Gone?' Vicki looked at her father's ghost. He nodded guiltily.

'Oh shit!' she muttered. 'Dad, what have you done? Where have you stashed it? Oh!'

The light shone very bright and the wind whipped round the hut suddenly.

'Bring back my cup!'

The feather-light-figure retreated out of the door.

Vicki blinked herself awake. Jacob was gone too. She left the hut, pulled the door to and mussed up the leaf-litter to cover her tracks. The robin led her across the wood and over the Greenway, onto Tower Moor. She didn't want to go there, not yet, but the robin chirruped loudly and landed in the path ahead of her. She followed reluctantly.

The tower loomed up on its promontory of rock. The moor was wild, reeds standing out of the peat marsh, gorse bushes and low, bent thorn trees all pointing away from the west wind. The path wound up through the heather. Vicki climbed, her thoughts in another time, until she found herself at the top.

The robin sat on the scaffolding. Vicki peered down into the pit. A breath of dank air met her but there was nothing there.

She followed the bird up to the yew tree by the waterfall. It had been a favourite childhood thing to climb into the tree and sit astride a branch right out over the fal ... her flying horse. Now she climbed out onto the branch again and sat hidden in the tree. The fall roared below her.

There was a movement below. She pulled herself further into the yew tree as she watched Sylvie and Julian emerge and stand arguing at the pool's edge. After a couple of moments Julian turned his back on

Sylvie and went off towards the Greenway. She stood glaring after him. Then she found a stick and went tentatively into the water. Vicki waited, watched.

After a few minutes she came out, looking very frustrated, and stood staring up the fall. Vicki turned her thoughts off and sat as still as the robin beside her. At last, with a final glance up at the fall, Sylvie turned away and followed Julian back to the village.

Vicki climbed out of the tree and looked at the robin. He flew off to sit on a bush by the rock face.

'What is it?'

He watched her out of each eye in turn. Vicki's mind felt like fog, she knew he was trying to tell her something. But what?

He pecked at the branch, then flew into the bush. Next minute he was out again, looking at her.

'What?' she sighed, exasperated. 'I don't understand!'

The robin did his act again, flying into the bush, waiting a moment, then flying out.

'But there's nowhere to go,' she said. 'It's solid rock.'

The bird let out a long trill of song.

'I'm sorry!' she sighed. 'I just don't speak robin.'

The bird came and sat on her hand, pulled at her sleeve. He flew up, holding on with his beak, as though he was trying to pull her with him. Vicki went along. The robin let go and flew into the bush again. She began to pull branches aside, swearing as she pricked her fingers.

'I suppose it had to be a damn holly bush?'

The robin sang to her again. She felt he was laughing.

Then she saw it. There was a gap behind the bush. She pushed through and found herself in the mouth of a cave. She made to take a step forward, into it, and felt as if she'd walked into a plate-glass window.

'What now?' she asked, rubbing her nose.

The robin was silent then, suddenly, he trilled again and she stumbled forward into the cave, the barrier gone.

There was the spring, bubbling up into a natural rock basin in the floor of the cave. This was it, the source of the spring, the owl woman's water, the cave where she was killed. And no-one had known it was there. She looked around her, awed.

The water flowed out along a channel which disappeared after a few feet so the water went into a hole in the rock. It was going in the direction of the waterfall. And the waterfall itself spewed out through a hole in the cliff wall.

Half way up the channel the waterway divided. A slab of rock sat at the divide. As it was set it channelled the water down to the fall. If you turned it the other way the water went off at an angle, down another channel, back into the rock. If only Dad had known about this, she thought. I'll bet it's all you need to divert the water away from Julian's bottling plant.

Light flashed, she was blinded. A voice in her head said, 'No!'

Vision came back, she felt stunned and collapsed to sit on the cave floor. The robin came and sat on her arm, rubbed his beak against her hand. She began to get herself back together again.

'What is it?' she asked him again.

This time he flew to perch on the slab. It moved. The water flowed away into the rock and the song of the fall died. The robin flew up, the stone moved back. The water flowed back into its usual channel and the song of the fall resumed. He did it twice more then chirped, head on one side, questioning her.

She put her own hand on the slab. Nothing happened. Then she felt a voice in her head.

'Wait!' it said, sounding like the wind, the voice of the light-feather-figure, again. 'You will know when.'

'I see, I think,' she whispered.

Funeral Games

Consciousness dances through all Space-Time.
All the pasts, futures, and all the possibilities.
Bob Toben
Space-Time and Beyond

Funeral Music

'Hello Merle. Can you do the music for Dad's funeral?'

Merle heard Vicki's voice on the answer phone and picked up the receiver. No preamble. No 'how are you'. Straight to the point as she always had been. He remembered it like yesterday.

'Hi there. I wondered if you'd call.'

'What else? Who else?' she chuckled. 'Vera's told me you're back playing the organ again. I couldn't have anyone else do the music. Nor could Dad.'

'Of course I'll do it. What d'you want?'

'I don't really know. There's so much … you choose. Bring me some stuff. We can talk about it.'

'Today?'

'Tonight. Come about nine-ish. There's so much to do.'

'I know.' He paused, then, 'Vicki, I'm so sorry.'

'Merle don't. Not from you. I can't bear it.' Her voice broke.

'OK. It's OK. I understand,' he said softly. There was silence for a moment. 'I'll come about nine then?'

'Yes.' And she was gone.

Merle put the phone down, leaned back in his chair and breathed out heavily. Goldy watched him from her usual perch on the window-ledge beside his desk. He could read the old-fashioned look in her eyes, met it for a moment, then his eyes dropped. She knows me far too well! As well as Vicki perhaps and yet, he thought, perhaps much better. Do Vicki and I know each other at all, despite living together most of our lives?

He went to the Bechstein in the sitting room, pulled some music out of the piano stool and sat down with it. His fingers trailed over the keys as he looked through the sheets and he realised he was playing Lord of the Dance. Why not, he thought, Jacob loved the song and they'd done it before in church.

Getting the music together for the funeral was both good and painful, choosing pieces that Jacob would want, and would bring him to mind for the village. He wondered if they would be the same ones Vicki would choose, he'd find out tonight when he went up to the manor. She was bound to want Crimmond. He wanted her to want Crimmond. He wanted to hear again that velvet alto of hers changing, soaring into the descant. It was always a shock, even when you knew she could do it.

He took another sheet of music and began to play it properly. Towards the end his own tenor was ringing out '… And did those hills, in ancient time …'. He came to the end laughing, it was fabulous, pretentious and absolutely true. Yes, Jacob would love to have that at his passing ceremony. He went to put the music away but a scruffy yellow sheet escaped. He bent to recover it and stopped. It was in his own schoolboy hand, the melody and words of the song they sang at the well-guardian ceremony. It had last been sung the day Vicki became well-guardian, in the footsteps of her grandmothers before her. Tentatively he picked up the paper and put it on the music stand. His mind slipped back eighteen years as his fingers searched out the notes.

It was August and hot. He was seventeen, going up to Magdalene College for his first term in the coming October. She was thirteen, her birthday, the day of the village festival, the day she became well-guardian. He had led the pipe and drum band, won the race to lead home the owl woman as the village legend said. It had felt like being in an ancient play which, of course, it was. They sat on the clapper bridge now, in the moonlight, not talking as usual. The barn owl she had rescued the previous spring came down to sit on the stones beside them. Vicki fumbled in a pocket and came out with a slightly squashed dead mouse. Olly took it hungrily, although she was perfectly capable of catching her own.

'That was quite something,' Vicki said into the silence. 'I didn't think I'd really feel it, I know it too well, but it's weird actually doing it. When

John Smith asked me if I'd go out in the Lady's name I felt like … like … I don't know …' she ended lamely.

'Like lightning gone through me.' Merle answered for her, again as usual.

'That's it! It rooted me to the ground. I thought I wouldn't be able to move but then there I was, walking the maze.'

They sat silent again. Merle thought about his race with Julian. He hadn't expected to have competition, and especially not from that quarter. It had been a close thing.

Olly roused them, taking off and swooping low over their heads to go hunting.

'I'd better go.' Vicki said. 'We're both falling asleep. We'll fall into the river and drown!' She nuzzled him, he kissed her …

Merle dragged himself back to the present. He didn't want to go any further down that memory. He collected the sheet music together and put it in his satchel to take up to Bridewell later.

He parked the car and something told him to go round to the conservatory, despite it being January. He found her there, with Hecaté, the doors open. The night was warm, muggy, quite unlike it should be for the time of year, but his nose told him it wouldn't last, there'd be frost later and hard at that.

Vicki had got some decent claret but Vera must have done the sandwiches. He looked at the neat edges, quite the opposite of Vicki's 'doorsteps' from their childhood picnics.

'What've you got?' Vicki pounced.

Merle fished in the satchel and brought out the music.

'Jerusalem, Lord of the Dance and Crimmond,' he said. 'And these. I can't make up my mind which to do for the intro and the outro.' He offered her the sheets. Chopin's piano sonata in B-flat minor was on top.

'Oh no! Can't hack the funeral march.' She handed the Chopin straight back. 'It's so hackneyed, like having Mendelssohn at your wedding.'

'Jacob loved it,' Merle said simply.

'Since when?' She rounded on him. 'Mummy used to like it but Dad always went out when she put it on.'

'Chopin always went straight out after he'd performed that piece, so

Jacob was in excellent company," Merle replied. 'I played it for him a few years back and we got to talking about it. I told him what Anton Rubenstein said, that the last movement was like leaves blowing in an empty churchyard. That caught him. He got me to playing it for him a few times, then he bought Artur Rubenstein's version.'

'He never told me that ...' Vicki looked away from him, her mouth grim. 'OK ... I guess I didn't know that about Dad. But I want the coffin to come in to Bach's Toccata and Fugue. I can't hack walking into church with the Chopin playing, you can do that while we're sitting. What else?'

Merle looked at her for a moment. He'd forgotten that side of her. They stayed staring at each other for a moment and then she looked away. Merle let out his breath silently. He'd been able to hold Jacob's wants.

'I'd like to do the Dies Irae for the outro, when they take the coffin out. Can you stand that?'

She looked at the score and started to chuckle.

'Yes. Thunder and crash and Hammer horror films, Dad'd like that.' She paused, smiled ruefully at him, 'I'm sorry. Didn't mean to bite your head off.'

'Bollocks!' Merle snorted. 'Of course, you did! You can't bullshit me into believing you've changed that much. Who d'you think I am? One of your damn computer clients?

She grimaced, held out her hand. 'Truce?'

As it got cold they went inside. He wandered over to the Pleyel in the library and began to tinkle Rachmaninov tunes. She came and leaned on the side, so he played Summertime and was rewarded by her singing it along with him. He went on to Scot Joplin's piano rags and was further rewarded by her dancing to them, just as she always had. He managed to keep on playing tune after tune for half an hour before she realised what she was doing, stopped suddenly, yawned ostentatiously and made noises about being up early in the morning. Merle took his cue and left.

Goldy eyed him askance from the depths of the rocking chair as he opened the kitchen door.

'I know!' he told her. 'But what can I do?'

Goldy declined to reply and curled her tail over her nose. He could hear her thinking, 'Humans! Who needs them?' as he trundled up the stairs and fell into bed.

Message from the Dead

Vicki shut the door on Merle and stood leaning her forehead against it for several minutes. It felt like a thread from her was stuck to him, rolling out in his wake as he drove home. She felt herself travelling along it to Bridge Cottage, knowing when he arrived at his own gate. There she stopped, pulled herself together, back into everyday reality, and went to wash the plates and glasses.

'Ye gods!' she said to Hecaté, who had retired to the washing basket early in the proceedings, 'What the hell am I going to do?'

The cat looked up at her from green eyes, half hidden under her black tail, with an *I told you so* expression.

Vicki looked back at her, then crouched down and buried her face in the soft fur. Hecaté purred consolation and reassurance, as she had ten years ago when Vicki left.

'Thank the gods you're still here,' Vicki mumbled into the cat. 'I don't know where I'd be without you.'

The phone interrupted her.

'Hello …' she said cautiously.

'Vicki? Vicki is that you?' Faye's voice echoed down the line as if she was under water.

'Oh! Thank goodness! I hadn't a clue who could be ringing at this hour.'

'I heard that. What's up, girl? Have you seen him?'

'He just left.'

'Aha! Well, I dare say that accounts for it,' Faye chuckled.

'Bitch!' Vicki growled.

'That's better! You sound alive again. From the wispy little voice I got just now I thought you'd died too! Have you seen it, I mean her?'

'Yes. No. Well, not to speak to.' Vicki felt better already, Faye's acid tongue brought back a sense of normality. 'But I'm hearing things about her. And Julian. Vera's sort of full of it but there's not been time for her to tell me much yet.'

'Uh huh! Well … do you know any more what happened? Why Jacob had the accident? Was he just careless, or what?'

'No-one knows. There's a real live Agatha Christie policeman snuffling about and being mysterious, but it may all be nothing. Vera says Dad had supper with Merle that night, but I couldn't bring myself to ask him anything and he didn't volunteer.'

'Why was he there, with you?'

'He's doing the music, for the funeral. He's church organist. We were getting it all together. Funeral's in a few days.'

'Honey, I wish I could be there with you! When are you coming home? Do you know any more?' Faye asked.

There was a pause.

'Do you think you'll come back to London?' Faye continued, changing her question. 'Or will you be staying home now?'

'I just don't know … It's so different, actually being here. The place calls to me. I'd forgotten. This is my home, my roots, but I don't know what I'm going to do. It's all too soon.'

'I know, love. It's just I miss you. Hey,' Faye put a lighter tone into her voice, 'how would it be if I hopped in the car and came down for a bit of a holiday? I could sure use one.'

'I don't know … could you get away?'

'We've got David on line here now, and the students. They should be able to hold the fort for a couple of weeks or so.'

'I don't know,' Vicki repeated. 'I'd love to see you but … Call me after the funeral, Faye.'

'Two's company, three's a crowd?'

'Oh shut up, Faye! I don't know. And he hasn't said anything.'

'Bet he's looking though! OK! OK! I'm off. Go to bed, child, I'll speak to you soon. But call me anytime, day or night, if there's trouble. I'll be with you as soon as I can drive there! Love you!'

She stared at the phone after Faye had gone. It was like an umbilical cord to normality had been cut, again.

Vicki replaced the receiver and went down the corridor to the study. Hecaté climbed out of the basket and followed her. Sat in Jacob's ancient swivel-chair, her hands turned again to the papers in the desk but she couldn't concentrate on them.

Her mind went back twenty-three years. She was standing by the gaping hole. Her father was down in the grave, with Dick. They pushed the lid off the stone coffin.

'Double-up!' said Dick excitedly. 'Must have been important to have a lead coffin inside the stone one.'

'If it really is my ancestor, of course they're bloody important!' Jacob snorted.

The lead coffin had the Caer-y-troiau, the Celtic Troytown maze, inscribed on the lid.

'Shit!' Jacob stared at it, then grinned at his nine year old daughter crouched above them, beside the hole, watching. 'Don't you go telling Mummy I said that!'

Vicki giggled.

'You'd better go now,' he told her. 'We have to open the lead coffin and, if the seams aren't broken, it'll stink to high heaven. Two thousand year old liquidised-human-soup.' he answered her puzzled look. '

'Yuck!' she said.

Fortunately the seals had been broken. The contents were dry, mummified. It was the body of a young woman, dressed in a fine silk robe. The remains of her red-gold hair could still be seen clinging to the skull, along with the gold threads of her head-dress. Sunk into her chest was a bronze tablet giving her name, Iwerydd, and the legend of the gold cup.

The British Museum was over the moon. Jacob's career progressed into the fast lane. Dick rose along with him and their staff increased. Vicki remembered him telling Mummy about his interview with the boss, David Ranley-Hall.

'He said "Jacob, you can't refuse me on this!". He really was pleading with me,' Jacob laughed to Caroline. 'All exasperation and beseeching. He knows his control of the purse strings is his only lever with me.

"You're a bloody madman," he told me. I just grinned. He's OK, just stuck in the bloody admin. I never want to rise to that,' Jacob took a turn about the room. He was elated.

'You know,' he stopped beside Caroline, crouched beside her taking her hands, looking into her eyes. 'This discovery, a potential British grail, is going to hit all the newspapers. I'll be a damn national celebrity, at least for a bit. Ranley-Hall doesn't know whether to be pleased or horrified. Discovering myths to be true isn't at all the sort of thing academia appreciates.'

'What did you tell him, about this woman?' Caroline asked.

'I said I supposed I couldn't refuse him,' Jacob grimaced, 'although I'd bloody like to. I've got all the help I need on this dig without some damn fool American wanting to be in on the act. Probably got a crush on Arthur or Merlin judging by the way she writes. I don't need that!'

'She's head of department, did you say?' Caroline was watching him carefully.

'Yes. Professor Sylvie Villiers of the University of Pennsylvania, for god's sake!'

'Well, can't you put her on to cataloguing or something. That ought to keep her too busy to be bothering you.'

'That's what David suggested,' he chuckled. 'I just threw up my hands and stalked out. He took that as agreement. Probably glad I made so little fuss. He knows I'm stubborn but he thinks, maybe this time, I can see which side my bread is buttered. As I went out I heard him call in his secretary. Later I saw a copy of the letter, inviting the silly bitch to join the team. *And* he's told her she'll be on cataloguing!' Jacob grinned like a schoolboy. 'If she comes after that she's totally obsessed. No-one with her qualifications would do a job like that.'

She had come.

Things had gone well, at first, but Caroline never liked Sylvie, wouldn't have her to stay at the manor as Dick did when they were working at Bridewell. Sylvie had taken a room at the Green Lion in the village. After a year the finds were catalogued, and written up, and there had been some muttering about Sylvie's name going on the papers. The dissension got so bad the team was downsized, and Sylvie was one of the ones no longer needed. The mood at home had lightened when she left but it didn't last. Caroline's death had followed within the year.

Sylvie went back to Pennsylvania, but rumour had it she returned to Britain when her husband died, got a post at Liverpool University. Vicki knew her father had been right, Sylvie was obsessed with the cup. She needed to be nearer to it than the other side of the Atlantic.

Then suddenly, a few years back, Vicki discovered Jacob was running an affair with the woman. She hit the roof, especially when she heard Sylvie had bought Well Cottage and moved in to Bridewell. Although she came up to the manor, Vera had told her Sylvie never slept the night there. And Jacob would never have her live there. Vera said he would go down, when he was at home, and visit her at the cottage.

But, while Sylvie lived at Bridewell, Vicki would only come home for a day or so, when she was away somewhere. There can be only one mistress of a house.

Vick shook her head, forcing herself back into the present. The past twenty four hours had been choc-a-bloc with visitations and, after the owl woman's disclosures that morning, she had to know what the hell he'd done with the cup.. But how had he got it?

Among a heap of utility bills she found the notebook. The first date was over two years back. He'd been investigating the tower, as usual, and Bill Warrington had been down with his geo-phys kit to map out the site. The notes referred to walls and shapes and potential tunnels or drains. Jacob's scrawly sketches looked like the work of a demented spider on methedrine.

'Where's the actual maps, for god's sake?' she grumbled, turning to the computer.

There were a dozen or so files in the folder. Vicki changed to thumbnails. She clicked on the first fuzzy green blob and got an aerial shot of the tower. She was just about to close it when she saw the depression in the grass. Like a path. And leading south. She closed it, thinking.

The next one was a geo-phys map. At first it looked like a mass of fuzzy green lines. She leaned back in the chair and squinted at the screen. After a bit she began to see more clearly. There was the tower. It was hard, at first, to read the rock formations from the masonry and walls, but she was getting used to it. The path she'd seen in the aerial shot was much clearer now. Vicki scrabbled among the papers and found the Ordnance Survey map. The path ran straight as a die between the tower and the Wilderness.

'Tunnel?' she breathed.

She opened Jacob's email and found a draft message dated the day he died. It was addressed to her.

Vicki darling, she read. *I know you've said you won't come home any more, not while Sylvie's in the village, but I do hope this'll change your mind. I've found it! She's on my tail all the time, tried to get in here the other day when I went out for a walk. Vera surprised her, saw the bushes moving on the other side of the lawn. Never thought we'd have to lock the doors here! All my fault, I know. Oh my dear, I'm so sorry! You were right and I was wrong. I don't really know why I did it. Some crazy spur. Hormones? I suppose! I can't even say I was lonely. I don't know, and maybe it doesn't matter. But I want to share this with you. Will you come? Your favourite wizard, Dad.*

Vicki stared at the screen. Why had he not sent it? She read the message, read it again, then pressed print and watched the sheet of paper emerge, with his words on it.

A fluttering and banging against the window startled her. She turned in time to see the white shape dive towards the glass. This time it stopped before it hit. A white owl.

'Gwenhwyfar?' she breathed.

'Kriee-i!' cried the owl, as it perched on the ledge. Then it opened its wings and was gone.

Vicki sat motionless for a time, hoping it would come back. When it didn't, she took the sheet of paper from the printer and curled up by the fire, in his favourite chair. Hecaté climbed into her lap and lay up her chest with her paws round Vicki's neck, purring. They were still there next morning when Vera came to clean the room.

Wake

Vicki walked alone. The coffin preceded her on the shoulders of six large village men. Another four walked alongside. There had been a lot of vying for who would get to carry the Professor down the old track from the manor to the church. Jacob was going out in style, walked from his home to his grave in the old way. The men were softly singing the corpse song, the Lyke Wake Dirge. John Smith, the village blacksmith, old and grey now but still sprightly, walked behind the undertaker, beating his drum. Everyone's feet took up the rhythm, but all were out of step.

'As we should be,' Vicki thought. '*Fire and sleet and candle leet,*' she took up the refrain, '*and Christ receive thy soul.*'

The men smiled to hear her singing.

They turned the corner from the Greenway into Church Lane and came in sight of the square, the church. A large crowd stood to either side of the lychgate. Suddenly the tableau reminded her of Hieronymus Bosch. From this distance the people seemed somehow featureless, formless, all eyes and dark, lumpy shapes, merging together, waiting, watching in hungry anticipation. She shook herself. It was the village, her village, in their Sunday best. She'd known most of them since childhood.

'They respected Jacob.' Vicki said to herself. She took a deep breath and followed the coffin to the lychgate.

The Reverend Martin Drinkwater stood behind and to one side of the crowd of mourners. Tall as a lamp-post, with his prayer book in his left hand, he was just as she remembered him. Like something out of Dickens, a force to be reckoned with.

'My dear girl!' He loomed up out of the crowd to meet her, nodding his long, gaunt head and taking her hand in both of his. 'Come. We must follow the coffin and lead them in.'

They walked up the yew lined path. Inside Merle was playing Bach's Toccata and Fugue in D minor.

The church was full of shadows. The Chartres blue stained glass of Iwerydd's window, in the south wall, blazed. More colour shone from other windows, painting the dark aisles. The bright clerestory overhead sent shafts of dust strewn light into the nave. One hit a face on the end of a pew, holly leaves spewed out of the mouth, the eyes shone at her. She caught her breath, remembering. It was good to be greeted again. Drinkwater handed her into the first pew on the north side.

The church filled up behind her as Merle went on to Chopin's funeral march. He's right, she thought. Hackneyed or not in other times and places, it worked here, today. She could sense her father laughing.

Under the stone on which his coffin now lay, Jacob had hunted for the gold cup which legend said was buried with the body of the saint. It had been his consuming passion. He had bent all of his resources, as a keeper in the British Museum, towards finding it. And, although as far as people knew he had never found the actual cup, his discovery of the tablet and the body of the priestess had made his name. Now his earthly remains lay in a wooden box on top of the place of his greatest triumph.

Drinkwater began the service, his warm voice echoing around the bright stone pillars of nave and choir, fading into the dark alcoves around the altar. The sun shone out through the clouds and some low, sideways light came through the clear spot in the Iwerydd window. An optical trick gave it the shape of a cup on the wall above the coffin.

Vicki felt the church crowded with mourners and many of them stood up to speak about her father. In spite of the loss of the water, it seemed he was still loved. She glanced sideways across the aisle to where Sylvie sat with Julian. The pew behind them was unoccupied, unlike the one behind herself, which was full to the gunwales. It seemed no-one wanted to sit near them. Vicki wondered how things were in the village, now that the bottling plant was making money and giving employment to some of the young people.

Crimmond came to its glorious end. The village had not forgotten she could sing. Satisfied smiles grew as they listened to her ethereal descant soaring up into the vast roof. Her voice died away with the organ notes, amongst the saints and rafters. Tears snagged at her cheeks as Merle began the Dies Irae. She stood as the coffin was carried past her, leading the way to the west door.

'The door of death.' She heard her father's voice.

A rush of wings went over her head as the verger opened the door. A barn owl swooped from the top of the rood screen, down the aisle, and out into the blinding sunlight. No-one had seen it until then. A soft whispering ran through the mourners.

Vicki followed it, following the coffin. Sylvie followed her, on Julian's arm. She felt the ice-blue eyes on her back all the way down the nave.

It was cold, the sun was fairly blazing down but it couldn't warm the air, their breath came out like puffs of steam. She felt the crowd behind her now, trooping after the coffin like a flock of black-feathered ducklings, herself the mother duck.

As the coffin climbed the hill on the bearers' shoulders, Vicki's mind ran riot. How would it be if, when they got to the grave, they just tipped the coffin and the body slid out through a flap in the end? Like Mozart's in the film. A couple of shovels of lime on top. But it was sunny. The lime would be quick, alive, it would destroy the flesh. In the film it had been raining, the lime had been slaked. Quick lime destroys, slack lime preserves, she thought. Mozart's body would have been preserved, like his music. Not Daddy.

She wished he had been burned. That was her style. But he was afraid of fire. His was a watery death and an earthy grave, slow, lingering. She preferred the speed of fire to slow choking and mouldering. She was afraid of worms and corruption.

They arrived at the grave. The bearers lowered the coffin decorously. This was no pauper's grave, the family plot went back time out of mind. It was set aside from the rest of the graveyard but there was no mausoleum, just a greensward around an ancient, twisted yew tree. Great grandfather, fed up with the continual maintenance of headstones, had set up a simple granite slab with names and dates.

The first name, Iwerydd, was the woman who Jacob had found in the grave, just as legend said he would. She'd been a fourth century Romano-British noblewoman, a priestess for the water-shrine. Her name, Iwerydd, was the name for the goddess, the ancestress of the Ivernian race, and her priestess would always take it. Later, even down to Victorian times, ordinary women took the name too, corrupted down to its phonetic of Urith. Vicki remembered Dad reading to her from the Black Book of Carmarthen, his mouth solemn but his eyes twinkling,

I have been where Bran was slain
Iwerydd's son of widespread fame

Now this latest son of Iwerydd was being laid to rest among his forebears. She wondered how he was taking to meeting them all at last.

'Dust to dust … ' Drinkwater said the old words.

A huge bumblebee droned past her, wings an invisible blur, flying over the grave.

'You shouldn't be able to fly!' she thought.

'In Egypt, the bee is the symbol of the soul.' She heard her father's voice again, in her head, the only place she would ever hear it now.

The ritual ended. She took the customary handful of earth and threw it onto the coffin where it landed with an echoing thud, loud enough to wake the dead. But not this one. The crowd melted away, leaving her alone, looking down into the pit at the shiny brass name-plate.

A rustle behind disturbed her.

'Are you going to the wake?' Julian's smile was sardonic.

Vicki turned on her heel and walked straight past him down the hill across the square. As she went his face came back to her from childhood, laughing, taunting. She had run from him then. This time he didn't follow her.

She arrived at the Sunday School room where the village had organised the feast. A pretty woman in her early thirties guided her to the great wing chair at the head of the room, brought tea and a slab of cake. This must be Olive, she thought. She hadn't met Joe's wife yet but Jacob had told her of the gardener's whirlwind love affair.

Merle came to stand beside her chair looking taciturn and handsome. It was where the village would expect him to be, taking care of her, taking her cup when it was empty and filling it again for her. He caught her eye and smiled wryly, the thought had obviously crossed his mind too.

She looked about the Sunday School, pulling her mind off him. How different it was to be here now, in the tall room, to when she had come here as a child. The church-style windows, too high to see out of, let in the grimy light. It seemed cleaning them had as high a priority now as it always had.

The woman who taught them catechism had been tall and gaunt, but she had been kindly. Dead now. She'd owned Well Cottage. It must have been her executors that Sylvie'd bought it off. What was her name? The smell of old leather hymn books came back to her as she remembered hiding in the cupboard once, when Julian had been hunting her. Miss Bakewell, Dorothy Bakewell, that was it. She'd torn Julian off a strip for disturbing her when she was writing up her lessons. He hadn't come looking for Vicki again there.

The village always looked after its own. They had insisted on organising the wake. Now, one by one, people came up to speak to her, perfectly choreographed, no-one pushed in or interrupted.

They've arranged it so I'm holding court, Vicki smiled wryly to herself. Chief mourner, enthroned in a sagging 1950's wing-chair, sipping tepid PG Tips, my hand squeezed, the damp peck on the cheek, listening politely to sincere platitudes.

'My dear, I'm so sorry!' The voice belonged to Julia Courtney. Vicki remembered playing in the apple orchards as a child.

'Thank you. How are things?' Immediately she regretted her question. The woman's face fell from sincere sympathy with Vicki's loss to worry about her own.

'Bad, my dear. Very bad,' she caught her breath. 'Without the water and now Brian's gone ...' the sentence trailed off.

Vicki reached out a hand, shocked by the desperate sadness in her eyes. Julia realised again where she was, drew her hand gently out of Vicki's and looked around her.

'Are you all right for tea?' Julia fumbled for words, trying to ground herself again. 'Oh you're taking care of her, Merle.'

'I'll come and see you very soon, Julia.' Vicki said as the woman drifted away, melted back into the crowd.

Vicki shook her head, trying to regain focus. She felt as if she was in between worlds, one minute at the wake, the next in the past. Another person came to offer condolences.

'He were a good man, your dad, in spite of everything. There was n'one like him. T' village'll miss un!' The old farmer pulled a smile into his bushy whiskers, remembering the child who had ridden her pony in his fields. How she's grown, he thought, realising it had been many years since he had seen her.

'Thank you, Mr Philips,' she replied.

'Ah, 'tis Ted, girl. Don' y' remember? Will y' be around for a while then, Vicki? Or is y' rushin' off back to London?' T'd be good to see a bit of y' again. Mother'll have some tea for y' an' y' stop by. Any time.'

'I don't know ... It all depends ...' her voice trailed off. 'I didn't realise things were in such a muddle here. Dad never told me anything!' she told him, exasperated.

'Eh well ...' Ted Philips looked up at Merle, 'you'll be bringin' 'er up to date no doubt?'

Merle nodded. 'That's right, Mr Phillips.'

'Well, you mind an' you come by now,' Phillips insisted.

'I will,' she promised. He moved away.

Trevor Biddacombe sat down beside her as she dumped the plate of heavy slab-cake on the floor. They smiled to each other as somebody's

Sealyham wolfed it down.

'I don't suppose you remember me?' Trevor said.

'Oh yes I do! I used to race my chestnut against your bay on Honeybeetle Moor.'

'So you did,' Trevor grinned back. 'And we was neck and neck most times. Weren't much as could catch that little red horse o' yours, 'cept your black.' Trevor caught Merle's eye, both men laughed.

'How are you, Trevor? How's Mrs Biddacombe?' Vicki asked.

Trevor's face fell at that. again Vicki felt the sadness. Was anything right in the village now?

'Mother's going blind, Vicki.'

'What?' she gasped.

'It's as she can't have the water for her eyes. The cataract's growing, she can hardly see a thing now. The doctors want to operate with that laser thing, but I don't want 'em to. She's too old. It'd be too much for her. She's eighty-five.'

'Oh god! Can't you buy the bottled water from Julian?

'Oh aye … for a price! He's asking near two pound a bottle and that's just for half a litre. And anyway,' Trevor's eyes held hers, 'it don't work.'

'What d'you mean, it doesn't work?'

''Tis as I say. We tried it, even though it was breaking the bank. But the water in the bottle don't do the trick.'

Vicki stared at him. The water from the village spring had always cured cataracts. Doctors and scientists had confirmed it, although they could none of them find what they called the active ingredient. Vicki had her own opinions on this, as had Jacob, and Joe.

'Trevor,' Vicki put her hand on his arm. 'I don't know what to say. May I call on your mother? Does she hate me?'

'Nay! A' course she don't! You come on down any time, she'll be glad to see y'.' Trevor was falling back into the Devon dialect. 'And don't y' worry too much, we'll find a way. Somehow!'

Trevor stood up as Pat Elworthy from the Green Lion came to claim Vicki's attention. Vicki found herself embroiled in a round of remaking old friendships. Her misgivings on seeing the crowd by the church were gone. She had come home.

The crowd thinned. Vera helped Olive and Joe with the washing up. The Sealyham waddled over to the kitchen for more scraps. Olive leaned down from the sink to rub his muzzle and tell him it would soon be time to go home. Good God! Was it hers? She went over to them.

'Don't bother with coming over to the manor tonight, Vera. I'll be fine on my own.'

Vera looked at her.

'Really,' Vicki put her arms round Vera and whispered. 'I want to be alone, to think.'

Vera raised her eyebrows and glanced over to where Merle was standing. Vicki coloured slightly, but shook her head.

'All right then. I'll see y' in the morning,' Vera turned back to the washing up. Vicki went back to her sagging throne.

Merle was across the room. Vicki caught his eyes, saw them smile to her while his mouth carried on the conversation with Mrs Partridge, from the post office, who'd been serving tea. Delighted, she folded up the moment storing it away for later.

She felt it again, the old in-tuneness with him. He would know she had cried as the thundering dissonances of Bach creaked out of the old organ. And that she smiled thinking of the mourners as a flock of ducklings. It was the sort of quirky image they had shared as children. The tears began again. She wiped at them with a miniature square of lace, quite inadequate. She should go.

'Are you going home?' Merle was there again, still taking care of her. 'Can I give you a lift?'

She shook her head, then nodded, uncertain for a moment where home was. Merle walked beside her, running interference, talking inanities in his quiet voice so that people left them alone as he gave the greetings for her. She was being managed, but she was too disoriented and tired to care. She took his arm without thinking. He made no demur, but didn't press closer. The inanities turned out to be a short monologue on Bach fugue. Probably fascinating, she thought, as he always had been, although she hadn't taken any of it in. They arrived at the Range Rover, Vicki stood uncertain for a moment. Merle opened the door for her. She got in. They drove home in silence.

'You must be tired, need a change,' Merle stopped in the stable yard but didn't turn the engine off. 'There's a very tolerable restaurant over at

Buckland, can I take you to dinner? We can talk music, jazz, computers, Pyrenees, physics, owls. More restful than the radio?'

'Thank you.' Vicki watched Merle's lopsided smile droop down the left side of his face keeping up with his eyes this time. It was a thing she had forgotten. It tugged at old strings now.

'I'll come about seven-thirty then?'

'Yes, please,' Vicki smiled back at last.

She climbed out and slammed the door.

He turned the Range Rover and accelerated out of the stable yard up the drive to the road, not looking back.

Julian

Julian watched Vicki retreat down the steep hill, through the gravestones. He followed slowly, as far as the lychgate, then stopped. Sitting on the bench under the canopy he felt inured to the cold. The last of the afternoon sun reached him there, before it sank behind the Sunday School on the other side of the square.

Julian muttered to himself as he sat. It was an old habit. As a child there had been no-one but his sister to talk to and she soon found it more fun to be with other children than with him. Lizzie giggled at him, and nudged her friends in the ribs. He never knew what it was that was so funny. Vicki always rejected him too. Again, he never knew why.

His mind went back eighteen years. He had been leaning against the lychgate then, watching, waiting.

All the village was gathered in the square. From within the forge Merle's pipe and drum band started up with the village song. The blacksmith led out the little chestnut horse with Vicki on his back. Her face was hidden by the ancient feather-mask of Iwerydd's owl. The long skirts of her costume, white, red and black, hung over the horse's back and he stepped out proudly. A pretty mediaeval picture, Julian's lip curled.

The blacksmith led the procession, widdershins, once round the square then up Church Lane and the Greenway, to the old track which led to the Wilderness. The village followed. Julian brought up the rear.

94

The smith stopped at the gate into the Wilderness.

'I bring the owl woman!' he called. 'Give us passage!'

Then he opened the gate and led the pony through. They turned up a ride, the children dancing and everyone singing. Beech trees arched overhead like a huge cathedral nave.

Everything stopped at the entrance to the glade, in the middle of the wood. Here was the stone circle and, within it, the turf-maze, the Troytown. At its centre stood the hag-stone, the hole in its top dark against the whiteness of the stone in the sunlight.

The blacksmith lifted Vicki down. Julian edged his way to the front of the crowd.

The smith stood barring Vicki's way.

'And will you go out in the Lady's name?' he asked her.

'Aye, 'til I be fetchèd hame!' she gave the ritual answer.

'And who shall go to fetch thee hame?' called the smith.

Merle came forward. Julian stepped up at his shoulder. The two boys glared at each other.

'I see we have a contest,' the smith laughed. A soft chuckle went through the village, several people hooted encouragement. This was real sport, not just a pretty festival.

'Aye, well. Then this is what y'll do,' he told them. 'Vicki, you go on to the centre now. And then, when you give the whistle, these two lads will race to get you.' He looked long at each of the boys. 'And there'll be no fouling, mind!' he finished.

The pipe and drum band began, Martin Drinkwater led the villagers singing the old pagan song, Vicki set off into the maze. Julian flexed his running muscles. Merle stood still as death.

As the villagers finished the last chorus Vicki arrived at the centre. She paused a moment and then put two fingers in her mouth. The whistle shrieked around the clearing.

At the same moment Merle leaped into the path. He raced round the first arc, Julian at his heels. They turned round the top of the pattern and Julian barged Merle off the track, taking the lead. The village growled. But Merle was up and running again. They came thundering down to the bottom corner, neck and neck, then Merle shouldered past Julian and sprinted ahead. Round the spiral they went again. This time, as they rounded the top corner, Julian shoved his way past Merle and got the advantage. Merle raced round the outside track and caught up with him at the beginning of the final arc. Julian looked back over his shoulder and tripped. Merle leaped over him and ran up the home stretch. He caught Vicki up and swung her round and round, both of them laughing. The village cheered. He put her down and led her on the straight path out of the maze.

'You are a fool!' Julian's sister told him as he sat in the grass, leaning against one of the stones and holding his foot. 'Come on! Let's enjoy the party.'

'Later!' growled Julian. 'I twisted my ankle.'

His sister left him.

The party was in full swing when Julian finally arrived and went to lean against the door of the conservatory to watch the dancing. Vicki had changed out of the mediaeval dress into a mini skirt. She danced and danced. Julian watched and watched, until the bottle was empty, then he went for another one. When he came back she was nowhere to be seen.

He wandered around the party, drinking and joking with some of the boys from the town who had girlfriends here in the village. Dusk fell, it was ten o'clock, but she wasn't there. He got another bottle and wandered down the Greenway, back to the village. He stopped and sat in the lychgate, staring out at nothing, in a melancholy stupor. When the bottle was empty he left it by the step and set off slowly towards Penny Woods. The moon was full and he caught sight of his reflection in the windows of the old school house. Strange. He peered closer. It wasn't at all like his face. What were those streaks, like horns, growing out his forehead in the reflection? Had he got straws in his hair? He ran his fingers through but could feel nothing. Drunk, he thought. Shit! He kicked a stone and carried on up the lane.

Penny Woods were full of shadows and he fell several times going down the rocky alley to the clapper bridge. Arriving, he saw them sitting on the central stone, watching the water rush away downstream. Julian stood still.

He had never known why he wanted her, but he did. He didn't even like her. She was into horses and books and mediaeval music and dancing. She loved animals and they would come to her when she called. Stupid child, he thought. Julian enjoyed heavy rock music, clubs, drinking and girls. He wanted to go to London as soon as he could. But he had always wanted her, and she had never looked at him.

He watched as Merle gave Vicki a hug and set off home across the clapper bridge. Vicki watched him go, gave a final wave as he turned in the gate and then came back across the bridge towards the path home. And Julian.

He stepped back silently behind a big alder tree on the edge of the river. Vicki paused as she passed, her nose wrinkling as though she scented something, but she shook her head and carried on up the hill. Julian waited.

He found her in the old quarry, just past the top of the rocky alley, where the paths divided. She was lying under the oak tree in the grass of the clearing. The fox cubs were playing with her, one rolled around her hand, chewing her fingers while the vixen watched indulgently. All her attention was on the foxes.

The vixen saw him first and let out a sharp bark. Vicki rolled over and sat up. The foxes backed into a ring behind her at the edge of the clearing.

'What do you want?' Vicki's eyes were wary.

'You!' Julian's mouth curled in triumph. 'And now I have you.' He came slowly towards her,

Suddenly the vixen barked. She and the cubs ran off down the hill towards the bridge, howling. Julian laughed.

'See?' he said contemptuously. 'Even your little friends won't stay to help you when you need them, see how they run!' He hurled a stone after the fleeing foxes.

'Bastard!' Vicki spat at him, crawling backwards towards the oak tree. She found an old branch and grabbed it.

Julian came closer, crouching down beside her. She hit out at him with the branch, he blocked it with his hand. It broke.

'There!' he mocked her. 'Even the trees won't help. So much for all your kiddie-car magic. This is the real world, and in the real world I get what I want.'

He leaned towards her grabbing her shoulders. She punched him in the face. He laughed, slapped her back and twisted her roughly over, pushing her down into the long grass. His left hand held her throat, choking her.

He put one knee into her back while his other hand pulled her skirt up and fumbled in her pants. She twisted and fought, but he had her now. He could take her. Then she got her mouth round to his wrist and dug her teeth in. He let go. She screamed.

Julian never heard the blow coming. The next thing he knew he was on his back, with his head against a tree root, and a boot landing in his ribs. A shadowy figure towered over him for a moment. Then it went away.

Slowly, painfully, he propped himself against the tree. Nothing seemed to be broken. He looked across the clearing.

Merle had Vicki in his arms. She was crying. Julian made to get his trousers back together.

'If you ever come near her again I'll kill you!'

Merle stood over him again. Julian lay very still. He continued to lie very still for a long, long time after Merle had taken Vicki home. Eventually he got up and found his way back through the woods to the village, and the Cider Press, just as dawn was breaking. The foxes followed him all the way. There were far more of them now than had been playing with Vicki, must have been twenty at least. They dogged his steps, bit at his heels, then ran back, barking, herding him along Penny Lane and all the way home. Now they sat in a long row by the gate, tongues lolling and eyes fixed on him. He slammed the gate shut and ran.

Julian shook his head to clear away the memories. The sun had sunk down behind the rooftops, cold blue shadows crept around him where he sat in the darkened lychgate. Creakily, like an old man, he got up and walked slowly across the square and down Forge Alley to the bottling plant.

There was still a light on when he got there. He went through to his office, nodding to the foreman and a couple of lads who were clearing up at the end of their shift. He lay back in his chair and picked up the latest sales figures.

Here, at least, was something he could feel proud of. The sales for Bridewell Spring Water climbed steadily each quarter. It just went to show, he'd been right all along, whatever Jacob said. People did want the water. And wasn't it better to make it available to anyone who wanted it, and could pay for it, rather than hoarding it in the village? The locals had been swilling their washing in it, peeing in it, putting it on their gardens and making cider with it for two thousand years and more. Now was the time when it should go out into the wider world.

The door slammed open, breaking his reverie. Two hulking great lads barged in making the office feel all of a sudden much smaller and crowded. It was Trevor Biddacombe from Ash Farm with his cow-man Peter Alcock. Trevor walked up to the desk and stood looming over him.

'Now' he said. 'What's y' got a say about this, maister?' and he thrust a piece of paper under Julian's nose. ''Tis Mother. The doctor says she'll lose her sight. Her've been goin' downhill ever since you took the water.'

'I never stopped her having the water!' Julian protested.

'Come off it! How do y' expect her to pay your prices, a poor old woman on 'er pension? An' her never 'ad to pay for 'un afore. Twas all well until y' took our water. 'Er never 'ad a minute's trouble with 'er sight until then. And,' Biddacombe's eyes narrowed, 'what 'ave y' done wi'it, anyroad? It don't work no more, not out o' the bottle. What've y' done wi'it?'

Biddacombe leaned across the desk. Julian could feel the hot breath on his face.

'An' my cottage be fallin' down.' Peter Alcock added his two penn'orth. 'Subsidin'. There be great cracks in the cob, an' the windows out back is comin' apart from the frames. Tis all acorse of y' takin' the stream out o' it's natural bed.'

The two men stood over Julian.

'I'm a askin of y' again, maister. What be y' goin' a do about it?' Biddacombe's face hung in front of him, round like the moon. Julian shrank into the back of his chair.

Biddacombe and Alcock came round the desk and took Julian under the arms. They carried him out of the office and down to the vats where the water was stored before bottling. Trevor held him from behind, grasping both his upper arms and pulling them back, while Peter Alcock reached over and pushed the lid of a vat to one side. Julian dared not struggle, he felt as through the slightest movement would break his arms. Then Biddacombe pushed Julian forward and both men got hold of him, lifting him, to throw him into the vat.

Now he struggled. And found his voice. He managed one yell before Biddacombe's great ham fist slammed into his mouth.

There was a roar behind them and suddenly Biddacombe let him go. The foreman and the two lads from the bottling plant had come to his rescue. They slammed about them with bits of two-by-one from the packing cases. Alcock and Biddacombe gave up the fight and ran.

'You all right, Mr. Julian?' Wayne Driver, the foreman, held his arm, worried in case his boss would fall over.

'I'll live, thanks to you.' Julian managed a smile through cut lips, but his mouth hurt horribly and blood still tracked down his face onto his shirt.

'You'd best get off home, Mr Julian. That looks like a nasty cut you got. Don't you worry about all this. We'll clear up,' he said, pushing his boss gently towards the door. 'And lock up,' he added as Julian showed signs of hesitation.

Julian walked across the yard and up Forge Alley to Well Cottage. The light had gone now, just a touch of red behind the cottage roofs forecast a cold night and a fine day tomorrow.

Ahead of him something white glimmered in the dead grass at the bottom of the garden wall. As he got closer he saw it was a doll. He picked it up. Now he could see the long blackthorn sticking out of its groin. Ye gods! He held it, turning it over and over in his hands, accepting it, unable to let go of it. It had been a female doll, a rag doll, but someone had stitched a bright pink tube where the penis would be. It was through this that the blackthorn was fixed. Whoever it was had even gone to the trouble of daubing spots of red ink down it. Like blood.

Merle

Merle accelerated up the drive then stopped and sat at the exit, staring into the glass of the windscreen and out at nothing. He was seeing again the slight, black-clothed figure, the red hair standing out like an aureole under the wide brim of the hat.

Their relationship had slipped back onto him like an old, favourite shirt. It fitted like his own skin. It was just as much of a problem though, now, as it had been ten years back. I don't need a woman right now, he told himself severely, knowing he might as well whistle down the wind. It wasn't the right time. Perhaps it never would be the right time for them. And, even five years after his divorce, he didn't want any more to do with commitment. However, life doesn't seem to share my views, he thought sourly, as the image of Vicki still played before his eyes.

He put the Range Rover in gear, turned left and slid quietly down the lane past the top of the Greenway. Now he saw only bare tree branches and sleeping hedgerows through the windscreen. Somewhere there was the smell of wood smoke.

He gathered speed down Firebeacon Hill and tackled the ford at the bottom stylishly, water spraying up around the tyres but not reaching the windscreen. In spite of all the rain the level of the river was low, the Owlwater on its own couldn't fill it. Julian's bottling plant had affected the water table and the Bridewell was as low as in a hot June.

Merle turned into his lane, drove through the gate and parked. He locked the Range Rover and walked across the yard. There was a sound of movement on the other side of the kitchen door as he unlocked it and a soft rush of wings greeted him. The long yellow talons gripped his shoulder. Carefully he picked up the heavy leather glove and coaxed the falcon down onto his wrist. Goldy, curled in the rocking chair by the Rayburn with her nose under her tail, watched with interest. As he passed he reached down to stroke her and saw the remains of a mouse by her paws.

'I don't suppose you thought of sharing with Seabhac?' he asked the cat. 'No. I thought not.'

He made his way to the pantry and carefully placed the falcon on top of the fridge door while he got a chick leg out of the box. The bird was back on his wrist in a flash, but he wouldn't give her the food until he had flown her. As he carried her across the study and out of the French windows he saw the answer-phone flashing. 'Kate!' he thought, and carried on out into the orchard.

The merlin perched in the top of the old apple tree, watching as he unwrapped the lure and began to swing it. Then she stooped, her pointed wings slicing the still air. He watched the low sun glint off her brown underbelly and light up the bars on her tail, admiring her perfection. After four or five passes he allowed her to take the lure. She landed on it with a slight bounce, ripping at the leather with her curved beak, staring at him with wide golden eyes and calling softly. He called her back to his wrist and gave her the chick leg. She tore at it thoughtfully, then looked him in the eye.

'Yes, I know,' he answered her. 'But I'm not ringing that woman up tonight.'

He brought Seabhac home and set her on the perch beside his desk. In the kitchen he made a pot of tea, then followed Goldy into the study. Albert de Seligny's fax was there on top of the specifications, he settled down to read it. The job was coming together, Albert had ordered the hardware, now all that was needed was for Merle to test out the database. Then he could go and set up the first trials. The thought of a visit to Toulouse in February smiled at him. Warmth, wine, relaxed company. But the cloud of red hair overlaid his image of the café by the bridge in the old city. He shook his head but the image took its own time to fade. He settled into some calculations. The teapot was dry when the phone rang. He waited to hear who it was before picking up the handset, but it was Albert.

'I'm sorry to call you now. You had the funeral today didn't you?' the Frenchman's voice was careful, friendly but detached.

'That's all right. It went well. I'm just looking at your stuff now,' Merle replied. 'I wondered if you would prefer ...' and he launched into details about the design of the database which was going to keep track of vintages and sales of the Jolys wine.

'I look forward to seeing you then,' the Frenchman said finally and hung up the phone. Merle looked at the receiver in his hand for a minute, not seeing it, then put it down. Goldy climbed into his lap and set her paws on the keyboard. A splurge of numbers raced across the screen.

'No!' Merle lifted her off and set her back on the window ledge. 'I don't think we can get Albert to agree to an alternative set of costings like that, even if it did mean I wouldn't need to work for months!'

He tidied and saved the costings. Stretching stiff shoulder muscles, he went upstairs to turn on the bath. Goldy followed and sat between the taps, flicking her tail, her eyes slitted as she cat-napped off into another realm. Merle followed her in his own mind.

Again the halo of red hair came into his mind but this time he pushed it resolutely aside. Kate took its place. He watched her beautiful face, the fall of flaxen hair half hiding the twisted eyes. Even here, now, Merle could see that they belied the smile on her mouth. She wanted something, of course. As the warmth of the water relaxed his muscles he found himself remembering.

He had got back a day early from a trip to France. He'd caught a late flight and, arriving at the flat, dumped the cases and gone straight to the kitchen to fix himself coffee. He took the steaming cup back to the living room to relax on the sofa for half an hour and turned the radio on softly. He hadn't been especially quiet, Kate said it disturbed her more if he tiptoed about. Finishing his coffee he went to the bedroom.

They made no attempt to dissemble but were lying curled in each other's arms in the manner of long habit. Merle stood in the doorway for a moment, his mouth hanging open, then he backed out, shutting the door. Shortly after, Nick came out and stood lounging against the table.

'Well, old man,' he said. 'I suppose you always knew it would come to this.'

Merle hadn't known any such thing but he didn't say so. Kate had been getting distant for some time but he hadn't realised it was as bad as this. She said he called her Vicki in his sleep.

'I'm afraid she's told me all about it.' Nick continued into Merle's silence. 'How you call her by your old girlfriend's name when you're asleep. And sometimes when you're not too. Not good, old man, not good at all. Doesn't do anything for a lady's confidence. Makes it quite obvious she's not number one.'

Merle didn't answer.

'She needed someone to talk it through with. So she could decide what to do.'

Nick paused, waiting. Merle still didn't respond.

'I think she's decided.' Nick told him. 'It was just a matter of timing, old man.'

He stood up and stretched. Then, as Merle still wasn't responding, he headed back to the bedroom again.

That was too much. Merle grabbed Nick by the throat and, much to his and Nick's surprise, flung him out into the hallway, slamming the door. He went back to the bedroom, collected the rest of Nick's clothes in a bundle and flung them out after him.

When he came back Kate was looking sultry and interested. He fished a suitcase out of the wardrobe and slung some of her clothes in it, added her handbag. Then he pulled her naked out of the bed and half dragged her across the flat to the front door. Opening it, there was now no sign of Nick. Merle threw the suitcase into the hall and shoved Kate out in its wake.

'What am I supposed to do now,' she snarled furiously.

'Honey,' he said slowly. 'I don't give a damn!' and he slammed the door.

The water was cooling as he found himself back in the bath again. He yawned clenched jaw muscles back into a more comfortable state. Goldy looked him in the eye.

'Oh, Goldy girl. I don't know! I just don't know!' He answered her as he climbed out of the bath.

The cat watched his thin, brown body drip onto the mat. What's she thinking? Merle wondered as he towelled down. Am I too thin? He looked in the mirror and stared at his rib cage, no spare flesh, good leg and shoulder muscles. A runner's body, he grinned at Goldy who was still watching. So don't you go thinking comments at me.

'Do you think she'll notice?' he asked the cat directly.

Goldy stared at him with unblinking silver eyes.

She knows who I'm talking about though, Merle thought as he headed for the bedroom and clean clothes.

He took Seabhac to her mews, as he grandly called the converted potting shed by the garage. She settled easily, flicking an eye open as he left, giving her gentle whistling noise. The sky was dark and bright with stars, frost nipped his nose. He headed for Bridewell Manor.

Dinner

Vicki watched Merle drive away, then turned back to the house. The door squeaked and groaned, the knocker rattling as she pushed it open.

104

Dropping hat and gloves on the pew by the door, Vicki went down into the library where the last of the sunset flickered off the high ceiling. She kicked off her shoes and unlocked the French windows, flinging them open. Wind stirred the frost-blackened leaves of the climbing rose and she closed her eyes, breathing it in, remembering the heavy scent. Tears began again. It was so long ago. She hugged herself, toes squirming down among the frosted grass stems. Then the wind caught her scarf and blew it against her cheek. Vicki screamed.

She was back in that summer of long ago. Julian's hand, cold and soft on her throat, his body above her, he pulled up her skirt, fumbled in her pants. Vicki stumbled forward, gasping for air and reality. Her hand closed on the rose thorns, ripping her palm.

Back in the library, she wiped the blood off her hands and shivered away the memory. Julian was at Well Cottage. With Sylvie. She was here, alone, safe, inviolate. She collapsed into the sofa with Hecaté. Together they slept.

The knocking reached her from the end of a long dreamless tunnel. Vicki stumbled to her feet wondering who it was. Hecaté preceded her through the back hall, up the stone corridor. She pulled the groaning door open and stared blankly at Merle. He had brought flowers.

'Am I too early?' he asked.

'Oh!' she peered past him into the dark. 'Come in, Merle, come in. I'd forgotten. I was asleep. Is it that time already?'

She let him in. He followed her down to the library where she stopped by the staircase.

'Wait for me while I splash water on my face, I'm all at sea.'

'I could put the flowers in water.' Merle offered, picking Hecaté up and draping her over his shoulders, giving Vicki time.

'Oh, yes, the flowers!' she was still feeling groggy. 'Thank you. There's vases in the kitchen. I won't be long.'

She went up the stairs.

Merle went to the kitchen, hunted in cupboards, eventually finding what he wanted. He took the kenzan, the round spikes, out of his pocket and set it in the flat, brown dish. He measured the stems of the bronze chrysanthemums, setting heaven, Shin, to the back, Hikae, earth, to the front and Soe, man, between the two. He added eucalyptus and stones.

Hecaté sat on the table, watching with enormous green eyes, contemplating the Zen garden he had created.

'Oh!' Vicki cried from the doorway. 'It's beautiful!'

Merle stood up. 'Are you better now?'

'Yes. Thank you.' At last she returned his smile. Satisfied, he followed her out.

The roads were empty, in twenty minutes they were at Buckland. Soft light from the windows opened up the shadows around the lime-washed buildings. She hadn't known the restaurant existed. How should she? It had been ten years.

Dinner was strange, intimate. Merle offered her the menu as though to a stranger.

'You order.' She pushed it back at him like a friend.

He talked about wine, computers, Bach's organs, the little owl on Crete, the sounds of sheep bells in the Pyrenees. Nothing about himself. No questions about her.

'How come you're back?' she said into a pause.

'I was in between things, jobs, everything. ...'

Vicki cocked an eyebrow at him. 'Don't bullshit me.'

'OK ...' Merle swallowed. 'I split up with Kate. It ... wasn't working.' He jolted to a stop, then restarted himself again.

'You know my parents died. I'd just come back from London, the divorce. It rather wrecked the company as Kate went off with Nick. I lit out on my own. They didn't tell me mum was dying. She and dad jumped off Hurlestone Point together, although everyone said it was an accident.'

Merle jerked to a stop again. He was talking like a learner-driver, kangaroo-foot on the accelerator. He went to drink some wine, then took the water instead. He looked at Vicki. I needed you then, his eyes told her. Where were you ...?

Vicki looked away.

'I inherited Bridge Cottage,' Merle got going again, 'and started my own computer consultancy, working from home. With the old contacts it soon got going. I'm doing quite well now.'

He stopped.

'You saw a lot of Dad too, didn't you? Vera told me.' Vicki broke the silence. 'Tell me about it.'

'It began again after my parents died. I was out in the orchard when along comes this car, far too fast, trying to drive through the ford. It stalled and Jacob clambered out. He stood there, up to his knees in the river, swearing. I was very impressed by his fluency.' Merle grinned at her. 'I don't think he repeated himself once. When things seemed to be dying down a bit, I poked my head up over the hedge, ready to duck again if it seemed a good idea. He saw me straight away and grinned, saying he was a bloody old fool and would I mind giving him a hand. I pulled the car out with the Range Rover. He came in for tea and stayed for dinner, eventually leaving about midnight after a couple of bottles of claret. After that he used to come over a couple of times a month, and I would go up to Bridewell. It was just like old times, except I was now grown up.

'He was very good to me. I think the stalling in the river was a set-up.' Merle was looking away from her now. 'I really didn't know which way was up at first, kept forgetting basic things, like eating. Jacob made sure someone would come round every day and check me out. He'd come himself too, always with something plausible he wanted me to do for him. I realised what he was at after a while, and then I could manage for myself. There's so much to do when someone dies,' he stopped and looked at her. 'I know the ropes, if you need any help,' he offered.

'How did he get off with Sylvie?' Vicki changed the subject.

'You don't know? He never talked about it to you?'

'It was a sore point. He never told me about her, I found out by accident and stormed round to his flat. There was the hell of a row and I told him he was a stupid fool. We didn't speak for a couple of weeks, then he called me, invited me over to the flat. Delagardie was there too, you remember the solicitor? He had the will out all over the coffee table and was showing me that Dad hadn't changed it in Sylvie's favour, that I still inherited. Dad was adamant that he wasn't going to marry her, they were just very good friends and surely I didn't begrudge him some fun and companionship in his old age. Anybody'd have thought he was ninety not fifty-eight!' Vicki smiled again. 'I suppose I did begrudge him, in a way. But I wouldn't have minded if it had been anyone else, it was just that it was her … you understand?'

Merle nodded.

'We were like a pair of cats, stalking round each other, ready to spit and claw,' Vicki went on. 'Delagardie managed to get us around, but we never talked about it again. In fact, he's never mentioned her name to me in all the time since.'

'Not wanting a row?' Merle quizzed her.

She couldn't help herself, she grinned at him.

Merle made a face back.

Damn! This is far too bloody easy, she thought.

'Well,' Merle went on. 'It was all rather crazy and odd, just what you'd expect from him, really. He was at some conference, Oxford, a whole bunch of boffins arguing their theories about possible British grails. He must have told you about that?'

'Yes, hilarious. But I didn't realise that's where he met Sylvie again. Makes sense though. She would be there!'

'Indeed she was. Hanging on the coattails of anyone she thought would offer her a lead, still totally obsessed on the subject. She soon noticed Jacob. He was there with David Ranley-Hall. David saw her and made the mistake of smiling to her, you know how absent minded he is at times! Saw a face he knew and he smiled at it, never thought about whose it was. Of course, that was just what she wanted. She galloped over and gushed madly, and was then impossible to get rid of for the rest of the conference!'

'Ye gods! I didn't realise.'

'He said Sylvie had some ideas that really did help him. They began to see a lot of each other and the inevitable happened. She's a very attractive woman, knows how to play her stuff. Then she bought Well Cottage, living "on site" as it were, and they saw each other most days, unless he was in London. I didn't see much of him then. Sylvie doesn't like me any more than I like her, so I didn't go to dinner, but he still came down here once a month, on his own of course.'

'So what happened next?' Vicki asked him.

'It was a bit over eighteen months ago,' said Merle. 'They broke up. She was so damn keen on finding the cup Jacob got suspicious, began to hold stuff back from her. He started to tell me something once, then clammed up. He was cooling off her too, and I was seeing more of him again. He said she'd blow hot and cold, one minute it was all darling and love-me-do, next it was go away, I'm busy, sick, fed up. It all came apart at the seams when he discovered she'd taken up with Julian Courtney. That's when they had the fight.' He stopped and looked at Vicki.

'Vera told me about that, she said it was about some papers. But it was about the water, wasn't it?'

'Yes. Vera gave you the authorised version. But you're right, it was the water. She had Julian living with her in Well Cottage then and, within a month, they'd set up the bottling plant. You know the old sheds, opposite Well Cottage, the other side of Forge Alley? Well, they bought them. Still the village didn't catch on until the day the water stopped flowing. Up to then everyone thought it was a joke.'

Merle paused. Vicki poured more coffee.

'Jacob was away lecturing in America, it hit him on the nose as soon as he got back. And it made him mad. He called her up to the manor and they had a blazing row. He told her she had no right to take the water and she laughed at him. She'd brought Julian with her and he said it served Jacob right for being such a thieving old fart and not giving Sylvie all the credit due to her. So Jacob punched him on the nose, laid him out. That's when she stabbed Jacob with the poker. I went up to see him when he was convalescing and he told me he'd decided to find the spring and redirect the water into the village. Give it back. He got Dick and Joe to do some dowsing and apparently there is water, just where he thought, but it could be one hell of a job getting it.'

'I think I'm sorry I left home,' she looked away from him.

'What d'you mean?'

'Well, if I'd been here Dad wouldn't have got off with Sylvie. She wouldn't have got off with Julian. And they wouldn't have taken over the well. I think I've reneged on all my promises.'

Merle gave her an old-fashioned look.

'What's that mean?' Vicki glared at him.

Merle pretended to back off.

'I've been back five years now. I play the organ. I also ring the bells. This gives me respect from the church wardens. I'm no longer the *enfant terrible* who went off to London-town to make his fortune. Now I'm the prodigal returned.' His eyes twinkled. 'They tell me the inner secrets.'

'So tell me what the village is saying,' Vicki demanded crossly. 'No-one else will. I heard snippets at the wake but even Vera's havey-cavey with me!'

'You haven't yet achieved prodigal status,' Merle pulled a face, teasing her. She glared at him. 'Jacob blamed himself entirely,' he went on, 'and, I think, with justification for the effect his affair has had on the village.'

'And what is that effect?'

'People lost their water supply, had to go on the mains, and it cost them dear. Jacob tried to help, offering to pay fees but he was most often refused. He was seen as the cause of the trouble, almost before Julian. They have their pride and don't want to be bought off. There have also been several cases of cataract, old people who'd had never had trouble with their sight while they had the water, like Trevor told you. And you heard about Brian Courtney's suicide?'

'Suicide?'

'Jacob didn't tell you?'

Vicki looked away, her face grim. 'No,' she said. 'I heard he was dead but nobody told me it was suicide. No wonder Julia looked at me that way. I thought it was just because the orchards were going to pot. What happened?'

'It began a couple of years back. Brian asked the bank for a whacking big loan to modernise the cider press. Everything was looking hunky dory and the bank gave it him. Of course, he spent it. No-one was thinking anything could go wrong. Then Julian got kicked out of that job with the advertising agency in London and came home, with his tail between his legs. And, of course, Sylvie saw him. And he saw her.' Merle rolled his eyes. 'Well, that was it. She was tiring of Jacob, he wasn't coming up with the goods. Julian set up the bottling plant and the water stopped flowing. There was nothing Jacob could do. Well Cottage owns the well and there is nothing, anywhere, that says they have to keep it flowing to the village. Delagardie turned over every stone. The damage began quite slowly. No-one noticed until Peter Alcock found he couldn't shut his windows. Then the subsidence really took off, his cottage is unliveable now. They took his old mum off to a home in town. Peter's gone to Ash Farm. Trevor made one of the attics in the main house into a tiny flat for him.'

'Next thing was the orchards. The stream ran dry, the leaves went brown in May and all the fruit dropped in June, not just the usual excess. And no water for the leat to run the cider press. Brian was really struggling, every penny he had went to service the damn' loan. Olive Miller … you know Joe's wife?'

Vicki nodded, although she'd never met her until the wake.

'Well, Olive carried on doing the books, for no pay, just to try and keep things going, but it just got worse. Brian went to Julian. Begged him to put the water back, even a couple of days a week. Julian laughed. Julia says Brian came home with that queer, vacant look, like he'd lost his arm or something. He told her what had happened in a dead, monotone voice, then sat in front of the TV. Wouldn't have his dinner. Didn't even seem to hear her speak. She went off to bed leaving him sitting on the sofa. She woke up again about four o'clock and found he still hadn't come up, so she went down. The sitting room was empty, but the kitchen door was open. She went out.'

Merle's voice was getting choked.

'There was a moon that night,' he continued, 'so she didn't bother with a torch. She searched up and down the roads and finally in the orchard. There's one old tree there, they say it's the first one was ever put in the orchard, and there he was, swinging from it. Hanged himself. I think Julia stood there for a long time just holding his body and crying before she went to get help to cut him down. She said he was quite cold and the doctor said he'd been dead about five hours when they found him, so Julia thinks he went straight out and did it, as soon as he was sure she was in bed. Sort of thing he would do too, not wanting Julia to guess and talk him out of it.'

They both sat silent. Vicki was finding it hard to take it all in.

'Julia's going to sell up,' Merle continued after a while. 'She feels she has to. Brian's suicide rather jinxed all the insurance and there's no money to pay off the loan or anything else. She called Jacob and he said he'd try to help. Now he can't, of course.'

They looked at each other.

'Won't Lizzie help?'

'Seems not. She married an American and they live there now, don't come home much. She did make it for her dad's funeral, but was off again the next day.'

Merle had so far managed to keep hidden the fact that Jacob had left an odd looking package with him on the night of his death. After all, he hadn't seen Jacob arrive with the package nor had he seen Jacob leave without it. And it was quite reasonable to suppose that he wouldn't go ferreting around in his sack of potatoes looking for something he didn't know was there.

He wondered how he was going to tell Vicki.

'I suppose some would say that it's not all black,' he picked up the conversation again. 'The people who work for Julian are all for it. They don't care about conservation. Or trees dying. Or that the otters and kingfishers are gone. Or old people losing their sight. The whole place seems to be dying …' He stopped.

Vicki looked at him. 'You're still one of the old ones.'

'Oh yes!' Merle's smile drooped again. 'Always!'

'What you're telling me is that the village is split. Some few are happy with what Julian has done. But others, the majority, are not. Are they angry? At Jacob? At me?'

'Jacob, yes. You? I don't know. They're waiting to see what you'll do. They've not seen you for many years. Maybe you side with Julian? You look foreign, like city-folk, short skirts, designer clothes. Maybe you don't care either. Do you know they have a new name for the Wilderness?

Vicki shook her head.

'They say ''T'aint no bloody Wilderness no more. Tis bloody Wasteland!''' His voice took on the broad burr of the country as he spoke and his fingers reached to touch hers. 'An' what'll 'er do? Will 'er do ought to set'n to rights?'

The drive home was silent. On the doorstep Merle took her hand, kissed the tips of her fingers and was gone.

She stood alone, safe and inviolate, on the threshold.

Hardacre

Detective Inspector Hardacre sat at the back of the church, behind the villagers, close by the font. He didn't follow the coffin to the grave but lingered in the west door until Vicki had gone down the hill to the wake. Then he watched from the shadow of a yew tree while Julian sat in the lychgate. Only after he had seen Julian sink into what looked like a fit of the dismals did he leave the churchyard and go to the wake. He drank his cup of PG Tips and ate his slab-cake. Then he went to give his condolences to Vicki.

'Miss Bryde, this is a very difficult time for you,' he said. 'Please be assured I am doing my best to make sure the facts of your father's death come to light.'

She smiled slightly at him and nodded, gave him her hand. A part of him had wanted to kiss her fingers but he had restrained it. She was far too lovely for anyone's peace of mind.

He left the wake but, instead of driving back to town, he lingered again, hiding, in a gap between buildings in Forge Alley. The lights were still on at the bottling plant. As he watched a figure came up the lane. Small, neat and quick, it went to the wall of the garden at Well Cottage and dropped something. Then it returned the way it had come. It didn't see him.

Hardacre slipped along the Alley and peered down at the thing. It was somebody's old rag doll, but with a difference. This one had a penis, with a blackthorn stuck through it. Hardacre's breath hissed. The chapel knew about witchcraft and curses. He'd been told to avoid things like that from Sunday School. His police training also told him not to touch, to leave it where it was, to watch. He looked up in time to see the small figure come out under the streetlamp where Forge Alley joined the bottom of Owlpen Hill. He recognised the figure. He had met it in the kitchen of the manor on the occasion of Jacob Bryde's death. It had been at the funeral, and the wake.

'What on earth's she think she's doing?' he asked himself.

Inheritance

We influence our futures (and pasts) directly with thought.
Bob Toben
Space-Time and Beyond

Thoughts of a dry brain

Sunlight shafting through the gap in the curtains danced a jig across Joe's eyelids. Lying on his back, his first thought was, 'I wonder if I snored?'

Screwing up his eyes against the grit of galloping middle age, he gingerly opened one eyelid. Instant agony! He fumbled across the bedside table, feeling for the bottle. There was a slight crash as he found it, but Olive didn't stir.

'Artificial tears, indeed!' he gently let the healing liquid into the corner of his eye, 'I'll have to produce artificial snot next!'

The eyebright did its job, Joe could soon open his eyes without pain. He rolled quietly out of bed and went to the loo. Meditating, or perhaps, he thought, less pretentiously, just in a daze, he stared at himself in the mirror as he waited for the pee to come. He stuck out his tongue, it looked white and furry. His acupuncturist would have something to say about that. Probably just the wine from last night, though, and insufficient water. It had seemed right to celebrate Jacob's passing with a bottle of the best claret. He and Olive had enjoyed their quiet evening at home after the bustle of the funeral and the wake. He'd had no chance to speak to Vicki yet. He'd forgotten how slim she was. If she stood beside a flag pole, she'd be marked absent, he mused. There were a lot of things he wanted to talk to her about.

Thinking about Vicki, he reached out a hand to the handle on the cistern and caught it back just in time. Damn! He'd nearly forgot himself and flushed the loo.

'Mustn't flush!' he admonished himself. 'Wait 'til you've done number twos and then use the bucket. Christ, what a way to live on the edge of the twenty-first century. Buck Rogers eat your heart out!' Pulling the dressing gown around his body he made his way downstairs.

Arriving in the kitchen, still thinking of other things, he turned on the tap. It coughed at him, perhaps even snarled. It must be getting fed up with his not remembering there wouldn't be water in it any more. Not until he'd pumped it up. Then his feet began to shout at him that they were feeling the cold of the flagstone floor. As usual, he'd forgotten his slippers. He ferreted about under the kitchen table and found the spare pair, pushed his feet into them.

'Water, water, everywhere, nor any drop to drink,' he chanted mournfully. 'Water, water, everywhere, except the kitchen sink! Don't know what Coleridge would think, be off on the opium again without a doubt! Poor bloody Mariner wouldn't have a chance here!' Pissed off, Joe reflected, would be a good term if he had been able to get a drink of water and so work up some more pee. As it was, however ...

He went over to the fridge, only to find there was nothing but sparkling water left. Sparkling water, first thing in the morning, was not to his taste, despite growing up in France. Come to think of it, the French didn't go for it much either. Coffee in the mornings, Perrier, with the wine, in the evenings.

'Avec gaz!' he smiled to himself, and then, 'Ah well!'

How much of his life could be described in those words, Ah well? Stop mucking about and get on with it, he told himself. 'There's tooth cleaning, face wiping and dish washing to be thought of, not to mention loo flushing. And how to organise it?'

He had to speak to Vicki.

What had Jacob been up to? What had he found? What were they going to do? There were times when he really didn't appreciate the competent, pater familias image he had invented for himself during his later life.

'All very well grumping about it now,' he thought, 'but how do I stop?'

His wife, friends, Jacob, had all come to build their lives around this image. Even in the village, he was looked up to as a second string for Jacob, despite being an 'in-comer', not village born. Now Jacob was gone he wasn't looking forward to the responsibilities that might be pushed his way, but he was at a loss to see how the intricate web of relationships, going back more than half his fifty-odd years, could be

115

dismantled without a lot of grief on all sides.

'What is the matter with me this morning? Usually I just go onto auto-pilot and get things moving but this morning ... what's so different about a little minor catastrophe like the death of a dear friend in unusual, to say the least, circumstances? And,' he muttered, ' a complete loss of water which has been going on for months now. It's all throwing me off kilter!'

He picked up the tray he'd made for Olive. He liked to bring her breakfast in bed every now and then, it was like the foreplay to making love, he enjoyed giving her attention and she enjoyed receiving it. He was pleased with the tray. He had found orange juice, and some apricot jam for the bread. He stood mesmerised at the bottom of the stairs with the tray in his hands, looking at it with pride, then shook himself awake again.

'I'm ruminating like a cow! I must be getting old!' and he set off up the stairs again.

Olive was sitting up, her arms curled around her knees under the duvet. Joe sat down carefully on the edge of the bed and put the tray between them.

'I found some orange juice,' he announced with a certain quiet triumph. 'And some apricot jam.'

'Are you going to speak to Vicki today?' she asked.

'I hope so. I hope she's going to speak to me.'

'What d'you mean?'

'I don't know, Olive. I was watching her yesterday, at the funeral and after. There's something different about her.'

'She's just lost her father,' Olive said.

'Yes but there's something more than that.'

'Well, you haven't seen her for years. She'll have changed.'

'I don't know, Olive. I can't explain. Just a feeling I have.'

'Men's intuition,' she chuckled, stroked his hand.

Joe sat looking out into space.

'All we want is our own water back,' she continued, twiddling a bit of her hair between her fingers. 'Vicki's all we've got now.'

'I wish she'd come home before. You know, I should have written to her. It makes me feel a bit odd now. Will she stay? Does she want us? I felt her yesterday, at the funeral, and she was all there, just like she used to be. It was just this strangeness, like a cloud hanging over her, I just felt I couldn't get through.'

'Ye-es.' Olive didn't know Vicki from the old days as her husband did. He had helped bring her up when her mother died. It had been he who had found her, there in the car, covered in blood. He said she hadn't spoken at all for days and days.

'I wish she'd been here,' Olive went on, 'when the trees fell down, and the stream dried up, and great cracks came in the fields. And the cottages. They're just cob, mud and plaster, but now the walls lean at every angle, windows no longer fit and the roofs are coming apart. People who've lived here for generations are losing their homes.' She jounced up and down aggressively in the bed, straightening the covers. 'And the apples. I don't know if Julia will cope now Brian's dead,' she finished miserably.

'I'll phone Vicki now. And anyway we have to go over for the reading of the will.'

Joe kissed the top of her head and left her with the tray while he beat a hasty retreat down the stairs. It wasn't the first time they'd talked like this. But what good did it do? They needed a miracle to get Julian to give the water back.

He stood at the sink, staring at the uncooperative taps, then went for the pump outside. He came back with a bucket of sweet, brown water and filled the big kettle on the stove preparatory to washing last night's cups and glasses.

Bridewell apple orchards had been famous for more than two thousand years. The Romans had known them. Then a thousand years later, when the Conqueror came the village, its orchards were noted in the Doomsday Book. Jacob had taken them to Kew, shown them the Bridewell entries, and translated the asides in the margins from the old Norman-French. It seemed the conquerors knew their apples, various nobles had tried to outbid each other to their Duke for the valuable land. In the end, Jacob's Saxon ancestor had sworn fealty to William and kept Bridewell Manor for himself.

Time out of mind folk had come to the village for the water. The legends said it cured cataract, and modern doctors supported this, but it seemed to do good to other things as well. There'd been several cancer sufferers who said they were still alive, long after their 'sell by' date, as a result of the water. Joe wanted more research done on its effects on the immune system, but then Julian had taken the water, so all that had gone out the window.

Joe's mind slid back to his first meeting with Jacob. He'd read about the old walled garden in a book. It told about the work Jacob's mother and grandmother had done there following Rudolph Steiner's precepts. Joe was fascinated. His own parents and grandparents had followed Steiner too. What was this place? He came to Bridewell and sneaked in, through the Wilderness, to get a look. It was derelict. Something had flipped in Joe at that moment. He limped across the stable-yard to the front door and banged on it, hard.

Jacob opened it.

'Why,' Joe demanded,' after everything your grandmother did, and stood for, are you not using it? Why is it in wrack and ruin, and after everything she did and stood for.'

Jacob took off his specs and stood wiping them, staring rather bemusedly at this angry young man on his doorstep. Doing the absent minded professor. Then he smiled and invited Joe in for tea. A week later Joe had moved into the Owl House and begun putting the garden to rights. That was twenty-five years ago.

'It was a miracle he didn't throw me out on my ear!' Joe grinned, taking the boiling kettle off the hob and pouring water into a bowl. He got the crockery together and began washing up.

After the crash, his career as a racing driver was in ribbons. No Formula One company would look at him any more. He could still drive the pants off any jack-the-lad, even with the short leg, but that would never satisfy him. And no way was he content just to tinker with engines as a mechanic, or even as a consultant. He'd left cars and petrol and speed and gone to hide in the middle of Exmoor. If you heard one car an hour here from two miles away everyone stopped to see where the fair was.

Since that beginning, Joe had built up a flourishing business supplying herbs to herbalists. He'd also learned the art of herbalism and produced his own remedies, like the eyebright with which he doctored himself so successfully. 'Now it's all threatened by Julian's antics,' he muttered. 'Damn the boy!'

'Oh yes!' Joe rattled the plates together in the sink, 'Julian's very happy to sell us the water at a discount price. Like three quid a litre. It's outrageous!'

But he could command the price because of the water's reputation. It was selling like hot cakes at every supermarket in the country. And abroad, Joe snorted his disgust. It was exploitation. And he was seriously worried. Over the past years, he'd built up regular orders for his remedies. Now, he wasn't sure how he could fulfil them. 'Bugger Julian!' Joe sighed.

'I'm being middle-aged and jaundiced,' he admonished himself. 'There must be some young people, successful young people, in business, who care about the world, but we don't seem to have them here, that's what's so irritating!'

It had been custom since before Saxon times for the owners of Well Cottage to keep the water running to the village. And no-one, including Jacob, had ever considered making the arrangement legally binding. Not until they lost the water. Then, of course, it was too late. What had happened to Jacob that he didn't get the measure of Sylvie? Everyone else had.

'Lost his bleedin' marbles!' Joe muttered.

The phone startled him out of his reverie. As usual, he didn't make it in time to beat the answer-phone. He turned the volume up. Don't want to speak to some clot at this hour, he thought, but it was Vicki. As usual, he forgot to turn the volume down again when he picked up the hand-set, so there was a dreadful honking and squawking in both their ears until he got it fixed.

'Bloody thing!' he cursed down the phone, 'but what would I do without it?'

'Good morning Joe!'

'I'm sorry Vicki, it's one of those days.'

'How's the head?' she asked, and that set him off again.

'I don't have hangovers!' he replied testily, thinking how does she know about the claret? 'I take vitamin C before I go to bed.' Then he calmed down, got the phone onto his comfortable ear, and managed to speak to her intelligently. 'Sorry Vicki, I'm very crotchety today! No water this morning, have you tried making tea with Perrier? It's ghastly! Hang on.'

'It's Vicki,' he called up the stairs to Olive, only to discover her standing behind him.

'I know, dear, you said.'

'Asks what time we're coming for the reading of the will ...'

'Whenever you're ready,' Olive said pointedly, taking the phone out of his hand. 'Hello, Vicki? It's Olive here. What time would you like us to be there?' she went on. 'Yes ... OK. Can Vera manage, would you like some more help? No? OK ... We'll be there at noon.'

Turning to her husband, she pushed him gently up the stairs to get dressed.

Sylvie

Sylvie sat with the rag doll, the poppet, in her hands, allowing her fingers to stroke it, feeling the rough cotton against her skin. Julian had been shaking when he got back to the house, after the funeral, clutching it. She'd mended his face and given him a potion to calm his nerves. And sent out a curse on the damned yokels who'd hit him. His past rising up at him again, her lip curled. But who had done this? Sent the poppet. An image came.

She was standing at a sink, a child's paint box on the drainer in front of her, painting the blood onto the penis. Sylvie tried raising the eyes she was looking through to see out the window. It worked. She was now looking out into a cobbled yard, bright with flower boxes. At the far side, over by the gate, was an ancient oak, encrusted with ivy. Sylvie looked up further. She could see the tower. Ah! Now she knew. She was at Greendown.

'Vera!' she hissed, and felt the other woman become aware of her, no longer standing at the sink but now, in real time, sitting by the fire with her cat.

'You ...' she whispered. 'So that's it. The child you had never had by the father you always loved. You'll protect that child forever, won't you?

120

Against me, me, who *has* had him. Ha!' she laughed. 'I am forever your enemy. As the child is mine.'

She felt Vera listening, watching, but refusing to respond, giving Sylvie no chance to hold her, enchant her.

'Yes, you would know these things,' Sylvie's mouth smiled, her eyes narrowed. 'And, now Vicki is come home, you're very much on your guard are you not? But it's no use, don't you see? The cup is mine. She left, She deserted the owl woman. I am here. She will come to me now.'

Sylvie's right hand made a cutting motion before her face. The image disappeared. She was back in Well Cottage. Her mind turned back to Julian and the story of how he had tried to rape Vicki after the well-guardian party. Her lip curled. What a fool he was sometimes, certainly had been as a boy. He had grown somewhat with her but not, apparently, enough to leave the damned poppet well alone. Or maybe Vera was slyer than she'd thought. Maybe there'd been some alluring charm on it as well. She pulled it apart, her nose wrinkling as she found the old tissue inside, amongst the stuffing. Yes, that would be what she'd used, a tissue Julian had blown his nose in. Ugh! But it's good, she thought. And I'd love to have seen her lurking around, watching him. And hunting through the waste bins round the village for a filthy old tissue. But, she stopped, stared into space. This happening showed Vera was determined and would stop at nothing if she would get something as filthy as that to work her will with. She sat back again, put the disembowelled poppet down. Yes, I must keep watch and be careful of her.

She pulled herself back to the present. Delagardie had called her to the will reading and she would go. In itself it was nothing, just Jacob's spite, revenge for her betrayal of him with the son of his best friend. He would magnanimously give her back the research papers she'd sweated over, and which he had refused to return once they had broken up. But Vera would be there. She could check her out. And, she smiled viciously, Vicki would hate it, be terrified Jacob had disinherited her. That would add sauce, an hors-d'oeuvre to the main course of taking the cup from her. Permanently.

She sat for a few moments savouring it, then looked at the doll. Vera had laid it out for her lover, to entrap him. And had succeeded too for, despite all her training, the stupid boy had picked the damn thing up, accepted it. But now she knew whose hand it was at work, and would have her revenge later. As for Julian, she would do what she could to protect him, starting with destroying the doll.

Sylvie got up from the desk and tossed the poppet onto the open fire. It began to blaze. The flames sprang up giving a smell of wormwood. Satisfied, she went upstairs to dress her part for the reading of the will.

Reading the Will

Merle followed Vicki into the dining room, balancing three carving dishes full of sandwiches, and made straight for the polished rosewood table.

'Not on there, Merle!' Vera scolded, coming up behind him. 'I dunno how many times I got t' tell y'! I spend half me life polishing and you go for to wreck it with not putting a cloth down first. D'you think I got nuthin' better t'do?'

'I'm sorry, Vera.' Merle froze.

'Here!' and she swept an acre of white linen along the gleaming wood. Vicki laughed. But Vera was determined. Even if there were only to be half a dozen of them for the reading of the will, the cold buffet would be 'done right'.

They were ready when the first arrivals knocked on the door.

'Sorry, are we early? Do you need any help?' Joe and Olive were on the doorstep, the Sealyham in tow. They found chairs in the library, close to the fire. The Sealyham curled in a ball at Olive's feet. The room smelled of wet dog.

There were a few moments of awkward silence before they heard another car pulling up. Vera went to open the door and they all heard Martin Drinkwater's voice, a moment later he followed Vera into the library.

'Vicki,' he took her hand. 'Are you well?'

'So far,' Vicki smiled wryly.

Vera offered him sherry. He sat down at the other end of the sofa to Merle. Silence ensued again.

Another car arrived.

'Place is becoming a parking lot,' Merle muttered.

Drinkwater heard him and smiled.

Vera answered the door and they heard female voices for a moment, then Julia Courtney walked into the room.

'Vicki,' she began. 'I don't really know why I'm here. Your solicitor phoned early this morning and said I should come.'

'Julia,' Vicki embraced her. 'You're always welcome.'

'Come and sit down,' Drinkwater led her to a chair by the fire, got her some sherry.

The place was filling up. Good thing Vera made all those sandwiches, thought Merle, we'll need 'em! The fire crackled into the silence and the grandfather clock began to chime midday.

'Hullo-ullo-ullo?' Delagardie's voice trilled down the stone corridor from the stable-yard. A moment later the man himself arrived, clutching his venerable briefcase. Vicki steered him to the table and put a glass of sherry in his hand.

'Thank you, my dear!' Delagardie pretended to fuss slightly while he took in both scene and atmosphere. They exchanged glances, Delagardie smiled slightly and nodded.

Merle watched their performance. She's truly queen of this particular castle right now, he thought.

'Now! Now! Are we all here yet?' Delagardie settled himself, counting faces from behind the slightly nonplussed expression he habitually wore as a mask. 'No Mrs Villiers?

Everyone stared. Vicki turned to Delagardie as one betrayed.

'She is mentioned in the will and I have informed her as such.' There was a decided twinkle in his eye. 'There's nothing for you to worry about, Vicki,' he relented.

They heard a car pull up and Vera went to open the door. Heeled shoes clacked down the stone corridor.

'Mrs Villiers,' Vera announced, as if she'd taken poison.

Sylvie sailed into the library, with Julian behind her. The Sealyham gave a weak growl. Olive hushed him with her toe.

Delagardie stared at Julian over the top of his spectacles. 'I think you had better wait outside,' he said. 'There is no mention of you in the will.'

Everyone held their breath. The flush rose up Julian's neck and through his face. He turned, looked about him and noticed his mother by the fire. One hand went to her mouth, with the other she began to reach out to him. He turned on his heel and went out of the room. They heard the door slam.

Sylvie paused, like a Hollywood actress. For just a moment she was in charge of the room, not Vicki, then Vera came up with a glass of sherry. The two women's eyes met, held a moment, then Sylvie looked away. She took the glass of sherry and went to sit in a wing chair on the other side of the room, watching Vicki from under her eyelids. Vera's face relaxed into a slow smile.

Silence reigned.

'Vicki! Ladies! Gentlemen!' Delagardie looked up, allowing the silence to continue while he gathered all the eyes. 'I believe we are all here now.'

The Sealyham wheezed quietly from the fireplace.

'We are gathered here to read the last will and testament of Jacob Owen Bryde,' Delagardie intoned. 'All the beneficiaries are here, except Mr Richard Fischer-King.' He glanced round at his audience and paused briefly at Sylvie, his mouth smiling, his eyes weighing the opposition and recalling his time on the bench. 'I have spoken to Mr Fischer-King this morning with regard to his legacy.' He paused again for effect. 'The document is quite long; if you are sitting comfortably I will begin.'

The room was warm, womb-like. No doubt, thought Merle, come the end of the several pages flapping in Delagardie's hands, he would hear he'd got some small thing or other that he had admired when Jacob had been alive. He closed his eyes.

'... and finally to Merle, the son of my dear friends Dr and Mrs Hollyman, I give the package I left in his house when I last saw him. May he use it for the benefit of all and find within everything that his heart desires.'

Merle jerked awake. Everyone was staring at him. Vicki looked as though she had swallowed a mouse. Joe watched him from half closed eyes. Olive looked away, bending to make a fuss of the Sealyham. Julia stared at him. Vera's mouth hung open. But Sylvie caught his eyes and held them. He felt as if he were looking down the twin barrels of a gun.

The room was silent for what felt like an age, then Delagardie continued, as though nothing had happened.

124

'There are various bequests to charities,' he was winding down now, but his hooded eyes watched everyone over the top of rimless spectacles. 'The Woodland Trust, RSPB, Cat's Protection League. If any of you are interested in details I can explain, but that about wraps it up.'

Delagardie shuffled the papers together and stuffed them back into the briefcase, then stood by the table wiping his glasses on a silk handkerchief. Vera came forward with more sherry for everyone and the solicitor took a glass as she passed. He caught Vicki's eye and they went off together to the study.

Merle watched Sylvie leave. Her face was a frozen mask. A few moments later they heard the door slam and the car go off down the drive. There were tears in Vera's eyes as she offered him sherry. Joe and Olive held hands and smiled sadly. Julia was openly crying with Drinkwater comforting her.

And me, Merle thought, what have I got out of the will but more trouble, by the looks of it. And how am I to explain not having told her about the package last night at dinner? What the hell is in the damn package anyway? And why's it come to me and not Vicki? From the look Sylvie had given him it seemed she might at least have a guess. Gloomily, he followed the others as they trooped into the dining room.

'You were asleep, Merle.' Olive steered him towards the sandwiches. 'You missed all the action and haven't a clue what happened have you?'

'No!' he grinned at her. 'Bring me up to date?'

'Well you were an excellent last turn. Delagardie is a showman, he was obviously delighted to have that to finish with. But you weren't the only show-stopper.'

'So ... tell me about it?' Merle liked this woman.

'We all were!' Olive's eyes were alight with mischief. 'Jacob made a codicil to his will. Well, several actually. And he must have done yours in the last few days.' Olive too paused for effect.

'Really ... ?' Merle put down the plate of sandwiches and took two glasses. 'Red or white?' he asked her.

'Red,' she smiled ruefully. 'Hair of the dog! Joe and I finished a bottle of claret in Jacob's honour last night.'

Merle poured for them both, then steered her over to a pair of chairs

125

set round a Buhl table in the bay-window.

'Now,' he quizzed her. 'I'm all agog!'

'Ah! Well, to begin at the beginning, I think you dropped off just after Delagardie did his listen-with-mother bit?'

Merle chuckled and nodded.

'Yes. Well … the main part of the will was quite straight forward. Vicki inherits the manor, the money and all the attendant problems. Vera got a legacy and confirmed at Greendown for her lifetime. No surprises there. Drinkwater gets a goodly sum to invest for repairs to the church, plus a whole set of historical papers which catalogue the church history. Then the fun starts. Julia Courtney gets a sum to pay off that blasted loan, thank god, so she should be able to begin again now, if she wants to. Joe and I,' Olive paused and swallowed. 'We got the Owl House at a peppercorn rent for our lifetime and a legacy to do Joe's herbal research. And then there was Sylvie.' Olive paused, drank some wine, nibbled on a sandwich.

'Can I get you anything, more wine?' Merle asked solicitously. Olive was spinning it out and he enjoyed playing along.

'No, thank you,' she replied, her eyes twinkling. 'Now it seems there was some substance in the tale of the row over the papers. Jacob detailed a great long list of documents Sylvie is to have, with caustic thanks for her assistance with his work. Then he stated that she has no rights on Iwerydd's land, nor to Iwerydd's property. That last was all a bit cryptic but I saw Sylvie's eyes narrow, perhaps it meant something to her. Vicki and she held eyes for a moment, and then she looked away. She never said a word but upped and left once Delagardie came to a stop. And there, apart from you, you have it! So … what is in this package then? Do tell!'

Merle fumbled with a sandwich, feeling his ears get red. 'Really, I haven't a clue, Olive.'

'Oh, come now, you must have a guess. It's not the cup is it?'

Merle gulped, choked and Olive patted him on the back. When he was conscious again she looked him in the eye.

'Is it …?'

Merle pulled himself together, 'No,' he said. 'Honestly …,' and he met her look. 'I don't know what it is.'

Vicki came back into the room at that moment and saw Merle with Olive. She hesitated for a moment, caught his eye and then looked away. She went over to join Delagardie who was talking to Joe, Vera, Julia and Drinkwater. Merle felt uncomfortable.

'I think I'll be going,' he stood up. ' I really can't talk about it before I've seen Vicki.'

Olive looked at him quizzically. 'Not going far, I hope?'

He frowned at her, puzzled.

'Rats, is it?' she quizzed him. 'Leaving the ship? But I don't think this one's sinking quite yet.'

'I'm going home. Bye, Olive.'

'Merle! Phone me!' he heard Vicki call as he shut the door.

Aftermath

Vicki closed the door on the last of her guests and leaned against the jamb. Now the reading of the will was over she felt flat, wondering what to do. Why had her father left this mysterious package to Merle? Why not to her?

Delagardie had taken her off to the study to give her the tale of Jacob's flying visit to his London chambers. Jacob had grinned when Delagardie asked what it was all about, and refused to say.

'Just a precaution, James. Just a precaution!'

He'd scribbled the codicil, hopped from foot to foot while it was typed, insisted on Delagardie hauling in a couple of staff to witness it. Then clapped his hat back on his head and disappeared out the door. What the devil was he up to?

Grumpily, she mooched back to the kitchen, where Vera was in charge, and began to try to help with the washing up.

Up to her arms in suds and crockery, Vera clucked and bustled at the sink. She was even tinier than Vicki and far more aggressively assertive. Vicki stood looking vacant, a pile of dirty plates in her hands. Vera looked at her.

'You leave'n all to me. You've 'ad enough with all them people, and her, 'angin' round, trying to steal the spoons. I tol' you afore, I'm 'appiest when I got summat to do.' Vera took the plates away from her. 'An' you want to get a look at that there package.'

'Fat chance of that today, I think,' Vicki snorted.

Vera looked at her sidelong. 'He still loves you, you know.'

'I know no such thing!' Vicki glared. 'But it's not only that.'

'What then?'

'How well did he know Dad, Vera?'

'Pretty well, I'd say. Like I told you, Mr Jacob was often down to Bridge Cottage of an evening this last eighteen months, when he was home from London, an' since he broke up with that woman. Stay down late he would, an' he used to tell me about it next morning when I come in to get his breakfast. Allus seemed to enjoy his self.' She added thoughtfully.

Vicki watched a blackbird hunting worms on the bit of frozen grass outside the kitchen window. Vera watched her.

'Anyway,' Vicki changed the subject, 'I can't demand to see the package, not now it's been left directly to Merle.'

'What you going t' do then?' Vera turned back to the dishes.

'I don't know.'

'Why don't you just go an' set down in the library for a bit, put a bit o' music on, read a book or something. Stop stretching your mind where it don't want to go. You bin buzzing like a spinning top ever since you come home. Get on!' Vera took her by the shoulders and marshalled her into the corridor. 'You get out o' my kitchen. I'll bring you a pot of Lapsang in a minute.'

Vera found Vicki in the library, her feet up on the sofa and Hecaté purring on her chest, when she brought the tea.

'I'll get Joe to drive me back to Greendown when I's finished up 'ere. You don't have to worry, I won't be walking back in the dark.' Vera said softly, so as not to disturb her. Vicki opened her eyes and smiled.

It's too much for her on her own, Vera mused to herself as she did the last of the tidying and hung up her apron. It was fortunate in a way that her car was on the blink, it gave her the opportunity to chat with Joe without it seeming too contrived. She would speak to Joe about Vicki as he drove her home. What Vicki needed was Merle, someone she could really talk to, who would really be useful to her. Not like these flibbertigibbets in London. Not that Vera had ever been to London, or met any of Vicki's London friends, but she knew what the city was like.

Vera clamped her hat on her head and went round to the walled garden to knock up Joe. Wills or no wills, she knew Joe would be out checking his garden afore he had his supper and there she found him.

Poppets

'It's all too much for 'er,' Vera repeated to Augustus at home in the kitchen.

Augustus, her tabby cat, was purring round her legs for food, which she gave him, somewhat absent-mindedly as her thoughts drifted round the happenings at the will reading. Sylvie had looked at her, they'd held eyes. And then Sylvie had broken away. But she knows I sent the poppet, Vera thought. No matter, done is done. What's needed is to get them two young 'uns back together. Augustus butted her leg, she picked him up and went over to the chair by the Rayburn.

'I dunno, boy,' she told him.

She sat remembering Sylvie's visitation, that morning, while she and Augustus were sitting over a cup of coffee by the fire.

Suddenly, the cat stopped purring, his coat bottled and he hissed. Vera could feel the cold settle round her. Her breath began to come out like steam in spite of the heat in the kitchen. She sat perfectly still, hardly breathing, her eyes fixed on the grandfather clock opposite and her brain just counting out the numbers round its dial. She knew not to think, to be still as death. So, she would give Sylvie no holds. She could hear Sylvie thinking, willing her to move, but she was not such a fool.

After a little while it went away. Augustus' coat returned to normal and he relaxed back into her lap.

'Ugh!' she said. The cat licked her hand.

'She knows it were me,' she told him.

He looked back at her, his big golden eyes unblinking, then sat upright in her lap. There had been a knock on the door.

'Who is it?' something told Vera it wasn't anyone she knew.

'Detective Inspector Hardacre,' said the voice.

Vera tucked Augustus under her arm and went to the door. Hardacre stood in the light from the kitchen holding his hat.

'Good evening, Miss Gardner, I'm sorry to trouble you again, but maybe you could help me with a few things that are puzzling me about this case.'

Vera looked him in the eye, there was something about this man. He looked like someone who had one time seen the fey, or something of that sort. But he kept it pretty well hidden most of the time. She stood back from the door.

'You'd best come in, then.' She made for the kettle.

'I don't need any coffee,' Hardacre said quickly.

'Mebee not, but I need some tea,' Vera said tartly. 'Sit yerself down. What be'e wanting?'

'I had a funny experience yesterday, after the funeral,' Hardacre began. 'I didn't stay at the wake too long, but I thought I'd go for a little walk around the village after. Well, I got to the alley that leads to the bottling plant, and I was just wondering which way to go, when I saw something whitish lying in the ditch.' Hardacre stopped and looked up at Vera. 'It was a doll,' he continued, faintly smiling.

Vera raised her eyebrows and looked back.

'Well,' Hardacre went on after a little pause, 'it was a strange sort of doll. Somebody'd sewn a sort of penis onto it and then stuck a thorn through that. Looked like something out of Denis Wheatly.' He stopped again.

Vera was looking at him quite hard now, from under half-closed eyelids. 'Did you pick it up?' she asked him.

'No-o-o,' he replied. 'I didn't touch it. But not too long after, I saw that young man who owns the bottling plant come out and head up the lane. Looked as if he'd been in a bit of a fight too. Well, he comes along and sees the doll, and he picks it up. He stood there staring at it and, do you know, he went quite white.'

Hardacre stopped again but Vera didn't jump to fill the silence. I might have met my match here, he thought.

'I didn't know really what to make of the whole episode,' he picked up his monologue again. 'I was hoping you might be able to tell me something about it. I've only ever seen anything like that in books.'

'Poppets, they call 'em,' Vera said quietly, looking away from him. 'It's a hexy thing, wishing bad luck on someone.'

'This one seemed pretty specific, considering where they stuck that thorn.'

'I dare say. Young Julian picked it up, you say?'

Hardacre nodded. 'That means something to you?'

'I can't really say. He b'aint much liked in the village.'

'How's that, Miss Gardner? His family's respected isn't it? Owns the cider press.'

A cloud settled on Vera's face. 'He killed his father,' she said.

'I thought he committed suicide.'

'Aggerravated!' she scowled. 'Ain't that what you perlicemen call it? Julian took away his father's lifeblood and laughed in his face. That's why Brian Courtney hanged hisself. That boy was always a nasty piece o' work.'

'I don't know much about him,' Hardacre lied.

'An' you ain't missin' a thing! I dunno how Brian and Julia got a boy like that, he's not a bit like either o' them. He was always a solitary boy, not interested in the place, nor his family's business, but allus wantin' to be off to the city, and the bright lights, and the women. And the money. An' he's a fool too, he'd a had a goodly fortune an' he'd stuck with his dad. The cider press was doing very well and allus had been. Now ...'

Vera stopped, realising she'd been coaxed into giving out quite a lot of information. She looked at the policeman, something in her confirmed what she'd seen when he arrived at her door. Mebee this man was all right, mebee he wouldn't harm Vicki, nor Merle. Vera smiled at him for the first time.

'What are these ... poppets, did you call them?' Hardacre smiled back. Softly, softly, catchee monkey, he thought.

'Witch-dolls, I s'pose y' could say.'

'How d'you make them?' Hardacre used the *you* deliberately, would she notice? Would she answer in such a way as to disclaim making the doll? He was sure now that she had made it, he wanted to know why.

'Y' can take a doll, any old doll will do, and put something o' the person

131

you wants to hex inside it. Blood's best, but skin or a bit o' toenail'll do. Even a bit o' handkerchief they've used or clothing. It's got to 'ave the smell, the dust, or the juice o' the person on it. Y' don't want nothing new-washed. Then whoever was doin' it'd give the doll the name of the person and say some words over it, bout what they wanted to happen. An' mebee other things, like if they wanted to take away the heart, the courage, of whoever it was they'd stuff some wormwood in it.'

She realised half way through, thought Hardacre. I wonder if she'll back off from me now?

'What about this thorn?' he asked her.

'Black did y' say it was?'

Hardacre nodded.

'Blackthorn's nasty. Some people do get a rash off even a scratch from 'un. But some'un who used it like what you said is thinking nasty thoughts for young Julian. Where it gets stuck is where them as is setting the spell will want the damage done.'

'Who might hate Julian that much, would you know?'

'There's plenty o' they!' Vera replied grimly.

'I'm getting the feeling you might be one of them, Miss Gardner,' Hardacre ventured.

'One of several hundred,' Vera grinned at him. 'I'm not sure how many people there are in the village but, apart from they as work for 'im, I don't think there's many good words said there.'

Hardacre raised his eyebrows. Vera responded.

'Like I said, he weren't popular when he was a lad. He used to shoot up animals, and people's cats and dogs, for a lark. And he was always after Miss Vicki, almost had 'er once after the well guardian party, but Mr Merle put a stop to that. And there was all sorts of other stuff. Then he went off to London, and I think even his parents thought good riddance. But he managed to snarl that job up too. 'Twas quite a good un, as I heard, advertising, and him having all sorts o' posh accounts, as they call 'em. An' then he come'd home again. Seems like he got some good severance pay as he didn't need to go lookin' for work around here, and he had that flashy car. An' then he saw her, an' it weren't long afore he was eyeing her. He's a good lookin' young chap, an' her seemed to be not getting what her wanted with Mr Jacob. She took young Julian in with her, and weren't one bit worried about all the gossip she caused. Nor all the heartache either.'

'Well, thank you, Miss Gardner,' Hardacre prepared to leave. 'You've explained quite a bit I wasn't at all clear on and given me some good background.'

'You think there's summat else besides Mr Jacob slipping and fallin' into the pool?' Vera asked as he was getting up.

'I still can't say,' he said. 'But I'll be sure and let Miss Bryde know as soon as I find anything, either positive or negative. I know she must be wanting to set her mind at rest.'

Vera let him out of the door and watched him get into his car. He drove off up the Greenway. Augustus twined round her legs again, purring.

'You don't think I said too much then, boy?' she picked him up and went back to the chair by the stove. Augustus purred louder. 'Well, I dunno but what I've changed me mind about him. I think he may be all right after all.'

Hardacre drove to the end of the Greenway and stopped, wondering whether to turn right or left. There was still a touch of red where the last light of the setting sun crept over the hills. He turned left.

Sliding down Firebeacon Hill, he felt the woods close around him. It was a strange place, only fifteen miles from the old Saxon town of West Milton and yet the whole feel of the place was of another time. At home, in his comfortable little house off East Street, he was conscious of being in the normal world of television and advertising and fast-food. Here, he seemed to be surrounded by legends and witches and ancient mysteries.

He parked carefully in a gateway near the bottom of the lane, out of site of the clapper bridge, and walked down to the river. It was dark now but his eyes had grown accustomed, he could see the trees, the bridge, the water. He crossed carefully and stood in front of Merle's gate. There was a light on. Something told him to wait. He went back across the bridge. There was a meadow off to one side, he brought the car down and parked behind some bushes, out of sight but now able to see the bridge, and Merle's gate. Something was going to happen.

The Wilderness

It had been a strange evening. Vicki had fallen asleep, woken again hours later. She tried ringing Merle but he didn't pick up the phone so she left a message, knowing he was there but respecting his need to be alone. She was hungry. Wandering down to the kitchen, she found the sandwiches Vera had left for her under a cloth in the pantry. She took them back to the library, with a glass of wine, and sat comfortably in the hearth, with Hecaté, listening to Prokofiev. It grew late. The fire sank to sleep, just glowing wood.

Vicki sat up, suddenly wide awake. Hecaté was fussing, purring, she too wanted to go out.

'What is it?' she looked into the green eyes.

Hecaté purred even louder and playfully batted her ankle. "OK!' Vicki scooped her up and took her down to the cloakroom to get a coat, scarf, boots.

The old clock clanged midnight as she followed the cat across the stiff, white-frosted grass of the old stable-yard. Everything was frozen monochrome in the moonlight. Dead grass, dead sticks, dead heads of teasels, dead thorn bushes. Hecaté led her into the Wilderness.

The trees were sleeping, brooding, watching, their branches reaching for the sky. The mist, like dragon's-breath, flowed across the grass, swirling around her ankles. It rose higher and a sense of a presence grew at her back. It felt as though she was walking through a tunnel of mist.

At the centre of the wood, Vicki set her hand on one of the stones, asking permission to enter. She felt a pressure release and Hecaté led the way into the maze. They walked it through, coming to the central hagstone. Vicki stopped and listened. Yes, this was the place. She tucked her coat under her and sat down with her back to the stone and Hecaté in her lap. A wall of mist formed around the edge of the circle, closing them in. They waited.

An owl flew round the circle, then sat on a stone, watching, blinking, staring. Vicki wrapped her scarf around the sleeve of her coat and held out her arm. The bird glided across and gripped it, stood looking at Vicki. Vicki looked back.

'What is it?' she asked.

She felt the tickle of words in her mind.

'Help me.'

Vicki looked at the owl, and was caught again by its golden eyes. She felt herself sinking, through the earth, and found herself in a cavern. The floor glowed. Mist, full of light, spread across it. It seemed as if the owl, who still sat on her wrist, was its source. Vicki tried to get up and found she couldn't move.

The owl looked at her and then pointed down with its beak. On the floor was a circular stone, with a knot-work pattern around its edge, surrounding a double-ended tree, whose roots and branches were plaited together making a circle. In the centre was the word *Tinne*.

'Holly!' she breathed.

It looked like a lid.

Everything went hazy and she felt she was shooting upwards. With a slight jolt, she found herself back in the middle of the Troytown again. The owl blinked at her. Vicki screwed her eyes shut, then opened them again. The bird nibbled delicately at her fingers, she stroked its soft neck feathers.

'What was that?' she asked softly.

The golden eyes closed slowly, opened again. 'Remember!' she heard in her head, then the owl was gone.

Hecaté led her out of the maze. At the entrance, she stopped, bottling her fur. Vicki nearly trod on her, then peering into the mist, she saw someone leaning against a tree.

'Bloody hell, it's him!' she whispered to herself, recognising Merle's shape. 'What's he doing here?'

'Is that you?' he croaked. His voice sounded hoarse and he looked as if he'd been hit on the head with a brick.

'What are you …' she began, then thought again. 'It's a bloody cold night to be standing around here. Let's go home and get a hot drink.' She led him out of the Wilderness.

WALK ON WATER

Merle stood in the kitchen thinking, his mind still on the reading of the will. He had left as soon as possible, not speaking to Vicki, needing time to think. Olive's questions had unsettled him. Who knew what about the cup? Jacob had never spoken of it with regard to his diggings. His whole focus had been on his ancestor, Richard, who had built the tower as a folly in the seventeenth century. Of course, Jacob had always been driven by the legend, the gold cup, to which the woman in the grave had been priestess.

Merle fumbled about in the sack of potatoes. The lump felt square, not that that meant anything. Jacob could have put it in a box. He pushed it away. He couldn't open it. Not without her.

He thought about what Olive had said, again. Who else was thinking it might be the cup? How many people would know about the package now, after the will-reading. He shook his head hard, trying to get clear.

'You really can trust all the people in the room,' he told himself. 'Jacob would have known they would be there. He would have foreseen this.'

Then he recalled Sylvie's eyes, like the barrels of a gun.

He felt cold. He piled the potatoes back on top of the lump and pushed the sack back under the counter. He hadn't turned the light on and was glad of that now as he passed his hand in a circle, three times, over the sack and muttered a charm. He shut the door of the larder firmly on his way out.

Goldy sat there, waiting for him.

'I know,' he told the cat glumly. 'Here I am, doing all my old tricks again, and she's only been back a few days. What am I going to do?'

The cat blinked her silver eyes and went to the door.

'You're right. A breath of fresh air would be good.'

Goldy stretched herself up the jamb of the door and yawned.

'Come on,' he opened the kitchen door and followed her out to the potting shed mews. Seabhac turned her head as they came in, the bells on her jesses sounding softly as she moved along her perch.

'Shhh, girl. It's me,' he told her. The falcon was all alert as he took her on his wrist.

They went to the orchard where no-one would find them. It was an old habit. Shadow, the grey feral tom-cat joined them. He pretty well lived with them now, Goldy accepted him, occasionally he would even allow Merle to stroke him.

Seabhac was ready, Merle threw up his wrist and she soared. For a few moments the cats and the man watched the bird as she sped off into the north, then Merle walked over to the old tree stump and settled himself to wait for her return.

'Call me!' Vicki had almost ordered him as he made his get-away after the will-reading, after Olive's searching. But he hadn't. He had no idea how to tell her about the package. There were two messages showing on his answer-phone, probably from her.

Goldy was playing with Shadow, batting him round the head and running off, then stopping to make sure he followed her. The falcon was skittish too. He could sense the electricity in the animals and the bird. And in himself. Something was happening, more than the feelings which were stirring in him for Vicki. Oh yes, the old chemistry was there, had been when they chose the music, despite the spat. And at dinner after the funeral. And again this morning. But this was different, seemed not to be from her, although he could sense it touched her too. He felt he would make static, sparks, if he just touched a tree-branch. The hairs rose on the back of his neck.

A heavy, rank smell assaulted his nose. He looked up. A young dog fox stared at him from the hedge, just an arm stretch away. Merle sat very still. The fox was in his prime, well fed, his coat glistening red and black in the low winter sun with a white flash on the breast. He sat down, his tongue lolling over gleaming fangs. Merle remembered the foxes when he had rescued Vicki from Julian eighteen years ago.

'What can I do for you?' Merle whispered.

The fox's nose twitched. 'Hhhn!' he snorted softly.

A picture formed in Merle's mind of the package in its hiding place and the skin crawled up his back. He knew immediately someone was searching for it. Not physically, not as yet, but thinking about it. His eyes focused on the fox again, it reached out its nose, brushing Merle's hand, then streaked away over the hedge in a flash of red fur.

The cats returned to butt his legs, Seabhac's bells sounded and a moment later she stooped to his wrist. They returned to the cottage and he checked there were still several pounds of potatoes on top of the package. His wards had held.

Later, in bed, Merle left the curtains open so he could see the clear night sky. The falcon was perched on top of the wardrobe, quiet now but watching. She had refused to settle in the mews so he had brought her back to the house. Goldy too had refused her usual couch in the corner of the stairs and come to lie beside him on the other pillow, her watching eyes half veiled in her tail. Even Shadow wouldn't go out but was curled at the end of the bed, an unheard of occurrence. Merle glared at them all, settled himself against a pile of pillows with a book.

He still hadn't phoned Vicki, had ignored her messages, but her face kept mingling with the words on the page. He couldn't concentrate. He gave it up, turned off the light and rolled over to watch the moon emptying light into the room, bathing him in silver. Sleepily he tracked ice-snakes down the frost-painted glass. The sheets hugged him, his thinking closed down, a thick fog shrouded his brain and he shut his eyes. Sleep, big and black and warm, rose to envelop him.

He came out of it like a shot. Waking in the middle of the night, the light was so bright he was amazed she didn't see it, hear it too. But she was not there, not with him in the bed, but away on top of the hill in her own bed, in Bridewell Manor, or so he hoped. He shook his head, trying to clear the fog.

Light painted the room silver, ironing out the bumps in the cob walls with its brilliance. He shook his head again but the humming noise continued, grew louder, it was almost like tinnitus, but not quite. The light and the humming beat at him, he had to get up.

He rolled out of bed, knocking the alarm clock off the table, banging against the chair as he pulled on jeans, dressing hurriedly. Nothing stirred. Goldy slept on by the pillow, Seabhac and the grey tom didn't move. It seemed only he was awake. He stumbled down the stairs, tripping and cursing softly.

In the kitchen he groped his way, in the dazzling light, to the sink, splashed water into his eyes and peered out the window. At first he could see nothing but the bright darkness, then he saw the window-pane seemingly etched with frozen owls and flowers of ice, obliterating the view.

'What the hell?' He pulled on a coat. He had to go to her.

Ice grated on the step and clung to the wooden frame as he pulled the door open. The door seemed to shriek as he finally got it unfastened. The stone pig, guarding his gate, grinned up at him as he passed but nothing else stirred.

He skidded across the stones of the clapper bridge, nearly falling into the icy water. He climbed the slippery path through the rocky alley and came to the bridge. He looked up the track by the Owlwater, but that was closed to him. The steep path was like a waterfall of ice. He turned to Penny Woods, struggling and skidding on the frozen mud. The buzzing pylons at the top of the hill were alive with wild fire, streaking purple and orange round the wires. He arrived in Penny Lane and peered into the cottage windows as he passed them, looking for his reflection. But the windows were blind eyes, bleeding tears of runny ice. They didn't see him. He was invisible in the world and he knew it.

He skidded and shuffled his way across the square. Ice sheets covered the cobbles, like a frozen lake. If he hurried he knew he would fall.

'I'm walking on water!' he grinned to himself.

He slid across to the head of Church Lane. His woolly gloves stuck to the freezing stones of the churchyard wall as he clutched at it, trying to stay upright. He carried on up the Greenway. The ruts were like frozen waves, he took to the grass in the middle where, at least, it was less slippery. The ghostly shining lured him on, lighting the path in front of him but not to either side. He arrived, at last, at the entrance to the Wilderness.

There was a figure standing by the gate. He thought at first it was Vicki, then he saw the feathers on its face, like the owl-mask she wore at the well-guardian ritual. He was just about to speak when he realised he could see the trees through it. It seemed to dissolve, then sharpen again. He shook his head but it was no good, the apparition was still there, barring his way.

'Help me,' it whispered.

'What can I do?' he asked.

'She has me trapped and forces me to do her will.'

'Who? Where?'

'Sheeeeeeeeee,' it hissed, then it stretched out its hands towards him. They held a dish on which was a severed head. Blood dripped down the long white fingers.

'The king is dead,' it hissed, 'long live the king!' And it laughed, a weird shrieking sound.

Merle fell down backwards and sat in the freezing grass. For a moment he'd thought it was his own head on the platter, but then he recognised

Jacob Bryde, mouth open, eyes shut. Merle put his hands over his eyes, willing the apparition to go away. When he looked again it had gone, no trace of anything. He got up. The gate creaked open, ice fringes rustling, and let him through into the Wilderness.

Woods enclosed him on every side, mist curled out from the edge of the path to enfold his feet. It rose to knee-level. He waded on, through it, towards the glade at the centre. There was no wind, but the shadows wavered as though the tree branches were moving over his head. He stopped, looked up and found himself staring into a pair of bright, round golden eyes which blinked at him. The owl gave a loud khree-i. He ducked and stumbled as it flew over his head, the wind from its wings ruffled his hair.

The moment passed and he continued. There was no sound but the crunching of frosted grass under his feet. He didn't remember the rides being so long. Eventually he arrived at the glade. It, too, was full of bright mist. Things seemed to shift every time he looked at them them. He felt giddy, drunk, or as if he was looking at things through swirling water.

Was there someone by the stone in the centre of the glade? He wasn't sure, the mist threw odd shadows. He kept very still, watching. Then, for a moment, his eyes cleared and he saw her sitting in the middle of the maze.

Something was happening, although he couldn't see what. He tried to go forward into the maze but he couldn't pass the wall of mist, so he found a tree stump and sat down. There was movement and lights within the circle. His ears began to buzz, he shook his head. Was the damned humming going to start all over again? The buzz stayed, he could almost hear words, sounding slurred and unfocused. He tried to make sense of them. Failed.

He could see Vicki clearly now. She had Hecaté in her lap. Something else was there, on her arm, silvery-white, but he couldn't see it clearly.

He ducked again as a white streak flew straight at him. Then he saw Vicki coming out of the maze. He pulled himself to his feet, leaned against the tree trunk and shook his head, trying to clear the cobwebs. He nearly fell as the dizziness swept over him. What would she say? Was he trespassing? No matter, he was here now. He kept very still, trying to stand upright.

'Is that you?' his voice creaked.

She began to speak then changed her mind, took his arm, and hurried him out of the Wilderness.

'I had to come,' he said.

'Not here!' She was holding him up. Hecaté trotted beside her. He stumbled several times, hanging onto her arm. The way back seemed very short.

Arrived in the kitchen, the warmth befuddled him. He slumped into a chair by the old beech-wood table and watched her put the kettle on.

'What happened?' he asked absently, half asleep.

Vicki poured him tea. 'I think you'd better stay what's left of the night,' she said. 'You look dead on your feet. We can talk in the morning.'

She steered him up the stairs, along the gallery, to a panelled door. As she opened it, he could smell lavender and rosemary.

'Are you afraid of ghosts?' she asked, turning on the light.

'After tonight?'

But he stopped in the doorway. It was Jacob's room.

'This is the only other bed made up,' Vicki apologised, 'and I'm sure Dad wouldn't mind. Do you?'

'What do I do if he appears?' Merle avoided her question.

'Yell loudly! I'll come and sort it out. Here's towels,' she dumped the large fluffy bundle she'd collected from a cupboard along the way unceremoniously in his arms. 'The bathroom's through there.'

Vicki paused with her hand on the door.

'Next time,' she said 'return my calls!' And she left him.

Merle grimaced, then went to the bathroom. Putting on the light, he blinked at the glow of rosewood, brass fittings and white porcelain. He dumped the towels on the chair beside the bath and peered at himself in the mirror. The eye sockets were black pits but otherwise it was much the same face he shaved every morning. He soused his head under the tap and rubbed it hard with the towel. It made some difference, but not much. He could feel himself slipping, he needed sleep.

He went back into the bedroom and undressed slowly. The light was soft, diffused, and the huge, old four poster glowed. It was a warm, rich room. He stroked the ancient, silky wood and felt as if he were inhabiting a museum.

What would happen next, he wondered, groggily. It was like old times, weird happenings around Vicki. And himself.

'Goldy girl,' he whispered. 'I hope you're all OK down there.' He thought he heard a soft purr in answer.

He went over to the window and looked out. Was that a shadow under the laurel hedge? He scrunched his eyes tight shut, when he opened them again the lawn was empty. But the laurel leaves were swinging, just as though something had pushed its way between them.

'I'm seeing things,' he muttered, 'it's all too much.'

But he left the curtain open. Sufficient unto the morrow, Merle yawned and climbed into bed, pulling the sheets up around his ears and turning off the light. Sleep returned to take him over.

HARDACRE

Hardacre parked the car, climbed the steps and fumbled his key in the lock. At first it wouldn't turn. Had he got to his own house? He tried it again, it worked. Inside he managed his usual routine, getting the ice, the glass and the whisky bottle together before he crashed into the kitchen chair. It was gone three in the morning. He felt groggy. God! he thought, what an evening.

He'd fallen asleep, for a while, in the car and then suddenly woken up. It seemed there was a blaze of light all round him, but when he opened his eyes properly, and even got out of the car, it was normal night. The wind had dropped, it was bitterly cold but he still kept thinking he could hear the trees soughing, a bit like tinnitus, very disturbing.

As his instincts had told him, something was happening. He only just ducked behind the bushes in time as he watched Merle come out the gate and cross the bridge. He followed him, as carefully as possible, up through Penny Woods but it was hard going, slippery and steep. He kept his swearing, sotto voce, glad when they arrived in the village. He was a bit worried about Merle. At times, the man seemed to be walking as if he were on ice. Although it was cold and frosty, there wasn't any ice that Hardacre could see. He decided to follow anyway, and do nothing unless Merle was quite obviously in trouble.

At the entrance to the wood – Wilderness, wasn't that what they called it? – Merle stopped for several minutes. He seemed to be talking to someone but Hardacre could see nothing. At one point he fell over, then got up again. Finally, he opened the gate and went in. Following was more tricky now, the rides were wide and there was practically no cover. It didn't seem to matter however, Merle was acting oblivious of him, not even noticing when Hardacre tripped over a root, fell and skinned his shin. An oath escaped him then, but Merle didn't hear.

They stopped by the open space at the centre. Hardacre stood in the lee of an oak tree, peering round the edge. It was about then he decided he must be mentally deranged. He could see Vicki sitting at the centre of the circle with an owl on her wrist. Then she seemed to be going in and out of focus, or was it reality? And then she disappeared completely. It was just like those special effects in a horror film.

Hardacre clutched at the wood of the kitchen table, trying to make sure he was really here, in his own house, not out in that infernal forest. He took a swig of whisky. There was no way he could write up this report straight. It would have to be severely abridged. When the owl had finally flown out, straight at them, he'd nearly screamed. His nerves were a complete jangle. The brutal rapes and murders he'd seen in his past had never reduced him to this.

What on earth was going on? Thirty years of police experience, including the twenty good years in the Metropolitan force, told him that Jacob Bryde's death was an accident. But all his instincts screamed at him that it wasn't. The coroner had found nothing unusual. Vicki seemed not to be looking for any foul play. But he could tell she was worried about something.

And then there were all these odd happenings. The old-retainer housekeeper leaving a witch-doll for a young man whose reputation in the village seemed to be something worse than that of a diseased slug. The principle lady putting on a show tonight which would have got an Oscar for special effects at Hollywood. And the lead man doing a pretty good act himself. And who had bashed Julian's nose on the night of the wake? And what else was Vera not telling him, not to mention that gardener fellow, Millar. Ex-racing driver or something wasn't he? God! What a tangled web, he muttered.

He finished the whisky in his glass, feeling a bit more together now, washed up and went to bed.

Merle came back to consciousness knowing he had been run over by a bus. He lay paralysed, under the heavy, throbbing, engine, unable to move, his chest crushed. Opening his eyes, he found himself staring into a pair of luminous green headlamps, a couple of inches away and rather out of focus.

Something clicked in his head. He was in a bed, not his bed, and there was a window open. He coughed. Cold air always did that to him. He shut his eyes, opened them. Hecaté lay on his chest, purring. Gingerly he moved to prop himself on one elbow. Hecaté took no notice, clinging tightly to the duvet. He stroked her as he looked around the strange room, Jacob's room. Then he saw the open window and Vicki, sitting in the casement.

A red squirrel darted down the branch and onto her hand. She fed him nuts until his cheeks bulged, then he dashed back into the holly tree.

'I've not seen a red squirrel down here since we were kids,' he said. 'I thought the greys had pushed them all out.'

She shut the window. Merle was glad the icy blast was gone.

'Hardly anyone knows, but an ecologist friend of mine helped Dad get half a dozen pairs reintroduced into the Wilderness a few years ago. They're thriving.'

'Eh?' he gaped at her, 'tell me about it.'

She laughed and shook her head, 'Bath first, then breakfast. See you downstairs'

He splashed thoroughly in the giant cast iron Victorian tub. The rosewood glowed, the brass taps shone, the white porcelain gleamed, the ancient cast iron radiators chuffed and puffed and rattled away. He was warm now, sitting on the bed drying his toes, so warm he nearly dropped off to sleep again. He got dressed, still in something of a daze, and followed the coffee smell downstairs into the big kitchen.

'Here!' she thrust a toasting fork into his hand. He sat in front of the open Rayburn and began hassling bread to a reasonable shade of brown, while she cooked breakfast. They sat down together.

'Now,' she said, slicing the head off her egg, 'tell me all!'

'You really want to know?'

She nodded.

He made a business of dipping soldiers into his egg, then pushed his cup towards her for more coffee.

'It was the fox really,' he said. 'I was out flying my falcon and this fox came. Sat and looked at me and I got a picture, no a feeling, that someone was thinking about that package. I checked it was OK as soon as I got home, and it was.'

'Someone?' Vicki raised her eyebrows.

'Sylvie,' he said grimly. 'I think. Anyhow … things seemed OK for the time being so I went to bed. All the animals were round me, they wouldn't sleep in their usual places. I've got a merlin falcon again and one and a half cats.'

Vicki's eyebrows shot up.

'You'll meet them later.' Merle laughed. 'Anyway, they all wanted to sleep with me, which they never usually do. I was very tired, crashed out and then, all of a sudden, hours later I woke up. The room was full of light and an incredible buzzing, humming sound. Nobody else seemed to be awake. I crashed about quite a bit getting dressed but the cats never stirred. Somehow I found my way to the Wilderness and ..' Merle paused.

'And …?' she prompted him.

'There was a ghostly figure at the gate.' He looked to see how she was taking it. She raised an eyebrow, but stayed silent.

'She was waiting for me,' he continued. 'She stood on the other side of the gate, holding a severed head. She kept sort of dissolving and solidifying, like a ghost on TV. Then she spoke, asked me to help her, so I asked what I could do. "She trapped me," she said. I asked who and she hissed "*Sheeeeeeeeee*". Then she said, "The king is dead. Long live the king!" and cackled like a banshee. I shut my eyes and willed her to go away, when I opened them again it had worked, she was gone.'

'Who was it?' she asked.

'I thought it was you, at first,' he paused. 'It looked like the owl-mask you wore for the well-guardian ritual. But it was the owl woman.'

Vicki nodded. 'And whose was the head?'

'Jacob's.'

'Go on.'

'I got to the glade and I saw you through the mist. I tried to focus on you, but everything swam. I could hear bits of sound, but couldn't make any sense of them. Then the owl flew over my head and you were coming out of the maze.' He smiled at her. 'Was I trespassing?'

Vicki shook her head. 'You're welcome here.' The colour rose a little in her face, then she looked at him straight. 'In any case, I don't think it's up to me!'

'Who then?'

'The owl woman. You saw her, she allowed you to see her, came to you in fact. She was the owl who sat on my wrist and the woman at the Wilderness gate. ' Vicki put her hand on his. 'Will you help us?'

'Need you ask?'

'Thank you.' She gave him a strange look. 'What's this package Dad left you?'

'I think we'd better go and see.'

Treasure

Vicki stopped on the flagged doorstep of the old kitchen at Bridge Cottage, taking in the feel. It was the same and not the same. Merle had gone ahead of her, she followed him in now and began walking round, touching things.

'Go where you like,' he watched her, smiling. 'You'll remember your way around. I'll get the package.'

He wanted her to explore, to feel at home here again and took himself off to the pantry to grope in the potato bin, pulling the dusty tubers out all over the floor until his fingers found the package. He rummaged far longer than he needed to before piling the potatoes back, hoping she would make friends with his home again. Coming out, he found her sitting on the floor by the Rayburn, Goldy curled in her lap.

'She doesn't do that to many people,' he smiled down at them.

He set the package down on the floor and sat down beside her. They both stared at the sacking-wrapped lump, neither wishing to be first.

146

Goldy twitched her whiskers at the earthy smell and batted it with a paw, then settled back into Vicki's lap.

'It's yours,' Vicki turned to him.

He pulled a face, looked away and began pulling the sacking off to expose a box of dark wood. He opened it and lifted out the fragile cloth-covered package, unwrapping it cautiously. Inside was a leather-bound book. Merle's fingers tingled. Goldy got off Vicki's lap, bottling.

'I don't know how to do this properly, it's so delicate,' he held it out to her. 'You do it.'

She put the cloth on the floor and took the book, holding it with her palms on each side and its spine resting on the cloth, then, slowly, she let it fall open. A soft, ancient, damp smell rose to their nostrils.

'It's Richard Bryde's diary,' Vicki breathed. 'He did find it after all!' Her eyes filled up with tears.

Merle put an arm round her, she snuffled into his shoulder. After a little while the sobs subsided and she pulled away from him, fumbling for a handkerchief. He gave her his. She blew her nose, wiped her eyes and went back to the book. Where it had opened there was a piece of loose parchment. She took it by its edges and laid it on the cloth, studying it, her lips moving.

Merle tried to read it too but it appeared to be in some foreign language. He could make no sense at all.

'Gwyth ... gooy ... No! gooyth ... gooythboo ... Gooythbooyll!' she muttered triumphantly.

'What?'

'Here! Look!'

She was pointing at what seemed a meaningless jumble of letters, all consonants.

'Gwydd-be-wubble ...?' he tried.

'It's Welsh,' she laughed. 'Have you got a pen?'

He brought pen and paper and she wrote GWYDDBWYLL.

'It means game board, or chess board, or something like that. And I think it also means land as in Earth, or even a plot of land, or a domain,' she said.

'Eh?' he gawped at her. She reached forward, laughing, and pushed his lower jaw back to close his mouth.

'Dad tried to teach me Welsh. And Gaelic, and Breton, and langue d'oc, and god knows what. I wasn't very good.'

Merle was still looking nonplussed.

'Hellooo!' she waved a hand before his eyes. 'Anybody in there? Dad was a Celtic scholar. Had you forgotten?'

'You said land?'

'Well I think so but I'm not the one to ask. We need to take this to Dick, Dad's assistant at the BM.'

'What land?'

'I don't know.'

'Jacob would have been able to read this?'

'Of course!'

'D'you think he had read it?'

'Why? What're you getting at?' she frowned at him.

'If it's land, could it be anything to do with this land, here?'

'Oh …Umm … see what you mean!'

She sat thinking, then went back to the text. Her lips moved as she slowly pronounced the collections of consonants, half under her breath. One finger followed slowly along above the lines, not touching the delicate page.

'An gan gan dooy yoor kyuraniad,' she paused and scribbled a mass of unintelligible gobbledegook onto the note pad. 'Death by water is the due,' she translated.

The muttering and scribbling continued. Merle held his soul in patience, watching her. Vicki's tongue was between her lips as she concentrated. Goldy, sat beside her, had her tongue stuck out too, her eyes were on Vicki in unblinking concentration.

'Death by water is the due if ever you the spring betray. Then comes the wasteland. None but the blood shall take the water. I think that's what it says. I need Dad …' she stopped, began again. 'I need Dick to translate this.'

'That's what happened to Jacob,' Merle said, into the silence. 'Death by water in the Greenway pool.'

'And he betrayed the water.'

There was another pause.

'And so did I,' she finished.

The tension rose again between them.

'Let's go out for a bit,' he said. 'Seabhac needs to fly and you haven't met her yet.'

She wrapped the book in its cloth, boxed it and put the whole back in the sacking. He remembers the old things, she thought as she watched his hand circle over the potato sack, marking it with his ward. It was just so good, being with him again. His drooping sideways smile lit his face as he looked up at her. He's finding this easy too. I wonder what he wants?

Out in the orchard Vicki's mind wandered back to their childhood as she watched the falcon fly. It was summer. Merle was home for the summer holidays at the end of his first year at boarding school. They were in Penny Woods, along the river path, when they saw the young bird cowering in the long grass at the bottom of the tree. It knew it could not escape but it hissed bravely at the feet coming towards it. Carefully, Merle crouched down near the falcon. Again it hissed and raised its one good wing, trying to scare away these fearsome people.

'Pass me your sweatshirt, Vicki, but stay back,' Merle said.

'Here!' she whispered from behind him.

The bird was backed up against the trunk of the tree. Merle crept closer, gently put the sweatshirt over it. Now the bird could no longer see it huddled down, quiet. Carefully he picked it up.

'Wing's broken,' Dr Hollyman told them when they had it on the table in his surgery at Bridge Cottage. He held the wing and gently spread it open, the bird opened its beak but otherwise was still. 'There's pellet marks here. We'll take him to the vet.'

'Air rifle,' said the vet disgustedly. 'Damn the fool! Who on earth would want to shoot a beautiful creature like this?'

Vicki opened her mouth to tell them, then shut it again as Merle kicked her ankle.

'I'll speak to Brian Courtney,' Dr Hollyman said when they got home. 'It's time he knew, if he doesn't already, what he's got for a son. They should never have let him have that air rifle. He's injured several cats and dogs already. Now this falcon. He'll get a person next. It's got to stop.'

149

'I hate him!' Vicki exploded at last. 'I'll kill him!'

'Now! Now!' Mrs Hollyman hugged her as she burst into tears. 'We can't have that. But Dad will have a word with Brian.

'He's wicked!' she mumbled into Mrs Hollyman's shoulder.

Jack Hollyman and Jacob Bryde went together down to the Cider Press. Brian Courtney looked shocked but not surprised.

'I'll take the gun off him,' he said.

'And lock up all the others too, Brian,' Jacob added.

'Aye! I'll do that,' the men's eyes met.

Seabhac's bells called her out of the daydream. Merle was standing, holding up his arm. The falcon swooped down to him.

'Would you like to hold her?' he offered Vicki the spare glove.

She took it and held out a chick leg. Seabhac came to stand on her wrist, eyeing her as she tore at the meat. Merle watched as she stroked the bird's neck feathers.

'It's getting dark' he said. 'Shall we go back?'

'Can I use your phone?' Vicki asked as they went in.

He pointed to the study.

'Dick?' he heard her say, then, 'Oh damn! I 'spect you're out! It's Vicki. I'm down at Bridewell still. Looks like I'll be settled here for a while but I want to come and see you tomorrow. I'll try to be there by, oh, mid-day. See you for lunch.'

'Don't you want to leave him this number?' Merle called.

'Dick never calls back,' she laughed, coming back into the kitchen. 'I want to go up to Town tomorrow. See Dick. He's the best Celtic scholar around now Dad's gone, and he'll want to see this anyway. May I take it? Will you come with me?'

'Yes, of course, but …' he cocked an eyebrow at her.

'And can I stay here tonight?' She looked at him.

Merle's mind hummed. What did that mean? Should he get the spare bed ready?

'I don't want anyone to know about this or where I am right now,' she went on. 'Can I put the car in your shed?'

'I'll do it.' He held out his hand for the keys.

150

Coming back, he went to the wine rack, pulled out a St Emilion and opened it. He brought it to the sitting room where he found her by the fire, the book on the floor in front of her and Goldy perched on the log basket, overseeing the process.

'We should let it breath, but try it anyway.' He poured the wine, wondering what the rest of the evening would produce.

After dinner he went to the CD rack, looking through it. He looked back at her, she raised an eyebrow, a slow smile spread across his face and he turned back to the rack, chose a disk and put it on. He came back and stood looking down at her.

'What is it ..?' then the music began. 'Oh ... Brothers in Arms.' It was the first thing they'd danced grown-up rock-and-roll to, way back, when they were teenagers.

'You dancing …?' he asked.

He stood macho, one hand on his hip, the other held out to her, droog-suit fifties style. She had to laugh. She climbed to her feet, then,

'You asking …?' she gave the ritual response.

'I'm asking …?' he was grinning now.

'I'm dancing …' she gave him her hand.

It began slow with *So Far Away*.

'*Here I am again in this mean old town* ...' he breathed into her hair. The tears came and she was singing it with him by the end.

'*You're so far away from me* ...'

'Not any more ...' he whispered.

Money for Nothing began and he let go of her, stood back, knowing what she would do.

She slowly raised her arms over her head, just the faintest movement in her hips and fingers as Mark Knopfler began to sing. The drums began and she shook with them. Then, finally, with the crash of the guitar, she began to dance, every part of her moving differently to the heavy, pulsing rhythm.

'C'mon, babe, let's rock and roll,' he caught her hand.

At the instrumental he stood back for her solo, then caught her again, as the voice came back and they moved together, two parts of one whole.

The track finally came to an end and they collapsed laughing into the sofa.

'*And they flew pair and pair,*' Merle quoted the old song. '*Bide lady bide, there's no place you can hide ...*'

The tears were back again. She buried herself in his arms. He pulled her to her feet and they smooched around the room, her eyes watching him through the lashes. He felt the electricity between them. What did she want? Or he? She opened her eyes, questioning, then slowly closed them, opened them again.

'Goldy gives me eye-kisses too,' he said.

She chuckled. He picked her up. Static sparked between them as he carried her upstairs.

Later when all their clothes were joined together in a heap at the end of the bed and she was folded in his arms, he realised she was crying again. He traced the tear lines down her cheeks, his fingers stopping over her lips. She licked at the salt.

'What is it?' he asked.

'I don't know!' she buried her face in his shoulder. 'What am I doing here? What are we going to do?'

'Take each moment as it comes?' he kissed her again.

Suddenly they were rolling and playing like lions, first he on top and then she. Later, in the quiet time, she lay curled on her side as his fingers traced patterns down her skin. Then, once more, she turned to him laughing, and the fire burned up between them, dark and huge.

Dawn crept softly through the window, spilling sunlight on bare, brown limbs. His? Hers? It didn't matter. She licked his ear.

'Yes,' he told her. 'I want you, now and for always.'

Sylvie

Sylvie jerked bolt upright in the chair. She'd been dozing. Julian was down at the bottling plant, working late, finishing the accounts. Her neck was prickling, every hair standing on end. She looked up at the owl in the glass case on the mantle, it seemed to move, struggle to come alive again.

'It's no good,' she pointed her finger at it. 'You can't escape.'

But something inside her wasn't quite sure. What had woken her? She held herself still and looked inward. There! She could see them now, the black hair and the red hair mingling together, poring over the book.

'He found it!' Sylvie started out of the chair, stopped herself and sank back. She looked again, then glanced at the clock. Her vision seemed earlier than the five-to-midnight which the hands showed. Julian was late tonight, her mind rambled a little. Was he really still at the bottling plant, or somewhere else? She felt torn between looking for him and watching Vicki. Old habits ruled, she turned back to Vicki.

She tried fast-forwarding the vision and found them curled in bed. She left them there.

She tried to search the cottage. Where had they put it? She felt like a bodiless mouse scurrying through the rooms, searching under cushions, trying unopenable drawers. She had no substance in this astral form, useless! But she didn't feel up to going into her spirit-self, she'd done no preparation and she was tired, it would be too dangerous. Usually, she would suck the energy she needed from Julian when she wanted to walk the worlds. And he enjoyed it. Better than sex, he said, calling her his golden vampire.

Her grandmother had taught her the way of it, back in Philadelphia, when she had wanted to marry the handsome son of the most successful lawyer in town.

'Good girl,' the old woman told her when she'd come in from a date, glowing with the stolen energy. 'And you don't make babies that way, so there's no trouble with his parents. But he's hooked on you now. You'll be putting up the banns next week.' And so it had been.

She'd enjoyed living on the Main Road, in the old Palladian-style house and being the wife of one of the leading men in the city. She'd used the vampire trick to get herself promoted to head of department at Pennsylvania University, although her husband had found out about the affair later. After her return from England she'd found it best to be rid of him. Granny had helped with that too, along with her latest lover. Another younger man.

Good reasons for having a toy-boy, she grinned. Then she snarled, where is the bastard when I want him? Reluctantly, she gave up on the hunt for Richard Bryde's diary. Vicki must have guessed she would try to overlook them and guarded against it. Damn! The younger woman had got the better of her again.

Merle was still something of an unknown quantity. True she'd seen him about when she'd first come to Bridewell for the grave dig, but he'd seemed just a gangly youth whose voice was breaking. She remembered Julian too, his voice had already broken and there'd been hair on his chin. She smiled. But she knew Merle and Vicki had worked together, even as children, and that Joe had taught them as well as Vera. Both Joe and Vera were old ones. They would help Vicki scotch her plans, delight in it even. She thought again of Vera's poppet.

That would still have some effect even though she'd taken it off Julian as soon as he came in. But he'd been holding it, and it had been holding him, for a good few minutes before he got home. It would have set its barbs in him. The wormwood would still be sapping his strength although she had burned the damn thing. If she'd been less hasty she could have set it to work back on Vera. She'd been too quick there, throwing it in the fire. No matter, it was done now. Perhaps Vera would be wondering, watching to see if anything crept up on her. Well, thought Sylvie, I can exploit that, make her at least think I've done something.

She was tired. It was late. Where was Julian? Damn the boy, was he tiring of her too? She counted on his wish to settle scores with Vicki and Merle to keep him with her long enough. After that it didn't matter. If he was still here, well and good. If not, that was well too. But she didn't need him flouncing some village bint in her face, nor bringing her back to the house. At least Well Cottage was in her name and she could throw him out if he got troublesome. Damn the boy!

The door opened and Julian came in, looking white around the eyes. Sylvie came forward and kissed him, he didn't smell of drink. Nor of woman. She looked at him closely.

'Are you feeling OK?' she asked.

'Not really!' He collapsed into a chair. 'Is there anything to eat? I think I'm hungry.'

Sylvie brought him bread, ham, pickles and a glass of beer. He took it eagerly but, after a couple of bites, he went white as a sheet and ran for the sink, throwing up. Sylvie's eyes narrowed, she went to the dresser and brought out the vervain, set the kettle to boiling and made up a tisane.

Julian was back now in the chair by the fire, well away from the food. She brought him a cup of the tisane.

'Drink this,' she ordered. 'It's all right, you won't be sick again. Then I'll wash you in it. Come up to the bath.'

She took more vervain and ran the bath hot.

'It's that damn poppet, isn't it?' he muttered as he slid into the steaming water.

'Just lie back,' Sylvie began to sponge down his body.

Later she brought toast and a light gruel up to the bedroom. He was propped up on pillows and already looked better, his colour was back and he kept the food down.

'It's that damn poppet!' he said again.

'Yes, it is,' she replied. 'But the vervain will help with that and I'll make you up a charm-bag to wear.'

'Was it Vicki,' he looked at her, eyes slitting.

'Not this time. Vera.'

'That old bitch always had it in for me!'

'Yes, I think she does still. But don't worry, I'll fix it now I know who to go for. We need to think about something else.'

Julian pushed aside the tray and leaned back on the pillows. 'Tell me about it,' he grinned.

'It means work for you, are you up for that now?'

Julian's lip curled, his eyes slitted, he reached out slowly, took her hand and kissed her fingers.

'OK,' she sat cross-legged on the bed, pulling up her skirt to be comfortable. She saw he was looking.

'Later!' she laughed. 'First we have to organise what needs to be done. I saw them tonight, Vicki and Merle. They were looking at Richard Bryde's diary. Jacob had found it, as I thought, and that's what he left to Merle. I see why now, I wouldn't have looked there but for the fact that they made love tonight and that sparked off my alarms. After they went to bed I went looking but I had no power without you.' She stroked his hand. 'I need you for that you know, as well as everything else. I dare say that's why Vera's trying to bring you down, take the heart out of you, so you can't help me.'

'I'm here.' Julian's fingers gripped hers. 'We both have the same goals don't we? And I like what you do. When you suck my energy it's better than an orgasm.'

Sylvie gently pulled her hand away.

'I want you to go to London tomorrow,' she said. 'I got it from their minds that they're going. To see Dick, I expect. They'd want him to see the diary, get him to help them with it. He was up to all the stuff Jacob was. They'll stay at her flat.'

'You want me to burgle the place, don't you?' he grinned.

'Yes. And you look like you'll enjoy it too.'

'Just let me get my hands on Merle,' he said.

'No!' she smacked his cheek sharply. He glared, then calmed down. 'Come back to sense. There must be no violence. I want the diary. That's far more important than giving Merle a bloody nose. With the diary, and later the cup, we can make them wish to die while they go on living. Isn't that more to your taste?'

'Yes,' Julian whispered. 'But I want to feel him. To feel him hurting. Feel him physically. Feel his flesh.'

'You'll get your chance, but not yet. Will you do it?'

'Of course I will.' And he reached for her, pulling her down onto the bed beside him.

Riddles

Are the patterns in the brain the same as those of the Universe?
Bob Toben
Space-Time and Beyond

London

Vicki drove. The steady throbbing note of the engine was acting like a drum on Merle, lulling him to sleep. Good! she thought, I don't need him talking right now.

The little ginger cat had woken her, delicate white paws gently patting her cheek, the tiny pink nose pressed against her own and the steady throbbing purr. Her purr-to-weight ratio was extremely good, Vicki told her later when they crept down to the kitchen together to make some tea.

Merle had found them there, curled together in a blanket in the rocking chair. A light kiss to the top of her head had brought her back to the room, his cottage. The little cat had stirred, knowing him, stretched and rolled on her back in Vicki's arms. He crouched beside them tickling the cat's tummy and having his fingers bitten gently in pleasure. It was enough. No words for her to worry over, fence with. He pottered about the kitchen, made breakfast, got her a towel, fed Goldy.

While she was bathing, he slipped up the track through Penny Woods to his neighbour, at Stowford Farm, to ask him to look after Goldy, Seabhac and Shadow while he was away. The farmer, who was used to it and kept a tiercel himself, agreed.

'Off to foreign climes again is it? Tis all right for some! Get on wi' yer. I'll look in on 'em every day. They'll come to no harm.'

Vicki called Vera. 'I'm going to London, to see Dick. I'll be back tomorrow.'

'Be y' staying in Jacob's flat?' Vera asked.

'No, my own. You have the number? Merle's coming with me. Dick has to see this package, but I don't want people to know we're not here …' Vicki let the sentence trail away.

'No-one shan't know for me,' Vera said fiercely. 'But I'll tell Joe you gone away for a day or so, just so he don't ask.'

Vera was a continuity in life, Vicki smiled wryly as she hung up the phone. It was her ritual to be at the big house, pottering, cleaning, tidying, sitting, she went over to the manor every day. She would take care of Hecaté, for Hecaté was part of the family.

Vera had come when Vicki was born. Caroline wanted someone to help, someone to share the joy in her baby, someone more personal than the girls from the village who came and did the cleaning. She never married, knew who she loved but he wasn't for her, so she would just look after him and his family.

Vera came to us then, Vicki sighed, and she's never left.

'Err! Whoops!' Merle opened an eye as the car swerved.

'Damn! Sorry! Idiot came out of the side road without looking.' Vicki brought them back on track again.

'Ah, hmmm,' he closed his eyes again, feigning sleep.

The car swooped on over Salisbury Plain. The land-rover, which had come out of the side-turning, had not even looked to his right. Memories began to surface. Vicki's hands shook a little on the wheel, she let her foot up on the accelerator.

'Problem?' Merle opened his eyes again.

They came to a round-about and she pulled the car up the side road to the left. The mist was thicker here. At the cross roads she turned right and pulled into the verge before they got to what looked like a car park ahead. She cut the engine. Not looking at her, Merle reached behind for the coffee flask and busied himself for a few moments pouring, setting her cup on the dash, putting the flask away again.

He's too damn perceptive, she thought, taking a deep breath. There was no point in waiting for him to ask, they both knew.

'You know what happened. We were on our way to ballet class. A car came out of Honeybeetle Cross, not looking. Mummy swerved and went off the road. There was an old hay turning machine in the gateway. I heard a roaring as though the spear … ' she stopped, corrected herself. 'I thought the long connecting rod on the machine was roaring, wanted blood, but it was just the car engine revving until it stalled. The rod smashed through the windscreen. It went into Mummy's throat and out the back of the seat.' Vicki stopped, turned to Merle. 'She looked so surprised, her mouth opened and all the blood came out.'

He knew the story, of course. He sat still, waiting, what was she going to say?

'A woman got out of the car and came up to the window. She peered in.' Vicki's voice was flat, dead. 'I don't know if she saw me. Her face was horrible, mad blue eyes. There was blood everywhere. I froze, kept perfectly still. I was afraid she'd see me. She just looked for a minute or two, then went back to her car and drove away.'

Merle took her cup, poured more coffee, gave it back to her. He didn't look at her yet. This was new. No-one had ever talked about another car.

'It seemed like hours later when Joe's old van came. It wasn't really,' she sipped the coffee. 'He wrenched open the door on my side, it was sort of stuck, and pulled me out, then just stood there holding me, hugging me. Daddy stood there too saying 'Oh my God, Joe! Oh my God!'. They just stood there looking and crying to each other.

'They cried and rocked me. Dad tried to get Mummy out of the car. He got blood all over himself trying to push the rod thing back out of her neck. It was silly really. Joe didn't dare put me down and he didn't want to bring me too near. He kept trying to call Dad back and keep his voice calm and look after me. Eventually, he got Dad to hold me and get into the van, then he drove us back to the house. Then he got on the phone, police and your dad.' She stopped.

'I began screaming. I screamed and screamed. They thought I was going to die. Then the ambulance came and they took me with them. Dad came too. All of us, in this ambulance, with Mummy's body under a sheet. Bouncing and jouncing along the lanes to the cottage hospital. Your dad was there, he gave me a tranquilliser and the world went away for a long, long time.'

'When the car came out of the side road just now, was that when you remembered the other car, the woman?'

159

She nodded to him.

'I just realised who it was …' her voice trailed off, she stared blankly through the windscreen into another landscape, where he couldn't follow.

'Who?'

'Sylvie!'

'Wha…' He let his voice die away.

They sat still, on the edge of the side road in the middle of Salisbury Plain. Looking east, the weak sun began to dissolve the mist. Like the wrecks of teeth in an old man's jaw, Stonehenge solidified on the hill in front of them, against the leaden sky. The mist curled around the car. It felt as though they were in the middle of a shrinking universe, bounded by fog.

'What do we do now?' Merle asked eventually.

'I don't know. Nothing, I suppose. Certainly no-one would believe me after this long, and with all there is between Sylvie and me anyway. And what good would it do?'

'None. But we should be careful. Vicki,' he turned towards her, 'I meant what I said last night. Don't go and do something stupid now. I don't want to lose you again.'

She sat looking at him, hungry, wary.

'Do you want me to drive?' he asked.

She shook her head. 'Not insured.'

'Are you OK?'

'I can drive, if that's what you mean. As to OK, what's that?'

'It's less than a hundred miles now,' Merle studied the map as though he were a foreigner. 'We'll be there in time for lunch.'

That's it, boy, be practical, talk about food, he thought. He tried pushing what she had just told him onto the back burner, but it wouldn't stay there. Had Jacob ever known it was Sylvie who had killed his wife? It seemed unlikely. Later, leave it for now. Later, maybe she would talk again. He wanted her to talk to him, wanted the old intimacy of knowing her, knowing things she never told to anyone else.

Damn! he thought, I'm past all this crazy falling in love stuff. We've done it all before and look what happened! I've got a career, my own house, business, cats, falcon, the bell ringing, the jazz group. What do I want with falling in love? And with her again. She left me before!

But she was different now. He knew. He felt in tune with her like he felt in tune with his clarinet, his saxophone, his piano. She was a part of him. Always had been.

He watched her covertly out of the corner of his eye, not letting her see. Wouldn't do to act up at the moment. Slowly, relaxing all his muscles, he turned the word over again in his head. Murder. That's what he'd thought. It wasn't what she'd said but the word had jumped into his mind. He lay his head back on the rest, perhaps the way her mother had died had been a coincidence, but what are coincidences? Perhaps Jacob's death hadn't been an accident either.

The crawl through London ended at last. Vicki turned off the Old Street roundabout up City Road and into Vestry Street. She headed down into the residents' car park between a boutique selling expensive ethnic gewgaws and a health food shop.

'This is us,' she said. 'Neighbourhood's gone down a bit, the ethnic shop used to be a fresh fish stall.'

'Pity!'

'There's still the Italian bakery at the top of the road. They've been there since before the war. The old man, the father, came to escape from Mussolini. He's got a signed photo of the old fascist and some incredible stories, if you've the time to listen.'

Vicki parked. Merle got the bags out, she locked the car and led him over to the antique iron lift. He heaved their bags in.

'I'm glad it's not all ethnic drums and rattles,' he said, as they rattled their way to top floor.

'Oh they're not so bad,' she laughed. 'The guy who owns it makes the drums himself. Says he's a Peruvian Sioux, whatever that is! He has wonderful tales. But some of the people who look after the shop are a bit intense!'

The warehouse-flat was six stories up into the sky and full of light. She watched as he slowly turned round, looking at the great, open space. Enough room to hold a ball, he thought.

Vicki opened the floor-to-ceiling windows which filled one wall and led him out into a forest, the garden she had created on the flat roof. The freshness struck him straight away, Merle followed her through the plants to a seat by a miniature waterfall. The place was a retreat, hidden

161

even from the sky by trellis covered in winter jasmine. The scent took him.

He looked down over the wall into a cobbled courtyard. There were trees in great tubs and bulbs already poking their heads up. He turned back to her. She raised an eyebrow, quizzing him.

'Yes,' he said. 'I like it!'

Inside again, he asked 'What now?'

'I said I'd be with Dick for lunch. I'll call the restaurant.'

'Allo! Jardin des Gourmets!' came over the speaker-phone.

'Xavier? It's Vicki Bryde.'

''Ooo? Bryde? Vicki? Is zat you?'

'Yes, it's me. Dad died, did you know?'

'Yes. We saw the obituary. I'm so sorry.'

'Thank you, Xavier. Do you have a table for three, for lunch?'

'Today?'

'Please.'

'What time? No! Wait a minute, how many you say?'

'Three.'

'Vicki, I think it is already booked. We have a reservation in the name of Mr Fischer-King, for three, for one-thirty. That is the Professor's assistant, no?'

Vicki looked at her watch. It said nearly twelve now.

'Oh lord! I hadn't thought of that. We're running late.'

'It is fine. I will hold the table. We will see you then.'

'Thank you Xavier. Bye!' She hung up and turned to Merle, laughing, 'We'll have to get a cab!'

Merle wrenched open the old lift doors as they arrived in the cobbled courtyard, slammed them shut and ran after her down the alley into the street. He knew something was on their side as a black cab rounded the corner, with its light on, just as they reached the pavement. He flagged it, opened the door for her.

'British Museum,' he said.

Walking into the flat he could see the red flashing light straight away. It made him want to turn round and go back out again. He hated coming home to messages. Who was it? What did they want? It was an invasion of privacy just to leave the message. Nearly as bad as having to answer the phone. Only the one message, thank god. He shrugged out of his jacket, slinging it onto the chair, and went through into the kitchen. The coffee filter was ready to go, his routine held.

Armed with a steaming mug of black coffee he felt better able to address the machine. It was unlikely whoever it was would want him to return the call that night.

'Oh! Damn!' He heard the sound of Vicki's voice. Wished he'd been in when she rang. Why did I have to decide to go to the pub the night she rings? Life was like that, full of near misses. She didn't want him to call back but she wanted to see him tomorrow, at the Museum. Oh well. Midday and she'd suggested lunch. There was that Thai place in Museum Street ...

'No!' he thought.

He dialled 1471. At first he didn't recognise the number, then he thought again and called directory enquiries. He was right. He had known she wouldn't come alone. He picked up the phone and called the Jardin.

'That's done.' He took a CD at random from the rack, then lay back on the sofa, in the half dark. As the first notes of Mahler's Wayfarer songs filled the room, Dick remembered ...

Vicki tapped on the glass and pushed at the door.

'Hi Dad! Am I interrupting?' She put her head round the jam.

Jacob looked up, 'Vicki!'

He went to the door, shoving boxes out of the way with his foot so she could come into the room. They hugged each other.

'Here's Dick,' Jacob turned to him laughing.

Dick felt his stutter rising. He knew, Jacob had told him, she'd just got her degree, broken up with Merle and moved to London. But it was different. She'd grown up. He just shook her hand, not trusting his voice. She was smiling directly into his eyes, almost taller than he was. He moved papers off a chair.

'Thank you.' She flashed the smile at him.

He and Jacob had been pouring over photos of the Rillaton cup. The cup itself, which had been found on Bodmin Moor in 1837, was downstairs in the gallery. They were arguing, as usual, over whether the Bridewell cup – if they could ever find it – would be similar. They continued the discussion, Dick's stutter vanishing as he talked about work.

'The picture on the tablet,' Jacob thrust the bronze into Dick's face, 'is *exactly* like the Rillaton cup.'

'Well … I suppose,' Dick laughed, 'if you've had enough to drink!' He pushed the tablet back at Jacob. 'It's a stylisation. Got to be, it's so small. You just cannot jump to the conclusion, based on a miniature stylised etching, and one that's the best part of two thousand years old, that it has to be the same. Just because you want it to be. That's no reason at all.'

This was an old hobby-horse between them. Vicki sat watching. Dick noticed. He couldn't sit there with those luminous green eyes on him and think of four thousand year old gold cups. Jacob suggested he join them for lunch, but that was impossible. He needed a drink, not lunch, and time to breathe.

He had met her many times since then, with her father, in London, and occasionally she would come down when they were both working at Bridewell. He'd gone down for the funeral, intending to stay for the will-reading the next day. But he couldn't. At the funeral he'd been tongue tied, clumsy, unable to say what he felt. He didn't make it to the wake but ran away, as usual. He grabbed Delagardie on his way down the square.

'I c-can't d-do it,' he whispered. 'Got to g-go.'

'That's all right, my boy.' Delagardie's hooded eyes looked into his, seeing far more than they should. 'I'll call you in the morning, let you know what the will says. Take care, my boy. Drive carefully.'

He hadn't. He'd driven back to town, very fast, getting two speeding tickets. And once home, he got very drunk.

Now, here she was in town. It must be about that package Delagardie said Jacob had left to Merle. Professionally he was intrigued, personally he was flustered.

'Tomorrow is another day,' he sighed. He got up to make another pot of coffee and put another CD on. This time he made sure it was Mozart.

164

The taxi drew up outside the gates, Merle paid it off. Vicki nodded to the man on the gate, then took Merle's arm and set off across the vast stone plain to the Museum.

'I'm sorry about your father,' the young man on reception recognised her. 'Mr Fischer-King said to call when you arrived.'

The phone buzzed, a voice answered.

'Miss Bryde and a Mr Hollyman to see you ... You'll come down? He'll be with you in a minute,' he smiled apologetically. 'He's just got to come down stairs. Lifts are out again that side.'

Dick clattered across the hall, grinning through his beard. She heard him, turned and held out her hands.

'Hello, Vicki!' Dick gripped them hard, then turned to Merle and shook his hand. 'What've you got for me?' he asked her.

Vicki tapped her bag.

'Oh-ho! C-come on then, let's get up to the office and see, It's a bit of a hike,' he added to Merle.

Dick led them down familiar corridors, up marble stairs, then the rickety iron flight to the top floor and finally through a door whose glass was still etched Prof. J. Bryde BA(Oxon) PhD. He pushed the door open and led the way inside. Nothing had changed. Heaps of files and boxes still covered the floor. Making some space on the desk, Dick motioned Vicki to show him the treasure. She peeled back the sacking, unwrapped the bundle and opened the lid to show the leather book.

Dick lifted it gently out of the wrappings, his stubby fingers stroking the silky leather. He sniffed at it, and finally opened it, both hands carefully supporting the fragile structure while he peered at the delicate scrawl.

He cocked an eyebrow at Vicki.

'Yes,' she nodded. 'It's Richard Bryde's diary.'

'Whew! I wondered what it was he was so chuffed about when he blew in here after Christmas. Like a dog with two tails!'

'Oh, I think he had it long before that,' Vicki sat on the edge of the desk. 'I think this was behind the row with Sylvie.'

'R-really?' Dick looked at her. She knows something, he thought.

What's she not telling?

'Whatever it was at Christmas was different. But look ...' Vicki opened the book at the parchment.

Dick took off his specs and held the parchment by its edges. 'It's old, Vicki,' he breathed. 'Much older than the diary.'

'Can you read it?' asked Merle.

'Course I can!' he glared. 'But Vicki, I'd like to get other opinions. Dr Maygood at Oxford would be here like a shot if he knew and Alexander's coming over from New York ...?'

'No! There's a lot going on, Dick.' And she gave him a potted version of the last few days. 'Can you keep it here tonight?'

'Yes, of course. And I can work on it with all the references to hand. I think the parchment itself may originate from Roman times, but it's in two different hands,' he peered at it, 'and inks. In fact, I'd say this side was done much later than that. We can have a look later. I'd love to know where Richard got it from. This bit,' he pointed, 'looks like it's very late in the occupation, maybe fourth century. But that bit's much later. It's all in Welsh, but you know that, don't you? ' He paused a moment. 'I've seen nothing like it before. It feels like holding the original Virgil!'

Dick trailed behind them along New Oxford Street to Soho, Greek Street and the Jardin. Vicki had taken Merle's arm. The pavements were not wide enough for three abreast with the on-coming traffic and anyway he was thinking. He followed them to the table at the back of the small restaurant, glad he'd guessed right. The Jardin was Jacob's favourite. Dick stumbled as he went to sit down. Merle helped him. The stutter, which had gone off for the past half hour came back, full fledged. Dick gripped Merle's hand, mumbled something and slid clumsily round the table. Xavier brought the wine, a good Fleurie. Dick gulped some, told himself to stop thinking and enjoy lunch.

Dick left his stutter in the restaurant along, with his dreams. The realist and the archaeologist took hold again. Confident in his subject, and in Jacob's old office, he was in charge. Merle and Vicki sat the other side of the big oak desk.

'Like I said, the parchment is old, very old. And this,' Dick pointed to the least legible column of writing, 'is ancient Welsh. I dare say few could read it after the Conquest. They tended to kill off people who held to the old ways and language. But this,' his eyebrows shot up as he pointed to the other half of the parchment, 'is much newer. It's a – umm – er – perhaps I should call it a *free* translation, which I guess dates from the eleventh century, probably around Domesday time. It would have been done by a monk. The clerical profession had pretty well hijacked writing by then. It was no longer fashionable, or perhaps altogether safe, for aristocrats to be literate and learned amongst the Norman lords, although there were some exceptions.'

Dick read the first line of the old text to them. '*Allan o'r gwaed, Wyrianiad y dwy; Llifeiro'r dwr drwy'r gwaed.*'

Merle was peering at the text which was beautiful but more like drawing than writing. 'Can you read it just like that?'

'Yes. But let's try this.' Dick swept up the book and twizzled his chair round to face the computer. He put the book down gently on its silk scarf, then he grabbed the keyboard off the top of the VDU with one hand and jiggled the mouse with the other.

'Come on, baby, wake up call,' and the screen flashed to life. 'We're working on being in the twentieth century here,' he laughed over his shoulder, 'just as we're about to leave it!'

Typing rapidly, he put the old text in first. The red under-linings of misspellings covered the page, but Dick didn't worry, he inserted symbols to show â or ô in words. Then he began on the monk's version.

'I didn't know they did that.' Merle pointed at the symbols.

'They don't all, but I use symbols to show pronunciation. Now then …' Dick had both texts on the screen side by side, with a third column for his translation, line by line.

OLD TEXT	MONK'S VERSION	DICK'S TRANSLATION
Allan o'r gwaed,	*Allan or gwaed*	*Out of the blood,*
Wyrianiad y dwy;	*wyrianiad y dwr*	*the rising of the*
Llifeiro'r dwr drwy'r	*Lliuerior dwr drwyr*	*water; The water*
gwaed	*gwaed*	*flows through the*
		blood

'Now just look at what that monk's done here. His spelling is entirely his own!' Dick pointed to the old Welsh and read it out loud, then did the same with the monk's translation, they could hear the difference.

'There was no set spelling in those days,' he went on. 'At least not as we would understand it. It's all phonetic, like old English. Probably drive the poor buggers into a frenzy to have to spell things the same as some poet in the next valley who you thought was an utter prat.'

'Spell-checkers an anathema?' Merle grinned.

'Absolutely!' Dick laughed. 'The monk wouldn't have been able to read the old stuff. The poet would have been sitting beside him, chanting out the verse, word by word. The monk was undoubtedly a very unsympathetic and Latinised clerk. Probably thought the devil would carry him off just for copying down this heathen tongue!'

Gwaed rhudd genethau,	*Gwaed rhudd y genethau tal iachad*	*Ruddy blood of girls*
Tâl iachad pridd sych	*prid sych*	*The tally of health of the dry earth*

Dick read the ancient Welsh, then the monk's version and, with hardly a pause, he typed his own translation in the third column. Vicki came round the desk and leaned over his shoulder, peering into the screen. He could smell her perfume. He took a deep breath, trying to clear his mind, and wishing she would wear *eau de cabbage* rather than the rosemary and lavender mix which reminded him of Jacob as well as her. Sensing his discomfort, Vicki sat back, leaving him alone.

Gwaed cochion y gwauddau,	*Gwaed cochion y gwaydau keidwad y*	*Rosy blood of daughters*
Ceidwad y ffynon	*fynon*	*Keeper of the spring*

'Now that's interesting.' Dick breathed more easily. 'You have to pierce through the tangle of puns that lurk in the Welsh. For example, gwauddau means daughters, but it can also mean daughters-in-law. Welsh poets like to get a lot of mileage out of a word and put a lot of meaning in. I wonder if he not only means daughters of the blood but daughters that are within the law? Perhaps only daughters are within the law? And,' he went on, 'gwauddau can also mean weavers. It gives an extra nuance to the poem as it echoes the sound of gwaed, blood. What do you think the daughters, within the law, might be weaving?' He threw the question over his shoulder to Vicki, confidence flowing freely again for the moment.

168

'Go on!' she laughed. 'Let's see.'

'Well, perhaps the weavers and the daughters, in law, are the keepers of the spring. That bloody monk was definitely Latinised. He drops the double *ff* in ffynon, but keeps double *dd* in rhudd then drops it again in pridd. Clot!'

Merle chuckled. 'It makes you cross, the monk's translation?'

'I've got Welsh blood,' Dick muttered, typing like crazy.

Gwaed lân lodesi,	*Gwaed lan y lodesy*	*Pure blood of*
Llywodraeth daear a	*llywodraeth daear*	*damsels*
dwr	*adwr*	*Governance of*
Dros gwyddbwyll	*Dros gwydbwyll*	*earth and water*
tragwyddoldeb.	*tragwydoldeb*	*Over the game-*
		board of eternity

'There!' Vicki slid off the desk and crouched beside Dick. 'Gwyddbwyll,' she stuck her finger on the screen, pronouncing the word well. 'In the old stories, Gwyddbwyll means the land, the Earth, the guardians of the land.'

'That would make sense of the daughters-in-law, the lawful guardians,' part of him noted his stammer had gone on holiday despite her close proximity. 'But it also means game-board-of-eternity, like I typed. That means more than just the land.'

'That's what the game-board is! It is the Land!'

'Well …' Dick backed down a bit. 'It is the land, but it's more than just a parcel of fields.'

'But maybe the daughters weave the Land, the pattern, the threads … Oh! I can't get the words!"

'Yes …I think I see,' Merle was answering for her again. 'Like the woven carpet of the Land, like a Persian carpet, all pattern. Like a chess board.'

Dick and Vicki stared at him.

'You know … I think you've got something there,' Dick said. 'Let's see how it goes on.'

Y mynedfa hyn rhôf iddoch I ofalu hyd yr oesoedd, Dros cynhedliadau dirifedi	*Y mynedua hyn rhou idoch I oualu hyd yr oesoed Dros kenhedliadau diruedi*	*This gate I give you, To guard through the ages, For unnumbered generations*

'Gate …? What gate?' Dick stopped typing.

'The gate of the spring. The gate through which the water comes?' Vicki had found her own voice again now. 'It's that we're to guard in the village ritual. The Troytown maze is called the gateway of the spring.'

'But it's n-nowhere n-near a spring!' Dick spluttered.

'Well … I don't know. But that's what the tradition is.'

'C'mon! Tell us how it ends,' Merle interjected before they came to blows.

Angan gan yddi'r cyfraniad Os by'r ffynon byth bradychu: Dyna darfod y daear A dychweliad y diffeithdir	*Angan gan dwy ywr kyuraniad Os byr fynon byt bradychy Dyna darfod y daear a dychweliat y difeitdir*	*Death by water is the due If the spring is ever betrayed Then the death of the land And the return of the wasteland*

Dick's words fell like lead into the silence. Merle got up, collected cups, poured coffee, wondering who would say it first. Death by water seemed just a bit close to what had actually happened. Like he'd said to Vicki last night. Was it only last night? It felt like centuries ago. Dick took up his typing again.

Goddef neb heb y gwaed I dwyn y dwyr	*Godeu neb heb y waed y dwyn y dwr*	*Let none but the blood Take the water*

'*I dwyn y dwr* literally means to draw the dew. I just rephrased it to try to fit with the rest,' he said. 'The last bit's a refrain. Repetition and refrain are part of the tradition. Use of rhythm. Sort of like a drum-beat. But the monk hasn't really bothered with it. Probably as much as the poor poet, or whoever gave him the piece, could do to get him to take it down! I wonder how it came to be transcribed at all …?'

Dick pushed his chair back from the computer, musing.

Dwyn y dwy	*Take the water*
Dwyn y dwr	*Take the water*
Goddef neb heb y gwaed	*Let none but the blood*
I dwyn y dwr	*Take the water*

He chanted softly, then began furtling at the keyboard. Trying to write poetry at my age, he thought, half laughing at himself. But the verse insisted that it be allowed to come.

From blood the water rises, let the water flow through the blood.
The blood of daughters buys healing for the parched earth.
The blood of daughters is guardian of the spring.
The blood of daughters holds land and water for all time.
This gateway I give to you to hold in trust for all generations.
Death by water is the fee if ever water is betrayed.
The land will die, the wasteland come again.
Let none but the blood take the water.

'What d'you think?' Dick swung round from the keyboard.

'I can't get over it being just what happened to Dad.'

Dick swung back to the screen, uncomfortable again.

Vicki touched him on the shoulder. 'Thank you, Dick. Will you come round to Vestry Street tomorrow morning, early.'

'Yes, of c-course,' he said.

Really, Dick supposed, he was glad they were gone.

Visitation

'What's that?' Vicki froze.

Merle had been nibbling her ear when she'd suddenly pulled away from him. He had heard nothing. Now she sat bolt upright in the bed, her head moving from side to side, tracking the sounds he still could not hear, like an animal listening.

'C'mon!'

She was out of bed and padding along the sleeping gallery towards the stairs down to the living room, before he could think. He stumbled after her, still full of sleep and sex and warmth. Realising he was following, she turned, her finger to her lips.

'Thhh!'

It took a moment for him to realise she meant 'Shush'.

He chuckled internally, so she remembered their childhood spy-games, did she? And that the sibilant letter 's' would carry in the silent flat. He grinned, and followed her carefully. There was no light that he could see through the railing behind which they were crouched, but a pencil beam might not show.

'Thtay!' she mouthed, slipping back past him. A moment later she was back. Light from the skylight glinted on metal.

'Glad she's on my side!' he thought, recognising Jacob's old cut-throat razor from the bathroom.

'Third thtep.' She advised him, beginning her descent. He watched where she put her feet and tried to follow exactly. It was awfully tempting to hum Wenceslas but he decided she wouldn't appreciate it just now.

They made it to the bottom of the stairs. The warehouse flat opened up around them, big dark shadows. Still he could hear no noise but he watched her head track back and forth across the empty space. She stopped, pointing like a hunting cat towards the kitchen. He could almost have sworn he heard a rumble in her throat. Then she was off.

He fell over the sofa just as a yell erupted ahead of him. There was a terrific clattering and crashing and he heard her cry out. On his feet again, ignoring skinned shins and stubbed toes, he made it round and over the furniture into the kitchen. Not caring any more, he slammed on the light switch.

She was half in the sink, blood dripping down her arm.

'Are you hurt?' he yelled in her ear.

'Shit!' she spat. 'Bastard got away! But I nicked him. He'll have something to show for his work tonight.'

Absentmindedly, she began to lick at the blood on her hand. He turned on the cold tap and held her arm under it. There wasn't a scratch.

'It's not my blood,' she laughed up into his eyes.

'Good,' he managed, his mind racing.

He helped her climb out of the sink and held her to him. They stood together on the warm wooden floor. His heart was pounding. Then he began to cough as the cold air flooded in through the open window. She pulled away from him gently and went to fill the kettle.

'Shall I shut this or do you want to leave it for the police.'

She stared at him.

'Window,' he said. 'Fingerprints.'

Vicki shook her head.

'You know who it was as well as I do,' she was reaching for the coffee. 'There's no point in bringing the police in.'

She gestured for him to light the gas, then she saw his face.

'Why don't you get us blankets from the chest in the living room? I'll do the coffee.'

Merle went. He needed time to think. He had forgotten how it was to be with her. His life over the past few years felt quite tame, in comparison, and he found himself expecting her to react as would Kate, or any of his other girlfriends. He laughed at himself, knowing he was taking far too long to find the blankets. One of them, he decided, was in shock and he didn't think it was her.

Riddle Game

'I've g-got it!' Dick exploded into the room.

'Come in,' Merle stood back from the door.

'Sorry!' Dick stopped shouting triumphantly. 'It took a bit of hunting but I've found it. Jacob's translation of Richard Bryde's diary.' He flourished a tatty looking notebook held together with an elastic band.

'Sit down,' Vicki told him. 'I'll get us all some coffee.'

Dick sat on the sofa, grinning and looking very smug as he took the diary out of a chamois-leather bag in his briefcase and put it on the coffee table, beside the notebook. He waited for Vicki to return with the tray and then he opened it.

'Look!' he said.

'I can't make head nor tail of all those f's and s's' Merle said. 'Read it for us, Dick.'

'Jacob copied out the legend. This would be the version that was going in seventeen-hundred-and-spelling-mistake, when old Richard was around.' Dick coughed portentously and began to read …

'The daughter of Brydda [he pronounced it 'brother'] *was called Iwerydd. She was guardian to the spring and gave out the water in the gold cup to all who came. When the child was nine years old her mother was killed. After a year of mourning Brydda took another wife, a beautiful foreign woman, to be his priestess. But the stepmother was jealous of Iwerydd and did enchant the father so he would give to her the cup of gold which belonged to the goddess.*

One day the Hollyman came and knocked on the door of the chief's house. The daughter came and answered him. He called her to go with him to the forest and she did visit his house by the bridge in the wood. And the two of them would shift their shapes and go about the country

Soon after the girl's first blooding, as the days shortened to the turn of the year, the stepmother saw Iwerydd change into a mouse and go running through the barns with a black cat on her tail. As the seasons turned she saw the girl change into an hare and go racing through the bare fields chased by a greyhound. At the next season she saw her change again, into a silvery salmon who dived through the deep pools pursued by a great otter. But at the harvest season the stepmother saw her shift into an owl-shape and fly over the woods followed by a great falcon. The stepmother was a sorceress and knew that now the girl was in her power, ready to serve the water of the spring. And the stepmother was afraid, for the cup was gone.

She called out to the village that the girl was no longer a maid and that she had spelled both the land and the chieftain's wife to barren-ness. At first none would heed her for she was not loved, but when no rain fell and the crops died and the girl's belly began to swell all could see the truth of it. As harvest time came nigh so the daughter's belly too came close to bursting with its fruit. They asked the stepmother what they should do and she said the harvesters must cut down the false maid for she was with child to a demon. The chieftain was besotted with his second wife and said nothing but hid within the hut, for the woman was in her power and the village had someone to blame for their troubles.

Iwerydd came back from the woods. The stepmother sent her son to call the haymakers and they followed him. They saw her flying as an owl and followed her into a cave upon a tump at the top of the field. They hacked at her with their scythes. As she lay on the ground they watched her form change from owl back into woman. Where her blood fell a new spring came bubbling out of the ground and the dry earth was covered in bright flowers. Now they knew what they had done. Lightning came out of the clear sky and the earth opened wide and swallowed up the son. His mother ran mad. And the Hollyman came out of the wood. He held Iwerydd's dead body and listened to the owl who sat now within the cave and would let none in but he.

'Take my child,' it told him, 'and bring back my cup.'

He cut the child from out the mother's womb and took it to the village. The chieftain wept with shame at what he had allowed to be done. The Hollyman took back the cup and sent him out of the village, saying "Wander where you will but come not here again. This place belongs to the Owl Woman and your daughter's daughter be its guardian. The blood of daughters shall serve the spring and this for all time. And the Owl Woman shall guard them. Let none but the blood take the water or else shall come again the wasteland." And he took the cup back to the source.

'That's the legend,' said Dick. 'And there's more still.'

He turned pages again until he came to one he'd marked.

'Here, he says how he went "*down unto ye pitte to fynde ye treasor*". But it's this which might help us.' He scrabbled about in the notebook again, 'Jacob translated it,' he pointed to some lines of doggerel.

My handle's home
Is in coffin stone
High up in the wood.
My shaft you'll find
In tower blind
Deep within the wood.

But the key to me
You can only see
When owl-light burns
On the stone tree
In the middle of the wood.

'Who wrote it?' Merle asked.

'Richard. I think it's the clue to where he found the cup.'

'Oh my god!' Vicki exclaimed, 'That's why Julian broke into the flat, he wanted the translation.'

'Quite likely,' Dick said dryly. 'None of us in the Museum realised he'd found the diary, but she must have guessed. Known perhaps. As you said yesterday, her row with Jacob may have been about this.'

'She must have some translations of her own, I think. That'd be what Dad was giving her back, in the will. And I think he knew she'd got it wrong, that they wouldn't help her.'

'Have you seen those papers?' Dick asked.

'No. But why else would he give them back to her? He certainly wouldn't if he thought they'd help her. It's like a last, nasty joke. Two fingers from the grave. Take that, lady, and much good may it do you.'

'Yeah,' Merle said. 'It would also account for his jubilaté when he came to dinner with me. He said he'd stolen a march on her, and he really had, if she only had a wrong translation. And,' he looked at Dick, 'do you think she has that doggerel?'

'Nope,' he said, showing them the page in the diary. 'It was loose, I think this came from somewhere else. And I'm willing to bet only he saw this. See, both the paper and the handwriting's different from the pages either side. It's still Richard's all right, but it looks like it was written at a different time. And the ink's different too. I don't know where Jacob got this, maybe not even at the same time as the diary. But I think he put it in here, like the parchment, for you to find, Merle. And to show to Vicki.'

'Hmmm! Yes, it was safer than leaving it at the house.'

'Or with me at the museum,' Dick said. 'But he hints about it here,' he pointed, 'in the notebook. If I hadn't had the diary I don't know that I'd have made sense of it.'

'Sylvie knows. She saw us, last night, at the cottage. But she didn't get anything. She knew we had the diary. And that I would bring it up to you, Dick, so she sent Julian after it.'

Dick looked at her, wary. 'What're you talking about?'

'She's overseen us with it,' Vicki sighed.

Dick stared at her.

'Crystal ball gazing!' Merle chuckled.

'Oh shit!' Dick groaned and put his head in his hands.

'It's OK, Dick. We've got a shield up over this place.' Vicki was laughing too. 'She can't see in here.'

'But what about my place?' Dick looked like a terrified rabbit.

'She doesn't know where you live, does she? So she'd have to find you in the Museum and follow you home.'

Dick swallowed. That needed thinking about.

'What else is in the notebook?' Vicki changed the subject.

'His own thoughts, how he wanted to capture the spring and put an end to the bottling plant by cutting off Julian's supply and piping the water directly to the village. He got me to do some dowsing and then got Joe to confirm what I'd said, about there being a spring under the tump the tower's on. We both told him diverting the spring would cause even more ructions with the water table, but he had the bit between his teeth by then and I think he was too incensed to care. And anyway, he wanted the opportunity to get in under the tower.' Dick paused.

'Is there anything else about the diary?'

'Not really. The rest of it's about the dig, how to get the tower dismantled. Each stone had to be marked and stored so that it could all be put back as it was, and he made his own notes on this as well as the dig plans. He cursed his father for getting it made a listed building!' Dick laughed. 'But it was no use protesting. As a keeper, he could hardly flout the rules! Eventually they got going on the earthwork and found the steps down into the mound. He writes about that, and they are beautiful work but very creepy! You're quite certain that the place really was used for ritual once you've been down there. It's not just the old archaeologist's excuse for what he can't explain. Bill Warrington came down with the geo-phys kit and got a plan of the whole area which confirms the ditch and iron age settlement. And a stone tunnel going south to a circular feature, perhaps an underground reservoir. He writes about that too.'

'I saw that on Dad's computer, and an aerial shot of the tower which shows a depression going that way.' Vicki said. 'Did Dad get to see the tunnel for himself?'

'Yes. It's here in the notebook.'

'Good,' she said. 'And then he died.'

There was a general silence.

"So what do we do now?" Merle sighed.

'We follow that blasted riddle. In Jacob's footsteps, I suppose,' Dick muttered into his beard. 'I loath these treasure hunt things!'

'You'll come with us, won't you Dick?'

'I s-suppose s-so,' Dick growled. Why's she got to ask me like that, he thought, then, 'I don't m-mind theoretical archaeology, but after your adventures last night all this hands-on stuff seems a m-mite dangerous!'

Merle and Vicki began to laugh.

A Policeman's Lot …

Hardacre put the phone down and glared at it. Then he got up and went down the corridor, knocked on the door.

'Come in!' Chief Superintendent Haddick's voice called through the solid wood.

Hardacre opened it and stood waiting.

'Come in, Hardacre, come in.' Haddick's voice was pained, but he was trying to be polite. 'Sit down, sit down. Now what's all this Bridewell stuff about?'

Hardacre sat down.

'I'm not sure sir, I feel there's something more there but I just can't put my finger on it, as yet.'

'You and your feelings! I thought it was just an accident,' Haddick shuffled papers around on his desk. 'The old professor fell off a cliff and drowned in his own lake, isn't that it?'

'Well … yes, at first sight it appears so. But there's a lot of people involved. And a hornet's nest surrounding his ex-mistress and her toy-boy. The whole village seems to be down on them.'

'Good god! It sounds like a plot for a TV saga!' the superintendent glared. 'And you seem to be spending the devil of a lot of time on it!'

'I know sir,' Hardacre smiled apologetically. 'But there does seem to be a lot of twisted threads there. So many people with an interest, an angle. And the daughter, sir. She's just not taking it as personally as I would have expected. She's not asking me for information, not badgering me. Just not as I would have thought she'd be with her father suddenly dead, in strange circumstances. And then there's the village, and the water problem they're having, and that all seems to be tied up with Professor Bryde's ex-mistress and her new boyfriend. It's a very tortuous coil sir, I'd like to continue following it up.'

'I didn't think there were still places like that in the modern world. It's almost feudal,' Haddick stared at him.

Hardacre grinned back at his chief. 'Yes sir, it is in a way.'

'I've read the reports,' Haddick said testily. 'I still think it's all a mare's nest.'

'But could you allow me a few more days, sir?'

'Oh well,' Haddick sighed. Experience had taught him there'd be no point in trying to prise Hardacre away from this case, and forbidding him would be a total disaster. 'I suppose so. But you'd better come up with something soon. There's a backlog of real cases I want you on.'

'Yes sir.'

'And don't you go haring off now and forgetting to keep in touch with us here!'

'No sir.'

'That'll be all then.'

Hardacre closed the door quietly behind him.

'Three bags full, sir!' he muttered and slipped down the back stair to the car park.

Antic Hay

A ham on rye is merely a ripple, or fluctuation constructed
by thought in the quantum foam of space
Bob Toben
Space-Time and Beyond

But it sure do taste good ...
Elen Sentier ... *At lunch* ...

Stonechest Wood

My handle's home
Is coffin stone
High up in the wood.

It was a steep climb up from Merle's cottage to the top of Stonechest
Wood. Dick was by far the least fit of the three of them, his main form
of exercise being the lifting of whisky glasses. He struggled along in the
rear, hands deep in the pockets of his brand new Barbour, his pristine
green wellies were squeaking. Fortunately Harrods had been open late
the previous evening so he could kit himself out for country living.
Surely we must be nearly at the top by now, he thought between gasps
for breath. But looking up through the trees was no help, the woods were
so deep, the trunks so close together that, even through the bare branches,
he couldn't see a thing. At least, he puffed, they took the spades. Merle
had looked indulgently at him as he'd hoisted them over his shoulder.
'I'll take those, old man!' he'd said.

The woods smelled faintly of smoke from the Rayburn at Bridge
Cottage, mixed with an earthy smell that brought back childhood
memories. Dick, for all his affected town ways, had been brought up on

Salisbury Plain and it was all coming back to him.

It was so different now, coming to Bridewell with Vicki. Without Jacob. Despite his feelings of loss there was a wild excitement, an adrenaline rush. They had taken turns to lead down the A303 but from the Tiverton turn off he had left it to her. He recalled his delight as they had swooped along the narrow road, with the river rushing below on their left, only to stop every few yards as pheasants trotted into the path of the cars. There had been the notice at the beginning of that road which said 'Beware of pheasants'. For once, a road sign which made sense.

The climb over the moors, amongst the mist and sheep, had thrilled him too. Suddenly the mists would part and the whole great expanse of wilderness would open out in front of them. They dived into valleys, through sleepy villages, past ancient pubs, until they finally came to the hill trail that led past Bridewell Manor, with the Firebeacon rising out of the mist on their right. And down the final hill, through the ford beside the clapper bridge, and into Bridge Cottage.

At lunch they had gone over the riddle again.

Vicki and Merle were sure the rhyme meant Stonechest Wood, behind Bridge Cottage. The legends told of three witches who lived there, and who had buried their son in a stone chest at the top of the hill, after carving him up. Dick wasn't sure whether he hoped this was true or not, but he had to agree that 'coffin stone' did suggest it. And Richard Bryde's diary seemed to confirm it, with a drawing of the ancient tump at the top of the hill.

Now, here he was, struggling up a vertical hillside, in slippery ice-mud, through woods which didn't seem to take kindly to visitors at all. He was so deep in his thoughts that he ran straight into Merle before he realised they'd made it to the top of the hill. He joined them looking at a very small tump.

'Is that it?' he said, disgusted.

'Yup!' Merle grinned.

'Ye gods! Do we have to dig the damn thing up?'

'Oh Dick! I do love you!' Vicki was leaning on the other spade. 'Archaeologists are supposed to enjoy digging things up!'

'That's all very well,' Dick glared at her. 'I did my practicals in nice warm places around the Mediterranean, where they had civilised tavernas and lots of sun. I don't see any fun in digging frozen earth, in a dank wood, in late winter, in Britain. You know,' he continued, staring at the miniature tump, 'Jacob never saw this, nobody's dug that earth for millennia, well years, at least. We're following in Richard's footsteps now, not his.'

'If he never saw it I wonder how he knew …' Merle said.

'You're right. I think he didn't find that doggerel until after he'd found the cup. Or, at least, got well towards it.' Vicki said.

'Creepy!' Dick gave a theatrical shudder.

'Well … you're the archaeologist, get digging!' she pushed the spade at him, grinning. 'You can raise the skeleton of the murdered son!'

'Ugh! Disgusting!' Dick collapsed onto a handy rock. 'Anyway, I'm knackered after that climb …' he looked plaintively at the other two.

'OK!' Vicki took the spade back. 'I'll do the first turn. You get your breath back.'

She shoved the spade into the earth and then jumped on it with both feet. Surprisingly, it gave way easily and she was able to lift out the first sod.

'Hey! This just might be easier than we thought.'

And so it was. The earth seemed very content to be lifted and soon the spades clinked against stone. Dick could resist no longer. His trowel was out of his pocket and his knees in the mud before you could say knife. The chest was soon uncovered.

There was no lock, but the centuries had made the stone begin to knit together again and it took all three of their trowels to clean the slit so they could open it. Inside was a great pile of feathers and sharp holly leaves. They searched it thoroughly but there was nothing else.

'I don't believe it,' Dick announced. 'There has to be something here, it's just as Richard Bryde said. We'd best get it home, I want to spend the evening examining it.'

This was easier said than done.

After some discussion, Merle and Dick left Vicki sitting by the chest and went back to Bridge cottage for ropes and something to sit the stone chest on. The journey down was, in some ways, just as difficult as the climb up and both men did a lot of it on their backsides. After the second fall they were so wet and dirty that it became funny and they raced each other in bum-slides down the muddy banks.

Arriving at the cottage they found Goldy and the grey tom waiting on the step. A jingle of bells and fluttering sounds showed that Seabhac was awake and interested too.

'Do you mind falcons?' Merle asked.

Dick shook his head. He didn't really know, but he was determined to keep up with Merle now. He remembered the kestrel that had sat on his wrist at the falconry, near Andover, when he'd visited there with his father. Merle went into the potting-shed-mews and came out with the small but glorious merlin on his wrist. She stared at Dick out of great golden eyes.

'It seems like they all want to come with us,' he said.

They collected rope from the garage and Merle found a large tin tray to slide the chest down the banks. After their own experience in bum-slides this seemed the best way to move the heavy thing. Dusk was beginning to slide over the hill as they turned back to Stonechest Wood.

The falcon flew silently ahead of them and the two cats slipped from tree bole to fern to tree, keeping well out of sight. A kind of stillness seemed to have settled over the whole place and the two men slogged up the forty-five degree slope unspeaking. Dick's town mannerisms had fallen away from him, along with his stammer, he still puffed and sweated but no longer complained, even in his heart. There was something about what they were doing which infected him with a sense of purpose he'd not known for a long time. His everyday self reared up. Silly! he began, then stopped, and put all thought of judgement on hold for the duration.

They arrived at the top to find Vicki with the falcon on her shoulder and the two cats in her lap. Merle's eyebrows shot up.

'I know!' she said ruefully, carefully shrugging only her left shoulder. 'A merlin falcon never goes to any other besides her master, but she came swooping straight down to me ...' Vicki left the sentence hanging.

'Everything's strange today.' Dick interjected. 'Even I, solid and dependable Dick, who doesn't have fanciful notions, can feel it. Let's not bother asking questions shall we? Just get on with getting that blinking thing down this infernal hill!'

Hearing him be his irritable self helped, and Dick knew it.

They loaded the stone chest onto the old tea tray and tied it as securely as they could. Merle took the two front ropes, Vicki and Dick took a back rope each. This way they hoped to steer their unruly charge and stop

Merle being run over by it.

The path the two men had made in their extra journeys was very clear through the woods now. So too was the gaping hole left by the chest.

'What do we do about that?' Dick pointed at it.

'Nothing,' Vicki said. 'If they find it it'll be too late, we'll already have whatever is in the chest. And anyway, after you two've played ski slopes down here you don't need a degree in rocket science to guess what's been going on.'

The rope trick worked fairly well although they all fell at least once. The chest would suddenly get a mind of its own and skid off the path. The beasts didn't play about as they usually would but stayed steady, on each side of the chest and above it, never making a sound. Full dark had come down by the time they reached the bottom and crowded into Merle's kitchen.

'Where's the tea, mate?' Dick took charge of the kettle.

Merle pointed to a cupboard, then he and Vicki fell into chairs by the table.

Dinner had long gone by. The feathers and leaves, now collected into a plastic bag, had revealed nothing whatsoever. All three brains were weary of trying to understand the riddle. Vicki had shut her eyes for a moment hoping for inspiration but almost at once she heard the words inside her head, 'It's not for you!' She opened her eyes again and sat by the fire wondering. It was late now. They stumbled up the stairs on aching limbs and crawled into bed. *My Guardian's home is in coffin stone.* Dick found the riddle going round and round in his head as he fell asleep.

Dawn was creeping over the window sill when Dick came to. He felt as though he was suffocating, something soft covered his face and nose, and there was a strong smell of damp. In his befuddled state he thought he'd been buried alive. He opened his eyes.

'Oh my god!'

Just the glimpse he had through whatever was covering his face was enough to convince him he was barking mad. Something huge and grey and gnarled lay on his chest, and the room was full of feathers.

'Help!' he tried to yell and got a mouthful of earth and feathers. Now really scared, and believing himself to be lying in the ground, he struggled to turn his mouth to one side so the earth wouldn't fall in when he opened it. He yelled again, with real passion this time, and kept on yelling.

He felt a touch on his forehead and stopped yelling long enough to hear Vicki's voice.

'Steady! It's OK. We're here. Just lie still, Dick. We'll get you out from under.'

She carried on stroking his forehead while Merle struggled to ease the branch off Dick's chest. Soon he was able to sit up. Vicki sat on the pillow and hugged him while Merle got brandy.

'Jesus Christ on a Harley!' he managed to gasp after the first fiery gulp of Napoleon's best had trickled through him. 'What the bloody hell's going on?'

'We rather hoped you could tell us that,' Vicki sat back and let go of Dick now her worst fears were over.

'And what is this?' Merle held up a black wooden disk with what looked like a double-ended tree carved on it.

'Where'd that come from?' Vicki said sharply, her mind going back to her experience in the Wilderness.

'It was under the branch I took off Dick's chest.'

She held out a hand for the disk. Merle gave it to her and she turned it over and over.

Parts of Dick's dream, night-mare more like he thought, were beginning to come back now as full consciousness returned. The room was indeed full of feathers, and the large branch which had been lying on him. He wondered how it could ever have come through the cottage window. Merle was going to have enough trouble getting it out of the door and down the stairs.

'This is a hell of a mess!' Dick commented to the room at large. 'I think …' he began, then something cold crept up along his spine and he decided to shut up for the moment.

'Let's get you up and in a bath,' Merle offered.

Vicki took the disk and followed Goldy down to the kitchen. In another moment she heard the bath begin running and muffled curses and laughter as Merle helped Dick into it. Goldy eyed her, then chirruped, demanding breakfast.

'What do you think, eh?' she asked the little cat.

Goldy paused her purring-eating to look up at Vicki. 'Wait,' she seemed to be saying. 'You'll know soon enough.'

Vicki stroked the disk with her fingers ... stopped. She traced the pattern at its centre again then got a magnifying glass from Merle's study. Tinne! she whispered, the word for holly, just like in my dream.

She put the disk down and got on with breakfast. By the time the coffee was brewed both men appeared, looking clean, if somewhat shell-shocked.

Full of toast and coffee, Dick felt quite human again.

'I had a dream,' he grinned, thinking of Martin Luther King.

'We rather suspected you might,' Merle grinned back.

'Yes. Well ... Sometime in the middle of the night, or maybe early this morning, I thought I woke up. I was back in Stonechest Wood, at the top of the hill sitting by the hole. The chest was gone, just the hole. I was pretty damn surprised – well, all right then – scared,' he admitted as the other two raised their eyebrows. 'But I didn't seem to be able to pinch myself any more awake so I just kept still and waited. There was no wind, the night was perfectly still but full of light, although there was no moon. The light shone into the hole, but didn't make it any lighter, just showed it to be far deeper than we dug. A great gaping darkness, right at my feet. You can be sure I sat still! I was afraid any movement would tip me into the pit. Anyway, as I watched, something seemed to stir down in the bottom. That was when I found I couldn't move anyway. I tried to get up and run but my legs wouldn't work. I willed like mad, but I couldn't even feel my legs, let alone make them move.

'I'm glad it was a dream because I'm sure I would have pissed my pants at that point. It seems I didn't though.' He grinned sheepishly. 'The movement continued until finally this enormous owl flew up out of the hole. Yes! I know! It's all very well for you!' he glared. 'I'm just an archaeologist! These things only happen in scholarly books on fairy stories, nice and academic. They're not supposed to be real!'

'Oh, Dick!' Vicki and Merle collapsed with laughter.

'Well, anyway,' Dick glared again, 'there it was standing in front of me, about five foot high. I suppose,' he considered 'that's not really very big for what she could be according to the stories. But it was quite big enough for me! The next thing I knew it'd picked me up. Have you ever

186

tried yelling in a dream? Quite useless! It seemed I couldn't make any noise as well as not move. It carried me down into that damned hole, all the way down to the bottom, where it was all light, full of stars, like crystals, and a sort of twilight feeling. Very beautiful too. We were in a cave. It set me down and pointed at the floor. There was this thing, like a lid, with the same carving on it as this,' he put his hand on the tree-disk. 'As I watched, a hand came out of the dark and lifted the lid. Inside was the cup. I looked up to see Jacob. He reached down and took the cup out of the hole.' Dick swallowed, continued. 'He stood holding it, looking at it, for a moment and then he walked off into the blackness and was gone.

'The owl looked into my eyes, and then it spoke.

"Help me!" it whispered. "Bring back my cup!"

'I couldn't speak, but it seemed to know I'd heard.

'Next thing I knew we were back by the hole at the top of Stonechest Wood. A wind started up. It tore the feathers apart, so there was nothing of the owl left, and swirled them down the hole. Like water down a plug-hole. It even went the right way round for the northern hemisphere!

'I passed out then. Next thing I knew was really waking up, feeling I was being crushed and suffocated and getting earth and feathers in my mouth. I yelled. I was terrified,' he admitted. 'I was never so glad to hear a voice in my life. But what is it?'

'The gods only know!' Merle was exasperated.

'I think I know,' Vicki said tentatively.

Everyone looked at her.

'I think I've been there. The only trouble is, I'm not certain where there is … or how to get there.' She told them of her experience in the Wilderness.

Overlooking

Sylvie woke with a start and found herself sitting upright in the bed. She'd dreamed herself covered in leaves and feathers, it took a moment for her to believe her eyes, that she was not. Julian stirred beside her, his hand closed on her arm.

'Are you all right?' he asked.

'Ahhhh!' Sylvie clawed at her head. 'Dream!'

Julian put an arm round her and waited.

'Her. Them. Bridge Cottage. The owl got through.'

'Escaped the case?'

'Yes, I think so. The spirit is strong. And it wants Vicki. I felt that the night I sent it to kill Jacob. But I'm not letting it go until I've got that blasted cup.'

'What did you see?' Julian remembered how to question her so she could bring the dream back.

'Strange. Falling down a well. Coming up covered in feathers and holly leaves. I was inside Dick. It was his dream.'

'Can you see it now?'

'No.' Sylvie swung her legs out of the bed and pulled on a robe. 'I'm going down to the study. Something I've got to find.'

In the corner room at the back of the cottage she searched. Her hand found the old exercise book, its covers tattered and dirty. She opened it at the drawing she'd copied from the Philadelphia Masonic library.

It took her back to when her affair with Jacob was on a high. They'd gone to see Seahenge on the beach at Holme, in Norfolk, paddling about in a raging North Sea gale. Next morning, the wind had dropped and the sky was the clear pale blue of early winter. The sun rose out of the sea. They'd actually held hands, watching the first rays strike the roots of the upturned tree.

Sylvie shook her head. It was gone, stupid to think of it, an emotional aberration. When they got back to Bridewell, Jacob had cooled off again immediately, returned to watching her through half-closed eyes.

She turned back to the picture in the old notebook. It was the same as the disk in Dick's dream. The picture had haunted her all her life, set her on her archaeological career. She reached out to Bridge Cottage and felt resistance. Do you think I can't do it? Sylvie hissed. Grandma came from the Harz mountains, you stupid girl, there's magic and to spare in me, enough to best you!

The door opened behind her and Julian came in.

'Found anything?' he asked.

'I don't know,' Sylvie showed him the notebook. 'I saw this in the

188

dream, Dick's dream. But his mind is full of feathers, I can't make head nor tail of it. And Vicki has a guard up.'

'What is it you're after?' Julian sat down opposite her.

'I've told you, I want to be the one who finds the grail.'

'So did he. But there's more to it than that, isn't there?'

'I want to use it.' Sylvie whispered. 'Jacob never would, too scared of his history. But I will. I need to find the gateway.'

'Gateway?'

'Yes. There must be one. A way to the source. The place where all her power comes from.'

'Where the spring comes from?'

'Yes.'

'I thought that was a cave.'

'So it is. The cave's under the tower. Richard Bryde built the tower to hide it. That's what Jacob found in the dig, why he didn't want me near it. And that's where he found the cup. But every time I look, I can't see it in his hands when he fell. I was too late there. I think he'd already been down inside the tower and put it back. So I've got to get in there to get it back.'

'OK ...' Julian sighed. 'When?'

'Now.'

Blind Tower

My shaft you'll find
In tower blind
Deep within the wood

They had argued all through breakfast. Did the riddle mean the shaft of a key, or a well, or something else? Then Dick said he had to see the stuff on Jacob's computer so they'd packed up, cats, falcon and all, and returned to Bridewell.

'You'll be wanting some dinner later,' Vera met them in the kitchen. 'But I need to get home now and set things straight.' Vera gave Vicki a peck on the cheek and left them. They heard her car chug off up the drive.

Hecaté stared at Goldy and Shadow across the expanse of the hearthrug, then she came forward and touched Goldy's nose. Shadow came timidly up behind and received a greeting. Hecaté stalked back to her washing basket. Shadow followed and she allowed him to settle on the rug beside her. Goldy stayed by the stove. Seabhac took possession of the top of the dresser, well out of reach of any confloptions by the cats.

'The computer?' Dick queried. He knew where it was, of course, but this was Vicki's house now. It felt strange to be here without Jacob. And with her.

She led him off to the study. Goldy joined them, helpfully sitting on the notebook. Dick grinned and Vicki left them to it.

He resurfaced hours later and dumped a mass of paper onto the rug in front of the fire in the library.

'The shaft has to be the tower!' Dick was adamant. 'It's like a mine shaft down there,' he pointed to a mess of diagrams and geo-phys printouts. 'The riddle must mean we have to go down into it. But it isn't in a wood.'

' I thought you weren't very keen on tunnels?' Merle said.

'No m-more I am,' his stutter surfaced again. 'I'm claustrophobic, can't stand enclosed places, caves, all that stuff. But this ancestor of yours wasn't a pillock, he was an educated man, and I'll bet he was playing word games. They always did in the eighteenth century and being a druid and all would make it even more likely, I'd think.'

Dick fumbled through Jacob's notebook again, leafing pages fast, his tongue sticking out between his lips as he concentrated. He looks just like the cat, Merle thought.

'Look at this,' he pointed. 'You know it says "Gateway" in the old parchment?'

They nodded.

'Well, Jacob seems to think it had something to do with the tower. Richard built the tower for a purpose, not just a rich man's folly, although he wanted it to look like that, in order to hide the gateway. Jacob says the gateway *was* the tower. So,' Dick paused, 'that means we have to go and look at it. And here,' he fished out another piece of paper, 'Old Richard's going on about it, how it's built on top of a much older structure, just as

190

Jacob found. And … Richard describes how he dug out the well-shaft.'

'The what …?'

'Well-shaft,' Dick, grinned at them triumphantly.

'You have it!' said Merle. 'Well-shaft it is.'

'Yes!' Dick was gleeful. 'They dug it out, found steps going down to an underground chamber with a stone tree, whatever that is, in it. Under which he found … the g-gold c-cup! Tomorrow, first thing, we go to the tower.'

Well Shafted

Julian led the way down the narrow, ladder-like steps to the stone landing. The stones of the walls fitted so exactly there was no gap between them. Julian was breathing hard. Sylvie took the torch and shone it down into the darkness to show the second flight, like a spiral staircase.

'This way,' she said.

He followed her down to the lower chamber, twenty feet from the top of the mound. He felt suffocated.

'What now?' he managed.

'Help me down.'

Julian sat on the bottom step and eased himself into the pit. He realised the whooshing noise which had been frightening him for some time was his own breath. He tried to control the dizziness and managed to help Sylvie down beside him. Immediately she began feeling about the walls. Julian shone the light so she could see what she was doing.

'Don't bother!' she said.

He watched her fingers running over the stones until,

'Light!' she hissed.

He shone the torch but at first they could see nothing. She took it from him and held it sideways along the wall. Now they could see the relief carved into the stone.

'Owl!' she breathed and came back to sit beside him. 'There has to be a way in. This was a ritual place which guarded the power, the gateway into otherworld. Once I have the key I can use it to draw power. And then ...'

'More of your bloody magic!' Julian muttered.

'Oh, for the gods' sake!' she retorted. 'You were born here, you know what it's about. This is the gateway. It was opened because they sacrificed the girl, Iwerydd. Yes! I know they never say that, but there was a drought, and it was only *after* she was killed that the spring came up. Blood opened the gateway. You tried to do that yourself, unconsciously, when you went to rape Vicki. And it would have worked too, if you could have managed it.'

'The drought came because the stepmother seduced the father and stole the cup, trying to take the daughter's place. Just like you.' Julian spat back.

'Oh, are you changing sides now?'

'Of course not!'

The silence fizzed between them for several minutes.

'So why are we here?' Julian said sulkily. The claustrophobia was getting to him.

'To get into the cave. Where it all happened. This is an ante-chamber. It's not the end of the mystery.'

'How d'you know?'

'I dreamed it.'

Julian put his head in his hands and groaned.

'You mean you dragged me up here to fart about in one of your damned dreams?' he said.

'Don't you sneer at me!' she spat. 'This is the stuff Jacob stole from me. But I've got it now. The papers I got back from Jacob include Richard's letters to Sir Francis Dashwood, the Hellfire Club man. Richard was a member for a while. And he talks about the gateway. Even tells Dashwood about a ritual he performed, to the goddess, pouring a libation to her, from a golden cup.'

Resignedly, Julian shone the torch on the wall where the relief of the owl was. It seemed to stand out now, like a round knob.

Sylvie put her hand on it, twisted it. Nothing happened.

The Stone Tree

But the key to me
You can only see
When owl-light burns
On the stone tree
In the middle of the wood.

'Brrrrrrrr!' Dick shivered and made a fuss about the cold to disguise his dislike of going underground. But he led the way down now in an attempt to get over his fear.

They were kitted out in boots and waterproofs, Merle had brought rope and torches, but only Dick had any real idea of what it would be like down the tower well-shaft. He had been down the steps with Jacob to the tiny antechamber at the bottom, but he'd not been there when Jacob found the way in. Until the other day, he hadn't known there was a way in. Like all Jacob's colleagues, he'd thought the pit at the bottom of the shaft was the end of the story. Now he knew it wasn't.

They arrived at the bottom. The place was two yards square and three deep with the steps winding down the wall on three sides. There was only just room for them all.

'See what I mean? Dark rituals!' Dick teased. He pulled the notebook from his pocket. 'Now, let's see what Richard has to say. He burbles on about the excavations, day by day, for a bit then we get somewhere.' He began reading.

'Monday, 21ˢᵗ April - The space is clearing. Tonight we know the chamber is there, but it is not yet safe to go in.

'Friday, 25ᵗʰ April - I inspected the labours this evening and was impressed this is not a mere fruitless quest of mine. The staircase winds its way down into the bowels of the earth, a lasting wonder. ["Blah, blah, blah …" Dick turned another page.] *They have now uncovered the eighteenth step and the staircase winds its way down. There is a single large flagstone which forms the last step,* ["That's where we're standing now," Dick interjected] *and, from there, there is a drop of some four feet to the pit at the bottom. Some of the men thought it might be a well. I have allowed them to believe this, but it is not so. I had them do some cleaning and then sent them away, for I had seen It. When they were gone, I turned It, and the way opened out before me. A man may walk in there bent*

193

double. Tonight, I will find out where it goes.'

'Come on, Dick, how far have we got to go, bent double?' Merle peered over his shoulder.

Dick turned over more pages.

'Th-three hundred yards,' he said gloomily.

'Shit! Can you handle that?' Merle asked him.

Dick swallowed hard and nodded, not trusting his voice.

'But what did he turn? How do we get in?' Vicki quartered the smooth stone walls with the torch. She stopped, backed up, stopped again.

'Give it here,' Merle took the torch and stood holding the beam along the wall. They could see the owl carved in the stone.

Vicki reached up, grasped it, jumped back.

'Shit!' she gasped, clutching her hand under her armpit. 'Bloody woman! That was like an electric shock.'

'What is it? What happened?' Merle held her.

'Sylvie! Felt her. Through the stone. She touched it. Tried to put a ward on it so I can't use it.'

'What do we do now?' Dick said.

'Go on,' Vicki gritted her teeth.

'Let me do it. You hang onto her,' Merle pushed Vicki into Dick's arms. 'Maybe I won't feel anything.'

His fingers tingled as he touched the owl-figure, but nothing more. He twisted it, there was a grating noise and a stone slid aside, showing a three-foot by four-foot hole.

'Has she been in this tunnel?' Merle asked.

Vicki reached out with all her senses. 'No, I don't think so.'

'It's OK to go in then?'

'Yes.'

'Ugh!' Dick put his head into the hole then pulled back. They could feel the dank air, it smelled of earth.

'You'd better go in the middle, Dick,' Vicki said, after they'd all stood staring at the blackness for what seemed like forever. 'Or you could stay here and wait for us?'

'N-not a ch-chance,' Dick stammered. 'Have t-to s-see this if it k-kills me. Jacob d-did.'

'OK …' Merle took the rope and tied them all together round the waist. 'You hang onto the rope behind Vicki and I'll be right behind you, holding onto yours. And count all the way down the tunnel, like one-elephant, two-elephant. According to those notes of Jacob's it's a long way, can you do it?'

'I have to,' Dick said through clenched teeth

'C'mon then!' Vicki bent and started up the tunnel. 'Thank the gods we're none of us fat!' They crept into the passage.

It was difficult to breathe, walking bent double, and Dick had to keep reminding himself that he wasn't actually suffocating. He religiously counted elephants, or rather heffalumps, seeing the pictures from his tattered copy of Winnie the Pooh. After an endless time and several thousand heffalumps, which turned out to have been a quarter of an hour, he felt the tunnel open up around him and was able to stand straight again.

Merle handed out packets of orange juice, then went looking around.

Vicki stood quiet. This was the place she'd sunk into, from the middle of the Wilderness, the night Merle came. She recalled the aerial photo, with the path running directly from the tower to the centre of the Wilderness. It was also like the place Dick had described in his dream, where he'd seen Jacob take the cup. Was this it, the owl woman's cave? Not the cave the robin had shown her the morning she'd come home? Which was what?

'Tell me!' she called out silently to anyone who might be listening.

Then she heard it, the sound of water. It seemed to be coming from right underneath where she stood in the middle of the cavern. Then it stopped. Then it began again further away. She shut her eyes and listened hard, this time it was coming from over there. She followed her ears and found herself standing back at the entrance to the passage they'd just come down. She stood thinking. The hole in the robin's cave, where you could divert the water, did that somehow connect to the tower shaft? Yes … it brought the water into this cavern.

And the first sound? A vision came in her head. She saw a deep shaft, going down below the Wilderness. Suddenly there was light. And water. Bubbling up from a spring deep in the Earth, under the wood. Under the Troytown.

'Ahhhh!' she breathed, realising. 'So the maze really does mark the

195

spring. That's why we do the ritual there.

She felt a touch like feathers on her face, but it was Merle.

'Hello,' he said softly, kissing her.

She kissed him back. 'Let's see what else is here.'

They went on round the wall, widdershins. Suddenly Merle stopped, shone the torch.

'Hey! …' he called, 'Dick, come and look at this.'

There was the sound of feet, then a shout, then swearing.

'It's OK,' called Dick. 'Just tripped over some damn hole in the floor. I'm OK. Show a light. Where are you?'

Merle shone the torch. Dick made his way more carefully and found them peering at a small hole in the wall of the chamber. A draft of clean, cold air came out.

'Hey!' Dick breathed, 'I think, I think … it might just be …'

'What?' Merle asked.

'At Maeshowe,' Dick explained slowly, 'the sun, at winter solstice, shines down just such a shaft.' He stopped. 'Shaft? God damn! *This* is the bloody shaft, not the steps at all. Here, quick … Anybody think to bring a compass?'

Merle fished in his pocket, passed it to Dick.

'South-west, Lughnasadh. That's it! The harvest sun-rise. I'll bet you any money the sun shines straight down this light-shaft on Lughnasadh.' Dick's stammer and claustrophobia were gone. His nose was on the scent.

'But where does it come out from?' Merle said. 'Where are we? We've come three hundred yards, you said.'

'Put the damn compass in the passage then,' said Dick, 'see which way it goes. We know it was straight.'

'We're under the Wilderness,' Vicki said quietly. The others gaped at her. 'We're under the Troytown, in the centre.'

'How'd you know?'

'There's an aerial photo in Dad's files. It shows a depression in the grass running from the tower to the centre of the Wilderness. And there's a geo-phys shot showing a tunnel in just the same place. And anyway, the other night, when you came up to the Wilderness, I'd just been here.'

196

'Eh?' Merle stared.

'I was with the owl, remember? As I sat there I suddenly felt as if I was sinking through the ground and found myself here, in a cavern just like this. On the floor was a circular stone, like in your dream, Dick, and just like the disk you brought back. And I'll bet you any money the light from this shaft lands on just such a stone right here, for real this time. The stone from under which Dad took the damn cup.'

'So it *is* in the middle of the wood, after all,' whispered Dick. 'Here give me the torch.'

He took it from Merle and stuck it into the shaft. The beam hit the floor at the centre of the cave, shining on a stone disk.

'It's the owl light,' Dick whispered, going up to look. 'Shining on the stone tree.'

It was the same intaglio of roots and branches as on the disk in his dream. He lifted it up. The hole was empty.

Rooftop Capers

'No! I don't care!' Vicki put her head under the pillow.

'Yes, you do,' Merle pulled the pillow off her, then slid out of bed and pulled on his clothes.

Hecaté batted at Shadow and went to stand beside Goldy at the end of the bed. All three cats were bottling and growling. Seabhac was rattling her jesses from the top of the mirror.

'Arrrrgggghhh!' Vicki cursed. 'Bloody Sylvie!' but she got out of bed and dressed.

The noises above, up on the roof, didn't abate. In the corridor they met Dick with his shoes in his hand.

'On the bloody roof!' he whispered.

'Two of them, I think,' agreed Merle.

'It's Julian and some mate of his,' Vicki spat, exasperated. 'Stupid woman! Does she think I can't see? They'll come through the dormer window in the big attic. It's got a balcony you can climb onto from the roof. Sylvie's told them.'

They followed the cats up the attic stairs. Seabhac gripped Merle's shoulder, clicking her beak.

In the attic, they could hear the feet and muttered cursing on the roof over their heads. It came towards the balcony window. A shadow dropped in front of the glass, scrapings followed and somebody opened the window. Merle and Dick flattened themselves against the walls either side. The cats stood bottling but silent in the shadow of an ancient tallboy, while Seabhac sat on top of it. Vicki crouched beside them, a torch in one hand and her father's walking stick in the other.

The window opened. The first of the intruders climbed over the sill, then turned to reach back and help the other. Vicki let both get well inside then turned the torch on them.

The light hit the intruders full in the face. Merle and Dick flung themselves onto the men, one went down straight away but the other fought back. There was a loud thud as somebody hit the floor and Vicki shone the torch in time to see Julian climbing out. There was a flurry of wings and Seabhac was on his neck, ripping his jacket. Merle went out of the window after them. She turned the torch to see the three cats sat on the fallen burglar.

Vicki held the walking stick ready, but the man on the floor wasn't moving. Merle had knocked him out. There was a gash on Dick's face but he was coming round.

'Damn and blast!' he tried to sit up. 'Did he get away?'

'Merle's gone after him. With Seabhac.' Vicki grinned at him. 'Are you OK?'

'Jeese! On the roof, in this weather? Bloody kill himself!'

'I doubt it,' she began, then the cats growled and screamed. There was a yell of pain followed by swearing and scrabbling as the other burglar shot out the window, blood dripping from his arms, his trousers shredded.

'Shit!' Vicki stuck her head out the window. 'Look out Merle, they're both out there!' she yelled.

Various thuds and shouts followed, and a slate came skidding down the roof to shoot over the top of the window onto the lawn. A few minutes later Merle and Seabhac came back in.

'Got away!' he said grimly.

'I've got it!' Sylvie told him as Julian manhandled Wayne through the door. 'Your little diversion worked a treat. I got into the study and found Jacob's notebook.'

'Wayne got knocked out, by Merle, and near scratched to death by those bloody cats. And his fucking falcon nearly had my head. But we managed to escape. They were waiting for us in that attic, just as you said they would be. I hope it was all worth it.'

'Of course!'

'You got the diary?'

'No.' Sylvie spat. 'She must be sleeping with that, but the notebook's well worth it. Jacob would never let me see it.' She turned to Wayne. He looked groggy, bruised and bleeding. 'Bring him in here,' she led them through to the kitchen.

Julian made coffee, with brandy, while Sylvie put ointment on Wayne's bruises and lavender on the cat scratches.

'What's that?' Wayne ducked away as Sylvie went to put something dark on the cut on his face.

'Spider's web,' she said brusquely. 'Didn't your mama ever use them on you?'

Wayne shook his head, staring.

'It's OK,' Julian laughed. 'She hasn't killed me yet!'

Sylvie applied the web. Wayne shuddered as it touched him.

'The ointment smells nice,' he offered.

'She makes it herself, herbs in the garden.' Julian held out the mug of coffee.

'That smells good too,' Wayne took the mug more confidently, recognising the smell of brandy.

Later, in bed, Julian sat stroking Sylvie's toes.

'D'you need the diary itself?' he asked.

'I don't know, perhaps not.' She wriggled luxuriously and tickled his toes in return. 'Let's not think about her for once.' She reached up for more of him.

'You're obsessed!' Hardacre told himself. 'You just can't keep away. It's a disease, and it's bloody well catching. Old Professor Bryde was obsessed and look where it got him. That daughter of his is pretty wound up. And her boyfriend. And as for that Julian bloke, and his woman Sylvie … well. And now you're at it.'

Like Alice, Hardacre often gave himself good advice but rarely took it. Instinct was his strength. In the Met, his colleagues and bosses had learned to listen to his hunches, even if they seemed completely off the wall. He followed his instinct now, grumbling and complaining all the way, but that was how he always was.

He was lurking about in Bridewell again. Feel like I'm bloody James Bond, he muttered, shaken but not stirred. He sneaked into the churchyard. Ha! There was a place he could stand where he could just see both the front door of Well Cottage and its back entrance in Forge Alley. He had no idea why he'd felt he had to come out on a freezing January night and lurk about in the village, but something had called him. He'd been following that voice all his life, and it had never let him down yet.

A movement caught his eye. Two men were coming down the Greenway, one leaning on the other. He recognised the supporter as Julian Courtney but he couldn't see who the other was. They turned into Well Cottage. Hardacre hopped out of the churchyard and snuck after them. They left the gate unlatched, he took advantage and slid up the path behind them. As he knew, the kitchen looked out onto the square and he was able to get close enough to see in. Unfortunately, the cottage was double-glazed so he could hear nothing. Policeman's nightmare, all these new-fangled devices, he thought. Much better when windows only had one pane of glass and plenty of cracks. You could overhear really well then.

He watched Sylvie Villiers mending the cuts and bruises on the two young men. He still didn't know who the other one was, but he'd seen him around the bottling plant. Probably one of Julian's men. And one who was trusted too. That pair'd been up to no good this night, of that he was sure. Then they all left the kitchen. Hardacre scuttled away before the man was let out. He didn't bother following, nothing to be gained there.

As he watched, the downstairs lights went off too, no more to be gained here either, he thought.

They'd come from the Greenway. Everything in him shouted they'd been at Bridewell Manor. Obvious really, the lane went on up past the manor, and there was a footpath into the grounds. Wonder what's going down up at the big house?

No sooner thought than his feet were carrying him that way. It was dark, the trees began to crowd round him. He told himself strongly that he wasn't a superstitious man and didn't believe in all this modern paranormal gobbledygook. It didn't help at all.

There were lights on everywhere at the manor and he could see someone trudging about outside. They seemed to be checking the grounds. Looks like I was right, he muttered. That Julian bloke was burgling. I wish, oh how I wish, they'd trust me enough to tell me what's going on. He watched a bit longer but he knew, without knocking on the door, he wasn't going to learn any more.

A whoosh of wings made him fall over into the grass. He sat up, every hair on his head upright, to find a falcon, sitting in the grass beside him. The jesses on its legs told him it belonged to someone, he remembered that Merle Hollyman had a bird. This was probably it. Was Merle nearby? The bird looked him in the eye. His neck and arm hairs stood up again. He didn't know why but he felt the bird was trying to tell him something. Rashly, he put out one hand. To his utter surprise the bird didn't peck him but rubbed its beak against his finger.

'I'll come and see you tomorrow,' he told it. It flew off. Maybe she'll talk to me, he thought, perhaps that's what the bird wants as well. He got up, dusted himself down.

'What the hell do I think I'm doing, believing a falcon's talking to me?' He shook his head and reluctantly made his way back to his car, his house and his bed.

Oversight

They'd all slept in after the alarums and excursions of the night. Now, they were in the kitchen, having brunch. Hecaté had allowed Goldy to share her washing basket. Shadow purred on the rug below. Seabhac was on the kitchen table, wanting scraps but not getting any.

'Don't feed her,' Merle told them. 'She'll get too fed up to fly.'

'What d'you mean?' Dick asked.

'It's where the adage comes from,' Merle said. 'Raptors can't fly if they're too heavy. Weight's a continuous problem. They must have enough to eat to get the energy to soar. But if they go overweight, then they can't fly.'

Seabhac clicked her beak at him and turned to Dick.

'Sorry, old girl, Dad says I can't,' he grinned back at her. Then he turned to Vicki, 'How did Sylvie know where the notebook was?' he asked.

'Like I told you, she can overlook us, at least to some extent.'

'Oh shit!' Dick groaned. 'Go on, tell me about it.'

'If you put yourself into a sort of dream-trance, and you've got the training, you can eavesdrop and see what people are doing. I think she did that with you and your dream about the stone tree the other morning. You can sort of feel loose threads around, when another magician hasn't been tidy, closed the interface after themselves, shut down.'

'Can she do this anytime?' Dick asked. 'Can you?'

'You know enough about dowsing and such like to know that I can. So can Merle. So could you, if you wanted to learn.' Vicki laughed, then she sighed. 'I'll have to try and keep a guard round us all the time now, so she doesn't get to know what we know.'

'Can you?' Dick raised his eyebrows.

'Yes … but it'd be better if I had more help. Merle can help, and so can you. You sort of set up a high-pressure zone, like on the weather map, around yourself, this place. That way, as long as the pressure's high enough, the low pressure – that's Sylvie and her machinations – can't come in, has to go round the edge. Like the weather. But it's hard work, concentrating all the time, and we've got to find out what's happened to the cup as well. There's a friend of mine in London, we've worked together over the past few years and she could help look after us. I'm going to call her, ask her to come down.'

'Who is it?' asked Merle.

'Faye. The squirrel woman! And she's a shaman.' Vicki went off to the study.

'What the hell have I got into?' muttered Dick.

'Hah!' Merle snorted.

'I suppose it's like old times for you,' Dick looked at Merle.

'Yes and no, it's different. You've seen Vicki over the past ten years, I haven't. After we split up I rather let go of all that, it seemed to belong here, not in London. Since I came back, Jacob didn't go into that sort of stuff, just stuck with the archaeology, lots of weird theories but no practicals. It feels strange to be back here, doing it again. Apart from dreams, it really started up again the night Jacob died. Oh, I'd go for walks in the woods, along the river, feel things in the old way. I've always been able to talk to animals and birds. And I carried on with the garden biodynamics, with Joe's help, like my parents always did. But none of that has the witchy feel this stuff with Sylvie has.'

'Can Sylvie really do that, peer into her crystal ball, watch us, like Vicki said?'

'If she says so, yes. Vicki really does know this stuff. I dare say she's kept it pretty quiet in town, anyone would. But she knows it. And it sounds like this friend does too.'

'Does it make a difference to you two?' Dick dared to ask.

'No. Yes. I don't know. It's so normal and familiar to me. We lived it all the time when we were growing up so now, in some ways, it feels as if I've come home.' Merle stopped. 'When we split up I had no-one to work with, and I didn't want it, pushed it away, all too painful. I thought it would be painful to see her again, feel all that stuff. But it's not. It's like the past ten years were fake and I've only just now got back into reality.'

Dick watched him, wondering if he was envious, or not.

'Faye says she'll be here first thing tomorrow,' Vicki announced as she came back into the room.

'You know,' Merle smiled up at her, 'I ought to sort out de Seligny's contract. It won't take long. Will you come?'

'We'll all come,' she said. 'We shouldn't split up.'

Home to Roost

So time is flowing in two directions …
Bob Toben
Space-Time and Beyond

The Bad Penny

Arriving at Bridge Cottage, Merle let everyone in. Vicki and Dick got the cats out of their baskets while Seabhac took herself off to sit on the mantle, over the Rayburn. He walked through to the study. The answer-phone was blinking at him, on auto-pilot he turned it on.

'Hi Merle!' The silky voice slid out of the speaker. Merle froze, rooted to the spot.

'Something amazing has happened.' The voice went on, somehow he couldn't get to the off switch. 'I'm on my way to tell you about it,' it continued. 'I should be with you about six. Get some supper together for me, darling, and don't forget to open the Chianti as soon as you hear this message. I know you! You're off somewhere and you'll probably only hear it right before I get there. That wine has to breathe if we're to enjoy it together.'

He didn't really hear de Seligny's message which followed on. He did hear Vicki's footsteps behind him.

'Who was that?' Her voice was glacial.

Merle turned. There was nothing for it.

'My wife,' he said. 'My ex-wife,' he amended.

'You don't seem too sure of her status.'

'We divorced five years ago.'

'Really? I'd never have known!'

Merle made a slight movement towards her and saw Vicki draw away. Her eyes were steel. They stood across the room, fizzing like cats. Merle's

204

heart sank. Why the hell did I turn the blasted thing on, he thought, I usually know when it's Kate. They were at an impasse. Vicki looked at her watch.

'It's just coming up to six now,' she said. 'Shall I get the Chianti and open it for you. It seems she's not a woman who likes to be disappointed and you'll have enough to do getting some supper ready for her.'

Merle reeled, Vicki fought rough.

'I'll send her away,' he began.

'Don't be so stupid!' she spat. 'Of course you won't.'

She turned on her heel and went upstairs. Merle found her getting the case from the bedroom.

'I have work to do,' she stood and looked at him across the bed. 'It seems unlikely you will have much time for it while you're discovering the "something amazing". By the time you do, I suspect my work will be done.'

She picked up the overnight bag and headed out of the room. Merle was before her at the door.

'Let me past!'

'No! Not like this!'

'How else is there?'

The front door opened. 'Merle! Merle? Where are you?' The voice was even silkier when not distorted through the answer-phone. Then it changed 'Oh! Who are you?'

'Err … wh-who are y-you?' Dick stammered in response. They heard his chair scrape as he rose from the table.

Merle had to give up, go downstairs to rescue him. Vicki followed him, case in hand.

The cloud of pale gold hair shone like a nimbus. Long legs shimmered in sheer stockings from beneath a fox fur coat. One hand rested on the kitchen table, her eyes slitted as she took in all the participants in the scene she had just entered.

'Merle dear, have I interrupted a party?' Kate's smile grew as she saw the suitcase in Vicki's hand. 'Goodness, I would hate to break things up! Shall I dash back into that little town? I'm sure I saw a pizza place there. I could bring some back for us all?'

'Shut up, Kate! What the hell are you doing here anyway?'

Kate arranged herself in one of the chairs by the table.

'Aren't you going to introduce me?' She crossed her legs, looked demure. 'It seems a little rude to your friends.'

'No, I'm not! I didn't ask you here and I don't want you here,' Merle began.

Kate laughed and smiled apologies towards Dick and Vicki.

'I'm so sorry!' she said to them, pointedly leaving Merle out. 'You seem to have become involved in a 'domestic'. He can be quite unreasonable you know. Perhaps you'd like to withdraw while we sort this out. I'm sure he keeps some good brandy and, er, sherry somewhere.'

Merle made towards her, fists balled. Her eyes stopped him.

'You should listen to your messages, Merle! Then you'd know why I'm here. I've been trying to reach you for ages.'

'There's no need to worry.' Vicki addressed Kate. 'I was just going so you can sort it out between you.'

'V-vicki …!' Dick's anguished whisper reached her. 'D-don't leave me here!'

'Hurry!' she said curtly.

Dick dashed upstairs.

Goldy appeared from Merle's study. She saw Kate and a low growl escaped her.

'I'll be in the car,' Vicki called to Dick. She scooped up Hecaté and went out the door.

Merle stood transfixed. There was nothing he could do, he had to let her go. Any reparations would have to come later. If there was a later. His shoulders slumped. Gods! he thought, I am a fool! How could this be happening?

Dick slunk down the stairs, made some sort of a grimace and slid out the door. A moment later Merle heard them drive through the ford and accelerate away up Firebeacon Hill.

Cold Comfort

The drive back to Bridewell Manor was silent. Vicki unlocked the door. The house was warm, greeted her, made her want to cry.

'Shall I put these in our rooms?' he indicated their bags.

'Thank you.'

Dick headed for the stairs.

In the kitchen she began with the kettle, thought better of it and opened a bottle of Montepulciano. It ought to breathe, but she poured some into two glasses anyway, then began the pasta.

'What can I do?' Dick came into the kitchen.

'Chop onions,' she told him.

Vicki turned on Radio 3, for once not wanting silence. It came on with the beginning of the Sorcerer's Apprentice.

'Ye gods!' she said.

Dick made to turn it off.

'No, leave it if you can stand it. It's very appropriate!'

The pasta, tomatoes, onions, garlic and wine brought some semblance of life back into them.

'What are you going to do?' Dick asked her

'I must go on. What about you?'

'I told you, I took two weeks' leave as soon as you'd left the Museum. I want to stay. That is, if you want me to?' he added.

'Thank you, Dick.'

He wished she hadn't touched his hand.

'I'm going up to bed,' Vicki stood up. 'You do what you like. Feel free, use the kitchen, play music, whatever.'

Dick stood at the bottom of the stairs and watched her retreat, Hecaté in her arms. There was brandy, whisky and other comforts in the library he remembered, as well as the hi-fi. He poured a large tumbler of Courvoisier and allowed a good measure to slide down his throat. Riffling through the CD rack, he found Mahler's first symphony, put it on and lay on the sofa waiting for the music to begin. When it did, he found someone had

The drive back to Bridewell Manor was silent.

207

mixed the cases. Schubert's Death and the Maiden hit his ears. He lay there anyway, his eyes dry and his throat choked.

Some time later he came to and went upstairs. As he passed her door he thought he heard her, was she crying? He paused. Should he knock? All his life he had passed by on the other side, refusing to be involved. No answer greeted his knocking. He opened the door. Her curtains were open and he saw her curled in a ball around the cat.

'Vicki? Vicki?' He put one hand on her shoulder. 'Vicki, dearest, it'll be all right!'

There was no answer, but the crying stopped. He felt her shudder under his hand. Softly, he curled up around her in the great bed.

Later he dreamed. He opened his eyes and looked up into the slit pupils and luminous green eyes of a great cat. Her teeth were bared, her red mane stood out like a halo back-lit by the moon. The downy fur was silky against his thighs and the rhythm of her was insistent. He felt horribly alive, skin tingling, blood roaring in his ears. Life rose up in him and poured out. He was satisfied.

When he awoke it was dark. She must have put the light out. His eyes adjusted and showed him that he was alone, and in her bed. His clothes were damp, his body felt sticky, he remembered bits of the dream, pushed them away. He had to leave, now, at once, before she came back. He scuttled back to his own room.

Safely in the shower, he wondered how he would face her. Would she know he had dreamed of making love to her? Would she despise him? Had she lost him too, as well as Merle? He opened his window and stood staring out over the lawn, smelling the ghost of morning combined with vixen. His indecision spun out the moments and was rewarded by the sound of a car coming down the drive. Someone had arrived.

Past Life

Merle's sleep was troubled. Dreams, about which he could do nothing, plagued him. He knew he was dreaming but he couldn't wake up, had to go through with the whole scene again. He saw Vicki looking at him, saw himself turn away, watched himself walk out of Bridewell Manor, down

208

to Bridge Cottage, pack his bags and drive off to the Portsmouth ferry.

He was back in Marseilles, working in the café by the harbour. The sun was hot behind a haze of blue-grey cloud, it would thunder later. Then he saw her. She took one of the tables under the awning in the shade, next to the plate glass windows. She ordered tea and sat watching the boats.

He could see her reflection in the big mirror behind the counter as he made coffee and tisanes. One man stood behind her, the other sat opposite, astride a chair with his arms laid along the back. She looked afraid, but trying not to make a fuss.

'Attention, mon ami!' Jules, the patron, whispered to Merle from behind the coffee machine. 'Ils sont les revendeurs.'

Heroin, he thought, oh shit! He watched. It seemed they were more interested in 'pretty girl' than pushing drugs, perhaps they would go away. Everyone in the café was studiously looking the other way, or talking together in a suspiciously animated fashion. No help there. As he watched, the one standing behind her put his hands under her armpits and fondled her breasts. She squirmed and began to struggle. In a flash the other one slugged her under the chin, knocking her out. She went limp and the first man caught her from falling off the chair.

Merle flew over the tables. He arrived behind the one holding her, slipped an arm round his throat, pulling back hard and choking him, at the same time punching his knuckles into the man's kidney. The man dropped her as his fellow came to his rescue. Everyone else in the café departed at speed as the tables crashed and rolled between them. Merle's foot came up and kicked the other man in the balls. As he crumpled, Merle took him by the collar and belt and threw him through the plate glass window. The first man had got up again now and came at Merle, getting in a couple of good punches to the face and breaking his nose. Furious with pain, Merle gave the man a straight fingered chop to the throat. He went down again, and didn't get up.

Jules came over. 'Il est mort,' he said pointing to the one Merle had thrown through the window. He bent down and felt at the throat of the other one. 'Lui aussi!'.

The sound of sirens put paid to any further conversation. The flics surveyed the scene, examined the bodies and discussed it amongst themselves, then they called the Chef de Police.

Merle felt he was living in another reality when the slightly portly, pipe smoking, chief inspector climbed out of his battered Renault. He knew, at some level, that he was in shock but he also felt as if he was part of the cast of a Maigret film. The girl was in Jules arms, coming round and being given a sip of brandy. The policemen wouldn't allow him to go to her.

Maigret came over to him.

'I am sorry, monsieur, 'he spread his hands wide as he looked up at Merle. 'But we must go to the police station. I must have a statement. Two men are dead.'

The girl was being carried to an ambulance as they carefully bundled him into the back of the Renault and headed in the opposite direction, away from her. They arrived at the police station and Merle was sat in a battered wooden chair opposite the Chef de Police. Someone brought him a bowl of water and a napkin, he began wiping his face. The chief stuck his pipe in his mouth and came round from the back of his desk.

'It is broken, the nose, no? We will get the doctor to come to you shortly but first, we must have the statement.' And he returned to the other side of the desk. A young man came in with a notepad and pencil. Merle told his story.

'I am sorry, monsieur, but we will have to lock you up. An' I do not think it will be safe for you to be on the streets tonight. Those were heavy men that you have killed. Their friends will be waiting, watching for you. And,' he raised his hands around his ears, 'you have killed them! What am I to do? They were scum, yes, but murder is murder.'

'How's the girl?' Merle asked for the umpteenth time.

'She is in shock. They are keeping her in the hospital and she will be safe there. You need not worry.'

But I do, he thought.

'Can I know who she is?'

'No. Not unless she says. Not until we know too. Perhaps she was one of them. You see, monsieur?'

Merle saw. He hadn't thought of that.

'Take him to the cells and call the doctor,' the chief ordered the young policeman. 'Give him anything he wants and make sure the doctor has all he needs. This young man has done us all a favour, even though we cannot thank him for it.'

Three days later, his nose slightly askew, puffy and throbbing, Merle was back in the smoke filled office again.

'I am letting you go. It was a crime of passion and the men you killed were wanted by the police. But I strongly advise that you leave this town. Their colleagues will be after you and I cannot protect you. If you kill again I shall have to take notice.'

Merle went back to his apartment. There was a note from Jules pushed under the door.

'I have something for you,' it said.

My cards, I'll bet, thought Merle, but it wasn't.

'I shouldn't do this!' Jules said over a coffee. 'But you can come back if you want.'

Merle smiled at his friend. 'No, I don't think I should. If I leave they won't come back for you but, if I stay, they will.'

'Here,' Jules passed him a note. It was from the girl.

'She came in yesterday, looking for you,' he said. 'I wouldn't give her your address so she left this for you.'

The note had her phone number on it. In England.

It was mid-September. Jules gave him money. Merle packed up and went home. All night he stood by the rail on the ferry, watching the wake flow away from him and back to France.

The dream skipped time. He was at his parents' house when he called the number. Her voice was dark, sultry, quite unlike the pale silver-blonde hair he remembered.

He met her in a wine-bar in Covent Garden a few days later. Kate was in computers, and she knew his old friend, Nick, from Oxford days. It was a small world. Nick was glad to meet him again, said he wanted a partner. They joined forces. At first Kate was usually with Nick but gradually she came to spend more time with Merle. One night she was in his bed.

Merle felt as if he'd been set free. Vicki was gone, not here, not in his life anymore. No-one knew Kate, no-one had any expectations of either of them. It was a new life. Three weeks later they were married and he'd told nobody.

Faye & Dick

Faye drove into the courtyard. There was the famous one-handed clock Vicki had told her about. It was weird actually being here. The house didn't look seven hundred years old and it was hard for Faye, an American, to grasp that its foundations were from the thirteenth century. Vicki's family had been there even longer, since before the Romans came, and the site itself went back past four thousand years. That was truly ancient!

Faye shook herself, pulled her case out of the car, went up to the front door and knocked loudly. After a moment it opened and a bearded, bespectacled face peered up at her.

'Have I made it to Bridewell Manor?' she said.

'Err-umm-err yes' he answered. 'Err, who are you?'

'I'm Faye Morgan, Vicki's friend from London. Is she up?'

'Oh … ah … yes … she's … err … up and g-gone' the man smiled and stammered. 'Uh, come in.' He pulled the door wide and stood back for Faye. 'C-can I t-take your case?' he added, reaching for it.

'Why, thank you!' Faye gave it him. She was enjoying this, not used to gentlemen being gentlemen, but she could feel the tension in him, in the whole place. What was Vicki doing?

Dick shut the door and stood a moment undecided.

'I don't know which room she'll have put you in,' he said, the stammer disappearing for the moment. He put the case down. 'Perhaps you'd like some coffee, breakfast? There's a bathroom just down the hall here if you need it, but let me show you where the kitchen is.'

Faye followed him. The kitchen was just as she'd imagined. She looked out into the courtyard, the first snowdrops were pushing up under the old peach tree opposite, and the hellebores were flowering.

'I'll be in here, making coffee, breakfast,' Dick's voice brought her back. 'Shall I show you the bathroom?'

'Thank you,' Faye smiled, trying to catch his eye, missing.

Dick picked up her case again and she followed him across the hall and out of a door. They were by the staircase now, sweeping down with the tall window behind, again giving onto the courtyard. Faye caught glimpses of the mediaeval hall, what Vicki called the library, through the arch on her left. Dick stopped by the door to the cloakroom.

'Shout if you get lost, it's a bit of a warren,' he said and turned back to the kitchen again.

Faye let out her breath and stood looking round. White and blue and mirrors surrounded her. She felt grimy and all travelled-out. The big white towels tempted her. There was a shower in an adjoining room, as well as the loo. She took a quick shower, changed into fresh jeans and shirt. Feeling better, she left the case by the stairs and found her way back to the kitchen. The coffee was on the table along with bread, and cereals.

'Ah! Coffee.' Faye collapsed into a chair.

'I'm Dick Fischer-King.' Dick joined her on the other side of the table. 'Jacob's assistant at the British Museum. I forgot to introduce myself. It's, er, been a bit of a night!'

'I know!' Faye grinned back at him. 'Vicki called me late last night, told me Merle's ex-wife'd turned up. I guessed who you were. Vicki's talked about you.'

'I'm afraid I don't know anything about you,' Dick said. 'I usually saw Vicki with Jacob, and then it was shop or family talk. She said she'd worked with you. And that you're a shaman.'

'That's right, I am,' Faye grinned at Dick. 'But I'm also an environmental scientist, that's how I earn my bread. And how I got to know Vicki, years ago, when I needed a specialist database for some research stuff. She did the job for me privately. But I know about her weird side, it fits really well with my own shamanic work. I keep all that stuff well under wraps for work. Like she does. Companies and government departments don't take kindly to that sort of thing.'

'Err ... n-no, I s-suppose they wouldn't,' Dick's eyebrows scaled his hairline.

'Oh it's not a problem. I used to work for a conservation trust, when I first came over, but I'm self-employed now, doing woodland work and stream habitat assessments. Did a lot of work on the Thames, helped get the otters and cormorants back.'

'Ah ...' Dick said slowly, then, 'You know, I noticed that from my flat. It's right by the Thames and I've seen the cormorants again on the bridges and the buoys in the river.'

'Yes,' said Faye. 'It's good they're back.'

They sat silent for a moment, then Faye asked,

'What's been going on down here? Vicki's told me a bit but I don't really know. How are you involved?'

Dick gave her a potted history of events since Jacob's death.

'Vicki says you could help shield us from Sylvie, so we could get on with the search without worrying about her overlooking – is that the right word?' Faye nodded, he continued. 'Well, overlooking us then, seeing what we find.'

'Yes, I can do that,' Faye said. 'But what about you? You seem to know this stuff too.'

'Well, really, I'm sort of new to all this magical stuff,' he gave a rueful smile, 'but I could always dowse. Found it useful in the archaeology, even though you can't put anything like that into your papers. Everyone knows, but we keep it under wraps, like your shamanism.'

'I didn't know that. Sounds like sense to me. How did you get in with Jacob Bryde? Even I've heard of him, without knowing Vicki, after that sensational find he made in the church here. Were you in on that too?'

'Yes, I was!' Dick's stammer was on holiday again.

'Tell me about it!' she grinned.

I like this woman, Dick thought, but why's she asking me this? He came to a decision.

'You know, we're dancing round the issues here,' he looked her in the eye. 'Not talking about where Vicki's gone.'

'Yes! Stalling! I keep hoping Vicki will come back. Why, oh why, didn't she wait for me,' Faye said despairingly.

'Well … should we phone?'

Faye sat considering a moment, shut her eyes. Immediately, the picture of Kate and Merle was in her face. She opened her eyes and shook her head. 'Ugh! No! They're in bed!' Faye didn't mince matters.

'Who?' Dick raised his eyebrows.

'Merle and his ex. I think we'd better keep out for the time being,' she grimaced. 'I can't see Vicki at all, she must be cloaked. Someone will get through to us when it's OK again.'

Dick snorted. 'Times like this I wish I was back at work, with only office politics to worry about,' he said sourly. 'But I guess you're right. In the meantime …?'

'Why don't we enjoy a leisurely breakfast and get to know each other?

We might as well. We've got to work together in the not too distant … like later on today.' Faye smiled wryly.

'OK. Shall I do another pot of coffee?' Dick offered.

'Why not! And you start. How did you get to know Jacob?'

'Well, that was weird too ...' Dick took the pot over to the sink and began the next brew. 'It began before I ever met him. I was doing my PhD, on Celtic Christian shrines which had been built on much more ancient sites.'

'This sounds like a story,' Faye sat back, preparing to enjoy. 'Go on, Master Storyteller!' she said.

Dick coloured up. He brought the jug back to the table. 'All right,' he sat down, made a face at Faye. 'Don't forget you asked for this!' Then he cleared his throat, leaned back in his chair and half shut his eyes.

'I drove all round the country, all sorts of places, but the one which led to Bridewell is the old site at Kitnor, just up on the coast from here,' he began, then he noticed Faye's eyes bugging.

'It's, er, it's OK,' she said faintly. 'You tell me your story then I'll tell you mine.'

'OK ...' Dick hesitated a moment, then took her at her word. 'I drive a Morgan four-plus-four. Not really ideal for gallivanting round the moors, but she was the car of my dreams and I'd only just got her. I wasn't about to abandon her just for the PhD. She grumbled quietly in the lanes and over the moors and eventually she brought me to Kitnor. The way down's like going into another world. Silver-birch full of birdsong. And moss-green tree-root gargoyles.' Dick stopped. 'I feel like I'm teaching granny to suck eggs?'

'I – er – like eggs,' Faye managed. 'Go on.'

'At the bottom I saw the quaint little church-spire sticking up through the branches. I left the car by the bridge and took my first look at the tiny little church. The path through the graveyard is like something out of a Victorian novel, leaning gravestones everywhere. Inside there's that particular smell which says "church" to me. Like the smell of a library, only this one's a mix of damp hymn book, old leather, wax polish, tallow, spilled communion wine and mouse. It's a fabulous place. But you know that, don't you?'

Faye nodded. 'Go on,' she said again.

'Well, I was studying the Saxon window, the one with the face on the mullion. It's like a gestalt, but it really is there. I got my camera out and then I stopped. I felt I should ask if it was OK to take a picture and, as I looked at the face, the sunlight shifted, moved the shadows, and it seemed to smile at me. It wasn't scary or anything. I smiled back and took the shot. Then I took out my pendulum and worked the lines up the nave, and the spiral in front of the altar. When I'd done, I turned to go and touched my forelock to the window-face. I'll swear it grinned back.

'I stood for a minute saying "Thank you" to the church, then my skin prickled. Someone was watching. I turned and saw the crooked chimneys of the cottage. Gingerbread,' he paused.

'Just at that moment the cottage door opened and a little old woman wrapped in a shawl hobbled down the path on her stick. I nearly had a heart attack! At least it wasn't a broomstick! I wondered how quickly I could get the hell out of there should the need arise. And, I thought, what'll I do if she invites me in for tea?' he quirked an eyebrow at Faye.

Faye swallowed hard and tried to keep on breathing. This was too much coincidence. She nodded to him to go on.

'The old woman arrived at the cottage gate and opened it. I really wasn't surprised when it groaned. At that point I wouldn't have been surprised to see the cottage strutting about on fowl's legs. Anyway, she made her way carefully, one foot at a time, down the steps and came across to me.

'"Bin to see the church, have you?" she asked me. I told her, yes. She looked me up and down from the level of my chest. I'm only five foot seven, but she must have been under five feet. Like one of the little people. Then she said "Saw you coming, so I did. Kettle's on, have a cup o' tea?" She saw me hesitate. "There's ginger biscuits," she offered, and her eyes twinkled. You could have knocked me down with a feather, it was like she read my mind, which I'm sure she did. Inside was like a Disney film-set.' Dick paused again watching Faye.

Faye nodded slowly, indicating he go on, her mind picturing as he described the rocking chair, the dresser with the earthenware jars, the glass bottles full of brightly coloured concoctions, the spinning wheel, and the cauldron kettle hanging from a chain over the fire.

'She sat me down in an overstuffed armchair,' he continued, 'telling me to watch the kettle. She made the tea and set the places. And then

216

she put a plate of gingerbread men on the table. I tucked in. After a few minutes I realised, with a bit of a shock, that what I'd taken for animal sculptures were the real thing. Cats, squirrels, mice, a toad sat in the log basket and an owl on top of the grandfather clock. I stopped and looked at her.'

'College student are you?' she said.

'Sort of,' I replied. 'I'm doing my PhD.'

'Doctor, is it then? Well, doctor you will be.'

She went to a cupboard, brought out a silver bowl and filled it with water. "Look in there, deary, tell me what you see."

'At first it was dark, then a finger of sunlight came through the window and lit the water. The surface rippled. I wondered what, besides ginger, she put in her biscuits.

'I was looking at a great tall church standing at the top of a hill above a village square. I felt as if I was flying, like watching a film. I went up a lane and over a wood where the trees were laid out like a wheel. Then a long, white house. And finally a tower with a waterfall beside it. The water rippled again and I was staring at an elfin face with deep green eyes, surrounded by a halo of red hair.'

Dick stopped and looked away. 'I think,' he said, 'that was the moment I fell in love.'

'Anyway,' he continued more briskly now, 'she sent me on my way. A year later, almost to the day, I saw an advert for a post at the British Museum, as assistant to Jacob Bryde. I jumped at it. I'd read his papers and he seemed to work on similar lines to the way I wanted to go, especially on the Celtic theme. I sent in my application and waited. And waited. Then I got home one night to a message. I called him back and he invited me down to Bridewell for the interview. I'd forgotten how near it is to Kitnor. When I drove up the drive, I nearly crashed the car when I saw the house. There it all was, in every particular, just the same as I'd seen it in the old witch's bowl. Later, when he introduced me to the family, I saw Vicki and, although she was still a teenager, she was just like in the picture. Jacob and I got on really well, he took me dowsing in the kitchen garden, I stayed for tea, then dinner, and finally the night. I was a confirmed member of the family by the time I eventually left the next morning, and it all grew from there. I've been Jacob's friend ever since. And Vicki's.'

Silence hung between them. Then he looked at her shrewdly. 'You know that place and that old woman, don't you?'

Faye's mouth twisted wryly. 'I suppose I should be used to what people call coincidences,' she said. 'You see, that's my great aunt's cottage that you were in and she who gave you tea.'

It was Dick's turn for the double-take.

'Bloody ridiculous, eh?' Faye snorted.

'Will you t-tell me about it?' Dick's stammer reared its head.

Faye got up, walked over to the windows, stood looking out. Then she came back to him, her mind made up.

'OK,' she said slowly, tracing invisible patterns on the table. 'My dad died when I was eighteen. It was a bad year. I'd just flunked school, not a chance of a college place, and Dad was taken with a heart attack in the middle of the summer vacation. It was such a shock. No-one expected it. Mom was completely devastated and I just didn't know what to make of it. I was very taken up, too, with my own troubles, as I thought of them, although they were all my own fault. I'd had a very pampered childhood, no responsibilities, little-miss-rich-girl, living in Maryland, in a Scarlet O'Hara mansion in the middle of a wood. Servants, everything. Unlike Vicki, my parents never sent me off to learn from the housekeeper, and the gardener, and the groom who looked after my pony, so I was something of a spoiled brat. In consequence I didn't understand what had happened and I blamed my father for leaving us.

'We buried Dad. It was pissing down with rain that day, and I thought the coffin was going to float, the grave was so full of water. Looking back, it was a farce really. Everyone there, saying the right things, but all on the look-out for what they could make, even if it was only to score off another family member. The week after, Mom announced we were going to England. Dad's family came from there, and she'd always wanted to visit "the old country", so we packed onto the plane and flew over. Mom hired a car, and succeeded in driving on the wrong side of the road actually better than she'd ever driven at home.

'We arrived in Devon and put up at the George in West Milton, a real old-world English hotel. I queened it around the town, saying everything at nine thousand decibels in my best American accent,' Faye grinned ruefully. 'Yes, I was a complete pain! I think Mom didn't really notice, she was still in shock over losing Dad. We drove out onto the moor and

218

found Nether Stowey, where his family came from. Mom loved looking round the old village, and the bits of castle, and Coleridge's cottage, which she hadn't realised was in the same village. Mom didn't go in for poetry but, when she discovered Coleridge lived in "our village", as she called it, she began to read all his stuff. I did too and scared myself silly with the Ancient Mariner. And I began quoting bits of Kublai Khan, although I didn't understand a word of it. That's how we got ourselves to Kitnor.

'Your description of the church is just right. I felt it when I first saw it. Perhaps it was the first truly spiritual feeling I'd ever had, although I used to play with the fairies in the woods around home. I think I probably ordered them around in much the same way I did with the servants! And I suppose they let me off because I was a kid.

'We looked round the church, then we came out and stood by the porch looking round. Then this voice called out, "Marjorie? Marjorie Morgan, is that you?"

'Mom nearly fainted away on the spot. We turned to find this tiny little old woman standing at the churchyard gate. She beckoned us over. "How do you know me?" Mom asked her. "I'd know my nephew's wife anywhere," she said.

'Well, that's how it began. She told us tales of Dad's family going back into the ark, or so it seemed to me. We drove back to West Milton, promising to come again the next day. And so we did.

'Her cottage is fascinating, isn't it? And the valley too. It goes right down to the sea, you know, where Coleridge wrote that bit of the Kublai Kahn, or where he'd been when he took the opium and began to have the dream. I'm sure, too, it was Auntie's cottage where he holed up for the night. Mom had got a regular bee in her bonnet, wanted to go down to the shore and find the rock, and sit where Coleridge had sat, and all that stuff. Auntie told her it was dangerous and the tides were very fast. She told us, in her own way, about the Severn Bore but mom wouldn't be swayed.' Faye's voice caught a bit, she swallowed.

'Mom went off after lunch, despite Auntie's warning, and I never saw her again alive.' Faye stopped again, got out a handkerchief and blew her nose hard. Dick waited, knowing better than to touch her now.

'A while after mom had gone off for her walk, Auntie got out the silver bowl and began to watch in it. I came to look over her shoulder.

It was weird, like a sort of TV screen. Later, I learned that Auntie called it far-seeing. I could see Mom walk down the path by the stream and into the cave. She came out onto the shore and walked along until she came to the rock, then she sat down with her back against it looking out to sea. I saw a shadowy figure come up the beach towards her and she held out her hands in greeting. Then there was a roaring and the whole river seemed to rise up like a mountain. I know, now, it isn't really like that, not that far down the estuary. It's Gloucester-way that the Bore gets impressive. But this looked huge as we watched Mom. I don't think it was a real wave. It came racing up the beach and swallowed her up, her along with the shadowy figure. I cried out and fell down in a heap on the rug.'

She stopped again. This time, Dick touched her hand. After a minute or two, Faye squeezed his fingers back and continued.

'Auntie picked me up. She gave me herbs, which helped me come back to earth a bit. I asked her if it was true, if Mom was dead. She said it was. I wanted to go down and find Mom, find her body, where she was, but Auntie stopped me. We sat and waited until it grew dusk, then Auntie called the police and reported Mom as missing. Three days later, they found her body washed up on the Welsh shore, miles down the river.

'I didn't know what to do. I was completely off my head for a while. Both my parents were gone, and Mom in such a weird way. I stayed with Auntie, moved in with her. How she bore with me I don't know. I told you I was a spoiled brat and I really was. I used to commentate on everything I did, "I'm just putting this in the fridge," I'd tell her while she was standing beside me, watching me. "Really?" she'd say, "What you telling me for? I've got eyes in me head, girl! And a brain that still works!" Eventually I got the message, and stopped stating the bleeding obvious. It was a desperate call for attention.

'And with the animals. Auntie would always be talking to them and, whenever I heard her voice, I used to answer, as if she was talking to me. "Little Princess is it? You're not the centre of the bloody universe," she'd tell me crossly. "Very often you're the last person I'm talking to. Try to get that into your head will you?". Then, one day, I asked her, "How'm I to know when you're talking to me?". She tapped her head, "Noddle, nowse and knowing," she said acerbically. She was no soft option, didn't fuss over me, or allow me to make a drama out of my grief and sorrow and pain. But when she found me crying silently, off in a corner – and

220

she always managed to know, even if she was miles off in the woods or in the garden – she'd come sit with me and teach me how to cry properly. I loved her so much.' Faye's voice choked.

'After a few weeks I got better, stopped being such a pain. "You had too many servants and not enough service in your life," she said to me. "What you need is to work, and work hard, learn about the world, and the creatures in it, and the people." That's when I asked her, "Can I work with you?"

'She gave me an old fashioned look, over the top of her specs, and said, "You can work *for* me." And so I did. You're right. She was a witch. And she taught me.'

'As far as I know she's still there,' Dick said.

They sat silent for a while, digesting each other.

'When did Vicki go down to Bridge Cottage?' Faye asked.

'I don't know. I, er, saw her late last night, bed time. Then, when I got up this morning, she was nowhere about.'

The phone began to ring.

Breaking the Vase

Merle turned away from Kate. She came up behind him and put her arms round his waist.

'I'm hungry, Merle,' she said,

'Too bad!' He shoved her off roughly.

Kate staggered, regained her balance, went to sit by the table.

'Don't you want to know why I'm here?' she changed tack.

'Why then?'

'It's the French property.'

That brought him round to face her.

'Your uncle is dead. The notary eventually discovered he didn't know how to find you, so he wrote to Jean-Luc. He only had the address of our old flat, so the letter came to me. I've been trying to get through to you ever since but, as usual, it would be easier getting blood from a stone.'

Kate pulled a thick, unopened, envelope out of her bag.

As Merle took it, his hand shook a little. It was like a message from the grave. He stared at the cream, type written sheets, then began to read them. Kate sat quietly, not looking at him.

'It's about Barenton,' he began. 'I'd forgotten all about it.'

'Who?'

'Brittany, in the forest of Broceliande.'

'You mean Merlin's forest, like in the stories?'

'That's the one!' Merle grinned at her.

Kate stared at him, this was the side she had always shied away from when they were married and, fortunately, he hadn't wanted to go into it then either.

'Sounds like a fairy tale,' she looked away.

'So it is.'

Kate went back to the original subject. 'What's happened?'

'You know we used to go and stay there, when I was a kid. It was mother's house. Uncle Everard, her cousin, said he'd like to live there so they agreed. I'd forgotten. I suppose he'd be in his eighties now, if he'd lived.' Merle sat with the documents dangling from his hand, staring into nowhere.

'What does it say?' Kate dragged him back to the present. Merle finished reading.

'The house is mine now. Uncle Everard died in November. I dare say the notary took his time contacting people as usual. He should have known to write here, it's the obvious place. Sloppy!' he shrugged. 'But they always are.'

'You forget, you've kept well out of touch, too,' Kate said caustically. 'What's he want you to do?'

'He wants to know what I want to do with it and suggests I give him permission to sell it. That means he knows of a buyer and wants to make himself a cut. But I don't know if I want to. I'd like to go and see it again for myself. They've waited this long, they can wait a bit longer.'

'I'm going to scramble us some eggs.' Kate got up. 'I'm hungry and you are too. We can eat and decide what comes next later.'

Merle opened a bottle of wine. It wasn't Chianti, but then supper wasn't lobster either, thank the gods. However angry he was at Kate barging in on his delicate situation, and lousing it up, he was also grateful to her for bringing him the news of Barenton. What would Vicki think about this? Assuming he ever got to speak to her again. It added yet another spanner to the works and, as it was, there were quite enough already between him and the person he wanted more than anything else in his life.

Kate found plates, cutlery, glasses and set the kitchen table. Never at a loss, that one, Merle remembered. There was salad and potatoes as well as scrambled eggs. And smoked salmon. She must have brought that with her, for there was none in his fridge. For desert she'd got a French apple tart. In spite of the evening's alarums and disturbances Merle found he still had an appetite. Bridewell Manor seemed a million miles away, and impossible to get to. He wandered, in his slightly wine-befuddled state, if perhaps he had dreamt the whole thing. Kate, food and reality were right on the table in front of him.

'Where is this place, anyway?' Kate asked him later as they sat beside the fire in the sitting room.

He got out the maps and spread them on the floor, showed her the place on the edge of the forest of Broceliande. She leaned across, following the road down from St Malo. He could feel her breath on his hand, smell her perfume. He pointed to where the old house was, and the path that led up to the fountain. Their hands touched. Softly, she turned her head and kissed him. They both knew what they wanted. Old habits come to life in moments of despair, and now was certainly a despairing moment.

The past rose up to engulf him as he lay within her in the bed. Desperately his mind reached out to the aureole of red hair, the clear green eyes, but to no avail. Everywhere he looked he saw only the fall of flaxen hair upon the pillow and the deep sapphire eyes which ate hungrily into his.

He woke to the aroma of coffee. Kate had brought a jug to the bedroom. He could hear noises down in the kitchen and hoped to god she wasn't making breakfast. The dream was still with him, his escape from France, flight to London, Nick and Kate. All the killing, the running, which had brought him to her. He had run to France when Vicki had run from him to London. Then he had run from France because of the killing, straight into Kate's arms. And then, when he had found her with Nick, he had run again. Out of the marriage, out of the partnership with Nick and finally back to the moorland holt, where Vicki had been all his life. Only to find that his mother was dying of cancer. His mind finally brought him to the last scenes, his father holding the car door, his mother kissing him, saying brightly …

'I just need to go for a drive, dear, see the sea, we both do. Can't stay cooped up here all the time. We won't be very long.'

They had been forever. It was five o'clock in the evening when the police arrived at the cottage.

'I'm terribly sorry, sir,' the policeman said, 'but I have some bad news. Would you mind coming with us, please, sir'.

And he had gone. To the morgue in West Milton. The bodies were very little damaged, considering.

'They went over the cliff, sir,' said the policeman. 'At Hurlestone Point.'

It had been one of his mother's favourite places, she had gone there to think, to paint, when anything bothered her, usually alone. But this they had done together.

'I dare say she was a bit unsteady on her feet,' the policeman went on, 'what with the drugs and all, for the illness. And I expect he tried to save her and got pulled down with her.'

He's kind, thought Merle. He knows, but he's trying to make it seem to be an accident. And, indeed, there was nothing to show that it wasn't.

'Did they say anything to you, sir, before they left?'

'Only that they wouldn't be very long,' Merle said distantly. 'Mother said she had to go out, couldn't stay cooped up all the time. It was one of her favourite places.'

'I've seen her pictures in the gallery, in town. She had an exhibition most summers, didn't she? I bought one of the view from Hurlestone.' The policeman, too, was thoughtful.

Merle buried his parents and inherited Bridge Cottage, built up his business and remade his friendships with Jacob, Joe and Vera, and the rest of the village. He had rebuilt his life, or so he thought. Now Jacob was dead and Vicki had returned, only to be lost to him, again. He swallowed coffee and screwed up his eyes to hold back tears. When would the pain, the running, stop?

Footsteps on the stairs brought him back to the present.

'That was her, wasn't it?' Kate sat on the bed with her own mug of coffee. 'All through your sleep, and even before when we made love, you called me Vicki. Are you back together then?'

'Yes. No. I don't know.'

'I suppose my coming's put the kybosh on that.'

'Very likely!' Merle grimaced.

'Tell me about her, about what's going on here. I can see there's something up.'

'Her father just died so she's come home.'

But that wasn't enough, Kate wanted the whole story. Merle told her a little of Vicki, and the problems in the village with the water. It was nothing she couldn't have found out for herself, by asking in the pub or the post office and, he knew, she would do just that later anyway. It was her way, she always wanted to know everything about everyone, it gave her control. But he told her nothing of the diary or the cup.

'So you want to marry the land here as well?'

'It's not like that at all,' he tried, but it was no use.

As he told her about his childhood with Vicki, the funeral and how they had remade the old relationship, Kate heard his voice change. It was a note she had never heard before and she looked away from him now, into the middle distance of nowhere. He's gone, she thought to herself, he never spoke of me this way. Kate sat with the thought a while, not really hearing Merle's words at all, and then she made up her mind. He broke off as she got up from the bed, went to the door.

'You really mean it this time, don't you?' she said.

Their eyes met.

'It's all right, love, you won't see me again.' Kate turned and went down the stairs.

A few minutes later he heard her car accelerate up the hill. He listened until he could hear it no more and the only sound was of the wind in the trees.

'What can I do?' he said aloud, to anything that might be listening. Then he heard Goldy padding up the wooden stairs. He hadn't seen her since the previous evening when he put the falcon back in her mews. Goldy stopped by the bedroom door, stood up to stretch against the jamb and mewled.

'What is it?' he asked.

She stood looking at him and mewled again, more stridently, then trotted down the stairs, stopping at the bottom to look back at him. Grabbing a dressing gown and slippers, Merle followed.

Goldy went out of the cat flap. Merle opened the kitchen door to see her standing by Seabhac's mews. The door was open, Merle's heart stood still.

He crossed the yard at the speed of light. The old potting shed was dark, he heard Seabhac chatter at him and saw her sitting by Vicki's shoulder, guarding her as she lay in the straw.

The Owl Woman

So why are we here at all ?
Bob Toben
Space-Time and Beyond

Dream

Vicki dialled the number and waited.

'Be home! Be home!' she whispered, but the answer-phone came on. 'Damn!' she waited for it to stop. 'Faye? Faye! Pick up the phone! Be there! Oh Faye, please pick up the phone!'

Nothing.

Vicki replaced the receiver and sat on the bed hugging her knees. Hecaté jumped up beside her.

'I know! Oh Hecaté, I know!' She lay down, curled around the cat, hugging her. 'I've done it again. I'm so bloody stupid! I run every damn time if the going gets rough. I should've stayed. I was afraid of her. But I just ran. And gave all my power to her.' Hecaté licked her nose, that made the sobs worse. 'Merle didn't want her. I know that. I knew that then. He wants me. He told me so and I wouldn't bloody believe him. He was completely thrown by that message, and her arrival, and I deserted him. Again. Every bloody time I do it. He's had to face all the tough stuff without me and he needs me.'

The phone rang.

'Hello, hello, hello? Vicki? What's up?' Faye asked before she could get a word in.

'It's me! I'm such a stupid, selfish bitch!'

'Yes, dear!' Faye sighed, chuckled. 'We know that! Now … what have you done this time?'

'I ran out on him again. I just get him back, get myself back, start getting the ends together and something happens and I panic and run.

227

I'm useless, Faye, absolutely bloody useless!'

'Yes dear! I know you are. We all know you are!' again the throaty chuckle. 'But could you flesh it out for me a bit? I gather you've metaphorically kicked Merle in the balls again, is that it? At least I hope it was metaphorically? Really dumb to threaten your chances, for real, that way!'

Vicki began to giggle, snuffling, choking.

'There now … that's better,' Faye said gently. 'Bit of perspective coming back?'

The hysteria wore down. Vicki began to cry. 'I really am such a clot!' Gradually she got back some control and told Faye the whole history.

'Yeah! Seriously dumb!' Faye said. 'He needed you to support him, not run out on him. He didn't want the damn woman there. And, my girl, you don't even know what she came for now, do you? If you'd hung on in there, been queen of the castle as Merle wanted you to be, you'd know. And I bet you Kate is just the sort of woman to stir up a situation for the fun of it, especially with all the encouragement you gave her! I mean, wouldn't you?'

Vicki couldn't help it, she began to laugh again. 'You're right! I would! Especially if I had a drama queen like I must have been in front of me. I'd have played it for all it was worth.'

'And,' said Faye, with an old-fashioned look in her voice, 'I'll bet you've thrown them into bed together now!'

'Oh shit!'

'Yes, oh shit indeed!'

'You're right again, sister. He'll be so bloody miserable she'll only have to touch him to set it off.'

'And don't you go haring back down there now to make amends!' Faye admonished her. 'You're quite dumb enough, at times, to do just that. But you know very well you'd only find them in bed, and three's definitely a crowd there.'

'Ouch! Yes. Damn!'

'You can go down tomorrow. Not now! And I think I'd better come too.'

'Oh please! Everything's happening here. And I have to get into a tizzy about nothing at all, and build it into a super melodrama, and we've

228

got all this about the cup and Dad on our plates. Oh Faye, I'm really bloody useless at times!'

'Yes, darling, I know. We've done all that!' the chuckle was back again. 'Now, I'll be with you for breakfast, OK?'

'Please. I really need some help.'

'Hang on in there, girl. I'm coming.'

Four left feet isn't in it, Faye told the phone after Vicki had hung up.

The dream woke her. She turned to tell Merle but her hands touched something unfamiliar. Vicki opened her eyes. Dick was lying asleep beside her in the bed. She froze.

Memory pushed its way to the surface. She'd been crying. He'd come in, touched her, lain down beside her. She'd fallen asleep. She watched him now, his face flushed, snoring. Hecaté butted her hand, her eyes said 'Get up'. Vicki slid out of the bed and into some clothes, she went downstairs.

The car slid quietly down Firebeacon Hill. Vicki left it in the meadow while she and Hecaté walked over the bridge, up the lane, to his gate. Kate's car was still parked in the drive. She couldn't go in.

A soft whistle reached her from across the yard. Seabhac? Vicki called to the bird in her mind and felt an answering ripple, she could wait with her there, in the potting-shed mews. The sky was getting light, dawn was coming. She went back to the car and got a blanket, opened the gate silently and crossed the yard. Seabhac's door was unlocked, Hecaté slid in, she followed. The falcon whistled again. Vicki stroked her feathers, wrapped herself in the blanket and snuggled down with Hecaté in the straw. It was dark, her eyes were shut, but she could see perfectly, the mews appeared bright, shining with a pink-gold light, like the old moon. The silver cobweb hung in the air in front of her.

'Caer-y-troiau.' she whispered.

She felt herself being pulled into the pattern, the words of the village song coursing through her. Her feet ran the maze. She arrived at the centre and everything went dark.

'Hey, kiddo!' The woman's voice was soft, strong.

Faye? Vicki stirred and half opened her eyes. The long brown face hung over hers, she smiled up into the hazel eyes.

'That's better,' said the familiar American drawl. 'You've been gone from us for a while, girl. Come back, come home now …' The voice became a sing-song.

Vicki felt herself drifting upward. She could feel someone's arms around her, her head resting against a living, breathing person. She turned her head, felt wool against her face, smelled a scent she knew.

'Merle?' she whispered.

'I'm here,' Merle croaked, coughed. 'I'm here,' he managed again in a more normal voice.

'She's better. We can bring her indoors now.' Faye's voice.

Vicki felt herself being lifted up. Suddenly everything was very bright and she hid her face in the woollen jumper again. It was cold too. Then she felt herself being sat in a chair, a blanket round her. Things got a bit darker and warmer. She shivered.

Something jumped into her lap and began purring. Another something wrapped itself around her legs and a third climbed up gently after the first. She knew what they were, although they had no name in her mind. But they were warm and soft and strength poured out of them into her. A rough tongue licked her. She opened her eyes and stared into two deep green pools.

'Hecaté?' she whispered.

The black cat nuzzled her. Looking further she saw Goldy was the other weight on her lap and Shadow was curled round her feet. The cats were purring fit to bust and pressing themselves against her.

A human shape loomed into view. Merle held a mug to her lips and helped her drink. The tea was hot, sweet, brought her back to focus with a jolt. She sat up a little. Now she could see out into the room. It seemed very full of people.

'She's nearly back,' said Faye. 'Drink the tea, Vicki, it'll do you good. Joe's put Rescue Remedy in it.'

Merle put the cup to her mouth again and she swallowed. She was feeling more here, not that that's what she wanted, it had been quite pleasant being elsewhere. Now all these people would ask her questions. She shut her eyes again.

'No you don't!' Faye said sharply. She'd taken Merle's place with the mug. 'You get your ass back on in here! We need you to tell us what the hell's going on.'

Faye's voice pulled her back. Vicki tried to pull away. They tussled for a moment, then Faye said very clearly,

'Come on! Back you come. Open eyes. Look at me! Who are you? Come on, tell me your name. Come on, who are you?'

Faye wouldn't stop. Vicki sat up, pushed the cup away.

'I'm Vicki,' she grumbled faintly. 'And you're Faye,' her voice broke, 'and I'm so glad you're here.' She burst into tears.

'There, there. That's better.' Faye rocked her gently. 'She'll be OK now,' Faye told the room at large. 'She needs hot food. Can somebody get some breakfast together?'

Vicki heard the bustling and the voices but she stayed clinging to Faye. After a little while she began to doze.

'Vicki, breakfast!' the voice jerked her awake. Faye pulled her up and brought her to the table. She blinked at the light. There was Joe and Vera, Dick and Faye. And Merle.

'Where'd you all come from?' she croaked.

'I called them, I didn't know what to do,' Merle tentatively reached out for her hand. She didn't draw away.

"I'm so sorry I deserted you,' she whispered.

'So'm I!' he said wryly, but his eyes thanked her.

'What happened?'

'I found you, passed out in Seabhac's mews, with Hecaté. I couldn't wake you so I phoned the manor in the hope someone was there. Dick answered. He brought Faye and Vera, and she called Joe. None of us could wake you, only Faye.'

'I arrived at Bridewell for breakfast, like I said,' Faye took up the tale. 'Dick said you'd disappeared but I guessed where you'd gone. We were waiting for you to come back when the phone rang. Merle told us he'd found you, on the floor with the falcon sitting guard over you. We hightailed it down here. Dick damn near stalled in the ford.'

'I d-did n-not!' spluttered Dick.

'You did too!' Faye retorted. 'Anyway, we found you and I began to sing you back. And you deigned to come, thank the gods! Can you tell us what happened?'

'I had a dream,' Vicki began, smiling to herself as she repeated Dick's beginning from the other morning. 'I woke up and thought it was Merle beside me. I wanted to tell him the dream. But when I touched him I found it was you, Dick, lying on the bed, snoring. Hecaté told me to get up and come down here. She jumped in the car with me. When I saw Kate's car still in the drive I knew we couldn't go in but Seabhac called me, so I got a blanket and we went to sleep in her mews. And the dream started all over again. I was lying in the straw with my eyes shut and this silver cobweb hanging in the air in front of me. It was the maze, the Troytown. Then the song began, the words beating at me like a drum, and I was pulled into the web, running the maze, until I arrived at the centre. Then everything went dark.

'It stayed dark for a while and then I was in the cavern again, under the Wilderness. The light shaft was burning bluish, like moonlight, or rather, like the light in The King of Efland's Daughter. But it's the owl light and it shines right onto the stone tree. The owl woman was there.

'Then things began to run like a film. Dad emerged out of the tunnel and stood looking round. He found the light shaft and worked out where the light would fall. He lifted the stone tree and took the cup out of the hole, like you saw, Dick. The owl woman seemed very agitated, but Dad couldn't see her.

'Then the scene changed to the study. Dad had the cup and was looking at it by the fire when I saw Sylvie at the study window. She could see him and there was such a smile on her mouth. She saw me too and signed with her fingers so I couldn't move, couldn't tell Dad she was there. He put the cup in the priest-hole in the fireplace, then the scene changed again. It was night, up by the tower, and he was looking down into the pool with the cup in his hands. The owl shrieked, he let go the cup and followed it down.'

'But why here? Why did you have to come down to Bridge Cottage?' Merle asked.

'I think … I think because of the Hollyman,' Vicki said. 'It's he who sorts things out in the old story …'

'So you came to me …?'

Vicki looked up at him in silence, then

'Yes,' she said. 'I did.'

Back in the library Dick rolled his eyes.

'OK!' he sighed, 'So, Jacob found the cup. I suppose, if we followed Richard's diary right through, we'd come by how he did it, but there really doesn't seem to be any point. The damn thing's now in the pool and we have to get it out.'

'That seems to be it,' Vicki agreed.

'Gawd! It was much better when I just got fat and drunk at my desk in the Museum. All this practical stuff's making me tired! That's a bloody great pool! How the hell are you going to get the water out of it?' he began to chant, '*If fifty maids with fifty mops swept it for half a year, do you think, the Walrus wailed, they'd ever get it clear?*'

'*I doubt it, said the Carpenter, and shed a bitter tear,*' Merle aided and abetted Dick's court jester act. It helped Vicki, he could see she hadn't yet got over the dream, or Kate, or the knowledge that the she needed him. He was still feeling rather stunned by that himself, and coming so soon after the bust up over Kate. He would try to make it easier for her.

'Lewis Carroll'd turn in his grave,' Joe grinned, knowing what was going on, then, 'Vicki can you remember, in your dream, where it fell?' he went on.

She shut her eyes, '... Dad goes to sit on the stone seat. He sits there for a while. I can see the moon sinking. Then he gets up and goes over to the yew tree. You can see right down through the stone ring from there. The light's playing on the water, it's really beautiful.' She paused again. 'Now he's looking at the cup. No, at the light on it. There's something there, a white shadow, it reaches out to him ... Aaaahhhhh!'

Vicki had her arms over her head. Merle grabbed her, hugging her. Joe got the Rescue Remedy out again.

'It's all right, all right!' Vicki struggled out of Merle's arms, pushed away Joe's hand. 'It was just so loud!'

'What was?'

'The owl's cry. It went right through me.'

'Did you see how he fell?' Joe reminded her.

She closed her eyes. 'No. Can't see from that angle.'

'Damn!' said Joe. 'I expect it went right under the waterfall, the deepest place. I wish you could see for sure.'

'Sorry! No can do, angle's all wrong. You'd see much more clearly if you were down by the pool looking up.

'So, how're we going to do this thing?' Faye said.

'There's the old sluice gates, at the end of the pool, to drain off the water.' Joe said. 'But that's only good so far. We can drain the water off but it'll keep filling up again from the fall, probably almost as fast as it runs off. That's a big head of water.'

'I know how to sort that,' said Vicki.

'Eh?' Everyone stared at her.

'In the cave.'

'What cave? Where? You've seen it?'

Vicki nodded. 'A little bird took me there the other day.'

'What cave?' Dick repeated. 'I thought the cave was the place we went into the other day.'

'No, the cave where she died is up by the waterfall. A robin took me. I'd never been there before. I don't think anyone has.'

Everyone stared at her again.

Faye threw up her hands and sighed. 'Well … can we hear about it now?' she asked sarcastically.

Vicki made a face at her, not at all apologetic.

'It was the morning I got back,' she began. 'I went out for a walk and met a robin in the Wilderness. First, he led me to the old woodsman's hut and there was Dad. And the owl woman. That's when I first heard Dad had got the cup. The owl woman seemed pretty pissed about it. Then the wind came and blew her away, both of them disappeared. I came out of the hut and the robin took me up to the tower. I didn't really want to go but he was a very insistent bird! I climbed in the yew tree, like I did when I was a kid, and there, down by the pool, were Sylvie and Julian. He buggered off but she poked around in the water for a bit, glared up the fall and then went off herself. They never saw me. Anyway, then I got out of the tree and the robin kept on at me to go into the holly bushes that grow up by the rock there, so I did. You really have to really struggle with the branches, I got scratched to hell but, finally, there's the cave mouth. And then, something else stops you, like a force-field in Star

Trek,' she chuckled.

'But you got in?' Faye asked.

'Yes. The robin chirruped and field gave way, I literally fell in. The water flows down this channel which is divided by a slab of stone. He went and sat on the slab and it moved. The water changed direction and flowed down a hole in the wall and the sound of the fall stopped. He hopped up again and the stone went back the way it had been, the water flowed back down the fall again.

'Then I heard it the other day when we all went to the cavern under the Wilderness, but there wasn't any water then. But I think, when the water's diverted, it comes down the passage we crawled down. You know when you tripped over a hole, Dick? I'll bet that's a channel in the floor which takes it to the hole under the stone tree. The water runs into the hole and down to the village, to the well.'

'But that makes no sense of the story,' Dick complained. 'I thought she was killed in the cave, like you said before, and the water comes from there.'

'No. Think about the story again. The stepmother takes the cup and presumably that makes the water dry up, a drought, and the land becomes the wasteland. The daughter is killed and, where her blood falls, a new spring comes up. Then the Hollyman brings the cup back and everything's supposed to be all right again. And so it is, because bringing the cup back brings the *original* stream back. The one that begins from under the Wilderness. I saw that too when we were there. It's like the shaft you went down in your dream, only much, much further. There's a spring down there, deep within the earth. And that's the one the daughter served. That's why we do the ritual at the Troytown.'

'So the new spring is a sort of back-up job?'

'Yes, I think so.'

'So Jacob had the right idea in wanting to find the new spring and put it through to the village?'

'But the owl woman doesn't want that. She nearly blew my head off, while I was in the cave, when I just thought about it. She wants the old stream back. And the cup. Dad shouldn't have taken it. He found his way into the cavern following old Richard's cryptic clues and, of course, once there his passions got the better of him. He couldn't resist. Bloody archaeologists!'

'But … d'you mean to say no-one in the village knows about this cave?' Faye was incredulous.

'Nope.' Dick shook his head. 'Nor anybody else I ever heard. And Jacob never said anything.'

'In the village, people believe the cave is just a figment of the story, something made up to sound good.' Vicki said.

'That's right,' Vera put in.

'Isn't the cup perfectly safe in the pool?' Faye asked.

'I suppose …' Vicki stopped.

'But the owl woman wants it back,' said Merle.

'Yes. She does.' Vicki looked at him.

'So we have to drain the pool,' Joe said. 'And your robin friend seems to have given us the answer.'

'Will he let you in again, to turn the water off?' Faye asked.

'I think that's why he took me there.'

'Can you ask again now?' Faye eyed her. 'Be a good idea …'

Vicki laid back against the sofa again and shut her eyes.

'There's the gate, like the spider-web I saw in my dream.'

'Is the robin there?'

'Yes.'

'Ask him what to do'

Vicki shuddered. Merle looked at Faye, she shook her head. Joe sat very still. Dick found he was holding his breath.

Vera felt herself go cold, like an icy wind rushed past her. She looked at Vicki and it seemed she was enfolded in a shimmering white mist. Just then, the mist brightened and she was watching the film-show. Vera blinked a lot but the picture didn't change, in fact she could see more of it. She could see the spider-web Troytown-like gate hanging in front of her. Vicki moved forward and passed through it. Vera tried to move, couldn't. Then she heard the voice.

'Guard my gate through the ages,' it said. 'Let none but the blood take the water!'

Everything went dark and Vera lost consciousness.

Vicki was lying back on the sofa, she seemed asleep. There was a little smile on her face. Merle raised an eyebrow to Faye.

'She's OK.' She turned to Vera who was sat in the armchair by the fire, staring into space, a struck look on her face. 'This is the one we need to see to. Got your concoctions, Joe?'

Joe brought Rescue Remedy and Faye carefully opened Vera's mouth so Joe could put a couple of drops on her tongue. It worked a treat, she gasped, coughed and came back to the world.

'Gor! Bugger me!' she croaked.

'It's OK, love,' Joe had his arm round her. 'How're you feeling now?'

'Bit better,' Vera came to slowly. 'Have y' got anything to drink, my throat's parched.'

Dick got her a glass of water. Vera sipped at it, gradually coming back into the room.

'What happened?' Faye asked her.

'It were weird!' Vera stated. 'I saw Vicki an' I could see the cobweb. Then she went through but I couldn't follow. Everything went dark and I heard this voice coming out o' the cave. It said "Let none but the blood take the water," and somethin' 'bout guarding the gate. Then it all went black until I found meself back yere.'

Faye turned back to the others. 'Did anyone else see the web, the gate? Hear the voice?'

'Nope!' Dick spoke for them all.

Merle kept his mouth shut. He had seen Vicki shift into the owl woman. But he wasn't going to say.

'So what does it mean?' asked Dick.

'Just what Vera said, I think. Only Vicki can go into the cave,' Faye stopped and looked at Vera. 'But there's a very close connection between you and Vicki, isn't there?'

Vera looked her in the eye, nodded.

'It's almost like you're Vicki's mother?' Faye continued.

There was a silence for a minute.

'I allus wished I was,' Vera said softly, 'off'n felt like I was. She'd come to me. Oh, she came to her mother too but she'd come to me. Mrs

238

Caroline asked me to come an' live here right after 'er come home from the hospital with Vicki, as nanny and housekeeper. I had charge of Vicki from when 'er was only a few days old. Mrs Caroline fed 'er 'erself but I did a lot of the changin' and bathin' and such like. We was all three so close. It was terrible when Mrs Caroline was killed.'

'You were called, I think, by more than Vicki's mother. You were meant to be a part of her life and you still are now, aren't you? Even though she's been gone from home for ten years? You still look after her, don't you?' Faye looked at Vera.

Vera nodded again.

'I off'n thinks of 'er. An' I'd never want no harm to come to her, specially now ...' Vera shut her mouth firmly.

'Yes.' Faye met her eyes. 'I know what you mean.'

'So ...' Dick brought them back to the main subject. 'Vicki is the only one who can, or should, stop the water. You heard what the owl woman said, only the blood may take the water. That also means change its course, stop it flowing. Julian and Sylvie, taking the water for the bottling plant, denying it to the village, are out of order. They are not of the blood.'

'She bain't goin' on 'er own,' Vera said.

Again there was silence.

'Do you think you can actually go into the cave with Vicki, to turn the water off?' Faye asked her, a frown on her face. 'I don't think you should try.'

'I bain't letting her go on her own!'

'But you might get hurt ...'

Vera's chin went in. 'I'm going. Make up yer minds to it.'

She held Faye's eyes for a long while. Faye finally looked away, shaking her head.

'I know you shouldn't go,' she said. 'But I know nothing will stop you either. For the gods' sakes, take care.'

There was an uncomfortable silence.

'You know,' Dick said, 'the water was given to the village to repair a drought brought on by the greed and arrogance of the stepmother and the weakness of the father. What Jacob and Sylvie have done is like that.'

'But Sylvie isn't Vicki's stepmother,' Faye interrupted.

'Not for want of trying!' Merle said caustically. 'In the story the stepmother's son wants to have the chief's daughter. Julian took on that role very early. Now he and Sylvie live together, are in cahoots. It's like the legend's playing itself over again.'

Faye's eyes narrowed, a twisted smile took her face. 'I think you're more right than you might know,' she said.

'No, Faye … I know!' Merle's voice was soft but bitter.

Faye met his eyes, looked away.

'Well' she said, 'we'd better play the game out then. Tomorrow we drain the pool.'

'I must phone Olive, let her know what's happening, where I am,' Joe said.

'Would she come over?' Faye suggested. 'I could do with some help. Neither of these two should do anything for a while yet and we'll all need something to eat later.'

'I'll ask her,' Joe went off to the phone.

Olive

'Hellooo?' Olive stuck her head round the stable-yard door, her voice echoed down the stone corridor.

'We're down here!' a voice came back to her.

Olive followed the voice down the hall to the library and stood in the archway, smiling tentatively. A tall, red-haired woman sat cross-legged on the floor by the fire, next to Vicki. It looked like they'd been talking. Vera was in a wing chair.

'C'mon in, Olive,' Vicki smiled at her. 'This is Faye.'

Olive came on into the room, nodded to the red haired woman. 'Joe said there'd been a lot of excitement over here. What can I do?' she said.

'Oh, there has indeed! And we'd be very glad of your help,' Faye answered her.

There was a slight pause, Olive noticed the woman had an American accent.

'But we're all OK,' Faye continued, looking at Vicki who gave her a quick nod. 'How's about you sit down and I fill you in on events?'

Olive looked around, took a cushion off one of the chairs and imitated Faye's position. It took her back to her college days to be sitting on the floor like this. Faye told her about Vicki's journey and all their deliberations about turning the water off from the fall.

'And tomorrow we drain the pool,' she finished.

'Do you really think you'll find the cup?' Olive asked.

'Yes.'

Olive reeled inwardly. Faye had told her the whole story. It sounded like dungeons and dragons stuff, not real life. But here she was, sitting on the floor in the library at Bridewell, with three women who all seemed to think this was as normal as going to the supermarket.

'It's OK,' Vicki watched her face. 'You really *are* here and it *is* all happening, but you're going to be all right. Joe'll be all right.'

'I don't know you at all,' Olive looked at Vicki defensively. 'The only times we've met have been very stressful. And you don't know me either. Just now, I'm not sure *I* know me. Does this sort of thing happen all the time for you? How on earth do you manage to live?'

'Well no, not all the time!' Vicki chuckled. 'But I grew up with it, this house, the village, the legends, they're in my blood. Dad was part of it too, but it runs best in the women of the family. My gran was well guardian before me. She was the daughter of the house, her husband took her name rather than she take his. That happens in our family, so the name is never lost.'

Vicki stopped, looking troubled.

'It's OK love, it'll work out,' Faye put an arm round her.

Olive frowned. She wasn't quite sure what Vicki had meant. Joe had said she was back with Merle now … light dawned. If Vicki married Merle then he would take her name, come to live in her house. It sounded to Olive like he would be losing himself. Oh! she thought, so that's what all this is about!

'It's more'n that though,' Vera was awake again and reading her thoughts. 'Mr Merle's name, Hollyman, is same as they call the wizard who comes to our lady from the wood. He be like the Green Man in the stories, the man Gowan cuts the 'ead off in that poem Mr Jacob used to tell at the Christmas fair. He carries the holly, and that's for the robin who kills the wren at midwinter and brings the sun back to life again. When Doctor Hollyman came yere, back in the sixties, the whole village got to talkin'. He bought Bridge Cottage. Legend says it was there, in the wood, that the holly man lived and her did cross the old bridge to go visit with him. An' what happens? Dr Hollyman is friends with Mr Jacob, and their chil'ren grows up together, an' Vicki does cross the old bridge to visit with Merle. Everyone bin watchin' out for summat to happen all these years.'

'I didn't know all that,' said Faye softly.

'Now you do,' Vicki's voice was bitter. 'Does it make more sense to you about why I left?'

'Surely,' Faye looked at her. 'You could've told me.'

'No, I couldn't! I wanted to bury it, have nothing to do with it, stop it happening. As long as I wasn't here it didn't happen.'

'But you can't stop it, you know that!' Faye insisted.

'I know!' Vicki muttered. 'Like you know Dad's death was engineered so I'd come back and take up the guardianship again.'

'Are you saying,' Olive broke in. 'Are you saying that all this … this magic … is working now and making us all do things. That it caused Jacob's death? Ughhh! That's horrible!'

The other three women sat silent, in sympathy with Olive's disgust and turmoil.

'It's not quite like that,' Vicki said.

'But it is!' Olive burst out. 'How can you bear it? It's like being a slave, an automaton! It's horrible, something else ruling your life. And it sounds like you can't do anything about it!'

'No, we're not slaves, Olive.' Vicki looked at her directly. 'We get born knowing what we are, what we have to do. I always knew. So does Merle. I made promises on my thirteenth birthday, and I knew what they were about, I knew it wasn't just some pretty village custom. And then, when things got difficult, I just upped and ran. I ran away, wasn't here to help Dad. Then Merle upped and ran too, in the opposite direction. We left great holes in the village, after we'd promised to guard the water. It's not surprising, what's happened. I tried, oh how hard I tried and just kept on trying, to be normal. Like trying to live a soap-opera life – but that's not where I am, not my country.'

242

Olive was staring. 'You mean you're happy about having your life mapped out by some Great Power,' she was spitting the words. 'Not having any free will, not being able to have a life?'

'I think we'm all got lives, me dear!' Vera said.

'And we certainly have free will – look what I've done with mine!' Vicki added.

Olive saw the wistful ache in Vicki's eyes, but something burst out of her. 'Oh! I don't understand! And I'm not sure I want to!'

Vicki reached out to Olive, touching her hand gently, 'But will you help us?' she asked.

After supper, Merle stayed on in the kitchen. He picked up a tea towel as Olive collected the dishes off the kitchen table and went to dry up. She had her back to him at the sink. He heard a sniffling noise.

'Are you OK?' he asked. 'You're not, are you? Come and sit down for a minute, tell me what's up, what's going on.'

Olive came slowly, sat opposite, peering at him.

'I'm scared,' she looked away. 'For me, for Joe, for all of you,' she stopped. 'All of us,' she amended.

'Is that it?'

Olive looked away again, swallowed, then …

'I'm afraid of her, of Vicki. She's not human!'

Merle's answer surprised her.

'No, ' he said quietly. 'I don't think she is.'

'And you can love her?'

'I think that's why I love her.'

Olive stared at him.

'She told me what she'd told you, about being born knowing her fate, her destiny, how what she did would affect everything connected to her. It really is like that, Olive. It's so for me as well. And you're afraid for Joe too, now, aren't you?'

'He knows about all this, doesn't he?'

Merle nodded.

'He was with you two while you grew up. And he can dowse and things, do the biodynamics,' she paused. 'I've known all that, in a way, ever since I met him. I've watched him. I've even helped him do stirrings for the garden. But it was always like playing for me. Oh, I saw the garden grow, saw how well his herbs and everything else do, but I always told myself it was just the soil, the climate, Joe's own green fingers … anything but magic.'

'Magic, for you, is something which has nothing to do with everyday life, not scientific, not real. Is that how you see it?'

'Of course,' Olive nodded. 'That's what everyone says.'

'And they laugh at you if you think otherwise?'

'Yes.'

'And now, you find yourself in the middle of a completely crazy adventure, surrounded by people who talk like escapees from a lunatic asylum or a horror film?'

She grinned ruefully, it was exactly what she thought. Suddenly Merle's sideways smile caught Olive, and she could see what Vicki saw in this otherwise unremarkable man.

'I felt a bit like that myself,' he went on, 'when I came back, after my marriage broke up, I'd been away a long time. I'd made myself live in the normal world, where ancient gold cups and women who shapeshift into owls are figments of a psychotic imagination. But they're not, Olive. This is as real as anything else in my, or your, life. When Vicki came back, and I met her again, it was as though all the time without her was unreal. When she came, I felt I'd truly come home.'

'What am I going to do?' Olive looked at him.

'I don't know. But I do know you can't pretend it's not happening. And you can't pretend Joe isn't a part of it, or try to make him stop. That's the real issue isn't it? Joe?'

Olive nodded again, looked away.

'We really do need you, if you will, to help us.' Merle caught her eye again. 'Everyone's going flat out to get the cup, before Sylvie does, and we need you to help us keep our feet on the ground. Even just to feed us and be an anchor here.'

'Vera's going to be involved too, isn't she?'

Merle nodded.

'She's really is like Vicki's mother?'

'Yes. In a funny sort of way she is.'

'And you want me to hold the fort?'

Merle grinned at her turn of phrase, it seemed to suggest she was feeling better.

'Yes we do. Will you do that?'

Olive got up, went back to the sink. She smiled at Merle over her shoulder. 'Come on,' she said 'Let's finish that washing up so we can get back to the library and find out what they're up to.'

Hardacre

'Who can that be, at this time o' night?' Vera heard the knock at the door before anyone else. She went off down the hall and opened it, to find DI Hardacre on the step.

'I'm sorry to trouble you, yet again. But I'd like to ask Miss Bryde some things. May I come in?'

Vera looked him up and down. Yes, she said to herself, he's all right. She opened the door wider and stood back for him to enter. He followed her down the stone corridor.

'It's that there perliceman again,' she announced as they entered the library.

Hardacre stood with his hat in his hands, doing his best to look hot and uncomfortable in the warm library, but his hooded eyes were everywhere. So this was Bridewell manor, he thought, and the famous thirteenth century galleried hall with its two Tuscan columns. It reminded him of when he'd visited Southside House, in Wimbledon, with the column in the drawing room where Lady Hamilton did her *attitudes*. I wonder if anyone did anything like that here? He hushed himself. Vicki was getting up.

'Come in, Inspector.'

Vera took his coat. He gave her his hat as well, thanked her, and came over to the chair Vicki was indicating.

'What can we do for you?' she asked. 'Are you on duty or are you allowed some refreshment?'

Hardacre sat himself down, eyeing the bottles on the table.

'I'll take a Talisker, if you don't mind.'

245

Vicki poured for him. He waved away the water jug Merle was offering.

'No, I'll take it straight, thank you.'

He sniffed the golden liquid appreciatively and took a sip.

'Well,' he began. 'As you already know, from the autopsy results last week, there were no signs at all of foul play. I told you that when we released Professor Bryde's body for burial. The post mortem said your father drowned. Accidental death. Knocked himself unconscious on some rocks and breathed in the water. But,' Hardacre looked at her quite directly, 'I've still been conducting my enquiries over the past few days. And, if I might be so bold, I think you know it wasn't an accident and that there *was* foul play, although it's nothing as can be proved.'

His eyes stayed with Vicki but he could feel everyone else in the room watching him. It was uncanny, the last time he'd felt anything like this was back in the Met with a very strange case. It had never really been solved, not officially, although he knew what had happened. Like now, no-one in their right mind would have believed him, so he'd kept his mouth shut. Now, he hoped to be let in on this secret. He watched Vicki glance at Merle, and then across to the American woman. He hadn't been given her name as yet. It was she who replied to Vicki's look.

'I guess he's OK, honey! Feels good.'

Vera nodded. Merle smiled. Everyone else seemed to relax then, even Olive Millar.

'Where shall I start, inspector?' Vicki smiled wryly at him. 'It's a tortuous old plot!'

'Shall I just do my job and ask questions?' Hardacre's face softened, at last he was being allowed into the inner circle.

Vicki nodded.

'Right then,' Hardacre paused, putting his thoughts in order and coming to the conclusion that jumping in at the deep end might be the best way. 'Do you know who killed your father?'

'Yes,' Vicki took a deep breath. 'I did.'

That made Hardacre blink. 'Tell me about it,' he said.

'I was asleep, in my flat in London, when I found myself in a lucid dream. I'm pretty used to that but, this time, I wasn't in control, I was being taken, held,' she stopped. 'Enchanted. I could see the person doing the enchantment and feel them trapping me. I was inside a glass case, one of those ghastly Victorian things they put stuffed birds in. This one held a barn owl. Next thing, I found myself inside the barn owl. My ... essence?' she stopped, looking at Hardacre to see if she'd used the right words. He nodded. 'My essence then, was animating the owl. The person enchanting me directed me, as the owl, to fly to the tower where my father stood. I wanted to warn him so I called out, but all that came out was the owl screech. It frightened him and he slipped, fell into the pool and drowned.'

'And who was it enchanting you, Miss Bryde?'

Vicki swallowed. 'Sylvie Villiers,' she said.

'Bloody woman!' muttered Vera.

'You have some knowledge of Mrs Villiers, Miss Gardner?'

'Humph!' Vera spat, then went silent.

'Go on, V,' Vicki touched her hand. 'He's a friend.'

'Well I known her now for a good few years, on and off like. She first come down yere when Mr Jacob opened up the coffin and found the bronze tablet what made his name. I think she was wanting to make 'er own name on that, but y' didn't give 'er no chance. Mr Dick managed to get her put off the team so 'er weren't botherin' us all no more. But 'twas a difficult time. Mrs Caroline got killed, and Mr Jacob was in a terrible state. And Miss Vicki didn't talk to nobody for weeks. But 'er was gone, and we didn't see no more of 'er for years. Then Mr Jacob went to the conference in Oxford and he met 'er again. I think they was seein' each other for a goodish while in London afore she up and took it into 'er head to buy Well Cottage. I dessay Mr Jacob said he was thinkin' o' buyin' it hisself, and renting it out. Mebbe she said why don't she buy it and then it would all be the same thing. I know'd she was set on getting' a place 'ere, and wasn't goin' to trust Mr Jacob to look after 'er. And right she were about that too.

'When she come down 'ere it put a stop to Mr Merle comin' up to dinner. He and the professor'd been seeing each other most weeks, real good friends they was. But then Mr Jacob seemed to cool off Mrs Villiers and Mr Merle was comin' up again most weeks. Then there was the rows, and the final one when she got him in the leg with the poker. But Pat Elworthy was saying she was already goin' with young Julian Courtney by then, and I did think 'alf the row was really about that.'

'And what did you think when Professor Bryde was killed?'

Vera looked away into the fire for a moment.

'I knowed it was 'er,' she said softly. 'With Julian's help.'

'Is that why you put the rag doll out where he would find it?'

'What?' Vera turned on him.

'Well,' Hardacre continued gently. 'I saw you do it. And you told me all about these poppets, is that what you call them?'

Vera looked to Vicki. Vicki's eyebrows went up.

'I did it for you,' Vera whispered. 'I thought mebbe he was coming arter you again. An' I know she draws on him for 'er power. If I could stop him up then, mebbe, you'd be safe and they'd leave you alone.'

'Oh Vera! I don't think it was me they were after. Just Jacob and the cup.'

'Much you know, honey!' Faye broke in. 'Sylvie may well be more interested in the cup, but Julian isn't. He's after you. You and Merle. Vengeance, honey, vengeance. He's not forgotten the humiliation he suffered after he tried to rape you. Word got about, didn't it, Merle? You made sure all your friends knew, didn't you? He hates you, both of you, and is using Sylvie to get his own back. Vera's quite right to protect you, you are in danger. Sylvie will have burned the poppet, taken the sting off Julian, but she knows what you tried to do, Vera. Now you'll be on her list too.'

'Plenty of motive here,' Hardacre said grimly, 'but nothing I can put to my bosses. They don't go for the psychic stuff.'

'But you do, don't you?' said Merle. 'How come?'

'It's a long story, maybe I'll tell you one day,' Hardacre grinned. 'But while what Miss Bryde, and Miss Gardner, are saying is out of my league, I can at least believe it.'

'Can we drop the Miss Bryde bit at least?' Vicki smiled to him. 'This whole thing's got too intimate for that. I'm Vicki.'

'An' you can call me Vera,' she followed Vicki's lead.

'And I'm Faye, Faye Morgan, originally from Seattle but now settled here.'

'And I'm Olive, and this is my husband Joe,' Olive was not to be outdone by the other three women.

'Merle,' he pointed at his chest.

'And I'm Dick, Dick Fischer-King, Jacob's assistant at the BM,' Dick was getting used to not stuttering all the time but it still felt unlike himself. Maybe I'm getting a new self, he speculated. 'But to get back to the point, I think Faye's absolutely right about Vicki and Merle being targets. Do you agree inspector?'

'If we're going all informal, I can't be having with inspector either! My name's Jack. But yes, I do agree, from what I've heard. And what I learned when I went to interview them at Well Cottage. And … you've had a break-in here you haven't reported, isn't that so?'

'Clairvoyant as well, inspector? Sorry, Jack!' quizzed Merle.

'Nay! I was lurking about that night, on the off-chance, and saw young Julian half carrying his mate into Well Cottage. And, peeking through the window in good police style, I saw Mrs Villiers patch 'em up. They'd come down the Greenway, so I put two and two together so to speak.'

'We did have a break-in,' Vicki affirmed. 'But we decided not to trouble you with it.'

'Didn't want to set off too many unexplainable hares with the police, eh?' Hardacre gave her an old-fashioned look.

'Too right!' said Dick. 'I mean, how do you explain that you already knew a couple of local lads were going to break in, and how and where. And that you lay in wait for them, and there was a fight, and a chase over the rooftop. I say,' Dick stopped, looking alarmed, 'this *is* unofficial, isn't it?'

'Aye! I'd not be wanting to put any of this in a report, I'm not too far off retirement and I'd like to keep me pension intact! But what were they looking for, and what did they get?'

'Somebody … Sylvie… got Dad's notebook.'

'And what will Mrs Villiers do with that?'

'That's the trouble, Jack, she knew Dad quite well and can work out a lot from his notes.'

'And she can overlook us,' Faye threw in.

'Eh?' Hardacre was nonplussed.

'Overlooking is sort of crystal-ball gazing,' Faye told him, 'only I dare say she don't need a crystal ball to do it. Anyone can learn to watch someone from a distance. The Americans did, do, a lot of it in the CIA.

They call it far-seeing.'

'And so do the Brits and the Russians,' added Dick. 'And some archaeologists do a similar thing, to look into the past, to find where to dig. Like Bligh Bond at Glastonbury or Schliemann at Troy. But everyone keeps the lid on it or the media would have a field day! There's lots of debate about Schliemann being a con-man, always good meat for yet another pop-archaeology book! And the same goes for Bligh Bond. But we wouldn't know what we do without 'em. And both used forms of far-seeing or dreaming to get themselves started.'

'Well, there's cases of us policemen using psychics to help us and, like you, we keep them under our hats. But I don't think there's going to be any way I can use what you've told me to get justice for you over Mrs Villiers and Julian.'

'I don't think justice, in it's usual sense, was ever what I, or any of us, wanted,' said Vicki. 'Justice too often means punishment, revenge, and there's already been quite enough of that! But we're, er, constrained by what our legendary ancestor wants us to do. The owl woman has her own agenda and we've already messed with that too much, beginning with me absconding and running away because my love life didn't seem to be panning out as I wanted. I think that's the real reason my father had to die. Nothing else would bring me back. Sort of cutting the Gordian Knot so to speak.'

'That sounds so harsh!' Olive burst out.

'Yes, it does, doesn't it? But that's often how it is in this sort of stuff. It's so much easier if you're born an innocent and remain that way all your life. You don't have to take on these, er, responsibilities if you don't know they exist but, once you do, if you try to run away it all catches up with you, and places and people get hurt. And that really makes the gods cross! So,' Vicki finished, 'we're after a righting of wrongs, but not justice. And my father and I set up a lot of the wrongs that need righting so, although I absolutely loathe Sylvie and Julian, I can also see that it isn't altogether their fault. They're tools to get me back where I promised to be on my thirteenth birthday, damn it!'

'So what happens next?' Hardacre asked. 'Where are you going from here? What does this owl person want?'

'Owl woman,' Dick corrected him. 'She's Bridewell's legend and the ancestor of the Bryde family, the Big Boss,' he grinned at Vicki. 'She wants her cup back. It seems Jacob found it and took it. He'd always been obsessed with the thing ... well, so was I! It's pretty spectacular to find a real-live grail cup, and a gold one at that, if you're an archaeologist.'

'What's the cup got to do with it all, apart from its obvious value, and the kudos which would pertain to its finder?'

'The cup is the symbol for the water, and the daughter of the Bryde family is its keeper as well as being the protector of the water. Jacob found an old rigmarole, written about the time this house was first built, which tells it.'

Dick passed Hardacre the piece of paper.

From blood the water rises, let the water flow through the blood.
The blood of daughters buys healing for the parched earth.
The blood of daughters is guardian of the well.
The blood of daughters holds land and water for all time.
This gateway I give to you to hold in trust for all generations.
Death by water is the fee if ever water is betrayed.
The land will die, the wasteland come again.
Let none but the blood take the water.

Hardacre read the words aloud. Olive gasped, it was the first time she'd heard them. Joe and Vera looked grim.

'Sounds like Jacob got his come-uppance pretty straight, don't it?' Faye said dryly. '*Death by water is the fee if ever the water is betrayed.* And he betrayed it, from what you've told me.'

'I'm afraid you're right, sister,' Vicki grimaced. 'This latest little pageant is the original story updated. The water came back when the cup was replaced. Looks like that's what we've got to do now. When you came in,' Vicki looked at Hardacre, 'we were just making plans to get the cup tomorrow.'

'Might I help with that too?' Hardacre asked tentatively.

'Yes Inspector Jack. Provided you do exactly as we say,' Vicki said plainly. 'This is dangerous. Magic really does work. And you're the sorcerer's apprentice among us.'

'I'm good at following orders where I respect the giver,' he looked her in the eye. 'You tell me what I'm to do. But I warn you now, if there's any fighting I'm terrible likely to forget and muscle in to help!'

'Well, you be damn careful about that, Inspector Jack!' Vicki admonished him. 'It's just what could get you killed, and maybe us too.

Fools rush in where angels fear to tread!'

'Right you are, Guv!' Hardacre pulled his forelock, grinning.

Finders Keepers

HARDACRE

Hardacre woke up very early, wondering where he was. The room was strange and it didn't feel like his own bed. He turned over and found himself nose to nose with a small black cat. Her green eyes twinkled at him and she began to purr.

'How did you get in here?' he asked her, but all she did was lick his nose. He tickled her under the chin.

'I'd better get up,' he told her, after a few minutes.

He pulled the dressing gown Vicki had lent him round his body, one of Jacob's he assumed, and went round checking the doors and windows. All were shut. It was a mystery. He turned back to the cat but she had one leg skywards, doing her toilet, and no intention of offering him any solutions. Hardacre gave it up and went to run a bath. Later, dressed, he followed his nose and the coffee smell down the stairs to the kitchen.

'How do I get in touch with you if anything happens?' Olive was asking. 'You will take the mobile phones, won't you?'

'For what good they are around here,' Vicki laughed.

'It's impossible to get a signal,' Olive agreed. 'I can never reach Joe when I want him or else it's always breaking up.'

'I've got a satellite phone,' Hardacre wrote out the number. 'You'll definitely be able to reach me on that,' he said.

'Thank you!' Olive smiled appreciatively. 'I don't think I'm up to all this psychic lark, as yet. In fact, I'm not altogether sure I want to be. It's reassuring to have some nice modern technology to fall back on in case my far-fetching doesn't work!'

'Too right!' Hardacre agreed. 'All these witches and warlocks and whatnots are way out of my league!'

Olive waved them off to the tower. The house felt cold and empty all of a sudden. She jumped out of her skin as something soft touched her ankle and, looking down, saw Hecaté staring up at her, purring. Just behind were Goldy and Shadow. Olive shut the door. The cats led her back to the kitchen from where she could see both the drive and the track to Tower Moor. And the phone. For the sake of something to do she put the kettle on.

'I'm going to be awash with tea,' she told the cats. It seemed they grinned back.

'We should have a cat,' she told them. 'Joe would like one, I know. I don't suppose any of you are going to have kittens?'

Olive was certain she heard a voice inside her head saying 'No'. She stared at the cats, they were distinctly grinning.

'Any Cheshire ancestry?'

Again there was the feel, yes that was the word for it, feel of '*No*' inside her head. She sat down at the table forgetting all about the tea, what was going on? Nothing like this had ever happened to her before. The cats jumped up onto the table and sat looking at her. She noticed their eyes weren't blinking, they were very still, intense. Olive shook her head, for a moment there it seemed she'd seen Joe and Dick going down to the pool.

The little ginger cat, Merle's Goldy, patted her hand with a paw. Olive looked up and the cat caught her eyes again. It was like watching a film. There was Joe clambering down, reaching back to help Dick. She watched them arrive at the end of the pool and begin hunting through the tangle of dead undergrowth, looking for the sluice gate.

'Speak to him!'

Olive shook her head again but the feeling-sound didn't go away. Goldy was staring at her, eyes like saucers.

'You want me to try to speak to Joe?' she asked the cat.

'Yessssssssss!' The feel was sibilant, almost a hiss.

Olive pulled herself together and found the picture of Joe again in her mind's eye. He was looking back towards the house, slightly puzzled.

'J-Joe?' Olive tried thinking the name. Immediately the response came back.

'Olive? Is that you?'

'I th-think so!' she stuttered mentally.

'Hey! This is great. Hang on!'

He turned to Dick, she could see his lips move but not hear what he was saying, then,

'Olive?'

'Mmmm?'

'You are receiving me! This is wonderful. I just had to tell Dick what was going on. If you can transmit to me then that's great. What happens for you?'

'I can see you. It's a bit fish-eye-lens-like, but clear. I can hear you when you think to me but I can't hear when you speak to Dick. I just see your lips move. It's like a Technicolor silent film!'

'Can you keep watching?'

'Ye-es, but I'm not sure I can watch out here at the same time. I want to try something. I'm going to sort of hang up on you now, look around here, out the window and things, and then try to come back to you. Is that OK?'

'Sure! I'll be here. Just don't shout if I look like I'm standing on the edge of a cliff!'

'OK!' Olive opened her eyes and it was as if she had hung up the phone.

She looked back at the cats, they had smiles on their faces and were purring loudly. She looked out the window and her heart jumped into her throat. Sylvie and Julian crept into the yard and stopped. This window was the only one which looked that way and it seemed Sylvie knew, and was counting on it not being occupied. The window panes were small, there was no light on in the kitchen. If she kept still Olive knew they wouldn't see her.

She felt barely sheathed claws touch her hand.

'I know!' she thought to the cats.

'Don't think!' the command came into her mind. 'Mind blank! Mind blank!'

Olive stopped thinking. She stopped breathing too, just for good measure, and sat like a shop dummy, her mouth slightly open, watching.

Sylvie and Julian stood talking for a moment, heads close together, then slunk round the side of the house to the track up to the tower.

'Mind blank!' The command came again forcefully and she realised she'd begun thinking again. The barely sheathed claw was still on her hand, after a few moments, it lifted.

'Now!' came the command.

Olive flicked her eyes shut and straight away she could see Joe and Dick struggling with the sluice gates. She desperately wanted to shout but they looked like they were in a precarious position, so she gripped her hands together tightly and screwed up her face, determined to wait until it was safe. It would take Sylvie and Julian a few minutes to get to the tower. Unless she's got a bloody broomstick, Olive swore to herself. She waited until the water poured out the sluice gate and Joe and Dick were climbing back up, then she called.

'Joe!' she tried her best not to do a mental shriek but his head came up suddenly and she knew she'd been loud.

'What is it?'

'Sylvie and Julian. They just appeared. Went off down the track to the tower. It was a few minutes ago, I had to wait while you finished with the sluice-gate.' It all seemed to come out in a rush.

'OK. We'll tell the others. You keep watch, Olive.'

'Joe! Joe! Don't go yet. Try to call me back will you? We don't know if I can receive you without sending first.'

'Good thinking, Batman! Hang up, I'll try and call you.'

Olive hung up, opened her eyes and sat waiting anxiously. Hecaté tapped her with a paw.

'Eyes closed! Eyes closed!' she heard in her head.

With her eyes closed she could see Joe again, and hear him.

'Phew! Where'd you get to?'

'I didn't know to shut my eyes. Hecaté told me.'

'Hecaté? No, don't bother, tell me all later!'

'But I can't keep my eyes shut and watch out here!'

'Oh! No. Ummmm...'

'Hang on, Hecate's pawing me again.'

Olive 'slipped the link' and heard the cat in her head. Then ...

'Joe?'

'Yes?'

'Hecaté says, "I listen Joe. Tell you". I think that might work.'

'It will if she says so! Got her whiskers screwed on, that cat! Bye for now, love!' And Joe was gone.

Olive opened her eyes and sagged in the chair. She felt woozy and disconnected.

'Eat! Drink!' Goldy told her, so she searched through the cupboards, found the cake tin and ravaged her way through Vera's vanilla buns, with cherries on top, and a glass of milk. Then she cautiously crept to the window and peered sideways along the glass. She could see nothing, she turned to the cats.

'Can I go out?' she asked them.

'Wait!'

Olive came back to the table and shut her eyes. Immediately she found herself watching Merle and Julian. It appeared they were starring in what looked like a wall-to-wall action movie of the Bruce Willis kind.

JOE & DICK

'What d'you think of it all so far?' Joe asked Dick as they went to find the sluice gates. Vicki, and the belligerent Vera, had dropped out by the tower, Merle, Faye and Hardacre by the pool.

'Dunno!' Dick grinned. 'Never been in anything like it before.'

'I remember when you first came, Jacob brought you out to the walled garden. You'd dowsed before, hadn't you? Why didn't it work for you that time?'

Dick stopped and looked at Joe.

'Don't you know?' he said.

'Huh!' Joe began walking again. 'Love at first sight was it?'

'No. Second sight. I'd seen her face before in a silver bowl belonging to an old witch down at Kitnor.'

'You met Lilly Clocks?' Joe stopped in his tracks.

'Uh-huh. When I was doing my PhD research. She invited me into that gingerbread cottage of hers, *and* gave me bloody gingerbread for tea. Read my mind.' Dick laughed grimly. 'Then she made me look in her silver bowl. I saw the Wilderness, Bridewell Manor. And Vicki.'

'And you've lived with that, or rather without that, ever since? I'm surprised you're still here … in a way.'

Dick stopped, looked at him. 'I'll never be anywhere else, Joe. Especially now Jacob's dead.'

'Mmmm …!' Joe grunted, looked away.

They carried on to the far end of the pool and clambered down the gully beside a small fall which took the water into the next pool. It was three foot wide by about ten deep and the water came down fast. They got wet. Joe was glad, it stopped the conversation, he wasn't sure he wanted to go any further down that road, at least for the moment.

'Where is the blasted thing?' Joe swore.

They hunted through the soggy drift of last year's bracken and eventually found the sluice-gate. The latch was rusty, clogged up with mud and debris, and they were working away at it when suddenly Joe stopped. Dick watched, then Joe came back to him.

'Olive can somehow see us. And she can talk to me!' Joe's face was all lit up.

'That's good,' Dick said.

'Yes.' Joe grinned delightedly.

They carried on working and finally got the sluice gates open. The water poured through.

'Bunk me up!' Dick said. Standing on Joe's shoulders he could see the water level in the top pool sinking fast. The fall was gone. 'Vicki's managed to shut off the spring,' he said as he climbed down. 'It'll be flowing through the cavern now. Love to see it.'

He got down and they began the return climb.

'What we really need is a Lady of the Lake to stick her arm up, covered in white samite of course, and wave the cup at us!' Dick said into Joe's back.

'Wouldn't be very white coming up through all that mud,' Joe nodded his head at the greenish-grey sludge around the edges of the pool. 'Looks more like the great, grey, green, greasy Limpopo river to me! And get the pong!'

'Yuck!' Dick screwed up his nose. 'And we, or at least Merle, has to wade around in the stuff looking for the cup.'

'Life is very simple,' Joe pulled a pious and solemn face, 'But nobody said it was easy!'

'Grrrrr! That's awful.'

Dick thumped him in play-fight and they began mock-wrestling then, suddenly, Joe's head went up and he stood stock still. Dick waited, holding his breath.

'It's Olive!' Joe's face was grim. 'The proverbial's about to hit the fan! Sylvie and Julian just went past the house, heading for the tower. C'mon!' and Joe began to scramble back up the gully.

'Shit!' Dick crammed his specs back on his nose and followed as fast as he could.

VERA

Vera stood behind Vicki, shuffling her feet. It was cold, and daylight, and she was having second or third thoughts about the whole thing. Trouble was, she couldn't stop now. She knew that because she'd grown up with magic, albeit little magic like making poppets, herbal tisanes, bits of gardening or helping the dough to rise. This was rather bigger than all that and she wasn't really sure when she had agreed to it.

'*When you got born, woman!*' she heard inside her head.

'Backside!' she replied mentally, but it didn't do any good and she felt the chuckle tickle her brain again.

They were at the mouth of the cave, inside the holly bush. It had looked impossible but, somehow, Vicki had found a way through. Now she stood in front of Vera, waiting.

Vera came back to earth as Vicki touched her arm.

'I'm going to go in. I want you to stay here.'

'All right,' Vera said, but I be comin' with you! she muttered under her breath.

'I mean it, Vera ...' Vicki looked at her. 'You are not to come.'

They held eyes for a moment, then Vera looked away.

'I mean it ...' Vicki insisted.

There was silence between them, then Vicki turned away and took a deep breath. Now Vera could see the cobweb, silvery and shining, hanging in front of her. Suddenly it flashed blue-white, half blinding

258

them, and Vicki fell over the threshold. Tentatively Vera put her own foot where Vicki had been. Unlike her vision, there was no resistance. She followed.

It was warm inside the cave, soft light came off the walls. Vicki went straight to the water channel and knelt beside the stone, trying to move it. Vera crept closer.

At first, it wouldn't budge, then a movement from the back of the cave caught Vera's eye. Something came towards Vicki and, as Vera watched, she began to sparkle. She bent to the stone again and, suddenly, it was free. The water splashed up into Vera's eye, her vision changed and she could see.

With her right eye, into which the water had splashed, she could see the owl woman, the creature that had shapeshifted into Vicki, that Vicki had become. A tall white shape, with a heart-shaped face and great yellow eyes, surrounded by feathers, like eyebrows in a full circle. The nose was a beak but the mouth was human.

With her left eye she still saw Vicki, as she always was but with the sparkle.

The owl woman turned on her.

'What are you doing here, daughter of earth?' she hissed. 'You are not blood! You shall not draw the dew!'

Vera stood stock still, unable to move. The owl woman lifted an arm, a wing, and fingers grew out from the ends of the flight feathers. She pointed at Vera.

'Tell me,' she whispered. 'Which eye do you see me with?'

Vera's heart stopped still. Her hand moved without volition, pointing to her right eye.

There was a soft sound, like the "phutt!" of a damp squib, and the world went dark.

HARDACRE

Hardacre clambered his way down the steep stone staircase in the wake of Merle and Faye. He cursed as his feet threatened to take off without him. There's no way, he muttered, clutching at the wooden handrail, I can emulate these young people, skipping lightly down the precipice like bloody mountain goats.

259

Joe and Dick had scampered off ahead, down the precipitous steps, to fix the sluice gate. Damn it! he thought, Joe's my age, he ought to have to be as careful as me.

Hardacre arrived at the bottom, puffing, and pulled out his pipe. Don't suppose that helps with all this gadding about, he scowled, but I need a smoke, and some perspective, this is far too damn real for my liking. But I wouldn't have missed it for the world, he added. These were real people using their hunches, knowing things without logical reasons, and actually living their lives on this basis. He was quite envious.

He stopped at the edge of the pool. It was a strange, beautiful place. The black stone ring stood out. The cliff behind was shot through with lines of crystal, white and red. It reared up fifty feet above his head. He stood looking up at the top of the fall where the narrow ribbon of water fell twisting down like Rapunzel's hair. My! Getting quite fanciful, aren't we? he shook himself. But it wasn't really surprising, these people lived inside a fairytale and seemed to take it as normal. A part of Hardacre wanted that too and it was knocking in his head for attention.

As he looked up at the waterfall his vision suddenly blurred, then came back into focus and he was seeing Jacob fall, hearing the owl call out. It sounded like human speech, 'sheee-ee! sheee-ee!' He saw Jacob look up as it swooped over his head, saw his feet slip out from under him, and watched him follow the cup down into the pool. Jacob never called out.

'Merle! I saw it.' Hardacre shouted. 'He dropped the cup just before he fell. It came straight down by the ring, right where the fall comes through to the pool.'

'You saw?' asked Faye.

'Er, yes, I suppose I did,' Hardacre mumbled.

'So I should be heading right under the stone ring, when I can get in there, is that right?' Merle asked.

Hardacre pulled himself together. This was just like taking evidence, he told himself.

'Yes.' He shut his eyes. 'The cup went straight down. It fell through the water curtain, and into the bottom pool. There,' he pointed.

They watched. Suddenly the flow lessened, then stopped altogether and, at the same moment, there was a triumphal shout from Joe and the water level began dropping rapidly.

Merle pulled on his waders and went into the water, prodding his way with a stick, checking the bottom at each step. The water was slimy and the weed already beginning to smell. The mud sucked at his boots. It was silent, no birds, no wind, only the soft squelching of his feet. He felt as if he'd been walking forever.

He made for the stone ring. The bottom sloped gently towards the fall, making a basin some eight foot deep by fifty across. You don't notice how big it is when it's full of water, Merle thought. The rhododendrons at the edges, which normally had their lower branches in the water, now dripped from a couple of feet above the mud, making a quiet 'plish! plish!'

The stone ring towered over him. Without the water flowing through the hole in the rock looked huge and dark and empty. A gateway to hell, he thought grimly. He looked back, Faye and Hardacre waved.

Merle stood quiet for a moment. Where was the cup? He felt tendrils of himself, like root-threads, reaching out, searching the mud. Something pinged inside. There! He could feel it now. He crouched down and pushed his hands into the mud and pulled it up. He turned back to the others holding it aloft.

Just at that moment the waterfall started up again. Merle turned and Julian's fist landed squarely on his chin.

Hardacre saw Julian. He tried to grab Faye's arm and shout but nothing happened, his vocal cords were paralysed and his arm wouldn't move. He managed to turn his eyes enough to look at Faye and found her standing stiff, staring, mouth open, eyes fixed on Julian wading out into the mud towards Merle. Hardacre tried again to move but his feet wouldn't obey him. He looked up.

Sylvie stood at the top of the fall. Despite the distance he could see her clearly, she was smiling and pointing her finger at them. Out of the dim mists of childhood he remembered his mother saying 'Don't point! It's rude!'. Now he understood. Rude had nothing to do with it, Sylvie had transfixed them. Damn! he thought, what can I do? In despair he called out mentally to whatever might be listening.

He'd never had much faith in the Methodist god of his childhood but he prayed there was something out there now. And his prayer was answered. Something heard. He felt a current going through his body, like warm water in his veins. Something took hold of his arm and raised it, stretched out his first finger and pointed it at Sylvie. He watched as the bright light ran out, in slow motion, from the end of his finger and hit Sylvie right in the middle of her forehead. She fell down.

Suddenly his limbs were free and he crashed into the mud. Faye staggered, reached to help him. They looked to Merle.

The water was pouring through the stone ring again. It was up to knee level on the two men fighting in the pool, covered in mud and slogging it out, neither seeming to have the upper hand. Hardacre made to go and help.

'No good!' Faye pulled him back. 'By the time you could get there, even if you could keep your feet, it'd be all over.'

'Times like this,' he grunted, 'I wish we carried guns!' Then he realised that if the water was coming back Sylvie must have overcome Vicki.

'Vicki!' he shouted into Faye's face. 'We've got to get up there! Help her!'

'That's right!' Faye gave him an old fashioned look. 'She's the one we can help. Are you OK now? Up for it?'

Hardacre swallowed, nodded. Faye set off back up the stone staircase. He tried gamely to catch up.

MERLE & JULIAN

Merle reeled back into the water. Somehow he managed to hang onto the cup as he went under. He pushed it down the front of his waders, a small, hard lump against his stomach. He could see Julian's face distorted through the swirling water and scrabbled back, holding the last of his breath until he was under the fall. The water poured down his neck.

'Shit! Vicki! Where are you...?' his mind screamed. Nothing answered.

He tried standing up and Julian hit him again, banging him back into the rock-face. The cup slipped lower into the trousers part of his waders, crushing his balls. He crumpled over, then pulled himself upright again.

He ducked the next blow and Julian's fist slammed into the rock. The pain stopped him and he fell backwards groaning. Merle took his chance and gave Julian a left-right to the face, getting him on the eye but missing breaking his nose. Merle pushed himself away from the rock face. The water was up to waist level now, fast, muddy and swirling, threatening to take both men off their feet. Julian flung himself onto Merle.

They fell, went down to the bottom of the pool. Merle could see nothing, the water was thick with mud churned up by their feet. He gripped Julian's neck as hard as he could. Julian's hands were round his own throat. Merle's lungs were bursting, bright flashes coming before his eyes. There was a jerk as they hit the bottom, Julian lurched back away from him and loosened his grip. Merle flung his arms up between Julian's and burst free.

He kicked out for the surface. The water swirled around his shoulders as he clung to the rock under the fall, gasping for air. There was a splashing and Julian was beside him. They grappled each other again.

'I'll have you!' Julian hissed, his lips pulled back from his teeth in a frenzied snarl. He slammed Merle's head against the cliff face.

'You have her!' He took Merle by the collar.

'You have money!' His fist smashed into Merle's face.

'You have success!' Julian pounded him on the rock again.

'But it all goes once you're dead!'

Then Julian took Merle by the throat again and pulled him towards the deep water.

Merle stopped resisting and flung himself down on top of Julian, dragging him under. The water helped. Julian lost his footing. Merle kicked out for deep water. Julian was unable to direct himself. And loath to let go of Merle.

Merle sensed the rock and twisted so that Julian smashed right into it. The shock loosened the hands on his throat and Merle turned Julian and smashed his face into the rock. His body quivered. Merle smashed him against the rock again. Julian went limp. He hung in the water, mouth open, eyes staring.

Merle let go of the body and allowed himself to float up to the surface on his back, gasping and coughing. Joe's face hung over his for a moment and then the lights went out.

'He's alive,' Merle heard Joe say to somebody as the world came back again. He lay on his side, in the old leaf-mould by the edge of the pool, and coughed up water. A sharp blow between the shoulder blades fetched the last of it out of him.

'Vicki?' he managed. 'Vicki? Is Vicki OK?'

'She's alive, rough, but OK,' Joe told him. 'Vera's bad though. The ambulance is coming.'

'Shit!' Merle tried to sit up but was pushed back down again.

'You stay there, flat out. You nearly drowned.'

'Julian?' Merle whispered.

'Dead,' Joe's voice was flat.

Merle subsided and lay still.

FAYE

Faye scrambled up the steps as fast as she could. She nearly fell over Sylvie's prone body by the waterfall and, just beyond, was Vicki, with Vera out cold beside her. One of Vera's eyes looked smashed. The water was still pouring down into the pool. Faye wondered how she was going to turn it off.

'Don't bother,' Hardacre came puffing up behind her. 'It's all over down there.'

'What?'

'Julian's dead. Joe's there. He and Dick are pulling Merle out. What about these?' He pointed at the bodies.

'We'd better cover them up!' she said, pulling off her coat just as Olive arrived with a bottle of brandy and as many blankets as she could carry. She gasped at the sight of Vera's face. Faye took a blanket and covered her up. Between them they made the injured women more comfortable. Dick arrived and sat with Vera.

'What happened?' Olive whispered.

'Accident!' said Faye curtly. Then she put her arm round Olive. 'Try not to worry too much,' she said more gently. 'She'll live. The doctors'll see to her. And Sylvie's out cold. With any luck at all she'll be that way for a good long while.'

Hardacre used his satellite phone to call the ambulance, and his colleagues. He knew it would be best, for all of them, if he brought the police in straight away. He was determined Merle shouldn't be charged with anything if he could help it.

'We got Merle out of the pool. Joe's with him now.' Dick told him. 'We left Julian's body in there. Was that right?'

'Spot on,' Hardacre said grimly.

The sound of sirens rang through the air and Hardacre went to greet his colleagues. The medics brought Julian and Merle up to the tower, confirmed Julian was dead, and began on Merle's broken arm, cuts and concussion.

Hardacre talked to the detective.

'Looks like there was a bit more to this case than we thought, at first,' he began. 'The professor had found this gold cup and, apparently, his ex-mistress wanted the bloody thing too. Crazy archaeologists!' he laughed.

'Reminds me of that Agatha Christie one, you know, with old Poirrot, out in Afghanistan or somewhere.'

'Yes,' Hardacre grimaced. 'This case looks just as bloody tortuous! I suspect the Professor and his ex-girlfriend fought over this damned cup, and he fell off the cliff. Miss Bryde and Mr Fischer-King found some notes in his diary, that set us all off and we came looking to see if it had gone into the water with him, when he drowned. Then Mrs Villiers and that toy-boy of hers turned up. She had a fight with Miss Bryde and the housekeeper, up by the waterfall. Mr Hollyman was down here, in the pool hunting for the cup. He'd just found it when, next thing we know, there's Julian Courtney, in the pool and going straight for him. There was a fight and Mr Courtney was killed. Mr Hollyman was badly injured, nearly drowned.

'And what's happened to Mrs Villiers?' asked the detective.

'Don't really know,' Hardacre said slowly. 'She appeared up here while we were down there, at the bottom. Stood there at the top of the fall, staring down at us. Then suddenly she seemed to have some sort of fit and fell down. When we got up here she was out cold on the ground, like you see her now. We thought it best not to move her, but Miss Morgan wrapped her round in blankets to try to keep her warm.'

The doctor came up.

'I want to get Miss Gardner and Mrs Villiers to hospital immediately,' he said. 'Mrs Gardner's probably lost an eye and Mrs Villiers is in a coma. I'm very concerned there might be complications, bleeding in the brain. Can you ...'

Someone screamed. Turning, they saw Sylvie, awake now and sitting astride Julian, shaking him.

'Naaaa! Naaaa!' she shouted, slurring the words. 'Wake up! Wake up. Not dead! Come back!'

The doctor rushed over and managed to get a sedative into her. She sank back in his arms. Her eyes were wild, staring. Suddenly they fixed on Hardacre.

'You!' she hissed.

Her right arm began to rise, she struggled to make her finger point at him. The doctor pressed her back down again, getting between her and Hardacre. He waved to the paramedics to come and put her in the ambulance.

Hardacre mopped his forehead and rolled his eyes at the detective.

VICKI

Vicki moaned and choked as Faye dripped brandy into her mouth. She shuddered violently.

'Vera?' she tried to sit up.

'She's alive,' Faye helped her. 'She's out cold, which is a good thing as I think she's lost an eye. No,' she put a hand on Vicki. 'She's in good hands. There's nothing you can do and, when I looked, she was away off with the fairies.'

'O god! What have I done?' Vicki pushed Faye's hand away. 'I need to get my wits together.'

'What happened?'

'Vera was trying to protect me. again. I ordered her not to come with me into the cave. I thought she couldn't, but she did.'

'What happened?'

'Vera saw the owl woman. I'd changed, she shifted into me.'

'Oh shit!' Faye stared. 'What else happened?'

266

'I turned the water off, or rather the owl woman did, through me and, just as the flow changed direction some of it splashed up into Vera's eye,' Vicki shuddered. 'I turned on her, she pointed to the eye and … and … I put it out.'

'Christ!' Faye wanted to hug her but held back. Vicki wouldn't bear being touched right now.

'Then suddenly the owl woman was gone and Sylvie was standing there, in the cave, watching. She laughed. "Look what you've done to your mother!" she pointed at Vera. I just saw red, launched myself at her. Much good did it do me. She pointed her finger and out I went, like a light. Didn't know any more till you found me.'

'But you weren't in the cave when I found you!'

'I don't know, Faye. I doubt Sylvie pulled us out. Well …' Vicki stopped. 'I don't know. She might have. She'd not want anyone to know where it was either.'

'But how did she get into the cave?' Faye said.

'I think, fear, it's sort of Vera's fault. Somehow *she* managed to get into the cave, with me. And that could have sort of loosened the gate, made it possible for Sylvie to follow too. As long as we were in there.'

'Shit!' Faye looked away.

'What happened here?' Vicki brought her back.

'Merle found the cup, held it up, and right then the water came back on,' Faye told her. 'Julian had snuck up through the bushes and gone in after Merle. The policeman and me tried to shout out, but Sylvie was up here by the fall. She pointed the finger at both of us, froze us. Then the weirdest thing … the policeman somehow managed to move his arm, or rather I think it was moved for him. Lightning shot out of his finger and hit Sylvie smack in the forehead. She keeled over and went out like a light. We were free. The policeman crashed into the pond. I pulled him up and he was mad to go and help Merle but I managed to convince him we'd be too late. Then he realised that if the water was back on that meant you were out of commission. He fairly galloped up the steps behind me, wheezing and puffing like a grampus! We found you and he got on his satellite phone, called the police and the ambulance, and here we are.'

'I'd wish I'd seen Hardacre putting Sylvie out.' Vicki said, flatly. 'Bet it stunned him a bit too?'

'There's been no time to talk about it,' Faye said. 'He's being very circumspect. There's more there than meets the eye.'

'Yes. There's a lot goes on in his head he doesn't talk about.' Vicki paused, looked at Faye. 'I like him.'

'So do I. And I think he's doing his best to save Merle.'

Vicki's eyebrows went up.

'Well ... Merle killed Julian. In a fight, I know, but I dare say there's all sorts of things in the rule books about that, even if it is manslaughter, or justifiable homicide, or something. Oh yes,' she nodded to Vicki, 'Julian was out to get him. I don't think he gave a shit about the cup. He just motored on out there and began to do his best to kill Merle. Damn near succeeded too.'

There was an ear-piercing shriek. They turned to see Sylvie trying to shake Julian alive. The doctor grabbed her but Vicki saw her catch Hardacre's eyes, her hand moved to point at him.

'Shit!' she made to get up and fell back.

'It's OK,' Faye helped her up. 'The Doc's shot her full of tranquiliser. That should keep her down for a bit.'

'She wanted to kill our Jack too,' Vicki whispered.

'Did you know she's that good?' Faye asked.

'Yes, I did,' Vicki shut her mouth tight, then, 'help me up! I want to see Merle.'

Merle lay on a stretcher. Faye left them alone.

'Oh, my love!' She knelt beside him.

'Do I have to damn near get killed for you to say the word love to me?' Merle grinned wryly and attempted to kiss her with his swollen mouth.

'I guess you do!' she said ruefully. 'I could try and change that, if you'd like?'

'I'd like,' he mumbled.

The paramedics came to load him into the ambulance. Hardacre followed.

'You're not going to put him in the same wagon as Mrs Villiers are you?' he asked them.

'No sir, not if you think it's best.'

268

'I do. He can go with Miss Gardner.'

'Can I go with them?' Vicki asked.

'I'd, er, rather you didn't, Miss,' Hardacre looked at her, his eyes caught hers, then Merle's. 'I'll be back to see you as soon as I've done with them,' he told her as the doors closed.

'There's nothing you can do,' Faye put an arm round her. 'C'mon, lets go home.'

Resurrection

You cannot be aware of what is beyond space-time
but you can walk in this dream,
in contact with the higher consciousness that is the real you …
It will find you …
Bob Toben
Space-Time and Beyond

Bridewell Revisited

Hardacre pulled up in front of the clock-house, got out and, from habit, locked the car. He didn't want to go in yet.

'I need a smoke,' he told himself. 'Put my thoughts together.'

He took out his pipe, walked up past the stables to the duck pond, and stood watching the water swirl in figures of eight through each of the basins of the little waterfall. Gentle, he thought, not like the other one. He'd watched the fifty foot fall crashing down on the two men fighting, it had damn near got them both. Man was still no match for nature if she decided she wanted to overwhelm him, he smiled wryly. But this pool was different. Looking up he noticed the tall, wooden, throne-like seat, half hidden amongst the reeds and bushes. He went and sat in it.

Sitting in the chair, his feet were almost in the pond. He felt like King Canute trying to stop the flow of the tide. Not possible, he told himself and sucked on his pipe.

A flutter of wings made him look up to see an owl blink at him from a branch opposite. He felt a tickle inside his head and the words '*Thank you,*' shone out at him. He touched his forehead with his pipe, saluting her. She flew off towards the Wilderness while Hardacre walked back to the house, cleaning out his pipe.

Hecaté came and twined round his ankles.

'Thank you,' he crouched down and stoked her ears. 'I feel quite

270

topsy-turvy. Rather like it was my own family,' he looked into the big green eyes. 'You know that, don't you?'

Hecaté blinked slowly at him.

'Oh … come on in Inspector-Jack,' Faye said bleakly as she opened the door to him. 'We're in the library.'

Vicki was installed on the sofa, bruised and pale but otherwise looking OK. Joe was in a wing-chair by the fire. Olive sat on the rug, hugging his knees. She looked shell-shocked. He'd heard about how she'd discovered her telepathic ability. That's changed their relationship, he thought.

He went straight to Vicki and she reached up to hug him. Hardacre deliberately took both her hands and smiled ruefully. She raised her eyebrows, then nodded.

'Sit down and tell us what's happening,' she let go of his hands.

Faye got him a Talisker, he sipped it slowly.

'The doctor says Sylvie has a subarachnoid haemorrhage,' he began. 'He says the probability is that it will leave her with an altered personality. If she lives, and regains consciousness which isn't necessarily likely. She could go off with a stroke any time. Or burst another blood vessel in her brain.'

'And how do you feel about that?' Faye asked.

Hardacre looked at them all. 'You mean because I did it?'

'Yes.'

'Strange,' he said after a moment. 'In all my years in the Force I was issued a gun twice. Both times I never even drew it. Now I've seriously injured someone. If I told my superiors about it they'd have me sectioned and I'd lose my job. Probably spend weeks and months with a psychiatrist. I suppose I would keep my pension, end up medically retired.' He paused. 'It makes me wonder how many "cases" are really about this sort of thing but nobody says anything. Nobody dares.'

'You're absolutely right,' Vicki looked at him. 'But I don't think it's anywhere near time to "come out" on that. People believe what they can, not what is really there. But, what about Merle?' Vicki asked. 'And Vera.'

'I wasn't able to have much of a chat with Merle, not in the ambulance, with the medic-bloke there listening and all. Merle did it very well, went quite light-headed, gibbering rubbish. They rushed him into A&E, but

271

I was able to have a couple of minutes alone with him. The doctor had already said he had a concussion and might not remember everything too well. I suggested to him, strongly, that he have a real good concussion and not recall a damn thing until I'd seen him. He grinned woozily, rolled his eyes and began jabbering incoherently again, so I think he got it. I'm going back tomorrow and will try to see him alone. I'll go straight there from home, first thing in the morning, not call in to the station before I go. That should shake off my colleagues.'

'You're not going to do yourself any harm?' Joe asked.

'Not me! I've been at this game too long!'

'Did you see Vera?' Olive asked.

Hardacre's face went glum. 'Only through the window. They wouldn't let me near her.'

'D'you think they'd let me in to see her?' Vicki asked.

'I don't know. They were pretty cagey. And they were going to operate straight away. If you do get to see her, tell her not to say anything, not until she's seen me. She probably won't anyway. A wise lady! Now,' Hardacre looked grimly at them all. 'What's the story about her eye?'

Everyone was silent for a time.

'Did you ever read fairy stories?' Vicki began.

Hardacre nodded.

'Did you read John Rhys' tale of the midwife to the fairies?'

Hardacre shook his head. 'Tell me,' he said.

'It happens at Samhain,' Vicki began. 'This woman had a maidservant who would spin by the light of the moon, when the Tylwth Teg, the Faer Folk, would come to her, and sing and dance. In the spring she escaped with them. The maid's mistress was a famous midwife and one night a man came to fetch her to his wife. He took her to a large cave, the finest place the woman had ever seen, and she delivered the wife of a fair child. The man brought her ointment to anoint the child's eyes but told her, on no account, to touch her own with it. Later, one of her own eyes began to itch and she rubbed it. Her finger still had some of the ointment on it and suddenly she could see in two worlds. With her anointed eye she could see that the lady was her Eliian, her maidservant, and that the cave was rough, and that Eliian lay only on a bundle of heather. With the untouched eye she still saw all the finery she had seen at first. Later, the midwife saw the man again, in the local market, and she asked him "How is Eliian?" He answered her, "Pretty well. But with what eye do you see me?". The midwife said, "With this one," and the man took a stick and poked her eye out.'

Olive gasped and hid her head in Joe's lap.

Hardacre sat quiet. 'And what was it that Vera saw?'

'The owl woman,' Vicki said.

'And how?'

'I told her not to come, but she followed me anyway. I don't know how that happened. I managed to turn the stone and, as I did so, the water splashed up and some of it went into Vera's eye. Of course, then, she could see the owl woman,' Vicki stopped, looked away. 'She could see me.'

Hardacre raised his brows.

'The owl woman had shifted into me. I was her.'

There was silence in the room.

'She … I … asked Vera which eye she could me with. Vera stood stock still, transfixed, but her hand moved of its own accord and pointed to the eye. I put it out. Then the owl woman was gone. I was alone with Vera who, fortunately, had passed out. Sylvie was there. I think, when Vera broke her way into the cave, the guards were weakened so, when Sylvie came, she was able to cross the gate. Anyway, she stood there now, laughing at me, at Vera. I went mad, tried to attack her but she just pointed her finger and put me out too. We think she must have dragged us both outside, she wouldn't want anyone to find the cave either, so that's where you found us, by the waterfall, dead to the world,' Vicki finished.

The silence was broken by Olive's sobbing.

'It's terrible, the way you have to live,' Hardacre said.

An Eye for an Eye

Dick led the way up the Greenway. Faye walked beside him in comfortable silence, adjusting her long stride to his shorter one. When they reached the road Dick crossed it and took the ancient cattle drover's way across

273

the moor. Faye climbed in his footsteps. Sessile oaks overhung the green lane, old and gnarled and full of faces. Faye looked about her, she felt good, this was the land that her bones knew even if they had been born in America. It was her father's land.

They reached the Firebeacon and sat with their backs to to the stone cairn at its summit, looking at the views. You could see for miles in every direction.

Dick pointed south, 'There's the Wilderness.'

'And the tower,' she added quietly.

Dick's shoulder rested against hers.

'See that valley?' Dick pointed back north. 'That's the way to the Kitnor stone. It's only about five miles, shall we go?'

Faye stood up and held a hand down to pull him up.

A couple of hours later they headed down the bracken-lined path through the wood. As they rounded a corner they came to the huge upturned root.

'It's like the guardian of the gateway,' Dick said.

Faye put her hand on it. 'Pass, friend,' she heard in her head.

Dick led her into the grove. There was a single stone at its centre. The sun, slanting through the trees, poured shadows and sunlight in stripes across the clearing so, at first, she didn't see it. Then the face came clear.

A stone head reared out of the earth.

Faye went up to it.

'There's a mark in his eye,' she whispered. 'It's the Troytown.'

'Yes.'

They sat down by the stone and Faye pulled out her flask, offered it to Dick. He took a swig.

'What happened to Vera frightens me,' he said, after a while. 'What if I accidentally saw the owl woman?'

Faye said nothing.

'I suppose it's unlikely to happen, once the cup's gone back,' Dick went on.

'Vicki has the Troytown in her eye. Like the Kitnor stone,' Faye told him. 'Vera didn't. That's why none of us could go into the cave except

Vicki. And she told Vera not to go. She knew something would happen. But Vera wouldn't listen.'

'What really happened?'

'You cannot see, walk between the worlds, without the Faer Folk giving you permission. If you take it without them giving it, then they will take your eye in payment.'

Dick was digesting this when Faye pointed across the grove, behind the stone.

'Look!'

Dick saw the bright lights, dancing between the trees, on the far side of the clearing. He held his breath but the vision didn't fade. He tried shutting his eyes. The lights disappeared and he was in the red-dark of his own head. When he opened his eyes again, the lights were still there, dancing in the grove beyond the stone.

'What does it mean?' Dick asked.

'Wait,' Faye said.

They sat silent together, beside the stone, watching the lights come closer, dancing and singing around them. One came close, stood on Dick's hand, and he felt something spit in his eye. Now Dick could see the dark fairy man clearly. He turned to Faye. She was smiling, she too could see the Arthur-Rackham-like forms.

'Yes,' she said. 'They gave me the gift a long while back.'

'Aye!' laughed the fairy man. 'Tis a strange bond, between thee and we, given by the witch-woman of Kitnor.'

Then he held out an acorn cup to Dick.

'Drink!' he ordered them.

Dick drank and offered the tiny cup to Faye. She took a sip, smiling, and passed it back to the Faer.

'Tis the loving cup!' the fairy man laughed again, and smacked them both on the cheek with his wand.

Dick looked at Faye. She shone. He looked down at his own hands and saw them shining too.

The fairy man danced away, leading his people back into the woods, and was gone.

Dick leaned towards Faye. She kissed him, opening his mouth with her tongue. He began to kiss her back, then gripped her hard and pulled her with him into the grass beside the stone.

Penny Woods

'See you for dinner!' Merle waved goodbye with his good arm. 'I'll call the solicitor now and get the final document done.'

Vicki was standing in the middle of the clapper bridge, looking across at the island, when Faye caught up with her.

'He's going with you, you know that, don't you?'

'I suppose,' Vicki smiled wanly.

They crossed the bridge and climbed up the rocky alley between high stone banks and the huge tree roots which seemed to hold the stones of the wall together.

'I'll bet it's like a whadi, when it rains,' Faye tried to lighten the mood, but Vicki only grunted and carried on climbing.

Vicki was thinking. She'd wandered through all the rooms at Bridge Cottage, with Goldy beside her, touching the walls, the furniture. Faye and Merle were in his study, discussing its rental. It's his home, she thought, and he's leaving it. For me. Because I cannot run away again. Because I have to take up the promises I made, and keep them this time. He is giving up his home and his name. For me. And for the water.

Sylvie was insane, certified, in a coma, waking occasionally like a little child, other times violent. There was no possibility of her recovering. Vicki was buying Well Cottage from her executors. Delagardie had written the old injunction into the deeds. No-one would hijack the water again. And she'd gone there, at last, after all these years, laying old ghosts to rest. She'd found the barn owl, smashed the Victorian glass case, released the owl. She and Merle had burned her body in the middle of the Wilderness the previous night. The spirit was set free.

She'd visited Vera, on her own. Vera was getting better but refused to have a false eye, despite the doctor's pleas.

276

'Bain't no point,' she said gruffly. 'I saw what I saw. I should have done as you told me. 'Twas my own fault. And the false eye would never work, you know that.'

'O Vera! I'm so sorry …' Vicki hid her head in Vera's lap.

'There now!' Vera stroked her hair. 'Don' y' take on so. 'Tis done now. An' I should a listened to y' when y' told me not to come. But I thought I knowed best. I only did it acorst I thought y' weren't strong enough on yer own. I should've known better.'

Vicki stopped on the wooden bridge, waiting for Faye. The path divided here. Straight on took you up through Penny Woods into the village. Left took you back through the Home Wood, along the path of the Owlwater, up to Bridewell Manor.

'That's a pretty place,' Faye pointed to a glade backed by stone cliffs. She arched her back, stretching after the climb, glad to have got alongside Vicki so they could talk again.

But Vicki said nothing, stood looking into the shadows of the oak tree which dominated the glade.

'Sit down?' Faye suggested.

Vicki hesitated again, then took a breath and went to sit under the oak. Faye's mind clicked into gear.

'Was it here?' she asked.

Vicki nodded. Faye put an arm round her.

Suddenly Vicki's head came up, her nostrils quivered. Faye smelled it too. Then they saw her. A young hind stepped out of the trees opposite. Her coat shone red, the sun glinted off her swollen belly. She looked near to dropping her fawn. The two women sat still as death.

'Your belly will hold the future, as does mine,' Vicki heard the hind say inside her head.

There was a rustle and an owl came to settle on the hind's rump. Surprisingly, she made no move and the two creatures stood watching the humans.

'I want my cup,' said the owl. 'Bring it to me.'

A cloud covered the sun. The hind tossed her head, turned and trotted, stiff-legged, back into the forest. The bird flew off.

'Did you hear?' Vicki asked.

Faye nodded. 'What are you going to do?'

'Dick wants to put it in the Museum. It's the find of the century. He looks almost as obsessed as Dad. Or Sylvie.'

'So ...?'

'It has to go back. You heard her.'

'And you have to resume your guardianship.'

'Merle knows that better than me, it seems.'

'In that he's giving up his home for you, renting it to me, yes.'

'And what about you? You and Dick?'

'Yup!' Faye coloured up. 'We're an item. We made our promises at the Kitnor Stone,' Faye told her about the Faer Folk.

'Appropriate! And you're going to live in Merle's cottage?'

'Yes, if I'm to help you manage these woods. But Dick will be in London, at least part of the week, doing Jacob's old job. And we both need our own space too. It's not like we're kids, just fallen in love. We have fallen in love, but our eyes are open. And I can go visit him in London too. I think I need that. I'm not like you, prepared to bury myself in the country for ever and ever.'

'I don't think I'll be doing that either. I've still got Vestry Street. I'll like to come up to Town too.'

'And Merle?'

'Yes,' Vicki smiled, thinking of how he had liked the flat.

'And you're willing to be here, with him, now?'

Vicki sat still, then,

'Yes,' she said. 'Yes, I am.'

Conception

Merle stood by the French windows in the study looking out across the lawn. The sun shone, but it was cold for the first day of May. Spring had gone. Summer was coming, even if it didn't feel like it today. The lease with Faye was signed. He'd moved out. He felt empty and full at the same time.

Vicki was sat on the rug with Hecaté, Goldy and Shadow, watching the dragons dancing in the fire.

'What did Kate come for?' she asked him.

He turned to her, coming back to the present, sat down beside her in the hearth.

'It's my mother's property, Barenton in Broceliande. Her family had a place there, in the middle of the wood. She let it to my uncle Everard, but he died last year and the notary had been trying to catch up with me. He found Kate. She came to give me his letter, and the deeds,' he stopped, looked at her, 'now it's mine,' he finished.

'I remember. Your mum used to tell us stories,' she looked at him, raised an eyebrow, smiling. 'Do you want to go there?'

'One day. Would you come?'

'Merlin and Vivien going back to the Fountains of Youth,' her eyes twinkled. 'Like our childhood games.'

'And Barenton is the real place ...' He watched her.

'Yes, I'll come. But you know I can't run away again.'

'I know. It means I can't leave here either, at least not for ever. But we could go to Barenton for a holiday.'

'Aren't you afraid I'll imprison you in the crystal castle under the lake?'

'No,' he chuckled. 'And I don't mind if you do.'

They sat listening to the fire crackle.

'We made a child last night,' she said at length.

'I know.'

'It's a girl.'

'I know that too ...' He thought of the old injunction, the blood of daughters, and the potential being in her womb. It was the inheritance. The beginning again, after Jacob's death.

'I used to dream of us being married, having children, happily-ever-after and all that. But I never saw where we lived. I always saw us as we were, as children, you coming to play at my house, me coming to play at yours. Grown-up isn't like that!'

'That's why I ran away. You wouldn't come and live with me. I didn't know, then, what it meant to give up everything. So I ran. Abandoned you, my home, the promises I made, everything.'

'You've come back, now?'

'Yes,' she said softly. 'What else?'

'I don't know … what else is there?'

'For us, nothing. We are this place. It'll be the same for our daughter.'

'Does that worry you?'

'No … because I can't stop it. But I can help her, try to make it easier for her, so she doesn't have to run away too.'

'Do you think you can?'

'We can.'

'I don't know, Vicki,' Merle's brow was creased. 'I don't know if we should. Perhaps all the running helped us, we'd have been useless, naïve if we hadn't fought and run, got it wrong. I don't know. I don't think I can see that far.'

'And the road to hell is paved with good intentions, eh?'

'Too right!' he grinned. 'And parents who know best are complete pains in the arse!'

'OK, I'll try and keep my mouth shut. You'll have to help!'

'I'll kick your ankle every time I see you with some useful advice on your tongue!'

Merle was laughing, he took her by the shoulders, she pushed back, they wrestled on the hearthrug.

Later, lying together in front of the fire, he curled a strand of her hair around his finger.

'And the cup?' he asked. 'Dick's writing a paper on the findings, he wants it on display in the British Museum. But the owl woman has demanded it back, hasn't she?'

'It does its work best in the dark,' Vicki said. 'In the shadows. As a rumour, a legend, a myth. Out in the light it causes strife, murders, thefts and greed. It's better back in the dark.'

'That's where she wants it too. She's told you, hasn't she?'

'Yes. I'll give it back to her next year, after the child is born. After her naming, at Lughnasadh. She's agreed to that.'

Hardacre brought Lilly Clocks with him to the naming ceremony. They stood together, to one side of the dining room, watching.

'Like the thirteenth fairy, so I am,' Lilly cackled quietly so none but he could hear. 'But I got a good gift for her. An' this is better'n you coming down to tell me the story. I'm a part of it.'

Lilly crossed to the cradle and looked down at the baby girl who gurgled back up at her. The baby reached a chubby fist up to the old woman. Lilly bent and kissed her on both eyelids.

'There, little one,' she whispered. 'Come thee and see me when thee's older.'

The pudgy fingers squeezed the gnarled hand. They understood one another.

'What've you given her, Auntie?' Faye came up beside her.

Lilly looked up at her, grinning. 'Noddle, nowse and knowing,' she cackled. 'Like I gived you!'

Vera eyed them from across the table and brought a plate of sandwiches over. Lilly lightly touched the patch where her right eye had been.

'What did y' see, me dear?'

'The owl woman,' Vera told her.

Lilly nodded, looked into her good eye, smiled, then reached up to kiss her.

'I'll be seein' of thee,' she whispered.

'And I o' thee,' Vera nodded. She took the sandwiches on to Ranley-Hall who was boring Delagardie to death with his latest financing project.

Olive refused to go near the old woman. She'd tried commiserating with Vera, to no avail. Vera had looked at her out of her one eye.

'Don' y' worrit about it,' she'd said.

Olive could make no sense of it. She had tried to get out of coming to the naming ceremony but Joe insisted.

They all trooped down to the pool below the falls. The sun burned down on them as they stood on the beach getting ready for the ceremony.

'Do you really think this is a good idea?' Ranley-Hall whispered, tugging Dick's sleeve.

'Of course!' Dick grinned at his boss.

Martin Drinkwater took the cup from Dick's hand and waded out into the pool, holding it on high.

Merle picked up his baby daughter, took Vicki's hand and set off into the pool, followed by Dick and Faye. Drinkwater waited by the stone ring.

'Who stands witness for this child?' he called out.

'I do, in place of the goddess,' said Faye.

'And I stand witness in p-place of the god,' Dick said loudly, inwardly cursing his stammer for emerging at just that moment.

Drinkwater put his arm through the stone ring, so the water from the other side of the fall would fill the cup.

'In the name of Earth, Air, Fire and Water, I name this child Anny.'

He poured the water over her head.

Resolution

That night, Vicki dreamed she was in the cave. The stone moved and the water flowed away from the fall and down into the rock. She dipped her fingers in the water, took a sip. It felt like she was shrinking, folding up like a telescope, like Alice, until she was small enough to ride the water down through the hole in the wall. It was like a roller-coaster, a flying carpet, like riding a light wave. She landed on the stone floor of the cavern with a bump and all the air went out of her. The water flowed down the channel in the floor, to the hole in the middle of the cavern. Owl-light flowed down the shaft to fall on the stone tree. The owl woman stood where the light and water met.

'Bring me my cup,' she said.

Lightning jolted through her. She sat bolt upright in the bed. Merle lay beside her, his face soft and open, like the child's. She leaned over and brushed his hair with her lips, then slid out of bed and got dressed. Goldy and Shadow stood waiting at the end of the bed. Hecaté roused from her washing basket and followed them all into the study. Vicki knelt in front of the fireplace.

Merle dreamed too. He was back in the cavern under the Wilderness, a scene playing out in the air in front of him, like on some crazy cinema screen. He watched the Hollyman come out of the wood, stop and look at him from out of the screen. Their eyes met. He has my face, Merle realised.

The scene continued. Then, suddenly, Merle found he *was* the Hollyman, had shifted into him. He climbed up to the cave by the waterfall, the owl let him in. He held the dead body of his love in his arms, cut open her belly and freed the child within. The owl sat on his shoulder, whispering to him all the way back to the village. He gave the baby to one of the village women and stood at the door of the headman's hut. It was just where Well Cottage stood now. He called for him to bring out the cup and, a moment later, a misshapen man with Jacob's face came out and knelt before him, offering the cup. He took it back up to the mound.

He climbed down the steps and found his way into the cavern. His love stood there, shining and feathered, as he knelt beside the hole in the ground and placed the cup within it. Then he drew the stone tree back to cover the hole. Standing, he felt himself shift into a bright falcon, to fly up, with his love, into the dark sky.

Merle woke just as Vicki left the room. He waited a moment, then dressed hurriedly and followed her down the stairs to Jacob's study. He held his breath as she worked the mechanism. The panel swung open and he watched her take out the cup and wrap it in a dark scarf. He kept well back, guessing what would come, and followed her up to the tower.

Standing at the edge of the fall, Vicki heard the yew tree speak with her father's voice.

'Remember!'

Light glimmered off the rushing water, fracturing and splitting like a strobe. The shadows grew, making the brightness brighter. Something took shape in the laurel bushes on the far side of the pool. It rose up the column of water and hovered at the top, staring at Vicki from round, golden eyes.

'Return my cup!' demanded the owl woman.

The water thundered and shook the ground. Vicki offered the cup but the owl woman screamed and flew at her. She ducked and felt herself falling, falling, falling.

Merle leaped forward and grabbed her in a rugby tackle, pulling her backwards, stopping her fall. Lying beside her, their legs hanging out over the fall, he carefully inched himself backwards, dragging her to safety. Their blood dripped down, mixing with the water as it fell. Somehow, crazily, she'd kept hold of the cup.

She lay in his arms, silent, smiling, eyes open but not seeing him or anything in this world. He held her close not daring to move, trying to cover her with himself, to keep her warm. It seemed they stayed that way for ages.

He felt the movement, then she coughed, choked. He helped her sit up.

'Stupid girl! ' he scolded. 'You're as bad as your father! You got it wrong, again.'

'Huh?'

'Don't you remember the story?' Merle took off his jacket and wrapped it round her. 'It's the Hollyman puts the cup back, not you! I thought that's what you were going to do tonight. That's why I followed you, so I'd be here when you needed me. Then you went all dippy at the waterfall and damn near fell in. You'd have taken the cup with you and then I'd have had to do it all over again. Without you.' Merle broke off, his voice choking. 'You said you'd come back!'

'Oh ...Oh my god!' she hugged him. 'I'm sorry! I'm sorry! I nearly ran out on you again!'

They stayed that way, holding each other for a long while, then she pulled back gently. 'Tell me ...?' she said.

'It's the story. Who is it comes to the cave, after you're dead?' he grasped her shoulders, shook her gently.

'Of course!' she whispered. 'It's the Hollyman.'

'That's right! And I just did it in a dream,' he told her.

She sat staring at him.

'First I was watching the story play out, in the cave up by the waterfall, watching the Hollyman cutting the baby out of you. Then I found myself shifted into the Hollyman. I went to the headman's house and demanded the cup. He brought it. It was Jacob. He gave it to me and I brought it up here, climbed down into the cavern and put it back in the hole. The owl woman was there, she looked like you,' he paused. 'Then I turned into a falcon, like in the song, and we flew off together.'

Vicki watched him, a smile sliding sideways onto her face to match his own.

'We'd better do it right then, eh?' she said.

'Yes.'

'Do we have to turn into birds as well?'

Merle chuckled. 'Let's wait and see,' he said.

He led the way to the cavern. Owl light shone down the shaft. It was Lughnasadh dawn, the day she'd promised the owl woman she would return the cup. They'd completely forgotten.

The air shimmered and the owl woman was there. Merle held out the cup to her but she pointed at the stone tree. He lifted it. Underneath was a pool of water. He looked up at her.

She bent and dipped her finger in the water, touched his eyes. Then she took the cup, dipped it into the water, drank and held it out to Merle. He drank and offered it to Vicki. She drank and offered it to the owl woman. This time, she took it.

A wind came up from nowhere. It tore the feathers apart, so there was nothing of the owl woman left and swirled them down the hole, like water down a plug-hole. It even went the right way round for the northern hemisphere.

Bridewell

to Kitnor

Firebeacon Hill

Honeybeetle Common

Honeybeetle Cross

Old Drover track

Stonechest Wood

Bride Steps

Firebeacon Hill

The Greenway

Greendown

Tower Moor

Summer Moor

Bridge Cottage

The Owlwater

Clock House

Bridewell

The Wilderness

Mouseberry Hill

The Greenway

Penny Woods

Owlpen Copse

Owl House

vicarage

St Iwerydd's

Bridewell River

Penny Lane

Stowford

School Lane

The Well

Green Lion

Orchards

Cider Press

Orchards

Bridewell Stream